Alliance.125

Hirunda

The First Book

Raita Jauhiainen

ALLIANCE.125

HIRUNDA

The First Book

Publisher: Books on Demand GmbH, Helsinki, Finland
Manufacturer: Books on Demand GmbH, Norderstedt, Germany
ISBN: 978-952-498-697-7

The original book in Finnish: Allianssi.125: Hirunda: Ensimmäinen kirja
Cover and design: Raita Jauhiainen
Images: Raita Jauhiainen

1.

Jani gazed out of the train window at the dreary view rushing by. He didn't notice the passage of time nor the other passengers around him, and was only awoken from his thoughts when a monotonous voice broke the silence in the carriage by announcing:

"*Linai, Station West.*"

Jani got to his feet and walked to the doors. When they opened he stepped off the train onto the platform at Linai Station, held his head down, and began to walk towards the exit. A heavy, lingering smell hanging in the air wrapped itself round his face.

The journey from Gavialis, the biggest city in the world, took approximately fifteen minutes by train, but during that time Jani travelled from one kind of world to another. Linai was one of the four suburbs of the city, but possibly the grimmest one of them all. Gavialis'waste recycling was carried out in Linai, and the place with its facilities and halls did not even attract nulls to visit the place. The only reason to come to Linai was work, not to spend any spare time, if anyone happened to have too much of it in the first place.

Jani, however, did not serve in any of the waste recycling units, even though he came to Linai on an almost daily basis. His post was located in a relatively hidden control room in one of the facilities near Linai Station. Jani's job was concerned with human waste, but it had nothing to do with recycling. His job was to stare for hours at a display screen, which transmitted images from the infamous Cold Pit prison, where the most barbaric criminals were sent. The sociopaths who lived in the place had carried out such ruthless crimes against humanity that they were no longer allowed to remain on the same planet as the rest of the human race. Therefore, they had been sent away to spend the rest of their days thousands of kilometers away from Earth, on the moon.

He stepped through the doors leading inside the building where the command room was located and walked to the stairs. As he climbed one step at a time he yawned deeply. The grayness of weekdays numbed his mind and he had not felt anything lately, other than deep nausea, towards the monotony of each passing day.

He did not like his job, even though it was an easy one. In principle he had nothing to complain about, but there were moments when the ease of his working week did not interest him anymore; when he began to miss something else, like striving towards a goal of some kind. Sitting in the command room had lost all its charm after three and a half years. It seemed that the similarity of each day had the ability to blur the meaning of any work. That always happened, sooner or later.

He also did not like his own attitude. He knew his mediocre life would have been a subject of envy for someone else; after all, he was not a null, who no longer had anything to contribute to society. Damn, he was not even working in waste recycling, even if he had to come to Linai almost every day. So compared with many others he was lucky. In Gavialis he was not exactly a high flyer, but when he stepped onto the platform of Linai Station West, he was at least blending into mediocrity.

Jani opened the door, which alerted the man on the night shift. They nodded to each other without saying a word as Jani relieved him from his duties. Jani sat down behind his monitor and leaned against the back of his chair. Then he stretched, chasing the last traces of tiredness away. A new day in the control room had begun; the room every detail of which he knew intimately.

A new day was also dawning in Cold Pit prison where the prisoners were being woken up. The daily rhythm of the inmates followed Earth Standard Time, which was Gavialis time.

"Another day ahead," Jani sighed as he pulled his unfocused thoughts together.

He began to watch the screen, which was transmitting images from the main corridor of the prison. Cold Pit had been constructed 32 years ago and during its existence, it had become a big enough threat for those who were prone to commit crimes. Nevertheless, despite the long and threatening shadow of Cold Pit, there were always those in society who tested the limits of the law.

However, such testing came with a high price because the ones who had been sent to Cold Pit never returned to Earth. Therefore, every convicted felon would also die in the prison, approximately 400 thousand kilometers away from home. It also meant that Cold Pit was never entirely empty of inmates and that meant that Jani's job was never done. There were also a few guards and doctors working in the prison, but they remained in the isolation wing of the facility, since most of the prison guarding was carried out from Earth.

"*Linai?*" Jani suddenly heard above his display unit. "*Transportation ship Beloni asks permission to land.*"

He woke from his thoughts and he leaned toward the display in front of him. He changed the view to the Cold Pit's landing pad, which was also supervised from Earth. He noticed the lights of the landing pad blinking blue.

"Transportation ship Beloni," Jani said. "Permission to land granted."

"*Permission received, Linai,*" he heard the response. "*Beloni beginning landing sequence. Estimated time of docking; eleven minutes.*"

Jani switched channels in order to see the images transmitted by the camera situated on one of Cold Pit's unmanned monitoring towers. Then he waited for the transportation ship to appear on the screen as it descended to the prison's maintenance wing landing pad. He activated another window on his display unit so he could see the trajectory of Beloni from the moon's orbit to Cold Pit. The ship seemed to land at an optimal angle. Beloni had departed from Earth's orbit approximately 30 hours ago and now it had finally reached its destination. He guessed that the ship was most likely transporting guards as well as foodstuffs to the prison, but perhaps there were a couple of convicted criminals on board as well.

Finally, Jani noticed a light moon dust rising as the transportation ship approached close enough to the moon soil. Overall the landing appeared completely effortless to him, sitting in the control room. Nevertheless, the view on his display was still bleak simply because it was Cold Pit to where the ship was landing.

Jani had considered applying for the position of guard to Cold Pit a couple of times, because the idea of having a job on the moon somewhat fascinated him. Of course, there were important solar power plants on the moon as well, so the prison was not the only possibility of work there. However, staring at his display unit for some time, he realized he didn't have what it takes to leave Earth. He knew he did not have the required skills to work in a power plant, therefore there was no point in wasting any time on futile job applications, either.

Jani noticed as the Beloni made its touchdown.

"*Beloni landed*," he then heard above his display unit.

"Linai copies that," Jani noted. "Have fun," he added.

"*Always*," the captain of the ship laughed.

Jani swiveled round on his chair looking at the ceiling of the control room. The room was not a particularly glamorous place to work, but it was so much better than being inside Cold Pit.

All of a sudden he heard his display unit giving the signal indicating incoming communication. He swiveled round to face the display and activated the speech window from the bottom left corner. A serious looking man appeared on the screen.

"Jani 821771?" the man said almost immediately.

"Yes," Jani replied.

"We have booked an appointment for you in the Gavialis Main Hospital," the man said.

"Excuse me?" Jani asked him, baffled.

"We have booked an appointment for you in the Gavialis Main Hospital," the man repeated in a similarly monotonous tone.

"For me?" Jani asked the man. "Are you sure you have contacted the right person?"

"You are Jani 821771, are you not?" the man on the screen asked him blandly.

"Yes."

"Then you are the man I needed to get in touch with."

"Umm … alright," Jani replied. "It's just that I wasn't expecting this. When should I arrive there?"

"Today at 13:15," the man said.

Jani didn't know what to think.

"Today?" he questioned, confused. "I am working today. Why am I being summoned at such short notice?"

"You have been chosen as a test subject for one of our research studies," he heard the man explaining. "We have already checked the most appropriate time from your ID Account's week view and received confirmation from your immediate manager that you are allowed to leave your post. Your stand-in will arrive shortly, so you will have plenty of time to travel back to the city."

"What kind of study are we talking about?"

"A study which requires one visit to Sixth Circle and one visit to the Main Hospital."

"So, this isn't about an annual check-up?"

"I have uploaded access permission to Sixth Circle on your ID Account," the man informed him, ignoring Jani's question entirely. "The permission in question grants you four hours of visiting time."

"Alright," Jani replied.

"At 13:15," the man said again. "Please be on time."

Jani nodded, after which the man finally disconnected their communication link, and the view from Cold Pit's landing pad filled the screen once again. He didn't know what to think. Going to the Main Hospital was an unexpected turn of events, but a positive one.

"This is how small my life has become," he said to himself with a laugh. "That a mere visit to a hospital gets me in a better mood."

However, it was not just any hospital in the city; it was the Main Hospital. The facility in question was located inside Sixth Circle; a part of the city where Jani had no business without an official access permission, and now he had one.

Being able to step into Sixth Circle was a huge deal for a man like Jani. In Gavialis there were seven circles in total, from which the seventh formed the core of the city and therefore was the most hallowed one. From First Circle, where he lived, one could barely see the silhouettes of tall buildings in Third Circle during the daytime. So city circles beyond that were much too far away to be seen with the naked eye. He had, however, been to the inner parts of the city; Fifth Circle was the so-called free zone, and that was how far Jani had managed to get when it came to the inner circles of the city. Fifth Circle was dedicated to men's free time, but the number of Jani's Silver Wing marks granted him only three or four hours per week in that part of the city. If he didn't use these hours he was unable to save them for upcoming weeks, and for that reason alone, an invitation to Sixth Circle made him anxious, but also excited. He could barely believe his luck.

Jani checked the time. It was only 9:32. He would have liked to leave already, but his stand-in had not yet arrived. He activated his ID Account and checked all new incoming messages. There were none, neither written nor audio ones. He hadn't expected anything else, even though he would have liked to have heard from Lu. Lu, however, was still patrolling the northern border of the city and Jani had no idea when he would have some time off. Nevertheless, he decided to type a message to his friend.

Lu,

You won't believe what has just happened. I have been invited to the Gavialis Main Hospital. That means I'm going to Sixth Circle! Such an odd thing, so let's see what they want from me. At least I'll get out of work for a little while.

When you're online again, message me.

Jani

Jani checked the time again. It was 9:36. He was impatient. The mere thought of entering Gavialis' Sixth Circle felt even better than earning a Silver Wing mark. Therefore, all things between Linai and Cold Pit started to quickly disappear as the excitement of seeing the inner part of the city took over. He really was about to see that part of the city he could not remember ever visiting before, and soon there was no room for any other thoughts in his head.

* * *

Jani was standing on Linai Station West and he heard the train approaching. It didn't take long before it quickly appeared, moving at an incredible speed, but promptly slowing down once in the station. The train stopped at the platform and the doors opened. Jani stepped in as quickly as he could.

The carriage was almost empty. He sat down and activated the small news display, even though he didn't even glance at it. In his mind he was on his journey already; a journey he had not expected at all. He knew that the U train would go round Linai before returning to First Corner Station of the city. Before arriving at Sixth Circle, he would actually have to change trains twice. First, he would change at the border of the city onto the Heptagon Line, which circled the enormous Gavialis. Once he had arrived at Sixth Corner Station, he would take either train 6A or 6C, which ran between the Heptagon Line and Sixth Circle.

The train jerked slightly as they started to move. Moments later they reached maximum velocity as the train practically flew ahead and they raced between the Linai buildings and the blocks towards the south. They would stop twice before the train would finally head north again, taking Jani back to Gavialis. He felt pretty good about himself. He felt free, even though he only needed to make a quick visit to the Main Hospital on Sixth Circle.

Jani was pulled back from his thoughts. He turned his face and saw a dirty null sitting on the other side of the aisle. The man was filthy and he smelled strongly of durratin. Jani knew the man's face. The man in question often traveled on the trains which circulated between the city border and suburbs. He and the man had sat in the same carriages many times and in his mind Jani had started to call the man Null 497, because he had no idea what the man's name really was. The man remembered him only occasionally, though, because durratin had already caused considerable damage to his memory.

"Where are you heading, boy?" Null 497 finally asked him, because the train carriage was almost empty and Jani was sitting near the man.

He quickly realized the man was too intoxicated again to remember him, even though he had asked how Jani was doing no more than two days ago.

"To Sixth Circle," Jani finally said.

"They have women in there," the man stated as he stared ahead blankly.

"I guess they do," Jani replied.

"Those women," Null 497 said, inhaling deeply through his nose. "They always smell so sweet."

""I haven't noticed."

"Have you ever seen any women, then?" the man asked him, slightly amused.

"Couple of times," Jani said.

"Sixth Circle," the man stated. "It is a fine place indeed."

Jani took a quick glance at the old man and wondered if he had ever even been in Sixth Circle. If so, if the man had, at some time in his past, had permission to step beyond Fifth Circle, his current situation would be extremely sad. All the nulls were kept outside the city, in the so-called Circle Nil, and therefore many of them were often to be found on the R, E, and U trains, as well as on the Heptagon Line trains which ran along the city boundary. However, none of them could ever get beyond the station gates at the seven stations on the Heptagon Line from where the trains heading into the city leave.

"Your life is still ahead of you, boy," Null 497 stated. "Stay away from all intoxicants and you'll be fine."

"I'll try," Jani promised.

"Don't just try!" the man replied, and there was some anger in his voice. "Don't ruin your life! I used to have 497 Silver Wing marks back then. That's 497! Three more and I would have received the real silver one on my chest. Can you believe that?"

"I can," Jani assured him.

"My life would have become so much better," the man said. "I would have been given access to move to the inner circles of the city, but durratin ruined it all."

Jani watched the man as he spoke and nodded. He didn't know if the man expected him to comment on his story in any way, because when intoxicated, he wasn't really aware of the world around him.

"I was already living in Third Circle," he continued. "That's the third! I fought my way up there. And I was one mean fighter. A man has to be the best if he wants to succeed in this world. The best!"

"That's the way it is," Jani agreed.

"I had 497 Silver Wing marks," the man said again. "That's 497! All of them were taken away from me. Every single one of them. That's what happens when you crack under the pressure and find relief in durratin. It feels so liberating at first. Do you know what I mean?"

"I do."

"Do you like intoxicating drinks, then?"

"Not so much, no."

"Good," Null 497 growled, "because that stuff only brings you down. First you feel liberated when your head gets lighter, but look at me now, boy! I mean look! I am a prisoner. These trains are my prison. And here I am now."

Jani nodded, extremely uneasily though. He pitied the man, but at the same time he knew that his misery was his own doing. Some were meant to fail in order for others to succeed; that was how things were in the world. Nevertheless, the role of being a null was a dire one, but the man could only blame himself. Stupidity, incompetence, and laziness were characteristics which brought no one any good. To fall to durratin was utmost stupidity; there was no doubt about that.

"You, boy, are young and healthy-looking," the man said and Jani could smell his bad breath all the way to his seat. "You can even get your own woman. That's a woman! Women do like young men, you know."

"We'll see," Jani replied.

"I lost my chance a long time ago already," the man stated. "But you, boy, you must do everything in your power to be victorious and rewarded. Only the best of the rewarded can get it all."

"I don't think I'm one of those best ones," Jani said.

"You do everything you can!" Null 497 urged. "That's everything! Don't drop outside the city and start this kind of living on the trains. I can't even see First Circle from these trains. I said trains! But you still have a future to look forward to!"

Jani nodded uneasily and tried to block Null 497's smell out of his mind.

"I am a drunk and I did this to myself," man slurred. "I said I! I wasn't able to keep my head together and this is the result of that. You are young. You can take it. Just focus on succeeding."

"I will try," Jani promised, trying to get rid of the man.

"Don't try," the man told him. "Do it!"

"I will do it," Jani assured him, but only to make the man stop talking.

"There's a good boy," the man said, and there was a faint sparkle in his eyes. "That's the way to do it. Make sure you are the best and you will get everything you want in this world. And the best part of it all – you will get more than the others!"

"*First Corner Station*," the automatic announcement informed them and Jani was most relieved to hear its sound.

"To Sixth Circle, huh?" the man asked him.

"To Sixth Circle," Jani answered and got to his feet. "This is where I change onto the Heptagon Line."

"That is a wise thing to do," Null 497 said. "I can also take Heptagon Line trains, but they won't let me take the ones heading into the city."

Jani nodded and stepped toward the doors. Once he got outside he checked an information tablet on the wall in order to find out the platform he needed to get on a B train. Since Sixth Corner Station was located on the east side of the city, the fastest way to get there was to take a B train from the First Corner Station which ran around the city counter-clockwise.

The sound of arriving and departing trains as well as the noise of the people echoed across the station tunnels. When Jani finally found the right platform, the B train was already shutting its doors. He leapt forward and managed to get on just before the doors were locked.

"*Next stop – Seventh Corner Station*," came the automatic announcement.

Jani took a seat and faced the window. He stared at the dimness outside for a while knowing it wouldn't take long before he could see the view to Gavialis' First Circle instead. Finally, the train started to move and as they departed from the station into the daylight, Jani soon noticed them passing the building where he lived. Seeing it from the train carriage made him smile because this time he had not taken train 1A or IC in order to get home. He was on Heptagon Line now and it was great, but it also made him anxious. Jani tried his best to conceal his emotions under his cool exterior, because someone like him feeling nervous was ridiculous.

The journey to Seventh Corner Station took almost twenty minutes. Once there, Jani watched the moving crowd on the station platform. Everyone seemed to be in a hurry either leaving the station or changing to trains 7A or 7C. The trains in question ran all the way to Seventh Circle, which was where the World President lived, as well as the highest-ranking officials. Jani had always assumed that people taking trains 7A and 7C would have looked more important somehow, but in fact the majority of them seemed relatively ordinary-looking. Of course, there was a chance they were heading to Fifth Circle instead, where all the trains from 5 to 7 made a stop; Fifth Circle, being the free zone in the middle of the city, meant that all the men in the world had access through the station gates without any specific access permission.

They finally departed from Seventh Corner Station and Jani knew it would take another twenty minutes to get to Sixth Corner Station. Suddenly, he noticed a man on the other side of the train carriage whose face looked very familiar. In fact, it was a face he would never forget. The man in question looked a lot like his life instructor. Jani remembered the speech the man had given many times, in order to teach the children certain necessary facts of life.

"Here in the educational institution you learn the basics, but what will become of you depends on you and you only. It is a fact that only a handful of you will live in Fourth Circle or beyond. And another fact is that statistically, at least three in this group alone will live outside of the city border before you reach 30. These three shall end up there because of their laziness or lack of talent. However, the majority of you will stay in the First Circle because you will not learn how to demand more from yourselves. If you don't like the idea of staying here as losers do, work hard in order to succeed. If you want to become something, you keep your eyes focused towards the city center and you will tell yourself every day again and again – I will get there! It's going to require a lot of hard work but becoming something requires unquenchable thirst for improvement because right now you are absolutely nothing!"

Jani had hated his instructor. The man had loved badgering them, even publicly humiliating them as a part of the process of "improving" his boys to become fighters, which in his opinion the world needed. Boys who had cried in front of the others had received special attention from the instructor, because cowardice would lead nowhere. The memory of the man caused Jani to gasp silently. He lived in First Circle and he had not become notable in any way. If his instructor had seen him today, and if he had remembered him for some reason, the man would have most likely announced loudly and even maliciously:

"What did I tell you, Jani? You were below average then and that is exactly what you still are!"

Those had been the words his instructor had told him on the last day in the educational institution. It had been the day before his descent, which meant moving from educational institution to command training. Every 14-year-old boy in the world faced the descent, no matter where they had grown up, and Jani had stayed in First Circle. Therefore, the descent had not brought him any remarkable life change, since he had not accomplished anything notable during his years in the educational institution. However, now he was on his way to Sixth Circle. He was heading towards a place he had only ever seen in pictures, a place where men like him really had no business.

"*Sixth Corner Station*," the automatic announcement finally said.

Jani shook off his memories, stood up, and rushed towards the doors. Once outside he headed resolutely to the platform from where he would get on the 6A or 6C train. To get to the platform he had to go through some locked station gates. However, as unbelievable as it was, the gates leading to those platforms would today grant him access based entirely on his fingerprint. That was something unheard of for Jani and now that he realized it was really going to happen, he also started to believe that he really was heading to the best parts of Gavialis.

The sound of the locking mechanism of the gate opening made him smile. He rushed forward and headed towards the first station platform he was able to find. When he finally got on train 6A, he calmed down. He faced the window again and looked outside. The train was moving above the streets and it made him feel somehow important. He activated the small news display, which was integrated into the backrest of the chair in front of him, and he started to follow the latest headlines from around the world. Before he managed to set the display to filter headlines from Gavialis local news alone, he noticed that one theme kept appearing among the headlines more than others. It was a clear sign of the importance and topicality of the news.

Woman found dead in Erasmia

Jani selected the headline with his index finger and the complete article appeared on the small screen.

A 22-year-old Erasmian woman was found dead earlier today (Gavialis time) inside the Main Hospital of Erasmia. Preliminary investigations suggest that the woman was choked to death. The police have not yet commented on the case, but according to leaked information the police do not yet have any suspects. The Erasmian woman is, however, already the second one to be killed this year. Therefore this capital crime casts a dark shadow on the Yellow Guards ...

He didn't know what to think about the incident. A murder of any kind was very rare, so when the victim was a woman, it was something most exceptional. It was only natural that the suspicions were directed towards the Yellow Guards, whose job it was to protect women, even though the mere thought of a murderer inside the Yellow Guard was unheard of and scandalous. Nothing like that had ever happened before.

Jani closed the article and left the news headline feed running on the screen. Then he looked outside the window and watched the city. They had already crossed First Circle, so the streets beneath them were either in Second or Third Circle. He looked in the direction they were heading, but Sixth Circle was still too far away to be seen.

Jani lost himself in his private thoughts again. The case of the Erasmian woman reminded him of the day, many years ago, when he and his peers had advanced to human anatomy in their educational institution studies. He had been either seven or eight years old at the time.

Once day, their life instructor had told them – or even confessed in a way – that there were many kinds of people in the world, but that all of the people were either men or women. Then the children had seen two big Yellow Guardsmen entering the room with a third person, who had been somewhat small next to those men in yellow. This person had had longer hair and a much slender body.

This person was a woman.

"Hello boys," the woman had greeted them and Jani still remembered how strange her voice had been. "My name is Pomarina Tinamus and I am a grown-up human female."

At that moment, the life of every boy in that room changed and Pomarina Tinamus was the cause. They had been shown images of female children, girls, and told how humans procreated biologically with one another. They had been told that women had the ability to carry children inside them and therefore each one of them was very important for the future of the human race. The lesson had ended with a reminder of the fact that only those who succeeded exceptionally well in life could obtain permission to meet women in person and even get one of them to themselves. Jani had known then already that he would not be one of those boys.

Now, as he sat on the train, he was finally heading to the part of the city where there were also women. No one outside of Sixth Circle could really ever see them in real life. Jani wondered how Pomarina Tinamus would look today, and whether she had many children to take care of. It was very likely because the number of children correlated to how well-respected and valued a woman was. And if a woman was well-respected, the man she was committed to was more respected and valued as well.

Finally, the train left from Fifth Circle's 5.6 Corner Station in the direction of Sixth Circle. He browsed the headlines, but without concentrating on any of them. His mind was already focused on his destination; on the place he had never believed he would be granted access permission.

Then he saw it. Through the window he saw something he had never seen with his own eyes before. There was a tall building far away in the distance, whose silhouette was instantly recognized by all who saw it. It was Caput Mortuum, one of the tallest buildings in Gavialis.

Caput Mortuum stood in Sixth Circle and it was an exceptional building. The tower was constructed from the rubble of ancient buildings which had been bombed during the Great War, and therefore the building was very well known in every city in the world. Caput Mortuum had become a symbol of world peace and was deeply respected. Jani also knew that, above the main doors, were the following words engraved on the wall:

"THIS WE SWEAR – NEVER AGAIN"

These words referred to the tragedy of the Great War, which had almost wiped out the entire human race. At night the tower of Caput Mortuum was illuminated with bright red light reminding people of the blood that had been spilled for everlasting world peace. There, finally, stood the iconic building, in Jani's sight. He was amazed. This was something entirely new for him. In Fifth Circle he typically remained on the west side of the city. Now, as he approached the inner parts of Gavialis from the east, Caput Mortuum dominated the view almost completely, and the tower seemed to get bigger every passing moment as he got closer.

Caput Mortuum was not, however, the only thing worth seeing in Sixth Circle. Both Sixth and Seventh Circle were full of unimaginably tall buildings and towers, and the most advanced technology known to man. Jani was finally able to discover for himself what else there was to see. The closer he came, the more his own trivial life in First Circle started to annoy him.

He activated the city map on his news display and checked the location of the Main Hospital once again. He was glad the place was relatively close to 6.6 Corner Station, where he was due to arrive, so he could get off the train at the next stop.

"Sixth Circle, 6.6 Corner Station."

The announcement alerted Jani. He was finally at his destination. He felt his palms getting sweatier and his heart beating faster. When the train finally stopped, he stood up without delay and hurried resolutely towards the doors.

6.6 Corner Station was enormous and it was full of people. There were even two Yellow Guardsmen in the crowd nearby who passed Jani, but this time they had no women with them. The Yellow Guardsmen did not leave unnoticed, however, with or without women. Their yellow uniforms alone got most of the men on alert, because no one fooled around with these men.

Finally, Jani noticed the gate leading out of the station and once he got there, he pressed his thumb on the sensor next to the gate. The gate opened almost immediately, which made Jani smile. Of course the same thing had already happened in Sixth Corner Station on the Heptagon Line, but here the access to Sixth Circle felt even more real, because he was finally in one of the better parts of the city.

Jani descended from the station to street level and walked by a tall fence towards another gate. There was a queue there but, after waiting for a moment, his turn came to press a portable sensor, held by a guard, with his thumb. That was new to him. In First and Second Circles men did not guard station gates. The same was true of the gates in Fifth Circle as well. So here in Sixth Circle, men coming into the city were observed much more carefully.

"From First Circle?" the gate guard asked him.

Jani nodded.

"You have been given four hours," the guard informed him seriously.

Jani nodded again.

The Guardsman, relatively large in size, observed Jani from beneath his eyebrows for a while, which made him feel somewhat small, but that was most likely the Guardsman's intention. Finally, the man grunted and let him pass. Three steps later he was finally inside Sixth Circle of Gavialis and the first thing he saw was an enormous building across the street which rendered him speechless. He felt small again, but this feeling was different from being under the scrutinous eye of the Guardsman. The mere size of the building was out of this world and to actually see it made a huge impact on him.

Jani followed the crowd. He didn't want anyone to see him dumbfounded, but he couldn't prevent his jaw from dropping when he saw how different the traffic was in Sixth Circle. Unlike in the outer circles of the city, many men here had a zoona, a private vehicle which received power from the energy grid integrated into the roads. Zoonas moved silently, but the men who were driving them used their horns as they passed each other. Jani would have loved to inspect one more closely, because he had only ever seen pictures of them, but unfortunately he didn't have the time for it right now.

He continued walking. On the walls of the enormous buildings were lots of bright and colorful display boards. They brought much liveliness to the streets, even if it was not dark yet. The sound of people talking filled the air.

Unlike Jani, most of the pedestrians seemed to be in a hurry. Suddenly he saw couple of Yellow Guardsmen again. But, as in the station, there were no women with these Guardsmen. They were simply part of the crowd here in Sixth Circle. Jani would have loved to see some women as well, now that he was finally here. But Sixth Circle was huge, so seeing women during his time here was highly unlikely. Luckily, there also seemed to be lots of other interesting things to see.

He kept walking, crossed a bridge which provided the pedestrians a way across the wide street full of zoonas, and turned right. He tried to remember the location of the Gavialis Main Hospital and guessed he had about one more kilometer to walk. Therefore, he could easily get there and explore his surroundings as he went. He took a deep breath. He knew already that going back to First Circle would bring him down. Sixth Circle was an entirely different kind of world a place where he would love to live as well.

All of a sudden he saw a building nearby, which was made of some kind of stone. In front of the building there was a small crowd assembled in the street. He became a little curious. In the streets where everyone seemed to be in a hurry, a crowd standing still seemed somewhat odd. Then he took a closer look at the building and saw that it had three pointed towers and one big front door. So why these men were gathered in front of this unremarkable-looking building, quite small next to the other grand constructions which surrounded it, was anybody's guess.

Jani checked the time from a timekeeper reflected from a huge display across the road, and concluded that he was in no hurry yet. Therefore, he had the opportunity to stay here for a moment to observe the men who had gathered in the street. However, as he got closer to them, he also noticed that a few men were wearing yellow uniforms.

Yellow Guardsmen!

Guardsmen who had been trained to protect women. This time, however, Jani got the impression that these Guardsmen were not off-duty. He took a deep breath. He had been lucky, it seemed, because the presence of the Yellow Guard was a clear indication that there were women inside the peculiar-looking building.

He approached the crowd and could see how each man around him was constantly looking at the big front doors. There were men from all age groups present, but Jani guessed that the youngest of them had come here from other Circles. There weren't that many young men in the world who succeeded in life so quickly that they had the opportunity to move to Sixth Circle before their hair turned gray, excluding, of course, the boys who had been born to real women. Of course, there were those young geniuses to whom success seemed to come easily.

Jani remained standing next to the stone wall of the building and waited. He heard murmurings and laughter from the crowd. He had heard what reactions a group of women may cause in men, but he had never witnessed it happening with his own eyes. However, each and every man, Jani included, knew his limits. The reputation of the Yellow Guard was well known and they had the right to use force. There had been incidents where Guardsmen had even taken their weapons, so no one fooled around with them. During the past few years, a couple of men had been killed when they had tried to run towards women, ignoring the Guardsmen and their warning entirely.

The crowd was getting more anxious, and the restlessness was affecting Jani as well. Excluding Pomarina Tinamus, who had visited his educational institution, he had never seen a woman in close proximity. The memory of that visit returned to Jani's thoughts, and no wonder in the current situation. How many women were in this building right now?

Jani leaned back against the wall and tapped its cool surface with his fingertips. He was nervous now. Suddenly he realized that one of the Guardsmen was watching him. He was very aware of the stare, the threatening look he received under those eyebrows. He quickly thought about the best way to proceed. He did not want to give the Guardsman the impression of being one of those who would rush towards women when they stepped out of the building into the daylight. He understood that such an action would cause him nothing other than trouble in the form of physical pain. He didn't want that since he was not a rusher.

The Guardsman continued to glare at Jani, who tried his best to look as neutral as possible, so that the huge man would not get ideas of knocking him down on the pavement. Unlike the many younger men present, he had at least behaved calmly and in a civilized manner. Women might be a disruption, but one should never show that publicly.

At last, the big doors of the building opened, which caused a stir in the crowd. Yellow Guardsmen reacted immediately and everyone saw how they took out their weapons and activated them. Then a line of young women appeared from the building. They were walking in pairs and the men on the street started to yell and applaud.

Unlike many of the other men here, Jani was dumbfounded. Women were so tiny! Based on the images he had seen of them, he had not expected them to be so fragile-looking in reality. The distant memory of Pomarina Tinamus did not match the sight he was witnessing right now. These women barely looked human. They were more like some unrealistic characters from a fairytale.

The fuss continued and some of the men were knocked down by the Guardsmen. The women did not, however, seem to be distracted by the attention in the slightest. It was well-known that women were taught how to move and behave in public places without paying any attention to the men around them. Quickly and without fuss, the Guardsmen had led every one of them behind the darkened windows of a vehicle. The whole procedure was executed swiftly and in an extremely straightforward manner.

When the women were out of sight, the crowd slowly started to disperse. A couple of men compared the pictures of the women they had taken with their noters. Jani knew already that those pictures would end up on the information network within minutes. He had occasionally browsed sites where men around the world uploaded images of women they had observed in public places.

Jani took a deep breath and thought of Lu. He would have loved to share this with his friend, because he knew that seeing women would have been a memorable thing for Lu as well. But Lu was still on duty. Jani couldn't help but notice that Lu's shifts seemed to have become longer and longer during the passing year. He had not seen much of his friend in the city lately. That was not totally unheard of as, unlike him, Lu didn't like being in the city that much.

Jani took a moment to think about his options. Since the Main Hospital was nearby and he still wasn't in a hurry, he made a quick decision to peek behind the big doors where the women had come from; if a group of young women had visited this particular building, it had to be important in some way.

It was surprisingly cool inside and one could barely hear the noise of the city behind the walls. The room Jani found himself in was a big one; the ceiling was high above him and the white walls made the room look even wider. He walked slowly ahead and wondered why the women had been brought here where there seemed to be so little to see.

"Welcome to Hirunda Historical Museum," he suddenly heard behind his back.

Jani turned around and saw a young dark-haired man in a dark suit standing behind him. The man was slim and relatively short, but he seemed to be very self-confident.

"Have you visited us before?" the man asked Jani.

"I have not," Jani finally said.

"Excellent. So, I am the museum guide," the man informed him. "Please press your thumb on this device."

There was a thin data pad in the guide's hand and Jani pressed it with his right thumb. The device made a faint beep after which the guide started to read the data on the pad.

"From First Circle," he said. "If you wish to see the museum, it will take one of your seven weekly dinners."

"Is that so?"

"The museum is worth it," the guide whispered and winked.

"I have never even heard of a place like this," Jani confessed.

"Only a few have," the guide said. "Especially if you happen to live in the outer city circles, but this is the only place in the world where you can familiarize yourself with our history."

Jani watched the man for a moment and considered his offer. He was not interested in history at all, so why should he waste one of his weekly dinners to see what the museum had placed on display?

"This museum is worth one dinner," the guide assured him as if he had been reading Jani's mind. "And I can offer you dinner tonight. My apartment is in Second Circle, so my invitation would grant you access there for a few hours."

"You live in Second Circle, but you work on Sixth?" Jani asked him astonished.

"I am a lucky one," the man said and winked again.

"Very lucky," Jani stated.

He remembered his own little apartment, which didn't even have a private sanitary facility for him to use, so he had to wash and shower in shared bathrooms. And to cap it all, he had to go to Linai to work on an almost daily basis. The man working in this museum was definitely in a much better situation than he was, there was no doubt about that.

"So? Do I have the pleasure of your company this evening over dinner, let's say around seven?" the guide asked him and gave a sly smile.

"Thank you, but I have other plans," Jani lied politely. He wasn't interested in spending time with this man at all.

"That's too bad," the man said. "Would you still like to see the museum?"

Jani took a deep breath and reconsidered.

"Why not?" he finally said against his own better judgment. "I still have time before my meeting."

"Excellent," the guide said. "We have just had a group of girls here."

"Yeah, I noticed," Jani stated.

"Girls of that age tend to giggle a lot," the man said.

Jani nodded, even though he knew nothing about girls and how they behaved.

"I hope you'll enjoy your tour," the guide said.

Then he led Jani to the dark brown doors. He opened them and gestured him to step inside. He saw a big room behind the doors. He stepped in and started to understand relatively quickly why the women had been brought to that place. The room itself was definitely something to see. It was completely different from anything he had ever seen before. The ceiling was high and it was full of painted pictures. The building seemed much older from the inside than it had appeared from the outside. There was also an echo in the room, but otherwise the place was silent.

Jani realized that he was the only person in the room. He guessed that the building had been emptied for the women and now he was the first visitor after them. He hoped the guide wouldn't take him for one of those men who desperately followed women and collected anything they may have left behind. Such men truly existed. However, on the other hand why would he care what the guide thought of him?

Jani turned right and walked past the wall. First, he came to a picture of a building that was being demolished. One of the walls was already in pieces on the ground. Jani looked at the picture for a moment and realized it looked quite similar to the one he was in now; Hirunda Historical Museum. He didn't, however, understand why the picture had been included in the museum's collection, so he activated an information display panel next to it and started to read.

This is an image record illustrating a real situation during the early phases of the city of Erasmia. The building being torn down was called a church, one of the holy buildings of the ancient world's religions. Before the Great War, people would come together in great numbers in this kind of building; people who believed in the same supernatural spiritual entity. There were certain worship rituals which were practiced in all religions, and the church was one kind of building where such rituals were carried out.

All religions were disbanded and forbidden after the Great War because dictators of different eras used them to become stronger and more powerful and amassed the power of their respective peoples to fight against each other in devastating wars. The Historical Museum in Gavialis is located in the world's last remaining church, which was spared the mass demolitions of religious buildings, ordered by Gavo Hirunda. These mass demolitions were carried out during years 1–3 after the Great War.

He deactivated the display and took another look at the picture. He now knew that he was standing inside a building which had in the past been called a church. In this very place people had practiced some odd worship rituals and the mere thought of it was almost incomprehensible for him. He had not even heard about churches before, not even in his educational institution.

He moved to the next picture on the wall. He looked at it for a moment and realized it was a picture of an old-fashioned artificial womb. Next to it was a man holding a little baby in his arms. The caption at the bottom of the picture said

Pavo 000001 – GAV

The newborn child in the picture was the first living child in the entire world to have been born from an artificial womb, and the boy's name was still known all over the world. Jani stared at the man in the picture for a while and saw deep pride in his eyes. There was a good reason for that pride; artificial wombs had saved mankind, of that there was no doubt. Then he activated the display next to the picture.

Artificial Wombs

Artificial wombs play an important part in maintaining the population of the human race. The first artificial wombs were created to control the birthrate of men all over the world. Male children were favored because of the need to build and rebuild the world's cities after the Great War, and this required vast human resources. However, only about 34% of the first artificial pregnancies came to term. Because of the low success rate, the ethics behind artificial child cultivation was widely called into question.

The main reason why most of the artificial pregnancies failed was the primitive technology used. Artificial wombs using the latest technological advancements at that time made it challenging for researchers to identify different kinds of risks involving child cultivation. As the technology slowly matured, the amount of children born alive also increased. Nowadays up to 79% of artificial pregnancies produce a living human child. Contrary to just a few decades ago, artificial wombs are now mostly used to support the birthrate of human females.

Jani deactivated the display and continued his tour. Next, he came to a picture which illustrated an aerial view. Jani knew without activating the information display that the picture showed the early stage of Gavialis; the heptagon shape of the city was already relatively easy to decipher. In the next picture, the city had been developed further as the inner circles of the city were already complete.

Jani continued forward and he came to a huge world map. For some reason the map didn't quite look like the world map he was familiar with. The abundance of the color green in it was quite eye-catching.

He stared at the map for a moment and after a while realized there were also differences in the coastal areas of all continents. In addition, the South Land was entirely white. Jani didn't know what to think of it, so he activated the information display in order to know why the map was so different from the world map of his day.

The World Map

This is a world map which has been preserved from the era before the Great War. The map differs from the world map of today, nevertheless researchers assume that this is a precise illustration of the world's biosphere as it was in the past. The old names of different areas have been removed from the map. The name removal was carried out on the orders given by Gavo Hirunda, who accepted the map as a part of this museum. Therefore, this map is the only known record of the world's geographical state during the old times before the Great War.

The abundance of the color green on the world map suggests that the land masses between the equator and the two tropics used to be full of forests. Therefore, it can be assumed that people had also populated these areas. In addition, permafrost covered the South Land and modern researchers assume that there was no permanently settled area on the continent in the past.

Jani deactivated the display and took a deep breath. The thought of the areas between the two tropics being suitable for living completely baffled him. The world he knew was divided evenly between the tropics of Capricorn and Cancer and Jani had never even considered the possibility that it might not always have been the case.

Next, Jani noticed a glass display cabinet and a peculiar-looking device in it. Upon reaching the cabinet, he activated the information display attached to the item and started to read.

Book

The book was the predecessor of the reading device, where the physical storage material of the text-based data was paper. One book contained static text content, which was therefore always topic-specific. In other words, the text content and its physical location were inseparable components. Book contents cannot be updated dynamically, so if the owner of a book wanted to read other writing, the only way was to acquire another book. It is reasonable to assume that one person might have had many books in their personal book collections. The book inside this display cabinet is written in an ancient language, which is not spoken anymore in any part of the world.

Jani looked at the book for a while and wondered how heavy it was to hold. The mere thought of reading text from such a thing was an odd one. Luckily, things were different now.

Then he saw an even bigger glass display cabinet, which was standing a little further away from the wall. He walked over to the cabinet and saw an odd-looking object inside. It was an octagonal shaped barrel which was metallic and there were many kinds of attachments on its surface. There were also four panels attached to it which reminded Jani of solar panels. Jani activated the information display and read:

Satellite

This is an ancient satellite from the time before the Great War. When the war was over and space travel became more common, it was quickly observed that the Earth's orbit was full of inactive old wreckage. Gavo Hirunda gave the order to clean up the orbit, which took two years. This is one of the satellites which was brought back to Earth in one piece. The purpose of this satellite is still the subject of much speculation.

Jani gave a laugh. He was amused because the device behind the glass did not much resemble a satellite. Then he continued his tour and he arrived at the other side of the big echoing room where there was a huge light stone tablet hanging on the wall. The stone had been engraved with a text that Jani recognized. It was one of Gavo Hirunda's most noteworthy speeches. The speech was still held as one of the main factors that led to the founding of the unified world nation. Jani stared at the tablet on the wall and read.

The world owes us nothing. We owe the world everything. To future generations, our children, we owe everything.

We have a new direction, a new goal which will guide us through the days to come. This goal is world peace, which was never achieved by those who are now gone. We are better than they were; if we decide to do better. We will achieve the era of peace, if we want to achieve it. And when I look at the world today I wonder why anyone would want to continue on the path of destruction. Each one of us deserves peace. But world peace is not given to us. We are the ones who create it, if we choose to do so.

Murder has to stop. We can't define ourselves through those we hate. We must stop wasting our time on destruction! To those who tempt us to hate we will shout "NO!" A man is more than his brothers' executioner. We are defined by what we do, so it's time for all of us to do better!

The time to build has come. We will not be blinded by hatred anymore, but by glory, which we create from these broken pieces of the world! I know our future is going to shine brighter than any of those forgotten days in our history, if we only choose so! We who have survived will make an oath that our hands shall never be covered in blood again.

He read the speech again. Gavo Hirunda had been a great man and there had not been anyone like him since. The man was a legend and his strength was still like a shadow which had fallen over the entire world.

Suddenly Jani made a decision. Before going to the Main Hospital he would make a quick stop at the nearest Contact Point, because both Gavo Hirunda and Sixth Circle inspired him to make a change. For the first time Jani felt true excitement and he finally felt that he didn't have to stay in First Circle; there might be more in him after all. That was the reason why he was willing to check the open positions in the nearest Contact Point now. If it really frustrated him to repeatedly go back and forth between the city and Linai, why didn't he do something about it?

The answer was relatively obvious; he was lazy. He had not been bothered to go and actively seek out any change in his life. He had become numb instead and he had even accepted that. Now, however, things would change. He was in Sixth Circle now and he had seen what kind of life people were living in this part of the city. So why didn't he demand more of himself and do all he could do in order to get out of First Circle?

He took another look at Gavo Hirunda's speech before he turned around and left. When he arrived back in the foyer of the building, the museum guide said something, but Jani didn't bother to stay and listen. Instead, he waved his hand goodbye and stepped through the front doors back into the daylight.

He almost ran down the stony steps and once he had reached the street again turned left, which was the way to the Main Hospital. He didn't know where the nearest Contact Point would be, but he knew one of them would cross his path eventually, because typically there was a Contact Point on every street corner. Before he knew it, he saw the familiar-looking green sign he had been looking for on the wall of a building not so far away. He walked towards the green sign and on reaching it, he walked through some glass doors and entered a small room which was full of information terminals. Here he had access to the city's internal network.

Jani took a seat and activated a terminal by pressing a yellow ellipse-shaped sensor with his thumb and the network connection opened. He saw his ID Account information on the screen and he chose "Recruiting" from the top corner. An application form appeared on the screen with some of his personal information already filled in. At the bottom of the form was a search function of all the vacant positions in the city. When Jani activated it, a list of vacancies appeared on the screen.

Jani decided to look at vacancies in Gavialis only; spending so much time in Linai or any other suburb didn't really interest him anymore. In addition, in the city of 20 million people there had to be a job for him somewhere. However, this time he concentrated specifically on the inner circles of the city. He set his search terms to filter all vacancies from Third to Sixth Circles and activated the search.

The system filtered Jani's search results quickly and a long list of vacancies appeared on the screen. A substantial part of the results showed maintenance positions, which was hardly surprising, since skillful maintenance crew were always needed. He didn't, however, have the required skills for the job, as, during his years at the educational institution, he had not bothered to learn any extra skills. Now it was more or less too late.

There were plenty of positions available for nurses as well, but that was another job he had no training for. Information network maintenance needed more skillful workers as well, but Jani knew nothing about network technology. There were also possibilities to do cleaning in inner circles of the city, but the status of some of those jobs turned from "vacant" to "filled" even as he was still considering such a possibility at his terminal.

There were also positions for holders whose work involved spending time in educational institutions' departments for newborns and spend hours holding babies so that their psychological development would progress normally. Jani's credits would have been sufficient for the job, but he was not at all interested in applying. Alongside other boys, he had done plenty of baby-holding during his years at the educational institution; that had been part of their education. However, even though young boys were obligated to hold the babies, more men were still needed as holders.

Then Jani noticed that the city of Gavialis was searching for new men to join the Yellow Guard. It was a good sign per se, because a need for new Guardsmen indicated that the number of women was increasing. He laughed silently, because he knew that the qualification requirements for Guardsmen were extremely demanding. He decided, however, to take a look at exactly what those requirements were, even if he knew already he would never fulfill them.

He couldn't help but roll his eyes and shake his head. Men wishing to become Guardsmen had to have combat training up to at least level five, and candidates had to be sterilized as well. Jani had postponed his operation for a while now, so he wasn't eligible for the position in that way either. A candidate was expected to have a minimum of 80 Silver Wing marks from sports alone, from which some needed to be from running, some from team sports, and the rest from swimming. He had only 43 Silver Wing marks in total, from which he had earned only 12 from sports. In addition, the applicants had to know first aid, which was something Jani knew almost nothing about. Applicants were also expected to have top achievements from both basic and rescue training. The habits of the candidates had to meet the requirements of the profession. There was a special mention of the requirement that no traces of intoxicant should be found in the applicants' systems. That must have been the only requirement he filled.

Jani closed the application form and stared at the screen for a moment. The qualification requirements for Yellow Guardsmen applicants had been depressing reading. They had simply reminded him of the fact that all he could ever be was a faceless man in Cold Pit's control room; a man whose success rate would always remain at a low level. He had to be honest with himself and admit that his pointless wandering would never change, even if he could work somewhere else. As long as he didn't know which direction to go in, he could very well stay in the control room staring at his monitor and its images from the moon's North Pole. He knew himself and his own limits. That's why he would only be deceiving himself, if he expected to become something he obviously wasn't. His place was in the control room, where no one expected him to be a top achiever at anything.

He woke from his thoughts as two men stepped inside the Contact Point. He decided to leave because time was ticking and he needed to be in the Main Hospital soon. Therefore, tormenting himself with impossible vacancies was futile. Jani stepped out onto the street. If he remembered his directions correctly, the hospital was only couple of hundred meters away. He checked the time from a reflection on a building wall across the street. He had less than fifteen minutes to reach the hospital.

He arrived at the next street corner from where he could see a big white building. That was the Gavialis Main Hospital – there was no doubt about that – right next to a paved open space. Jani turned left and walked quickly towards the hospital's main doors. Once inside he found himself in a big entrance hall. One wall of the hall was full of registration terminals. He saw a free terminal and approached it as quickly as he could. When he reached it he finally pressed a yellow ellipse with his thumb and waited for directions. Instead of receiving directions where exactly he should go, a short message appeared on the screen.

Please wait here.

Jani didn't know what to think of the message, but did what the system said. The uncertainty of the situation made him a little worried. He watched all the other men who arrived at the registration terminals and, unlike him, each one of them got their directions immediately and continued on their way to the different parts of the hospital. Realizing this made Jani's anxiety even more intense. Why did he have to wait here in the hospital entrance hall? Why was his situation exceptional?

At last, he saw two Yellow Guardsmen approaching him. The yellow uniforms of the men made Jani's anxiety turn into pure nervousness. Was something wrong?

"Jani 821771?" one of the Guardsmen asked him.

"Yes," Jani replied.

"Follow us."

"Why?"

"We are escorting you to the women's side of the hospital."

"Women's side?!" Jani exclaimed. "Why?"

"I don't know why," the Guardsman said, "but I know those are my orders. So follow us and make sure you stay between the two of us. If you don't remain in your place, we will stop you by using force. Do you understand these terms?"

"Yes …" Jani managed to say.

"Good," the Guardsman said. "Now follow us."

Jani followed the men without any resistance. He soon realized that other men in the main entrance hall were all staring at them. His exceptional treatment was very eye-catching; there was no denying that. Why was he being taken to the women's side of the hospital? How typical was something like this? Why exactly was he here?

They arrived in a long corridor. The walls of the corridor were white and the three men kept walking towards a set of locked doors at the other end. Jani knew that once he stepped through those doors, he would arrive in a completely new world. He had never even dreamt that something like this would happen to him, not once.

When they reached the doors, the other Guardsman opened the locking mechanism with his thumbprint. The doors opened and they arrived in an elevator. Once the doors had closed again they started to travel upwards.

When the elevator finally stopped and the doors opened, Jani saw a well-illuminated waiting room. He stepped forward with the two Guardsmen escorting him and noticed a few women sitting on chairs here and there. They really were women. He really was in the same room together with human women. It was mindboggling, but very real nonetheless.

"Eyes forward," the Guardsman commanded.

Jani did as was told without hesitating. He did not want to make the Guardsmen angry in the slightest.

"Who's my doctor?" Jani asked the Guardsmen as he tried to forget being in the same room as women. Perhaps talking to the Guardsmen would help him in that.

"Doctor Mari Alauda," the man said.

"A woman?"

"Of course," the Guardsman stated. "We are on the women's side of the hospital."

Jani swallowed. He didn't know what to think about a woman doctor, but he kept his thoughts to himself. The only thing he needed to do right now was to concentrate on not making the two Guardsmen – here to monitor his every move – upset. The most important thing was to remain calm and keep his facial expression as neutral as possible. Even if he was on the women's side of this hospital, which was extremely odd in itself, he had to pretend that it was something quite normal to him.

2.

Mari Alauda stared through her large office window at the crowds of people on the street below. There was darkness in her eyes. The heavy sensation of great pressure in her chest had finally eased and now it was easier to breathe again.

Mari still felt slightly nauseous; however, as a doctor she knew it wouldn't take long until all her symptoms faded away. Being a doctor she also knew that she was suffering from anxiety disorder and the autonomic nerve system's symptoms which came with it. It was fortunate that she had the appropriate medicine within her reach which numbed her fits; she was able to treat herself without anyone else knowing what was going on.

Turning her back to the window, she sat down behind her desk. She took a deep breath and activated her calendar, without which she simply couldn't imagine living. Suddenly a familiar name caught her eye on the 13:45 slot; Saia Motasilla. Mari couldn't help but smile, which felt quite refreshing after the morning.

She had known Saia for some years now. Lately the girl had come to the hospital simply to meet her, even though there was nothing wrong with her health, at least not physically. The latest reason that had given Saia reason to visit her was the ID chip each woman wore on her arm. After the age of fifteen, the ID chips were typically exchanged for new ones and Saia had been complaining for months now how nasty her ID chip felt. Mari was not convinced of Saia's complaints, but she consented to take the time to meet her. Perhaps all Saia wanted after all was someone to talk to.

Saia was a peculiar person. She was quiet, which often gave the impression of indifference. However, Mari was convinced that this did not tell the whole truth about the girl. There was strength in Saia; strength she had decided to conceal. If she were more outspoken, it could have opened possibilities for the girl to become whatever she had wanted. But Saia kept things to herself and Mari guessed the reason was shyness. There was also, however, a possibility that Saia was still going through the tragedy she had faced four years ago. Her older brother had committed suicide, which was not only devastating for families in general, but also slightly embarrassing. So perhaps some of her quietness was a result of this particular incident.

Despite Saia's silent ways, the girl had always remembered her manners by being very polite. Compared to Mari's daughter Naja, Saia was different in every possible way. Even though Naja was Mari's daughter, she did not like the girl. Naja always needed to be the center of attention. Naja didn't know how to be genuine and, in addition, she was full of herself. She lied, was cocky and even lazy, and Mari didn't have the time or the will to invest in raising her daughter. The feeling was mutual. Naja didn't like her own mother either, and it was something Mari hardly lost sleep over. She had done almost everything wrong with Naja since the beginning and now it was too late for her to expect or even demand that Naja be something she was not. Perhaps making a commitment to a man would eventually fix her personality one day.

The look in Mari's eyes darkened again. She tried to remind herself she was in no hurry to go home. She was still in her office; one of the few places she truly felt she belonged in. Naja was old enough not to need her around anymore, and when it came to her husband, he had never needed her in the first place. No one missed her anywhere else but here in the Main Hospital and it was exactly what she had wanted ever since she had been a young girl. She was living the kind of life she had always hoped for and therefore there was every reason in the world to feel proud of what she had accomplished.

Mari had always wanted to become a medical doctor. The only noteworthy obstacle on the path towards this dream had been committing herself to a man, which was the condition for women to receive permission to work. Luckily she had realized the means she had to use in order to achieve her dream when growing up and she had gained more than she had ever dreamed of.

And now she wasn't just any faceless doctor in the Gavialis Main Hospital; she was Doctor Alauda, one of the leading fertility doctors in the world, as well as a pioneer in the field of artificial pregnancies. Her name and face were known in medical circles in every city of the world. She had power and she was respected. She had a huge office with a magnificent view and because she was a woman, she was protected, and almost all her wishes were granted. She was Mari Alauda; a woman who was admired by other women as well.

However, despite all her recent accomplishments, Mari had started to realize the high price her choices and wishes brought and she hated the voice within, which continually reminded her of it. She refused to acknowledge its whispering, because now it was too late to question the choices which had taken her to the top of the world. She was living her dream and analyzing the past would lead nowhere.

Mari was pulled back to reality once she noticed the sign of an incoming message blinking on her table. She activated the communication link and a familiar face appeared on her display.

"Doctor Alauda," said the man in greeting.

"Doctor Aix," Mari replied and felt a blush rushing to her cheekbones.

Mari tried her best to cover her excitement, but she just didn't know how to look at Doctor Aix without feeling anything. This man had the power to create chaos inside her and all Mari could do was to pretend that it didn't happen every time she saw him. This time, however, Doctor Aix was extremely serious.

"We lost another one this morning," the man sighed and shook his head.

"Are you serious?" Mari asked him, even though she knew Aix wouldn't joke about this particular matter.

"Three months and that was it," Aix said.

"What in the world is going on?" Mari wondered and shook her head as well. "What are we doing wrong? Technically there is nothing wrong with the artificial wombs."

"A fatal error occurs in some part of the process," Aix stated. "We just haven't been able to identify it yet."

"What would it have been?" Mari asked him.

"A girl," Aix answered.

Mari took a deep breath, closed her eyes and shook her head again. The loss of every single XX fetus was a much more bitter loss than two XYs.

"I'll upload you some statistics from the past five years," Aix informed her next.

"Statistics?"

"Please study them and contact me immediately when you have drawn your conclusions about them. I want to know if you reach the same conclusion as I."

"Alright," Mari said and frowned at Aix's vagueness.

Then she noticed that her workstation was receiving data which was being sent from Aix's ID account.

"I'll examine the numbers today and I will let you know as soon as I have concluded my analysis," Mari informed him.

"Good," Doctor Aix stated. "If anyone can solve this puzzle, it's you."

"You have high expectations of me," Mari said and smiled.

"Of course I do," Aix stated and winked at her.

The man terminated the communication link between them and Mari's personal calendar filled the main view of her display again.

Mari didn't like Doctor Aix's news one bit. It was something that both worried and angered her, because she took every lost fetus as a personal failure. However, despite the grim news, she was smiling now. All it had taken was the attention she had received from Aix; the man had noticed her.

Aix was the only person in the world who had managed to change something within her. It felt like he had liberated her. Before Aix had appeared in her life, Mari had felt nothing and she had always thought of it as an ideal situation to be in.

Aix, however, had changed everything. The man had forced her to face her emotions again. He was the only one who had found a way through the walls she had built around herself; walls, which concealed the true self she had not let anyone ever really know. Aix was her perfect partner, a person with whom she didn't have to be anything else but herself. He made her feel important, but most of all, beautiful. No individual person had managed to do that before. They were not committed to one another, though, which was a bitter fact Mari still had a hard time accepting.

It had been more or less three years ago when Aix had appeared in the Gavialis Main Hospital and without warning he had woken in Mari a woman she had not known before; a woman she had never missed before. Suddenly life had started to feel carefree and easy for her. Her days had been filled with joy which had given a new meaning to everything in her life. Before Aix, she had never really appreciated love or falling in love in general. She had never expected to experience it herself and she had not even wanted to. She had not grown up feeling lonely; she had been too busy for that because she had had goals. She had kept her heart closed because all she had time for was herself and fulfilling her dreams.

Aix, however, had ripped her heart open and Mari had suddenly observed how all the clichés of love had gradually started to apply to her life as well. For the first time in her life she had started to feel lonely. Having Aix in her life had also introduced her to this nagging feeling that she was missing something extremely important. Suddenly she had started to feel an odd desire to be seen as a woman first instead of a person, at least when Aix was concerned. She had found the sexual side of herself, which had only typically emerged when she had lain on her bed, alone, away from the eyes of the others. This sudden discovery of her sexuality was not just a part of her psyche she had to tolerate because of biology, now it had a purpose. Just the mere thought of being against Aix's body was enough to engulf her whole being in a warm feeling that simply swept her away.

Mari stood up and returned to the window. She tried to forget Aix for a moment, but her efforts were in vain. As rewarding as working with him was, it had its downside. Aix was a distraction to her, but the kind of distraction she could no longer live without. It wasn't a very functional equation, but neither could Mari let it go.

"Just focus on the relevant things," Mari sighed to herself before returning to her desk.

Then she opened the statistics Aix had sent her and started to study the numbers on her display. The file contained data of all children cultivated in artificial wombs during the past five years in all world cities from Gavialis to Parus. Mari let the numbers run past her eyes and she quickly began to see a worrying pattern in them. There was no denying the fact that, in recent years, a growing number of girl fetuses had died in the artificial wombs.

Mari leaned back in her chair and took a deep breath. The statistics were deeply concerning. She knew very well that on average, only 79 per 100 artificial pregnancies were successful and because of that, womb technology was constantly under development in order to increase the success rate of artificial child production. However, what Mari couldn't ignore was the gender distribution of the successful 79%. During the past five years an ever increasing number of the children born had been boys.

"What on earth could be doing this?" Mari whispered. "Why are our XX cases more prone to damage?"

Mari tapped the surface of her desk with her fingertips, a typical gesture when she was trying to figure out explanations to issues which first seemed to have none. Artificial womb technology was their only way of raising the number of girls faster than natural women were able to. Over recent decades, they had succeeded in increasing the number of females, but now something had started to go wrong. Why now? Even though they had constantly invested in the production of girls specifically, the amount of girls born alive in all children born was in an alarming minority. The statistics Aix had sent to her were relatively concrete evidence of the fact that it was not about some fluke in statistics anymore. So what were they doing wrong?

Mari sighed in frustration. Something was causing a deadly development in female fetuses and it couldn't be anything natural because at the same time the production of boys showed no indications of change. Could the artificial wombs be the source of the problem? That didn't make sense because, on a technical level, each womb functioned identically to the next. When observing the situation from a biological perspective, the gender of a fetus was not a relevant factor in pregnancies, no matter if the carrier was a woman or an artificial womb.

She searched for the latest statistic pertaining to natural pregnancies on a worldwide scale. She studied the numbers for a moment and realized that the gender distribution of natural pregnancies was weighted in favor of girls. This was expected, since many women wanted to increase the status of their men by promising them a daughter as their first-born. That was a promise Mari had also given her own husband back then. Therefore, many first "natural" pregnancies began in hospitals with medical doctors who placed fertilized ova in the wombs of mothers-to-be. In addition, among the miscarriages of natural pregnancies there was no notable differences in the numbers of male and female fetuses. So why were the artificial wombs rejecting female ones?

Mari wondered why she hadn't become aware of these statistics before. If anyone, she should have recognized the current situation of child cultivation a long time ago! Now, as she studied the statistics, she felt like she was seeing the numbers for the first time. However, that was impossible and she refused to even entertain the idea.

Suddenly Mari was pulled back from her thoughts when her workstation gave a signal.

"*Your 13:15 client has registered present and he has arrived,*" Mari's personal assistant informed her.

Mari's facial expression became somewhat sly. She closed the statistics file and pushed the artificial womb issue out of her mind for a moment.

"Show him in," Mari told her personal assistant and straightened her posture.

After a brief moment the doors of her office finally opened and three men entered the room; two Yellow Guardsmen and Mari's 13:15 client. This was a young man whose face Mari had pictured in her mind on several occasions. And now she finally saw him standing in front of her and she was pleased with what she saw.

"Please have a seat," Mari said to the young man.

The man barely looked at her. This was somewhat expected because many young men felt awkward in the presence of an adult woman. In addition, there were also two relatively big Yellow Guardsmen in the room with them, which most likely made the young man feel even more nervous. That was the point of the Guardsmen after all.

The man took a seat and the Yellow Guardsmen remained on each side of the doors.

"You may leave," Mari told the Guardsmen.

"Ma'am?" one of them said.

"I will call you immediately, if there are any problems," Mari assured the man. "He is my client, so he has the right to a private discussion, without anyone else hearing us. So leave."

For a moment there was an awkward silence in the room. It irritated Mari slightly, because Guardsmen were expected to do as she told them. Why didn't the men leave?

"Very well, then," the other one finally replied in a disinclined tone.

The Guardsmen left and finally Mari was alone with the young man who had come to meet her.

"So," Mari said, activating the man's personal information by choosing his name from her calendar. "You are Jani 821771?"

"Yes," the man replied, but without making eye contact with Mari.

Mari observed him as discreetly as possible. Jani 821771 sat on the other side of Mari's desk and he was apparently uncomfortable. Mari knew the reason; her gender made him nervous. Most likely he had not seen many women at close proximity, if at all. It was a fact which still made Mari wonder about the world sometimes, even though she had been born and had grown up in the world where it was an everyday issue. Many young boys were told about the existence of women when they were six years old and ready to start their basic education. For some boys, the truth about the other gender was revealed during their education.

"You live in First Circle?" Mari asked the man.

"Yes."

"You may look at me while speaking to me," Mari informed him just to lighten somewhat the charged atmosphere between them. "I am a doctor and what we discuss in this room will remain between the two of us. Do you understand that?"

"Yes ma'am," Jani said.

"You have 43 Silver Wing marks?"

"Yes," Jani 821771 answered, and Mari could hear from his voice that the situation was embarrassing for him.

43 Silver Wing marks for a man of Jani's age was undeniably quite unimpressive. It meant that Jani was not ambitious enough to compete, succeed and go forward. And that was a pity.

"You work in Linai?" Mari asked him next.

"I do."

"And the previous physical examination was carried out last year in First Circle?"

"Yes."

"You have been well since then?"

"I have."

"Good," Mari said. "Do you know why I invited you here?" she finally asked him.

"Not really," Jani replied. "The invitation was most vague about this visit's purpose."

"I am very pleased that you chose to come anyway," Mari said.

"Why did you invite me here?"

"We have invited others as well," Mari assured him. "We want a great variety of men from your age group to contribute to some research of ours; men from different kinds of situations in life."

Jani listened to her and nodded.

"As you may already know, each city hospital has a department dedicated to both carrying out child cultivation and to studying it."

"I do."

"One part of examining child cultivation is the continuous development of artificial wombs. It should go without saying that the work being carried out in this field is extremely important."

Jani looked quickly at Mari and nodded again.

"Male gametes are naturally an inseparable part of our research. Even though a notable percentage of children is developed and cultivated in artificial wombs, both male and female gametes are still required. Research in the field of artificial wombs carried out in this department is the reason for you being here today. From the point of view of our research, we perceive you as a so-called random sample. In practice, this means that we are asking you to donate some of your gametes for the research work carried out into artificial womb development."

"I get the right to reproduce?" Jani asked her, astonished.

"No," Mari replied immediately and tried to hide her smile. "Your donation will be used in research work only which will not result in a living human child. Research in this case involves optimizing the artificial wombs' functions. However, we won't use your gamete without your permission and approval. Therefore, we need you to participate in this voluntarily. So I am asking you; can we count on your help?"

"Of course," Jani replied slightly abashed.

"Excellent," Mari said. "So, I assume that your physical health is at the same level as indicated by research into the general population, which corresponds with the average physical health of all men around the world. Therefore, I need to ask you a few personal questions."

"Alright."

"Do you use intoxicants on a regular basis? Alcohol or drugs?"

"No, I don't."

"Good," Mari stated, "because I should remind you of the fact that self-inflicted physical injuries are not typically treated."

"Unless a man doesn't happen to have enough Silver Wing marks," Jani added.

"In that case a man would have to have quite a lot of them for us to waste our resources on treating him," Mari explained seriously.

Jani smiled awkwardly and nodded.

"Are you prone to depression?" Mari asked him.

"I don't think so," Jani said. "I don't use any intoxicants, so ..."

"Depression isn't necessarily a sign of drug use, though using intoxicants does lead to depression in many cases."

"My former next door neighbor got depressed because he used drugs."

"It is an unfortunate story of too many young men out there," Mari stated. "As a doctor I can't feel anything but disappointment towards cases like that."

"Well, it was his decision," Jani replied.

"From a medical doctor's point of view all drugs should be legally banned," Mari voiced her opinion, "but on the other hand, hiding intoxicants and even denying they exist could just stir people's curiosity, and in a worst-case scenario, we could have many more men being dropped out of the cities than we have now."

"So, each one of us makes our own decisions," Jani said.

"That's the way it is," Mari stated, and smiled. "And therefore I am glad to see a young man from your age group who has decided more wisely."

Jani stared at the desk between them and nodded.

"Do you suffer from any sexually transmitted diseases?"

"No," Jani answered uneasily.

"Good," Mari said. "And have you had any symptoms after eating certain foods? Like breathing difficulties, rashes or swelling of mucusmenbranes?"

"No."

"Alright," Mari said, adding the information to the appropriate form. "In other words you are in good health and you are able to work."

"Yes."

"That's good to hear," Mari said, and smiled. "Now you should confirm your approval to participate in this research here with your signature."

Mari activated a small screen on the patient's side of the table and a form appeared on it. Jani 821771's personal information had already been filled in.

"I don't have to come back here after this at all?" Jani then asked her.

"You don't," Mari said. "After this conversation you will be led to an isolated room, where a male nurse will take a sample from your scrotum. If you don't wish to undergo this procedure, you also have the option to provide the sample yourself."

Jani looked at her for a moment and Mari could feel how the awkwardness between them suddenly became more tangible.

"The first option sounds alright," Jani said.

"The operation is painless," Mari added. "It is comparable with giving a blood sample."

"Alright."

"Thank you very much for your help, Jani 821771," Mari then said and nodded. "We truly appreciate your input."

Then she pressed the notice button to inform her Guardsmen that she was done with her client and the door behind Jani's back opened almost immediately.

"You may escort this young gentleman to the sampling room D521.1," Mari informed the men.

The Yellow Guardsmen nodded simultaneously. Jani stood up and nodded to Mari, before turning and leaving the room with the two big men escorting him out.

Once the door was closed, Mari felt complete emptiness. She had not known what to expect from this appointment, but now that she really had met a person she had already been tracking for almost a year, she didn't know what she was feeling. He had given a relatively level-headed impression of himself, but his number of Silver Wing marks was anything but impressive. However, the most important thing was that Jani had believed her lie and volunteered to take part in research that didn't really exist. However, the end justified the means and Mari needed a sample of Jani 821771's semen. The young man in question was, after all, Doctor Aix's biological offspring.

Mari switched her calendar window to the main window of her ID account and chose her personal files. A list appeared on the screen with multiple files, from images to text-based documents, but only one of them was encrypted. Mari decrypted the file and the following heading appeared on her display.

Project Luna

Mari copied the personal health information of Jani 821771 and pasted it into the file. Then she closed the document. Mari smiled. Project Luna was progressing unexpectedly easily and soon she would have a baby girl, who would bring new meaning to her life.

Mari took a deep breath and leaned against her chair's backrest. She had already figured everything out a long time ago. When an egg, fertilized with Jani 821771's contribution, was implanted into an artificial womb, she would personally follow the development of the child in a most observant manner. Even though she was not a typical sight in the artificial womb room these days, no one would question her presence there; she was Doctor Mari Alauda after all. So she would have this girl child, one way or another. If the first embryo failed, she would start from the beginning and try again and she would start over as often as it took to get the baby girl she wanted in her arms.

Mari had been giving Luna's birth a lot of thought for a long time now. Even though she had destroyed her own ovaries after giving birth to Naja, she still had the chance to have this child which was biologically hers because she still had some of her own ova to put to good use.

Doctor Aix, on the other hand, had already been sterilized a long time ago, as was the custom. Aix had, however, told her once about one of his research projects during which he had applied and received permission to use his own gametes. It had been quite an exceptional arrangement, but Mari had been very glad Aix had revealed this particular story from his past. It had given her the certainty that there was at least one biological offspring in the world and therefore Mari had spent a lot of time searching for the genetic match with Aix's DNA. Finally, she had found Jani 821771. Any biological child of Jani 821771 would be almost identical to Doctor Aix's child.

Mari had decided that this time she would do things right. She would avoid all those mistakes she had made, and was still making, with Naja. The only reason she had given birth to Naja was for the sake of her husband. Luna was something she would do for herself and the child would be perfect. She was an honored and respected doctor, therefore no one would question her desire to be a part of a girl's life who was cultivated in an artificial womb. Many women had decided to take "artificial" girls under their guardianship, a fact which had provided the children with viable alternatives to growing up in an educational institution.

After careful consideration Mari had concluded that taking an interest in one child's life would not render her exceptional in other people's eyes. She wouldn't take the girl home because she still didn't have the time to raise a child. Instead, she would be a female life instructor for the girl; one who would teach and guide the child, who would do everything in her power to make sure the girl had all she needed to grow up into a perfect woman.

Mari stood up and returned to the window. She watched the crowd on the streets and took a deep breath. She was happy that Aix's biological son was not too short because short men typically had trouble advancing in the society. However, Jani seemed to be a little bit unfocused, if any conclusions could be drawn from the amount of his Silver Wing marks. However, Mari had the feeling that if a guardian had raised Jani, he could have become something else, something better. If Aix himself had raised

Jani, the young man could have ended up as a doctor as well. However, Jani 821771 was what he was, and soon Mari would have received all she needed from him. That part was dealt with, she didn't have to spend another moment thinking about his life.

Mari couldn't stop wondering how love for another person resulted in a need to expand her love in the form of a child, but she wanted Luna. She wanted something which was both hers and Aix's because there was nothing certain between them now.

Mari still didn't know what Aix wanted and what the man even thought of her. She felt his attraction, but she didn't know how deep it was. The limiting factor was, of course, her personal situation. She was already committed to one man. Therefore, it was no wonder Aix didn't gravitate towards her more intensively, even though Mari still wished he would. She wished for this each morning upon her arrival at the hospital. In fact, she would have done almost anything to be near him. She missed him and being close to him, even now, but how much did Aix think of her? Why couldn't they ever speak of their emotions openly?

The door emitted a sound which pulled Mari back from her thoughts. She opened the door from the locking mechanism on her table, and Doctor Aix entered the room. Mari felt an ache in her chest. She was emotionally bound to Aix whether she wanted to be or not, and she could only hope the man would give some kind of indication of his feelings; that he would let Mari come near him and by doing so, would free them both.

He was all Mari could ever want. He was handsome, intellectual and was ever-present in her life. Mari's official partner was never there and this was fine by her. They had made their commitment for purely rational reasons. Her taking a husband who was over 30 years older than her hadn't been exceptional by any standards, since a woman's first husband was typically decades older than she was, but in Mari's case, the exceptional aspect of the commitment had been the fact that she shared her life with a man who did not want to touch her. Their lives together had always been one elaborate façade. Their deal had improved her husband's social status and through their union, Mari had received official permission to enter working life. The partnership between them had been an agreement based on common sense, and it had served them both well.

"Doctor Aix," Mari stated.

"Did you manage to examine the statistics I sent?" Aix asked her while the door was still open behind him.

Mari took a quick look at the Guardsman who was glaring at Aix's back without blinking an eye.

"You may close the door," Mari informed her protector.

The Guardsman did as he was told and finally they were alone.

"I did examine them," Mari finally answered, taking a seat behind her desk, "and I find it very obvious that there is something seriously wrong with XX production."

Aix sat on the other side of the desk where his biological offspring had been sitting just a few moments ago; a young man Aix knew nothing about.

"How do you explain it?" Aix asked her.

"I can't right now," Mari answered, "and I did promise to contact you as soon as I have analyzed the situation."

"Perhaps I could wait a minute longer," Aix said and looked at Mari in a way which made her feel weak inside.

"I'm flattered," Mari noted and smiled mischievously.

She enjoyed the situation because she didn't have these kinds of moments with Aix too often. On too many occasions their private moments had been filled with business, even if Mari had practically suffocated through her need to be noticed by him. Aix was relatively erratic. There were moments when he more or less ignored her on purpose, but then there were moments when he practically demanded Mari's full attention.

"It is mind-boggling that this kind of risk didn't raise red flags decades ago," Mari sighed.

"What do you mean?"

"The one, who decided back then that artificial wombs were primarily targeted towards boy child cultivation, did not see far enough," Mari specified.

"And the structure of our society has become distorted," Aix continued.

"And now we are facing the consequences of those decisions."

"We should compile a report for the city's Internal Affairs Council, if not for the Health Council as well," Aix said. "These statistics are worldwide, not only Gavialis-centered, and the situation is quite alarming."

"The situation is very alarming," Mari admitted, "but what should we put in that report? We don't even have a hypothesis yet to explain why female fetuses are dying in the artificial wombs."

Aix looked at Mari with a calm expression on his face and waited for her to continue.

"The alarming decrease of girl children will come out eventually," Mari added, "and when it does, they are going to press us hard. When that happens, we had better have at least some idea of the factors that are causing this."

"I know."

"The two of us will be among the first ones in those hearings," Mari continued, "So, we must find an explanation for this somehow, and sooner rather than later. We have to identify the critical factors behind this, as well as the specific points on the pregnancy timeline where the development of XX fetuses fails."

"However, male fetuses are developing just as they always have," Aix reminded her. "How do you explain that?"

"The only explanation is there is nothing wrong with the artificial wombs, if the wombs which maintain the pregnancy don't differ from one gender to another."

"Such blips in the technology would have been found ages ago."

"Would they?" Mari asked him. "The fertility program was perceived as a success as soon as cultivated children were harvested alive from the artificial wombs. Have we really uncovered the entire development of a human fetus, from the implantation of the embryo to the harvesting of a living child? Do we really know every single detail of what happens inside an artificial womb during the 40 weeks of pregnancy? The development of a human child from an egg to nine-month-old child is an extremely complex process."

"What would make the wombs destroy female fetuses in particular? Why only during the last few years?"

"Are we absolutely sure there had not been any loss of girls before that?"

"In order to find out we should examine older data as well."

"I think we should do that."

"Alright," Aix said. "You're the boss. Should I assign a research group?"

"Don't," Mari said. "This should remain between the two of us for the time being until we are absolutely sure about what is going on. I will examine the statistics from 15–20 years ago, you take the ones from 10–15 years ago."

"Very well."

"We should be prepared, however, that the most current statistics will end up at the Councils at some point."

"It is going to happen sooner or later."

"They are going to demand at least one, if not two, purely XX years from us, and that is going to mean that, instead of the traditional 70–30 figures, all the fetuses in production will be expected to be XXs. So we have to find out what is causing this odd loss of girls and we have to find out before the media get wind of this situation. Someone will lose his or her job, even if no one has done anything wrong. When the media circus gets heated, there always needs to be a scapegoat."

"I know," Aix sighed.

"The only positive I can come up with from these statistics is the natural pregnancies; at least they have come off well," Mari said.

"We really do have to produce more girls. If we can't, we are going to be faced with the situation where we will be unable to fix the distortion in the world's gender distribution. There are not enough girls and even if artificial wombs eased the situation, the manufacture of the wombs is still laborious, slow and extremely error-prone. Once one is damaged, it cannot be replaced with a new one immediately."

"I know," Mari sighed. "So, we have to get started. We have to find all the pieces of this puzzle. If we are unable to fix this situation, it could lead to huge social problems in the future, and not just in Gavialis."

"Society will collapse," Aix said in a most serious manner.

"We have to find a solution," Mari sighed.

Aix nodded, before getting to his feet and walking towards the door. Mari followed him and as they reached the door, Aix turned around to face her one more time. All of a sudden he placed his hand on Mari's left cheek. Mari was surprised and in that instant, she felt her knees go weak.

"What are you doing?" she asked Aix softly.

"You know what."

Mari was taken aback. She felt the warmth of his touch and it made her feel an ache within her. It was yearning in its purest form. She needed to be touched so much it practically hurt.

"I would kiss you, if I knew I wouldn't be thrown in prison for it."

"I had no idea you wanted to kiss me."

"Yes, you did."

"What if I don't tell a soul?" Mari asked him and smiled.

"The Guardsman behind this door would find out somehow," Aix said.

Then he took his hand from her face and let it slid over her chest to her abdomen, and all the way to her thighs. Mari felt the heat between her legs and the sensation was pure torture. She wanted Aix more than ever, and she could tell by the look on his face that there was the same need inside him as well. The air between them became warm and Mari didn't hear anything else but their deep breathing.

Aix removed his hands, even though the look in his eyes revealed it was the last thing he wanted to do. Then he turned his back on her and opened the door. Mari felt her cheeks burning. She watched Aix going without blinking an eye, until the door was shut and she was left alone again.

3.

Saia was impatient. She wanted to leave for the Main Hospital, but it was still too early for that. Instead, she browsed the latest headlines in order to kill time and tried to think about something other than her upcoming meeting. However, the mere thought of seeing Doctor Alauda in person made her anxious.

Suddenly, the news headline about the dead woman in Erasmia caught Saia's eye. Saia froze the headline flow on the screen and stared at it for a while. She didn't know if she dared to read the content of the article because the thought of yet another woman being killed in such a short period of time made Saia shudder. She wondered how something like this could still happen in today's world. Shouldn't people's murderous tendencies have remained in the days of the Great War? Or was the existence of mentally ill men capable of murder always inevitable in human society? It was an interesting question, but Saia knew she had no one to discuss the matter with. Other girls simply wanted to forget about the Erasmia incident and the Yellow Guardsmen remained silent, since their job wasn't to talk in the presence of women in the first place.

Saia sighed. Women were supposed to be safe; that's why the Yellow Guard existed. How had the murderer got past the Guardsmen again? Or was the murderer himself a Guardsman? The possibility didn't please Saia at all, but she wasn't alone with her pondering. The thousands of readers who had commented on the news had raised the topic of the Yellow Guardsmen in the discussion about the circumstances surrounding the death of the young Erasmian woman. Was this the murderer's intention; to instigate fear and paranoia among women? Why? What could the motive behind his actions be? Why did he hate women? And how long would it take before this psychopath was caught and sent to rot in the Cold Pit?

Saia was pulled back from her thoughts when the signal of an incoming message beeped under her fingers. She opened the message and realized it had been sent from the Health Council.

"Well, there it is at last," she sighed.

Saia had been expecting this particular message for some time. Now that it had come, it stirred mixed emotions within her. The strongest emotions emerging on the surface were, however, extreme discomfort and anger. Unlike the majority of girls of her age, she had not been expecting this message very eagerly. The fact that it had arrived today was, however, an interesting coincidence because her upcoming meeting in the Main Hospital was closely related to the contents of this message.

Saia took a deep breath and started to read.

Saia Motasilla,

We congratulate you, young woman, on reaching sexual maturity! We have booked an appointment for a health check for you in the Gavialis Main Hospital on the second day of the tenth month at 9:10 (Gavialis Time). The purpose of this health check is to re-examine your ovaries and womb. If the doctor carrying out your examination finds your physical condition to be good, we will extract and store your ova for artificial pregnancies. This operation is carried out on every 16-year-old girl who has reached sexual maturity.

The ova donation for artificial pregnancies is your civic duty. Refusal to participate in this operation and the possible sanctions resulting thereof are recorded in Hirundian Law (Law 146.3).

Your health check will be carried out by the doctor responsible for the fertility program, Doctor Mari Alauda (female). If you need special transportation to get to the Main Hospital, please reply to this message.

We thank you for your cooperation.

Kind regards,
Doctor Dama / Chief of Fertility Research
Gavialis Main Hospital,
Sixth Circle, 60-3246
GAVIALIS

[Attachment: Message of the Fertility Campaign]

[In order to confirm the authenticity of this message, please open this stamp]

Saia hesitated for a moment before activating the attachment. When she did so, a beautiful dark-haired woman appeared on her screen. She was one of the most famous beauties in the world. Her name was Mrs. Timalii and she was the Education and Culture Council Chief's spouse.

"Hello, young women of the world!" Mrs. Timalii greeted the viewer and her dark eyes sparkled. *"My name is Minla Timalii and I want to tell you beautiful young women around the world of the great adventure which is waiting for you. This adventure is called motherhood."*

Saia's facial expression became sour. Mrs. Timalii was an admired woman, there was no doubt about that, but she had now agreed to be the new face of the fertility program as well? The Health Council obviously didn't fool around when campaigning for procreation.

"I have five wonderful children – four daughters and one son. My better half and I have already planned a new pregnancy for next year and luckily the leading fertility doctors of the world are supporting us in this."

The image on the screen changed to a well-illuminated apartment. Mrs. Timalii was sitting in front of some large windows while a group of children sitting on the floor were playing nicely with their toys.

"Motherhood is an extremely rewarding job. One woman can give her husband over ten children during her lifetime, so think about what a hundred women can do! Our advanced medicine will also make sure that most of your children will be girls, unless you choose otherwise."

Then a close-up of Minla Timalii's face appeared on the screen again and the wide smile on her face changed to a more serious expression as she continued her speech.

"Women who stay at home are the real heroines of this world. That is why I encourage you, young women, to think about your future seriously. Each woman is indispensable because we have the ability to shape the future in a way men never could!"

Next, Minla Timalii was playing with her children with a wide smile on her face. The children seemed to be happy having their mother with them. Then the following text appeared on the screen:

Motherhood gives life a purpose

"We women are amazing!" Mrs. Timalii stated and looked straight at the viewer with her deep dark eyes. *"We create life! And based on my own experiences I can assure you all that motherhood has made me a whole person. The thought of a*

working life is an alluring one, of that I am sure, but as a woman who has experienced both sides of life's coin I can conclude that there isn't a more rewarding job out there than being a mother! So join us mothers to create the next generation of mankind."

The announcement then ended and the following text appeared on the display.

Every woman is worthy of motherhood – you included!

Saia sighed. She was very pleased about the fact that artificial wombs had been invented; no matter how convincingly beautiful Minla Timalii talked about motherhood. Luckily, women had the freedom not to be committed to a man and had the choice not to procreate, at least in principle. However, Saia intended to hold on tightly to this right of hers, no matter if she earned only the deep disapproval of the others.

Saia deactivated the message and continued tapping the surface of the table with her fingers. She knew that many girls waited years for this message from the Health Council; it was considered a milestone of the passage into adulthood. Every woman in the world received this message, no one wanted to be different. Saia on the other hand didn't know what to think of it. She wanted to see it as something meaningless or insignificant; taking a multi-vitamin each morning, but it wasn't like that. The result of this operation would be her someday having biological offspring; children she would know nothing about. This thought disturbed her, even though she knew it shouldn't; she had never heard of anyone mourning her ova, but for Saia the entire procedure was somewhat disturbing.

Saia took a deep breath. She knew Naja had already gone through her egg donation operation. The girl had made such a fuss of receiving her invitation to Swallow's Nest, which of course referred to the Main Hospital's fertility department, that no one in their study group had managed to miss her boasting. Naja's need for constant attention had amused Saia. She had not let her true thoughts be seen then, but secretly she had laughed at her.

Saia simply tolerated Naja. She had to, because when Naja had succeeded in taking pictures of her a few years ago wearing only her underwear, saying she would leak the photographs to the public via the Yellow Guardsmen, Saia had settled for her part as Naja's trash bin. She didn't want her pictures spread around the men, because she wasn't physically beautiful. And even if she had been as slender as Naja, she still wouldn't want any man to see her almost naked. The mere thought of something like that was extremely humiliating. So she had agreed to Naja's terms. She had lied for her, written her study assignments, and kept listening to her shallow thoughts for hours, flattering her from time to time. She had taken the verbal humiliation time and again, but luckily she had already become partly numbed to them.

However, her tolerating Naja wasn't for nothing, because the girl had something Saia wanted, therefore she had partly agreed to this loose alliance between them, even though she often wanted to rip Naja's eyes from their sockets. Naja was Doctor Alauda's daughter, and Doctor Alauda was the only person in the world whose opinion mattered to Saia. Naja had opened the door for her into Doctor Alauda's life without anyone paying any attention to it. Naja had made it possible for her to get closer to Doctor Alauda's daily life, even though the woman didn't spend much time at home. So if Saia had to be the main target of Naja's nastiness, it would be a small price to pay for being a part of Doctor Alauda's life.

Saia didn't understand why Naja hated and despised her own mother so deeply. Perhaps Naja envied her mother because she was perfect. Saia's own mother, on the other hand, was an idiot who used a significant amount of time putting a dampener on her as well as judging her. Just yesterday she had said Saia wasn't allowed to have dinner, since she was already fat enough.

"Why can't you put any effort into your looks?" her mother had asked her more often than Saia could remember. "You are not pretty, Saia. Don't assume that being female alone will make you worth pursuing. Ugly and lazy girls are desired by no one!"

Saia didn't want to be attractive, because she didn't want any man to pay any attention to her. She had always wanted to be left alone. However, her mother was obsessed with her daughter's looks, and unlike Naja she hated the thought of the day when her name would be added to the Apertum list. Then she would be obliged to participate in meetings with old men, because some of those "successful ones" might want to get to know her better. What on earth would she have in common with men who were decades older than her? However, her mother thought otherwise. She thought it was only right that a woman didn't have to spend the rest of her life with the first man she was committed to. In fact, many women made a commitment to a man twice or even three times during their lives.

"Your second man may be one you like," was one of her mother's favorite arguments. "The first one you need only tolerate. Once you've given him a daughter, you can tell him to leave you alone."

Saia couldn't help but wonder what her mother had thought of the man with whom she'd had Ati with. Had Ati been just a prize to that man; a child whom the mother had not cared much about? Had her mother given Ati more reasons to go? If that was the case, Saia could never forgive her because life after Ati had been hard for her. She missed her brother because no one else in the entire world had accepted her as Ati had.

Saia pushed the memories of her brother aside because they only made her sad, but the feeling of hunger didn't really make her mood better, either. Saia wondered if her mother was still at home because she really needed to eat soon. Her mother had recently inspected her room and found the hidden food and taken it away. After the incident Saia had felt the atmosphere in the apartment getting even more tense. Her mother had made it very clear how much she disapproved of Saia's outward appearance as well as her habit of spending time on browsing the information network in her room. It was too boyish from a woman's viewpoint.

"It's a miracle you haven't grown a man's parts between your legs already," her mother had even proclaimed once.

Then there was this other incident when her mother had gotten so frustrated with her that she had pushed Saia onto the bed in rage and pulled her pants down.

"Does this look like a boy's private parts, Saia?!" she had demanded to know, as she pointed her finger between her legs, her face red with anger. "You are a girl! Are you really that stupid that you don't realize that?! What is wrong with you?! If you really want to be a boy, then go out there in the city without your Guardsmen and be a boy! I won't stand in your way; I'll push you out of the door instead!"

Even though that particular incident had happened in the privacy of her own room, Saia had felt deeply humiliated. Her two smaller sisters had laughed in the hallway, one of them telling their mother afterwards that she would never want to be a boy.

"Well, you're not the disappointment she is," her mother had assured the girl.

On that day Saia had hated her mother more than ever before. If she had been any braver, she would have left home, dressed as a young man, a long time ago. Even that would have been a better option than staying, but she was too afraid. She didn't dare to go outside without Yellow Guardsmen because, despite all that had happened, she was still a girl.

Saia sighed in frustration and closed her eyes. She constantly felt like an outside observer, a person who did not fit in. Why did she have to live like this? Why did she still feel that she hadn't found a place of her own?

A memory of her brother came back to her. Saia had often wondered if life would have been easier in their apartment if Ati were still with them. At least it would have been different, Saia was sure of that.

Ati had been gone a long time now. Saia still remembered him as he was when she had looked into her brother's eyes, as if it were just yesterday. She had given her all to keeping his memory alive. She had made sure she would remember Ati's face as long as she lived.

Saia stood up and walked to her bed. She lay down, closed her eyes, and let Ati's memory come to her without resisting it anymore, and with the memories, she went back in time to about four years ago. She could still remember their last night as if it were yesterday.

She had been twelve years old, Ati twenty. At that time they had no longer been living in the same apartment because Ati had already been through his descent like every other boy at the age of fourteen. Therefore, her brother had been living in Second Circle at the time, but he had occasionally dropped by to have dinner with them, and he had often stayed the night in his old room as well.

Over the years Saia and Ati had developed a way to exchange information at the dinner table; it had been a game which only they had been aware of. If Ati set his drinking glass to his left, it meant that he was in a bad mood. If he tapped his fork three times on his plate, it was a sign that there was a message beneath the table for Saia. Food piled on the top of the plate indicated that they would try to meet during the night in Ati's old room to talk about what was going on in their lives. This was the signal Saia had always waited for the most because the discussions she then had with Ati were the best memories from those years. Ati had told her about things she couldn't have learnt anywhere else, like old religions, certain psychological issues that were not widely talked about in public, as well as the Great War.

Then had come the night when Ati had put a knife in his mouth and then placed it sideways next to his drinking glass. At the time Saia hadn't understood the meaning of the signal but the next morning had revealed the truth. During the night Ati had committed suicide by poisoning himself.

Where Ati had gotten his poison from, Saia didn't know. She only knew that her entire world had collapsed. Saia had cried over her brother for a long time. When her tears had finally dried, she started to feel anger because Ati had left her alone. However, she had also felt deep disappointment because Ati had concealed his intentions from her. He had not trusted her, told her that there had been blackness in his heart. Perhaps he was too sensitive, perhaps just too unhappy. Saia hated the word "perhaps" and she still had not fully accepted that it was all she was going to get. Even today, the memory of her brother stung her deep. Ati had been her best friend; the only one with whom she had felt free to be herself. Why had Ati left her here alone?

Relatively soon after her brother's death, Saia had often sneaked to the men's side of the apartment during the night in order to spend some time in Ati's old room. She had dug around in his things to find a note, some kind of message that would have been just for her but she had found nothing. Ati simply hadn't wanted to leave any explanations to his actions and this had bothered Saia for a long time.

Saia swallowed. She felt the sadness tightening round her neck. Remembering the old times with Ati was still difficult for her because she had never truly stopped wondering why he had not wanted to live.

His departure had made a huge impact on her life for another reason as well. Once, during her secret excursions into his old room, she had found something extremely unexpected among his belongings. She had found a world that he had never talked about. When Saia had found it without even searching for it, she had known immediately what to do.

She had found out that Ati had kept another identity, which he had used in order to keep in contact with certain people around the world. He had been known by the name of "The Fly," who published messages online about topics people didn't talk about in public. Suddenly, all of their private discussions had been placed in a much bigger framework, and Saia had begun to understand that Ati had not told her about certain things just to entertain her, but also to inform her about real issues. There really were individuals around the world who were interested in many different things.

It had taken months before Saia had fully understood what exactly Ati had been doing and how his mysterious network really worked. Once she had learnt enough about both her brother's technology and his writing style, she had become "The Fly" without anyone in the information network even realizing it.

Saia rolled over onto her right side and closed her eyes. So much had happened after Ati's death, even though so little had changed from the outsiders' viewpoint, but Saia herself felt the change within her and that was the most important thing. Saia slid her left arm under the pillow next to her and felt with her fingertips the world map she had hidden there.

The map had originally been Ati's. It was the only object her brother had managed to hide in her room without Saia even realizing it at the time. What made this particular map so special were the black crosses Ati had added to it. Each cross had been drawn in an area which was labeled on the map as wasteland. The five black crosses would have remained a mystery for Saia forever if Ati hadn't attached a little note to the map. The note had not told her the reason why Ati had taken his own life, but it was still more than anyone else had received from him. Saia had read the note hundreds of times and knew it by heart.

Hi Kid.

Take a good look at this map and remember the areas with the black crosses I've added. Those are important locations despite the label of wasteland because I am sure that one of them is much more than just toxic and uninhabitable desert.

Terra Unionia. That is the name which belongs to one of these locations I have marked. On the day you find it I will be by your side.

Don't ever listen to those who say you can't or you shouldn't just because you are a girl. And don't you tell yourself that mantra either, because it is a lie. More importantly, don't listen to mom. She doesn't know you, even though she's your mother.

This is my legacy to you, sister. Go see the world, because if there is a way out of the city for you, you will find it.

Ati

Ever since Saia had found the map she had spent considerable time thinking about Terra Unionia, and finding the place had become extremely important to her. In a way, it was one way for her to respect the memory of her brother. Saia didn't know how she could ever get outside the city in order to explore the locations Ati had marked on his map but she had no intention of giving up. The more time passed, the more she had started to ponder what there was to be found; who the people were living in the place and how many of them were there in general. She was certain that, one day, she could resolve the puzzle and, by doing so, would gain certain knowledge of where Terra Unionia was exactly because Ati had believed in her. After all, Ati had left her only five possible locations to investigate and Saia knew in her heart that one day she would stand on Terra Unionia. And when that happened, she would be there because of Ati.

No one talked about Terra Unionia, though. People were aware of the fact that there had once been such a place on Earth but the area in question had been forgotten a long time ago. However, Saia was absolutely fascinated by the thought of the place which was isolated from the rest of the world. What was Terra Unionia's current situation today? Where there still people living in the area? What kind of lives were they living? Were they starving? What habits did they have? Or had they already disappeared from Earth generations ago, leaving only ruins behind? Those were questions Saia wanted answers to, but she would have them only by finding Terra Unionia. The subject interested her so deeply that she had even written an essay on it but her supervisor grading it had described it as "pointless nonsense" and made her write about another topic which was closer to reality and real science.

Suddenly, Saia heard a knock at the door.

"Miss," she heard her regular Guardsman calling.

"Yes?" Saia answered.

"It is 13:25," the man behind the door informed her. "It's time."

"I'm coming," Saia informed him, and got up.

Before she stepped out of her room she hid her map behind the back wall of her cabinet. She didn't know what she would do if her mother found the map during one of her room inspections and took it away from her.

∗ ∗ ∗

"Saia Motasilla," the lady behind the registration desk said. "Doctor Alauda is ready to meet you now."

Saia nodded and stood up. The door in front of her was open and she entered a big office full of light. Mari Alauda stood in front of a huge window and was watching the people on the streets of Gavialis. Saia was nervous. There were no words to describe how beautiful Doctor Alauda was to her. A significant part of her beauty was her posture and self–assurance. Saia wanted to be like Mari Alauda, she wanted that badly but she knew it would never happen. So all she could to was to admire the woman's nobility and be inspired by it.

When she heard Saia's steps, Doctor Alauda turned around to face her and looked in her eyes with a smile on her face.

"Saia," Doctor Alauda said. "Please, take a seat."

Saia nodded and sat down in front of Doctor Alauda's desk. She started to feel a bit more nervous because she knew she was about to tell the woman something she wasn't expecting to hear. All Saia could do was to hope she had enough courage to tell Doctor Alauda what was in her mind, and that she wouldn't hate her after this meeting was over. If she decided not to speak to her anymore it would crush her, yet Saia knew she had to take the risk.

"We must talk about the situation of your ID chip," Doctor Alauda said. "You have complained about it many times now and each time I have concluded that there is nothing wrong with the chip. If you can really feel it in your arm, the reason has to be more psychological in nature and not really about your arm."

"The chip is not why I have come here," Saia said and she saw how her words surprised the doctor.

"What is this about, then?" she asked her.

Saia took a deep breath and tried to summon all her courage together, so she could say what was on her mind.

"Saia?"

"This is about the fertility program," she finally said as her heart pounded in her chest.

"I see," Mari Alauda said, and leaned back in her chair. "Your first time to participate in the program is coming soon."

"I received the invitation today," Saia stated.

"As they probably mentioned in the invitation, I am the doctor who carries out the examination. Therefore, I can tell you that everything will run smoothly without any problems. Do you have any questions now concerning the operation?"

"Not really," Saia said.

"What is this about, then?"

Saia took a deep breath and forced the following words out of her mouth.

"I would like the operation to be my last one."

"What do you mean?" Doctor Alauda asked her, slightly amused. "You are a perfectly healthy young woman, so I don't see any obstacles regarding going ahead with the program at a normal pace, which means making a donation every two years until you commit to a man."

"But I don't want to," Saia stated shyly.

"Saia …" Doctor Alauda began. "Is that what this is about?"

Saia swallowed.

"Every woman produces an enormous amount of ova during her lifetime, from which only a few typically become fertilized and start to develop into a human child. With artificial wombs we can put otherwise wasted ova to greater use. Not to mention the fact that women don't have to menstruate for a couple of years and this is a relief for many women."

"I don't have any problems with my periods."

"Many women still want to get rid of them nonetheless."

Saia didn't know what to say next, so she let Doctor Alauda continue.

"Of course, we don't take donations from committed women during the years they want to have children with their men. What I am trying to tell you is that there are no drawbacks for women when it comes to these donations. In fact, we have observed many benefits with this practice. For instance, we have found many cysts in their early stages, which we wouldn't have necessarily found that early without the donating operations. "

"I understand that there are benefits when it comes to this program," Saia noted.

"Good," Doctor Alauda said, "because I know girls may tell each other all kinds of horror stories about this operation; they want to make the younger ones a little scared, but I assure you all that talk is nonsense – urban myths and nothing more. Donating ova is a quick and easy operation, from which women only profit. No one has ever complained about their operation."

"I want my ovaries destroyed," Saia finally informed Doctor Alauda.

Silence fell. Doctor Alauda stared at Saia for a moment, evaluating whether she had really heard her right. Saia swallowed. What was Doctor Alauda thinking?

"Saia …"

"I have heard about a substance, which makes ova production stop for good," Saia continued. "So, I know that a drug of this nature really exists."

"What on earth are you talking about?" Doctor Alauda asked her and gave a laugh.

"You destroyed your ovaries with this substance after giving birth to Naja," Saia added quietly, even though she was scared of revealing to Doctor Alauda that she knew about that particular personal issue of hers.

Now, in the blink of an eye, the last trace of Mari Alauda's smile disappeared from the woman's face and Saia knew she had her undivided and full attention.

"What are you talking about?" Mari asked her quietly.

"I know it's true," Saia whispered, even though she was afraid to do so.

Doctor Alauda was clearly shocked about what she had heard. Now, however, the two of them shared a secret. Now Saia had something that bound her to Doctor Alauda.

Mari got up from her chair and turned her back on Saia. Then she walked to the window and stayed there without saying another word. Saia swallowed. She didn't know how to continue, so she waited for Doctor Alauda to say something, but the woman remained silent. So did she hate Saia now? If that was the case, Saia would have ruined everything.

"I have read your health records," Saia finally confessed, even though she knew it was stupid.

"Excuse me?" the woman asked her and turned around to face Saia. It was clear from the tone of her voice that she was angry.

Saia saw the emotions on her face as well; Doctor Alauda was really upset now, and Saia couldn't blame her for it. She had committed a crime when hacking into another person's ID account, as well as into the Komeion System containing health records belonging to people from all over the world. However, she had done so in order to find answers, and once she had studied Doctor Alauda's health record she had concluded that there was nothing biologically wrong with the woman that prevented her from having more children.

"You have donated your ova like every other woman but only once. This happened before Naja was born, because you committed to a man at such a young age," Saia continued. "Your man is still alive, so if you didn't have any more children, there has to be some biological reason for it."

"What if neither of us wanted any more children? What if that was the reason?" Doctor Alauda asked her.

"Perhaps, but I don't think so," Saia said shyly. "Even though you had committed to your man a few years before Naja was born, according to your health record you checked in to this hospital only a year after giving birth. You were treated for complications. The official diagnosis had something to do with your intestines, but I don't believe that is the truth. I believe you destroyed your ovaries. I have also read about other cases where mothers have checked into hospital with similar complications and acute pain, which are quickly treated."

"Have you really hacked into the Komeion System?" Doctor Alauda asked her quietly, both disbelief and anger reflected in her dark eyes.

Saia hesitated. Did Doctor Alauda think she was blackmailing her?

"I have," Saia confessed. Lying wouldn't get her case any further.

"Why?"

"First of all, I want you to believe me when I tell you I won't say a word about this to anyone," Saia said. "Your secret is safe with me. Secondly, I also want you to keep my secret; if anyone knows I've hacked into the information systems I am in trouble."

"You can be absolutely sure of that!" the doctor informed her seriously. "Hacking into any information system is not an act to be taken lightly."

"I won't tell anyone about your situation," Saia emphasized, "if that is what you are worried about. I haven't told anyone and I won't, but what I do want is that particular substance, which some women have had, after my ova donation."

"Saia," Doctor Alauda said in a most serious manner, and turned around to face her again. "Do you really understand what you are asking me to do?"

"I do," Saia whispered.

"I doubt that."

"I am being serious," Saia assured her.

"Why on Earth would you want to destroy your only means of making something out of yourself?" Mari asked her stunned. "It doesn't make any sense!"

"I don't want to be committed to a man," Saia explained. "The mere thought of it is a nightmare for me."

"You have nothing to be afraid of," Mari assured her. "Don't you see that committing to a man can work to your benefit as well? How else could you enter working life?"

"I'd rather be alone at home than …"

"Stop it," Doctor Alauda said seriously. "You are still too young to make a decision like this."

"I am not," Saia insisted.

"Believe me – you are," Mari assured her and the tone of her voice was more serious than Saia had ever heard from her.

"If I make a decision to commit to a man," Saia continued, "my ova will still be here somewhere, isn't that right? Don't you keep records of those who have made donations?"

"We do examine DNA, of course, but we don't label the ova we receive. Only the samples which are biologically very close to each other, like the samples of family members, are physically stored near each other, so we can avoid inter-breeding."

"My ova could be traced and located by examining the DNA records? In principle at least?"

"In principle, yes," Doctor Alauda admitted. "It could be done because we have your DNA information stored in our systems, but it would make the already complex process even more complicated for nothing, not to mention the fact that it goes against current regulations."

"But the chance of giving a man a child through an artificial womb would still exist, even if my ovaries had been destroyed."

"Not all men are ready to accept such an arrangement," Doctor Alauda pointed out. "Only a few actually do. The majority of men want a woman in their lives so that they can procreate in a natural way. Not to mention the fact that the regulations governing artificial pregnancies are extremely tightly set. Artificial wombs are not utilized in cases where a committed woman wants to avoid the pain of delivering her child. Giving birth is the primary task of women in this world alongside raising the children. Artificial wombs are used only in situations were carrying a child is extremely dangerous for a woman. Otherwise the children produced in artificial wombs are the offspring of anonymous donors."

"If you are my doctor – and according the invitation I received, you are – you could claim I cannot carry a child. They would believe you."

"Saia," Doctor Alauda said in a deep voice, "don't be unreasonable. What you are asking me here is without doubt unreasonable."

"I don't want to be committed to a man and I don't want to give birth," Saia explained. "I'm not good with kids."

"How can you be sure you will still feel like this in, let's say, ten years' time?"

"I just know."

"You are only sixteen years old!" Doctor Alauda exclaimed. "You can't make a decision like this yet, which would affect the rest of your life!"

"I don't want to be committed to a man," Saia insisted. "The mere thought of those stupid meetings with men is humiliating for me. I already know that if some man chooses me, it means there are no better ones left for him."

"That is not true," Mari said. "You are a beautiful young woman."

Doctor Alauda's words hit Saia somewhere deep. She was baffled and wondered if she was making fun of her, but Doctor Alauda's face was full of sincerity and it confused Saia even more.

"That's a lie," Saia finally stated. "We both know I'm not beautiful."

"Don't demean yourself," Mari told her. "It's pointless."

Saia felt her cheeks burning as she blushed.

"You are kind, but we both know that if some random man had to choose between me, and let's say Naja, he would choose Naja in a heartbeat. That would be just fine by me."

"That wouldn't necessarily mean that Naja were the better choice," Doctor Alauda pointed out. "You have to learn how to see your own strengths. No man makes his final choice based on one Apertum meeting alone. The idea of these meetings is to talk face to face with men, and only to chat. After this, men and women may continue their conversations via the information network service. Only then do the two really get to know each other."

Saia took a deep breath and took a moment to think about what Doctor Alauda had said. She had never expected that Doctor Alauda would see her this way. She had heard her mother's complaints about her ugliness and boyishness as long as she could remember, so when Doctor Alauda saw her in totally different light, it felt surprisingly good. Doctor Alauda liked her and that was amazing. It made Saia speechless. She couldn't understand why Naja hated her mother so much.

"I still don't believe that I want that kind of life," Saia finally said. "It's such a repulsive thought for me. I don't want to get pregnant and I don't want to give birth and I most certainly don't want to be chained to some child for the rest of my life. If my ova were safe here, I would have carried out my civic duty, and there would still be a way for me to have a biological child, if necessary."

"Saia ..."

" Doctor Alauda!" Saia exclaimed. "Please take me seriously."

"I am taking you seriously."

"I have been giving this considerable thought for a long time now," Saia assured her.

"I understand," Mari sighed, "but do you understand that a job is also one way to measure a woman in this world. If you don't step into working life and you don't even have children, how will you spend your days? What will you do? You will remain in the custody of your parents and you'll be dependent on the inheritance they leave you, not to mention the fact that by spending your days without anything purposeful to do, you will most likely become seriously depressed."

"I know."

"Is that what you really want?"

"I'd rather settle for that life than move to another apartment and share my life with some old man."

"Saia ..."

"And this whole mating ritual is totally overrated. If committing to a man is a requirement for a woman to enter working life, it will promote the development of twisted relationships where women settle for a spouse who doesn't interest them at all. That setting can't possibly create anything but resentment in all parties involved."

"You are right," Mari said, and Saia was surprised by her honesty. "But it is how this society works."

"I know," Saia replied. "And I want to do things differently. This is a free world, isn't it? Don't I have the right to exclude myself from this tradition, if I choose to do so?"

"Of course you are free to make that choice, but you have to realize it won't necessarily be very wise. Do you understand that you could meet all kinds of men who have many different goals?" Doctor Alauda asked her.

"Different how?"

Mari took a deep breath before beginning.

"There are some men who commit themselves to a woman for status-related reasons only."

"And?"

"And in situations like that, a man and a woman can make an arrangement to commit to each other just to better their social status. Like you just said – the current system supports cases of commitments between men and women where neither one of them is interested in procreation, but you won't find or meet those men if you refuse to participate in Apertum meetings."

"Does something like that happen a lot?"

"I don't know," Mari said, "but it is possible."

"How can you be so sure?"

"Because Naja's guardian has never wanted me in his bed," the doctor said.

Saia's jaw dropped.

"I made a deal with him because I wanted a career in medicine and he wanted to improve his own social status. I made this deal in good faith believing that it was exactly what I wanted. I got exactly what I had been hoping for, as did he. We both truly believed we had made the best deal of our lives. However, as time goes by you start to realize how difficult being alone can eventually be. So think about what you are doing."

Saia sighed and stared blankly at the shiny surface of Doctor Alauda's desk. Doctor Alauda stepped beside her and placed her hand on Saia's left shoulder. The warmth of her hand felt good. Saia would have done anything to be Doctor Alauda's friend.

"I can postpone your first donation operation for one year, since you started your periods after you turned fourteen," Mari said.

"Postpone?" Saia asked her, baffled.

She stared at Doctor Alauda for a moment and didn't know what to think about the suggestion she had just heard. Finally she said:

"It would be embarrassing if I didn't donate my ova at the age of sixteen."

"I won't tell a soul about this postponement, so let's call this upcoming year a reconsideration period," Mari said. "In this way you will have time to consider this decision of yours."

"I won't change my mind," Saia informed her.

"You're a smart girl, so I'm going to ask you to reconsider. Participating in Apertum meetings doesn't have to lead to the end of your freedom; it may very well lead to the beginning of it."

"Alright," Saia finally agreed and looked up straight into Doctor Alauda's dark eyes, "if you will also consider granting my wish."

"Very well," Mari said. "Let's agree we will both do some thinking, but stay away from my ID account."

"Of course. I hacked into it only once and it was about a year ago," Saia explained, and there was a tone of regret in her voice, even though she knew her explanation had little value for Doctor Alauda.

"This will be the last time you try to twist my arm for anything," Doctor Alauda added. "Believe me, Saia, when I say that you don't want to fool around with me."

Saia looked straight into Doctor Alauda's eyes and nodded. The woman didn't give her any reason to doubt her words.

4.

Jani stepped through the main doors of his apartment building into the street. Today was his day off, but the feeling that had typically colored his free time was gone. The thought of spending the day in Fifth Circle unusually made him feel nothing, even though he always waited eagerly to get there, as he usually spent all his accumulated free days in that part of the city. However, even if Jani's mind was as gray as the cloudy sky above him, he knew that going to Fifth Circle was a rational thing to do. When he had a whole day off from the control room, staying in First Circle would have been downright stupid.

Suddenly Jani realized there was a crowd in front of the main doors of the next building. He took a bite out of his fish roll, which he had saved from his dinner yesterday, and started to approach the crowd.

"What's going on in here?" Jani asked a dark-haired young man as he reached the people furthest from the building's main doors.

"The police conducted a raid," the man said.

"In that building?" Jani asked him confused. "Why?"

"The word is that the police suspect gang activity in that building," the man explained.

Jani could hardly believe his ears. There were gang activities taking place in the next-door building? He took a few steps forward and tried to get in the middle of the crowd in order to see better how the situation in the building was progressing. Then one of the doors was opened and a number of policemen in their black uniforms emerged. They had three men with them and the crowd immediately started to whistle and yell.

"So long! Have a nice time in Gaskar!" someone in the crowd shouted.

Jani took his noter out of his pocket and started to record.

"Lu, you won't believe what is going on in the building next-door to mine. The police have just taken three men with them on suspicion of gang activity. I wonder where they got the tip from. Well, I guess I shouldn't be surprised about anything that happens in First Circle, but this is still quite unusual. I don't envy those men, if they are found guilty."

Then Jani saved his message and let the device generate a text-based message from it. Once done, he sent it to his friend's ID account.

Finally Jani turned and left. He was heading to 1.2 Corner Station and as he walked, First Circle was becoming increasingly annoying with every step he took. Why was he so lazy? Why didn't he put any effort in getting the right to move to Second Circle? Why was he too laid-back to do anything remarkable? The fact remained that he was only worth 43 Silver Wing marks. He was a young man who would most likely never collect more than a hundred marks during his entire life.

As he continued walking he kept thinking about the three men he had just seen being arrested. It was quite clear they were in serious trouble. The difference between interest groups and gangs was carefully defined and written in the law, so the police did not make raids to cease gang activity lightly. Jani was, nevertheless, glad that the three men had been taken away. He wasn't too keen on searching for a new building to live in just because there were illegal gangs committing criminal activities next door. Luckily he had not observed any criminal activities near his building so far.

Jani climbed the stairs to the station and once there he went straight towards the platform. A train was just arriving. It was 1A, which would take him to First Corner Station most quickly. Jani got on the train, but didn't bother to sit down; the journey to First Corner Station didn't take long.

When the train finally came to a complete stop at First Corner Station, Jani got off and headed towards the platform for the Heptagon Line. A trip to Fifth Corner Station would take almost 45 minutes on both A and B trains, which meant he could take the first train that arrived at the station.

A train arrived rather quickly, which was hardly unusual, since there was usually a train every five or ten minutes. Once Jani had boarded, he sat down and activated the news screen, even though he continued to stare out of the window, his hand against his cheek. His day off had not started in the most pleasant circumstances, that much he knew, and now he was in a bad mood.

When the train left the station, Jani took a quick look at the latest headlines on the small screen in front of him. There were still headlines about the murdered woman in Erasmia, but there was a headline about the upcoming presidential election as well. Jani browsed the headlines in order to see if the gang arrest he had just witnessed had already ended up in the news. Then it caught his eye in the news ticker. People were quick, but on the other hand publishing new headlines didn't really take much work; just a few tips to the news center and a new headline was already published and delivered worldwide.

Suddenly Jani smelled something nasty. He took a quick look over his right shoulder and saw Null 497 sitting nearby on the other side of the carriage. Jani wondered how many times the man had already gone around the city on Heptagon Line. Jani smiled and took a quick look at the information tablet near the ceiling. Suddenly he realized something that shocked him. Instead of sitting on a train on Heptagon Line, he had taken U Train and now he was going straight to Linai at incredible speed.

"I don't believe this," Jani sighed and shook his head in disbelief.

He had been so deep in his thoughts that he had walked to the wrong platform at the station. Instead of taking the train circling the city border he was now headed to the smelliest suburb of Gavialis. Jani sighed again in frustration. A trip to Linai and back again would take over half an hour. It was time he could have spent elsewhere than in a train carriage. In addition, the thought of going to Linai on his day off didn't make improve his mood. These days were supposed to be for him and for things he liked doing. On days like this, he didn't even want to know about a place called Linai.

"Going to work, huh?" Jani heard then.

Jani was surprised. Null 497 had to be almost sober, if he remembered him.

"I took the wrong train," Jani said. "Today is my day off."

"You are young," the man pointed out sourly, "So, why are you already forgetting things like that? Don't tell me you have started to drink durratin."

"I haven't," Jani assured him and turned his face away to conceal his smile, which Null 497's disapproval had caused.

"Durratin will only drag you down," the man stated. "It will take you straight to the bottom from where you can't get back on your feet again. You better believe it."

"I do."

"Back in the day I had 497 Silver Wing marks," the man said, "but I lost them all because of durratin. That poison sticks with you, but in the end it was me who ruined my life, no one else."

"That's too bad," Jani said.

"You don't want a life like this," Null 497 stated. "This is a dog's life! It isn't worth living. I breathe, I walk, and I take a dump, but I'm not alive. Sitting on trains without ever getting access back to the city is not life."

"Where are you heading today?" Jani then asked the man, because Null 497 being on the U Train didn't indicate anything about his plans for the day.

"To Linai," he replied. "Sometimes you can find some food near the organic waste facilities; food the folk in the city have not eaten because of their hurries, or because they didn't want to."

The man surprised Jani. There weren't many nulls out there who would voluntarily spend time in Linai. Then Jani took a look at the fish roll with durra casing in his hand. He had saved it as his breakfast but he had eaten only one third of it since he wasn't hungry anymore.

"Here's something to eat, if you want it," Jani said and showed the man his fish roll.

"What is it?" the man asked him.

"Fish in durra roll," Jani said.

Null 497 nodded and Jani stood up to take his food to the man. It was obvious Null 497 needed it more than he did. Jani knew there weren't many who would have understood why he gave up something of his own and giving it to a man who had given up his life and basic rights, but Jani couldn't help but see tragedy in Null 497's fate. He pitied the man. It was true that in a few hours' time, Null 497 would be intoxicated again, because nulls seemed always to find durratin somehow. When that happened the man wouldn't even remember the fish roll he had eaten. Occasionally Jani had wondered how it was possible for nulls to keep on drinking and he had come to the conclusion that there had to be some on-going durratin production on Circle Nil. However, despite his craving for durratin, Null 497 also needed something to eat. Why shouldn't Jani give his durra roll to a man who didn't know where he would find his next meal?

Jani took a seat in front of Null 497. The smell of old durratin combined with the man's dirty clothes stank but Jani tried his best to ignore it and gave the man his breakfast. Null 497 took it without hesitating and bit into it with obvious appetite.

Jani felt better about himself. Even if he lived in the city's First Circle, where men were being arrested for gang activity, he was onto a pretty good thing. He had a job and through that he had a purpose in the world, even though it wasn't a very significant one. But he had the right to live in the city in his own little apartment, and he was given food on a daily basis. The meals were delivered to his apartment building twice a day where they were distributed among the apartments, Jani's included. It didn't sound like a fancy life; he lived on the lowest level of basic services but it was enough. He knew Null 497 would have given his right arm to get access to the city again, if he didn't love durratin more than life's basic needs.

"The presidential elections are about to begin," the man stated. "It hasn't been that long since the last ones."

"That's right," Jani said. "Soon most of the news headlines will be about that and nothing else."

"Why are people so interested in the news?" Null 497 pondered. "I sit on these trains for hours every day and guess what I have come to realize? People constantly stare at the headlines. They are more interested in reading news than talking to each other, or thinking about the world in general, for that matter. Only a handful of men stare outside these windows while traveling on these trains. Most of them simply keep staring at the news screen as if every single headline from another side of the world contained such crucial information that the sky was going to collapse on them. It's ridiculous. I read the news once every second or third day and here I am. Life continues just the same as yesterday."

"It's true," Jani admitted and by doing so surprised himself. "We just keep staring at the news screen."

"Fools."

"Perhaps it is our habit, whether the news interests us or not."

"It's pointless," the man stated. "Utterly futile, but what do I know about it? My opinions have no value in this world anymore."

"There are as many opinions as there are men," Jani pointed out and Null 497 grunted quietly in response to his words.

"What are your plans for today?" the man then asked him.

"My intention was to go to Fifth Circle," Jani said, "but I accidentally took this train, so I have to go around Linai before getting back to the city."

"What are you going to do in Fifth Circle?"

"What is there not to do?" Jani asked. "They have everything a man could ever want in Fifth Circle."

75

"Really? What about women?" the man asked him.

"What would I do with a woman?"

"Surely you think about women?" Null 497 said. "You are a young man after all."

"I don't spend my time thinking about things which are out of my reach. That's the way to avoid being disappointed."

"Well, that's one way to live," the man said, "but it's not always that easy. I don't have any business in the city anymore, not even in First Circle, but the city, durratin, and women are always on my mind; separately or simultaneously. Women more seldom these days, though."

"Why?"

"Durratin, because I need it, the city because I want to get back in, and women because they exist."

"I try not to think about them," Jani said. "Women, I mean. Why should I waste any thoughts on them when I will never have a chance to see them closer than ten meters away?"

"So, you have given up," Null 497 said, "and that is a pity. You are young and you have the potential to be whatever you want to be."

"My options are limited."

"So, you don't care about competing?"

"I accept the facts."

"So, you have given up competing, because it is too difficult."

"Well, isn't it?"

"Of course it is, but by competing a boy becomes a man. And through healthy competition man has accomplished great things."

"Why did you give up, then?" Jani dared to ask the man. "If competing constantly made you a man, why did you start drinking durratin?"

"It happened before I even knew it was happening," Null 497 said. "No one who gets hooked on durratin ever plans it."

"Do you think you could have avoided dropping out from the city, if there hadn't been so much pressure forcing you constantly to try and gain more Silver Wing marks for whatever skill or knowledge?"

"What are you talking about, boy?" Null 497 asked him, and laughed. "That is the talk of a lazy man. Diminishing the value of the Silver Wing mark system is a sign of laziness. What would the world be like now if, after the Great War, all the men had decided that they were good for nothing and therefore might as well give up and do nothing? We would have never gotten to the moon. We would have never built these grand cities in habitable areas. We would never have developed technology, which is incomparable with anything man has made before. We would have died and all we would have left behind would have been pollution and our moldering bones."

"Competition does make development progress," Jani admitted, "but if the existing system was perfect, if constantly measuring effectiveness and advancement in all areas of life is a flawless strategy for all, why drink durratin? Or why run towards Albedo's minefield with a death wish, like I think they said on the news this morning?"

"The weak ones are weeded out," Null 497 stated. "There is nothing wrong with competing. Not everyone can take it, though. Lazy or stupid people are eliminated from the game and the strong ones succeed. That is the basic principle of how this world functions, and therefore we have created a system which is favorable to all."

"What about you?" Jani asked.

"I couldn't keep up the pace without durratin, and I made the choice which caused me to be withdrawn from the city. It was my own doing."

"Even though you have accepted responsibility for what happened, you still miss the city and want to be back in there?"

"Of course I do," Null 497 said. "Who wouldn't? I didn't realize how privileged everyone in the city is, until I was withdrawn. You are privileged to be allowed to walk the streets of Gavialis. If you make bad choices and ruin your life, if you don't even bother to test your own limits, you have no right to live in the city. That is the way of life and that is the way which is right."

Jani listened to Null 497's words and he heard from the tone of his voice how much the man meant every word he said. It was slightly confusing for Jani, because he had assumed that a man who had been withdrawn from the city would have criticized the system even more. Null 497 had accepted his part and he loved durratin more than the life he had left behind. Jani knew, however, that if he had been in Null 497's shoes, he would not have been as understanding. He was already irked by many things in the current system, a system which valued all things that were linked – however remotely – with advancement in society.

"In my youth Fifth Circle was closed," the man said, "just like the other circles are now. So when you enter Fifth Circle today, remember that you are privileged. There was a long-lasting political feud about opening the boundaries, so that anyone, you included, could spend time in all Fifth

Circles of every world city. Men who lived in Fifth Circles were obviously reluctant to open the gates for the others from the outer circles."

"That's understandable," Jani noted.

"And back in those days, when this 'organization of equality' introduced the idea for public discussion, people laughed at them. I think their campaign was called 'A Free city for free men,' and the majority of the men from the outer circles were obviously behind the idea, and that's why they supported it. However, men in the inner circles resisted the motion as long as they could. They even tried publicly to tarnish the reputation of this organization by claiming it was a gang. The game was over when the campaign became a bill for the World High Council. At that point, it was clear to all parties that all cities' Fifth Circles would be opened, but no one predicted that one city would remove its circles entirely."

"They played it dirty, if they really accused the organization of being involved in gang activity," Jani said as he recalled the incident he had observed earlier next door to his own apartment building. "Fortunately they opened the circle."

"Enjoy Gavialis," Null 497 stated, "and don't underestimate its outer circles either. Gavialis is the finest city in the world, every circle included."

Jani looked at the man and nodded.

"All world cities are like monuments to mankind's creative power," Null 497 said, "but Gavialis is the greatest of them all. Don't ever even consider moving to another city. You wouldn't settle down elsewhere, believe me. "

"Gavialis is a great place," Jani stated, even though he had never seen any other cities, but he had never felt the need to leave. There was nothing in the other cities that he couldn't find in Gavialis, possibly excluding Vireo, which was the city furthest east of all cities of Capricorn Tropic; a city which had no circles. Instead of city circles, Vireo was divided into sectors which were all open to everyone. The city was a place Jani would want to visit sometime but until now he had postponed it; not only because of the distance, but also because of his free time credits, which, for the time being, were all to be spent in Gavialis' Fifth Circle.

"Have you ever been in the Sixth or Seventh Circle?" Null 497 asked him.

"Sixth," Jani said.

"A damn fine place," the man stated. "When you walk the streets among those massive buildings, you feel as small as an ant. Everything is so enormous and the grandness of it all can make any man speechless.

Nothing in this world is greater than that particular feeling; when you walk there and witness with your own eyes what mankind has accomplished."

"Fifth Circle is pretty great, too," Jani noted. "Perhaps things are not as big and grand there, but there is a lot of action and different options."

"Fifth Circle is only a pale shadow of Sixth or Seventh Circle," Null 497 assured him. "Sixth and Seventh Circles are the greatest parts of the entire city of Gavialis. The air itself feels different there. The big wide world is right there."

"True," Jani said and recalled his day in Sixth Circle.

He wanted to be back there. Fifth Circle provided him with plenty of stimulation and he had not even seen the entire circle yet because of its size, but Sixth Circle was something else entirely. Jani didn't want to think constantly about the place but his memories of Sixth Circle simply weren't fading.

"Did you see any women," the man asked, "while you were in Sixth Circle?"

"I did," Jani said. "Twice."

"Well, I'll be damned!" Null 497 exclaimed. "You were lucky."

Jani laughed.

"And you still don't think about them?"

"I thought of them for a little while after I had come back," Jani confessed. "But I came to realize that there is no point in thinking about something you can never have. So why waste time on something like that?"

"Don't ruin your life with durratin or, let's say, with N1014, and you may yet be given permission to meet women," the man said.

"I don't think so," Jani said, laughing. "A man like me doesn't receive offers like that."

"How do you know that?"

"I know," Jani assured the man.

"That attitude of yours is starting to bother me," Null 497 stated, which got Jani surprised. "You simply don't understand how lucky you are and what you could be capable of, if you only had the will to try. Do you have a provider?"

"No," Jani answered.

"And has that given you the excuse not to even try?" the man asked.

The question was totally unexpected for Jani. Null 497's curiosity made him slightly awkward as well.

"Boys who have grown up with their providers may have an advantage in many situations," Null 497 noted, "but many of the young men like you seem to forget that all the cultivated ones are also the offspring of successful men. Half of your genes are not from some worthless man, but an accomplished one, so you cannot blame your genes for anything."

"I don't," Jani said to the man.

"Your life is ahead of you, so do something about it," the man instructed. "Take a good look at me and make the decision that you will do something with your life. You have everything it takes to do something significant if you would only start to hate the laziness and excuses which are preventing you from making things happen. You, like any other man with a provider or guardian, have the same chances to advance and become successful in this world."

Jani was about to shake his head in disagreement because he knew Null 497's arguments were pointless. He knew what he was and what he was capable of. Perhaps with a little effort he could have increased his number of Silver Wing marks over fifty, but it would not have changed his life in any significant way.

"Women; they are the treasures of mankind," Null 497 said. "So rare are they. It's so odd that there are not more of them."

"The Yellow Guard would be huge if there were more of them," Jani said with a laugh.

"The Yellow Guard would not even exist, boy!" the man said instead and laughed, too.

Jani looked at him and wondered what he meant.

"If there were as many women as there are men, or significantly more than there are now, the world would be different," the man added. "Women would be … more ordinary. They could walk outside by themselves, even in the outer circles, instead of hiding from the world."

"That's difficult to imagine," Jani said. "The world is what it is. What would ever change it?"

"The world changes all the time, but only for those who have enough Silver Wing marks," Null 497 noted.

"I think you're right," Jani agreed.

"That's why you shouldn't give up," the man added. "You are young and you have all the time in the world to collect your Silver Wing marks. Work hard for your own advancement and don't waste time convincing yourself that it's pointless to even try, because no one is standing in your way. Only you can block your own path."

Finally Jani felt the train finally slowing down.

"*Linai, Station West,*" the automatic announcement said.

"Finally," Jani sighed.

Null 497 stood up and walked towards the doors. When they opened, he left the train and walked slowly along the station platform. Jani was glad that the awful smell had left with the man.

"Don't touch durratin, boy!" Null 497 shouted from the platform.

Jani smiled and nodded, and the train started moving again.

Jani felt a little strange. For some odd reason the conversation with Null 497 had been more fruitful than he had expected. No-one gave him any Silver Wing marks for talking to a null, but despite that, Jani really felt like he had just done something worthwhile. The man obviously didn't have many people in his life to talk to. People in the city avoided nulls and for a reason; some of them had lost their minds because of durratin or N1014. Therefore, some nulls were even considered dangerous. Jani, however, wasn't afraid of Null 497. The man was one of the few in his life to whom talking felt easy. Lu was another. Null 497 had to be sober, though, for a real conversation to take place between them. When intoxicated he wasn't really aware of the world around him.

Jani looked at the view outside the window and he heaved a sigh of relief at not being required to spend even a single hour in Linai today. Then he was suddenly pulled from his thoughts back to his surroundings, as he heard footsteps approaching down the middle aisle. Jani looked in the direction of the sound and he saw a man walking down the aisle towards him. The man was dressed quite smartly, so most likely he wasn't a null.

Jani wasn't interested in conversation so he turned his face towards the window again and hoped that this man, who was moving from one seat to another, wasn't too keen on talking, either. Jani took a deep breath. He also hoped that the man wouldn't cause any trouble. Finally, the stranger sat down on the other side of the middle aisle opposite Jani, in his opinion on purpose as there was no one else in the carriage with them at the moment.

"Are you busy?" Jani heard the man asking him.

Jani took a quick look at the man and noticed that he was staring at the news screen in front of him, even though he had directed his words at him.

"Excuse me?" Jani asked him.

"Are you busy?"

"Why you are you asking?"

"Because if you are not busy, I have an offer that you may find hard to resist."

"No, thank you," Jani stated briefly.

He was quite certain that the man had to be either a distributor of N1014 or possibly a gang member who was recruiting more fools for their criminal activities. In either case, Jani wanted to know nothing about it.

"I am not a criminal," the man then said as if he had read Jani's thoughts, "and I am not proposing anything illegal either," he added.

"Not interested," Jani informed the man as bluntly as possible, so that the man would give up and leave him alone.

"*Linai, Station South*," the automatic announcement said and the train slowed abruptly.

Jani saw some men standing on the station platform, but none of them stepped into the same carriage as himself and the man in the dark suit. It was unfortunate, because Jani knew already that the empty train carriage would make the man continue his talk.

They left the station and Jani tried his best to ignore the man.

"You are not interested spending a night in one of the tallest buildings in Gavialis in Sixth Circle?" the man continued.

Jani sighed.

"If you are looking for company, I recommend a trip to the Lepus area in Fifth Circle," he said to the man. "I am certain you will find company on that particular street without needing to try too hard."

"I am not searching for male company," the man responded, "but I am looking for a man who has time to make a quick trip to Makaira today."

"Makaira?" Jani asked the man. "The ocean city?"

"That's right."

"Why?"

"I will tell you, if you say yes to my proposal."

Jani sighed again.

"No thank you," he said.

"Are you sure?"

"I don't want any trouble," Jani informed the man. "All I want is to spend my day off in peace in Fifth Circle."

"You can go to Fifth Circle any time you want," the man pointed out. "But how many times have you spent your free days in Makaira?"

"I'm not interested in leaving Gavialis and going anywhere," Jani informed the man as seriously as he knew how.

"Not even for permission that guarantees you 18 hours in Sixth Circle?"

Jani sighed in frustration. Sixth Circle interested him, that was quite clear, but he didn't want to get involved in anything shady. The man who had come to him practically oozed shadiness and therefore the promises he made couldn't be trusted at all.

"Good," the man said. "You are considering it."

"Why me?" Jani then asked the man.

"Because you are here," the man answered.

"And that is the only reason you offered me this trip to Makaira?" Jani asked him and took a quick look at the man.

"If someone else had been sitting here, I would have made them the same offer."

"To Makaira and back again, by train, and I get 18-hour-permission for Sixth Circle," Jani said. "To be honest, this proposal is a weird one, so I am cautious and skeptical."

"I would most likely have withdrawn my proposal if you had accepted it immediately," the man suddenly said.

"Really?" Jani asked him. "If that was an attempt to quieten my doubts, it didn't work."

"My proposal is still valid, but only for the next three minutes," the man informed Jani. "If you decide to spend your day off on a train to Makaira and back again, access permission to Sixth Circle as well as permission to spend a night on the 100th floor in Grus Tower's will appear on your ID account."

Jani couldn't resist being tempted. The man had made him curious, there was no denying that anymore.

"So, all I have to do is to go to Makaira and come back, and I get permission to spend a night in a room on the 100th floor of Grus Tower?"

"That's right."

"Why does this still sound shady and also too easy?"

"Perhaps because it may very well be easy," the man suggested. "All I'm asking for is your time and that you will make your journey precisely as I tell you."

"Or else?"

"Or else you will not have the opportunity to spend a night in Grus Tower."

Jani smiled slightly and deliberated for a moment. He had already planned to spend the next few hours in Fifth Circle, but on the other hand he could very well make the trip to Makaira, if his time would really be compensated with a night in Sixth Circle. Null 497 had been right; Fifth Circle was only a pale shadow of the greatness known as Sixth Circle.

"How can I be sure I will get access permission to Sixth Circle, if I do what you ask?"

"I don't lie."

"I don't know you."

"And for that you can be happy," the man said.

"Will this bring me trouble?" Jani asked him then.

"I don't know why it would."

"Then why don't you go to Makaira yourself?"

"Because I can't," the man answered.

"Why not?"

"That is none of your business," the man replied. "All I want to know is if you are willing to take a trip to Makaira or not. You won't receive any Silver Wing marks for it, but I am offering you 18 hours in a place you cannot otherwise get into. Your time in Sixth Circle would start at six in the evening and end the following day at noon. It is your responsibility to get out of the circle in time."

"And all I have to do is to go to Makaira?"

"So, you will do it?"

"And what you ask from me isn't illegal?"

"When has a trip to Makaira been against the law?"

"It's not, but I find it odd that you won't go there yourself."

"Like I said; I can't."

"But what you can do is approach an unknown man on a train and make this proposal to him?"

"One minute," the man said. "Soon this offer will no longer be on the table."

"So, I would go to Makaira and come back," Jani said. "Obviously you want me to do something during the trip, because otherwise none of this would add up."

"Of course I do, but my proposal still doesn't make me a criminal."

"Then who are you exactly?"

"A man who is making you an offer you really should consider."

"Hmm ..."

"Yes or no," the man said. "If you say yes, I will tell you what you must do and I expect you to carry out the given task without attracting any attention."

"So, that is the reason why you approached me," Jani deduced, "because no one pays any attention to a man like me."

"Exactly," the man stated.

"This assignment requires being faceless."

"You are correct."

"Alright," Jani said against his own better judgment. "I'll do it. I will go to Makaira if I get 18-hour access to Sixth Circle."

"Good," the man said. "But if you fail in your assignment, you will get nothing. Do you understand?"

"I do," Jani said. "But will failing get me into trouble?"

"No," the man stated. "Failing simply keeps you from getting to Sixth Circle and Grus Tower. I do expect, though, that the offered compensation for your time is enough for you to do your best."

"It is," Jani assured him, "and I agree to do it. What exactly am I going to do?"

"You will go to First Corner Station and take a train on the Heptagon Line. You will get off at Fourth Corner Station where you will get on the 10:54 train to the coast via Albedo. It is extremely important that you don't miss this particular train, because the one before or after won't do."

"Alright," Jani said.

"There are exceptionally four carriages on this train, because the first one is a closed yellow carriage."

"There are women on the train?"

"So, I have heard."

Jani coughed. He couldn't stop wondering about the odd coincidences he had experienced over the last few days which had taken him near women again and again. First, there had been the moment in Hirunda Historical Museum, then the unexpected visit to the women's side of the Main Hospital, and now the yellow car on a train he was supposed to take.

"You must take a seat in the second last carriage of the train," the man continued. "Stay in your seat all the way to Makaira. Near Makaira you will feel the train slowing down. This is partly because the area you will pass is still contaminated with ionized radiation, but also because the train track is being maintained in that area. When the train arrives at Makaira, stay in the carriage. Don't get off the train, even if you have to wait for half an hour before the train departs back to Gavialis."

Jani nodded and waited for the man to continue.

"On your way back the train will slow down again in the same place. When it does, check the time. As the train speeds up again, wait precisely ten minutes before you get up and leave for that carriage's sanitary facility. There, you will find a suitcase behind a wall panel. Take it with you, but don't try to open it. The contents of that suitcase are not any of your concern."

Jani listened to the instructions carefully and nodded.

"When you get back to Gavialis, take a train on the Heptagon Line and come back to First Corner Station. There, take a U Train to Linai. Once at Linai West Station, leave the suitcase under the stairs of the east side exit and continue on your way without looking back."

"That's it?" Jani asked the man.

"Do you remember precisely what you are supposed to do?"

"I do," Jani assured him.

"And do you understand there will be no trouble for you unless you open the suitcase?"

"I do."

"In that case," the man said, looking Jani in the eyes for the first time, "have a pleasant journey."

"*Linai, East Station,*" the automatic announcement said next.

The train slowed down and the mysterious man stood up. Then he turned around and walked to the doors. Jani followed him for a moment without knowing what to think. Had he really agreed to go to Makaira? He, who had no interest whatsoever in leaving Gavialis to go anywhere?

When the train finally stopped, the man stepped out and disappeared. Jani was suddenly quite restless. Instead of Fifth Circle, his destination was Fourth Corner Station now, from where he was about to leave the city and travel all the way to Makaira. What exactly had he agreed to do for 18 hours in Sixth Circle?

5.

Saia sat next to Naja, who had taken a seat next the window, and activated the screen in front of her to read the latest news headlines. Lator, Naja's trusted Guardsman, passed them as he inspected the safety of the train carriage. According to Saia's calculations, their study group had only one Guardsman per girl, which was normal even though they were about to leave Gavialis. Saia had expected the safety measures to be extra-strict on this particular trip, especially after all the attacks against women that people were constantly talking about. The dead Erasmian woman was still in the news headlines, since the case had stirred considerable ferment all over the world.

"Girls," their supervisor called them. "Please register as present on this trip using the armrest on your right."

Saia pressed the silvery gray sensor on her armrest with her thumb and the seat gave a peeping sound as a green light appeared on the armrest. The other girls, Naja included, did the same, and their female supervisor checked the attendee information from her display in the front section of the carriage. When she was certain that all the girls were present and accounted for, she gave a thumbs-up sign and sat down.

The group was also accompanied by their male supervisor who took a seat between two Guardsmen in the rear section of the carriage. Saia knew he was a former Guardsman. Therefore, it was quite likely he was comfortable being around Yellow Guardsmen and young women.

Saia checked the time in the top right corner of her display. It was 10:54. Suddenly the train jolted slightly as they started to move and Saia's heart began to beat faster. She was finally getting out of Gavialis. She could hardly recall the last time she had done so. Mom didn't take her on their trips outside the city anymore, so this study trip was a unique opportunity for Saia to see the world beyond Gavialis' borders. Therefore, she had decided to remember everything she saw today, no matter if she had to look at the world from behind the window of a train. The most important thing was her getting out from Gavialis' Sixth Circle and the rest of the city.

"So long, Gavialis," Naja sighed and closed her eyes.

Saia took a quick look at the girl. Naja was annoying her already. Without Naja she could have enjoyed this day to the full. So why hadn't Naja stayed at home? This study trip was not mandatory for any of them, so why couldn't Naja just have stayed at home on her vast bed doing nothing? That was about all she did during her free time anyway.

Saia tried to push Naja out of her mind and focused on browsing the headlines. There were a few words about the upcoming presidential election but, since Saia wasn't very interested in the story, or for that matter the dead woman in Erasmia, she decided to skip over it. She didn't understand why the story of the Erasmian woman had to be discussed indefinitely. The guilty party had not been found yet, that much she had read about the case, so she chose to ignore the articles on the matter. She wanted to trust in the fact that the police would eventually find the murderer and once they had, he would quickly be sent to Cold Pit, so that the rest of the world could forget about him entirely.

Saia looked out of the window, ignoring Naja who was partly blocking the view. They were moving rapidly into an area which was extremely empty-looking compared with the massive buildings of their big city. It was odd how quickly all traces of human life were left behind and, instead of the enormous, tall man-made structures, there was only an empty expanse as far as the eye could see.

The memory of her brother returned to Saia again. Ati would have been pleased today, Saia was sure. Ati had never complained about how privileged girls were; how girl groups were taken to see different places, whereas boys had to fight for their benefits despite their young age. Girls were treated differently, even though there were girls who didn't deserve such treatment or respect. Boys, on the other hand, had the freedom to walk in the cities as they wished. Boys were allowed to go anywhere they had access permission, and therefore Saia had always envied their freedom.

There had been many times when Ati's second guardian – who was Saia's late biological antecedent – had taken Ati out of the city. Saia remembered how unfair it had felt because girls couldn't be separated from their group which was guarded by Yellow Guardsmen. Today, however, she felt quite free, even though she was sharing this moment with the rest of the girls in her study group. Leaving the city was a better option than staying there, and for this reason she knew that Ati would have been happy for her today.

Suddenly Saia realized their train was slowing down.

"Ladies," they suddenly heard.

The voice was that of their male supervisor who was still sitting in the back section of the car.

"We are slowing down for a moment because we have arrived at Albedo," the supervisor informed them. "Albedo is perhaps the most significant suburb of Gavialis, and it is located approximately 30 kilometers away from the northern border of the city's First Circle. Albedo is the hub of the space transportation plant and now one of this planet's most remarkable locations can be seen on the left-hand side of this train."

Saia looked outside over Naja's shoulder and saw big light buildings in the middle of a wide expanse.

"We are slowing down because our arrival coincides most advantageously with a manned flight to Mars which will be launched any minute now," the supervisor continued. "The launch the spacecraft will be carried out on the launch pad, which encircles Albedo. The speed of the manned space vessel is not as fast as the velocity of unmanned cargo ships typically fly; those craft may circle the launch pad at the incredible speed of 10 km per second. The reason why the spacecraft – which will shortly appear on the launch pad – won't reach that incredible speed is because of its more powerful engines as well as the presence of the human crew on board."

Naja sighed and rolled her eyes. Saia was trying not to pay her any attention but it was challenging. Naja had the annoying habit of dominating her surroundings.

"The vessel departing for Mars bears the name Mintaka and its crew has been informed of the yellow train carriage near the launching ring. In fact, the message sent to Mintaka's flight deck informed the crew that young women of Gavialis have slowed down by Albedo's launch pad in order to wish the crew a safe and pleasant journey; a journey which will take about five weeks."

"Right," Naja stated sourly.

Then the train carriage started to judder and a low hum filled the air outside. Saia held her breath as she waited. She had never before had the opportunity to observe the moment when such a huge vessel was launched into the Earth's orbit. Then she saw a light-colored vessel appearing on the launch pad. The sight was impressive and Saia couldn't help feeling deep respect for the men – and possibly women – who had been involved in the development of vessels such as this in the past.

"Technical information," their male supervisor continued. "The length of the craft is 54 meters and the heaviest load the vessel may carry is 55,000 kilograms. The crew onboard consists of between four and twenty men ..."

"Who cares?" Naja sighed, frustrated, and started to tap the news display in front of her as she obviously didn't know what else to do for entertainment.

Saia ignored Naja's stupidity and focused on the vessel, which slid so lightly onto the launch pad. Suddenly the vessel increased its speed and Saia watched the sight, her eyes wide open. It was amazing to her that something so big was able to move so effortlessly.

The vessel accelerated rapidly along the launch pad. Even though its diameter was kilometers long, the vessel passed their train again in almost no time. It took another brief moment until it appeared in their sights a third time. Saia barely dared blink. The engines of the vessel increased their power and she was able to feel it inside the train carriage as well. After a few laps of the launch pad, the vessel was finally positioned in a tunnel pointing upwards, and in an instant the massive vessel ascended into planetary orbit.

"That is so ... marvelous," Saia whispered.

"What's so special about that?" Naja asked her sourly.

Saia didn't bother to answer. She just watched as the vessel soared higher and wondered how powerful its engines had to be in order for the vessel to ascend into orbit, despite the gravitational forces of Earth. She could still hear the vessel's engines humming loudly, which made the train carriage jolt slightly, even though the vessel itself was already far up in the sky. The jolting suddenly ceased as the vessel moved further away and soon, nothing more than just a bright spot – the light of Mintaka's combustion engines – could be seen.

"It would be great to know what that job were like," Saia finally said.

"Why?" Naja asked her genuinely puzzled. "You don't have to know anything of the sort."

"It would be great to go into space someday," Saia said.

"For what reason?" Naja asked her even more astonished. "You don't have to go there."

"Maybe I don't have to, but I would still like to."

"Grow up," Naja told her sourly. "Women don't have to make their lives too complicated. At least not beautiful women. I'm sure there is a man out there who will settle for you and provide you with everything you ever ask for. So why should you even consider having a job? "

Saia glanced quickly at Naja, and she felt the urge to say something nasty to the girl, but she couldn't make up anything witty enough. She simply couldn't understand why Naja wasn't interested in anything in the world except her own reflection and getting attention from others. Like now, for instance, she was wearing a skirt whose hemline barely covered her knees. This was provocative because, according to the dress code for women in public, they were expected to wear trousers. Skirts and dresses were primarily meant to be worn among female groups or during functions where she was representing her man at public events.

"It is a recommendation, not a regulation or law," Naja had informed the others when her choice of clothes had been criticized.

Saia, however, saw from the look on Naja's face, how much she had enjoyed receiving such reprimands. It was one of the reasons she had chosen to wear the skirt, Saia was convinced. Attention was attention and Saia already knew that Naja would figure out a way to ruin the day in Makaira, if she didn't feel like she was getting enough of it. It had happened so many times before, it would most likely happen on this study trip as well. Saia could only hope that at some point during the day she would be able to distance herself from Naja. She didn't want to get involved in her narcissistic tricks.

Saia fell back into her seat and looked up the middle aisle. Perhaps one of these days she would be rid of Naja, her mother, and even Gavialis, too. The mere thought of leaving everything behind and escaping made her heart race. That was how much she dreamed about a new beginning somewhere else. How she longed for it!

Then she felt the train speed up again. Suddenly Saia remembered the map Ati had left her. According to the map, there was wasteland on the northern side of Albedo. Saia changed channels on her news display to a general map service and chose Albedo's coordinates. When the space center appeared on the map, she scrolled the image upwards in order to see what there was further north. According to the information on the map, there was indeed wasteland in that area, but it wasn't any old wasteland; it was one of the five areas Ati had marked with black crosses on Saia's world map before his death.

Saia felt her heart racing. Was Terra Unionia in that area north of Albedo? Could it really be located so close to the world's space center? If that was the case, why didn't someone realize it? If there really was a settled area in the wasteland north of Albedo, one could assume that someone had already seen something. So it was somewhat unlikely that the wasteland in question would be the location of Terra Unionia, no matter that Ati had crossed the area as one of the possibilities. Nevertheless, Saia would have loved to go and see the area for herself, yet she knew it was pointless daydreaming about it. She was on a study trip now and the only place she would see on this trip was Makaira. Still, the wasteland in question was located titillatingly near her current location as they skirted the wasteland area to the north and turned west.

Saia took a deep breath, leaned back and switched the map view back to the news headline ticker. She remained still and followed the headlines across the screen. Then she took two small earpieces from her arm rest and placed them in her ears. She switched the text-based news ticker to news broadcasts and began browsing the more interesting topics which had been published over the last couple of hours.

Suddenly Saia's interest was pricked as she saw a headline mentioning Mars. The headline was a new one; it had been published about three hours ago. Saia picked it up, increased the sound volume and started to listen carefully to the man's broadcast.

"Early this morning, Earth Standard Time, a remarkable historical find was discovered on the northern hemisphere of Mars – part of an ancient man-made exploration device. This is the first time that man has succeeded in finding proof that mankind has previously sent its devices to Mars in the time before the Great War. According to the Space Affairs Council, this is a notable find, which also proves that man explored space during the old times as well, when mankind mainly focused on warfare. According to the Council's official statement, this discovery does not, however, verify that manned missions to Mars ever took place. Preliminary investigations support the assumption that the device found was most likely controlled remotely from Earth ..."

Saia was surprised, not only because such a purely research-related topic had ended up on the news. The most surprising aspect of it all was that the topic also had a historical aspect to it.

Suddenly Saia felt Naja poking her arm.

"What?" Saia asked her as she removed the earpieces from her ears.

"Why aren't you saying anything?"

Saia looked at Naja without knowing what to think. She usually said nothing. Their mutual dealings had always been based on the division where Saia had to keep listening to Naja's endless talks, which focused on her own looks, men, or the attention she was craving.

"Did you watch the news?" Naja asked her.

"I did," Saia answered quietly.

"What would it take for you to focus on yourself as eagerly as you do on the news? Aren't you interested at all in your looks?"

Saia was dumbfounded.

"What would it take for you to focus on the news for a change?" she asked Naja in return.

It was futile, though, because Naja wasn't interested in what she had on her mind.

"I'm watching the news, so leave me alone," Saia told her, and placed the earpieces back in her ears.

She could feel Naja's sharp stare but refused to look at her. Suddenly she remembered the claim Doctor Alauda had made about her being a better choice for a man than Naja. Saia couldn't help smiling because she had never even dared hope that Doctor Alauda would see her in such a positive light. Even though she didn't want to make a commitment to a man, Doctor Alauda's words had meant a lot to her. She had found strength in them.

Doctor Alauda meant so much to Saia; more than she would ever be able to confess openly. For her, Doctor Alauda was perfect. The woman's confidence had supported her in getting over Ati's death. Through Doctor Alauda, she had started to believe that there might be similar strength in her to that in the doctor. Her independence and self-confidence had made Saia feel a little less lonely, and she would have done anything to be part of Doctor Alauda's life, even if for just a brief moment.

And here she was now; next to Naja. If Naja had not been Doctor Alauda's daughter, she would never have had the opportunity to infiltrate Doctor Alauda's life so quickly.

Saia froze the headline ticker and continued browsing the news manually. Suddenly her heart missed a beat as she saw a familiar name in the headlines.

Mari Alauda.

Saia looked at Naja as casually as possible in order to ensure that the girl wasn't following what she was doing. When she realized Naja was fiddling with her noter with some other girl on the train, she activated the headline where Naja's mother's name had appeared. In the video clip, Mari Alauda was standing in the middle of a crowd of men and the caption at the bottom of the display said "Health Council Management Group."

"The Health Council has granted Doctor Mari Alauda an honorary award for exemplary work. Doctor Alauda, who has conducted groundbreaking work on the fertility program, is, according to the Statistics Center, the world's leading female doctor. Thousands of women flock to consult Doctor Alauda every year ..."

Saia closed the video clip screen, because she didn't want Naja to notice her watching news about Doctor Alauda. She knew very well what Naja thought of her own mother. The hatred Naja felt for Doctor Alauda often gave Saia the feeling she needed to defend the woman. Doctor Alauda was no monster. If Naja wanted someone to blame for her misery, she should look in a mirror first. The mere thought of all the nasty things Naja had said about Doctor Alauda got Saia on the verge of rage.

When Saia was sure Naja still wasn't paying her any attention, Saia selected the option below the headline which enabled her to filter out more news about Mari Alauda. In an instant, a long list of headlines appeared on the screen, some of which were already a few years old.

Mari Alauda appointed to new research group in women's fertility program

Doctor Alauda criticizes recommendations of Health Council regarding female fetus production volumes

Doctor Alauda reaps reward for career success

Doctor Mari Alauda appointed Doctor of the Year by Association of Medical Doctors

Doctor Alauda – "Artificial womb technology requires ongoing development"

Determined Doctor Alauda increases female birth rate

Mari Alauda speaks on strategic policy definition regarding Gallinula fertility program

Doctor Alauda – I will not leave Gavialis Main Hospital

Doctor Alauda appoints four new doctors to Gavialis Main Hospital fertility department

Doctor Alauda – "Doctors' evaluation group to undergo personnel changes"

Doctor Alauda follows registration of artificial pregnancies as general operation model

Doctor Mari Alauda – "Artificial wombs an inseparable part of mankind for decades"

Doctor Alauda on artificial womb use: "I give special rights to no one"

Doctor Alauda –Post-natal depression is real

Saia would have liked to read every single headline about Mari Alauda, but she didn't dare. Thanks to Naja's presence, she didn't even dare scroll the headline listing down further because she didn't want to give Naja any reason to attack her. She decided to continue with the headlines when she was back at home again. Some of the headlines she had just seen were already familiar to her, but there had been many headlines in the list she had not seen before.

"It's so funny how some men in my apartment building always shout at me," Naja said.

Naja's voice pulled Saia back to the train carriage and she quickly peeked at the girl. She felt her frustration rise because she already knew what was about to come. She would have to listen to Naja talking about men again; how beautiful she was in their eyes and how men wanted to get near her all the time.

"There is this creep living in our apartment building," Naja started. "Lator said that he lives in apartment 52."

Saia looked at the ceiling of the train carriage but said nothing.

"That man seems always to know my schedule, which means he has been observing me. Every time I go out he is waiting for me in the hallway and tries to approach me. Once, the Guardsmen – well Lator mainly – even threw him against the wall!"

"I see," Saia finally said.

"But he doesn't care," Naja said and laughed. "I think he's obsessed with me, which is pretty amusing but also very sad. The men's minds are so fragile."

Saia was now amused. She knew the situation was anything but sad for Naja. She enjoyed the attention because it boosted the already existent illusion she had of being the most beautiful and wanted girl among her peers. This status of hers naturally demanded that Naja belittle men's admiration; being the object of so much attention, she couldn't react to each individual case separately. It was interesting, however, how Naja seemed to keep detailed score of how many men had noticed her, where it had happened and especially when.

"Lator is so wonderful," Naja whispered.

"What?" Saia asked her, even though she had already noticed how Lator's name kept recurring in Naja's conversation.

"Lator is so protective," Naja stated. "And he is so good-looking."

Saia took a deep breath. She wasn't convinced at all that she wanted to hear any more.

"I want to have sex with him," Naja whispered.

Saia looked at Naja for a moment and wondered if she was serious.

"Is he capable of doing it?"

"Why wouldn't he be?" Naja asked her in return and laughed. "He's only been sterilized. All the original parts are still there."

"He would be sent to Cold Pit," Saia reminded her quietly.

"I know," Naja said and smiled slyly, "but it would be worth it."

"Maybe for you," Saia stated.

"Above all for him," Naja snorted.

Saia was about to scream.

"Sometimes I let Lator watch me when I get dressed," Naja said.

"Why?"

"Because it feels good," Naja explained. "When a man watches you like that, when he admires you like Lator does, it feels good. You obviously can't understand that."

"I wouldn't want to."

"Oh please," Naja snorted "Quit lying. You would give anything to be as beautiful as I am."

Saia took a deep breath and tried to block the ugly feeling Naja's words stirred in her.

"And when he watches me, his crotch begins to bulge," Naja said quietly and laughed.

Saia swallowed. Did she really have to hear all this?

"He has shown it to me," Naja added.

"Shown you what?"

"His erection."

"What ...?"

Naja laughed again.

"So, he has already broken his oath," Saia noted quietly.

"So?"

"If he gets caught, he will take the most direct route to Cold Pit."

"Gaskar at most," Naja laughed.

Saia shook her head. She was genuinely dismayed.

"I have given Lator my pictures as well," she added.

"Pictures?"

"Of me wearing my underwear ... and even topless," Naja whispered and smiled. "He does everything I ask."

"As a Guardsman, wouldn't he do so anyway without any pictures?"

"Not everything," Naja stated mysteriously.

"Like?"

"Deliver me stuff."

"What stuff?"

"N1014."

Saia's jaw dropped.

"You use N1014?" she asked. Her question choked her.

"Occasionally," Naja said amused.

Saia couldn't help but think of Doctor Alauda. Did the woman know what her daughter was up to?

"You can ruin your health with it," Saia whispered.

"I am beautiful," Naja reminded her. "I can afford to take it every now and then, because it won't kill me. I can get away with it."

"It didn't show up in your examination?" Saia asked her curiously.

"What examination?"

"In Swallow's Nest, when you donated your ova?"

"I didn't use the stuff in the month before that examination. So the quantity of it in my system was at a very low level."

"N1014 doesn't ever totally disappear from your system," Saia pointed out.

"Well, mom didn't say a word about it, so I don't think she even noticed it."

"What about if you get hooked?"

"Unlikely, but if I do, mom will fix me up."

"Are you sure?"

"What is that supposed to mean?" Naja snapped.

"I've heard how you talk about your mom," Saia explained. "According to you, she doesn't really care about you or any of your business."

"She is my mother," Naja said, "but most of all, she is a medical doctor. Women are treated for every possible inconvenience. We are pampered and given extra care, even when there is nothing wrong with us. So if I end up in a bad condition, I will be taken care of. Women's basic security benefit will ensure that."

"Maybe so," Saia said. "But why?"

"What do you mean?"

"Why do you want to use that stuff and give Lator your pictures?"

"Because it's fun," Naja said and laughed. "And because nothing feels better than a man's attention. That is the reason I was born into this world; to tease men."

Saia was dumbfounded.

"And if men don't give you any attention, it's a sign of you not being a real woman," Naja added. "That means there is something very seriously wrong with you."

"What next?" Saia asked her then. "What if Lator starts asking you for something else?"

"Like?"

"You are playing a dangerous game here," Saia said.

"Life has to be interesting," Naja pointed out.

"You could ruin Lator's life."

"He would ruin it himself," Naja informed her sourly. "I haven't forced him into anything."

"Is he forcing you into anything?"

"Me? Don't be ridiculous."

"Have you shown him … what's between your legs?"

"Not yet," Naja whispered and there was a sly expression on her face.

Saia took a quick look at Lator who was engaged in discussion with another Yellow Guardsman at the front of the carriage. Lator was in trouble, there was no doubt about that. Why was he so stupid? Didn't he see what kind of person Naja was? If he was playing these games with Naja, he would eventually get caught. Naja would betray him if the truth didn't get out in another way, because she was capable of doing something like that just for the fun of it. So Lator's career in the Guard was already in danger and he would end up losing everything. It would happen – it was only a matter of time – why didn't Lator see it himself?

Saia took a deep breath and shook her head. Lator made his own decisions. If the man really wanted to play dangerous games no one could do anything to prevent it.

"You're just jealous of me," Naja whispered then.

"Uuuuh … what?"

"It irks you that I am beautiful and that I get attention. That's why you pretend you don't even want attention, as if you wouldn't miss it at all. You just don't want to admit to yourself that you are not good enough and that is the reason why you want to dismiss the entire idea."

"Has your mother been home much lately?" Saia asked her all of a sudden, just to change the subject. She knew that Doctor Alauda was the most effective conversation killer for Naja.

"Why do you want to know about her schedule?" Naja asked her sourly.

"I'm just asking," Saia said briefly.

"You are weird," Naja noted. "I just wish I could commit myself to a man already, so I could finally start living a real life. It would have to be a powerful and remarkable man from Seventh Circle. I don't pay attention to mediocre cases from Sixth Circle."

"Did you carry out your Apertum plans?" Saia asked her.

"I did."

"And your mom approved?"

"Believe me – she didn't resist at all. She wants me out of her life as soon as possible and she has no intention of waiting until I turn eighteen or twenty."

"So, you will start seeing men?"

"Why wouldn't I? I am hardly the first 16-year-old who participates in Apertum. And when I told my mom that I added my name to the Apertum list, she didn't have anything to say about it. She simply said 'I see' and she was done talking about it. On the other hand I am quite a mature 16-year-old, so the quicker I find a man to commit myself to, the better."

Saia didn't know what to say.

"I don't think you are ready for Apertum yet," Naja pondered. "You're not mentally mature yet, or physically attractive enough. You have to lose weight, but luckily a lot can happen during one year. So if you buck your ideas up, you can make it happen. So quit being so lazy. Nothing is more embarrassing than being ignored at Apertum evening parties."

Saia swallowed but remained silent.

"By the way, I've got some new clothes from my guardian," Naja said, "and I'm talking about real rarities. Being special has its benefits and that's why I get whatever I want."

Saia rolled her eyes, but remained silent yet again.

"Just look at Beatra," Naja snorted and nodded towards the middle of the carriage. "She copies me."

Saia took a quick look at Beatra and waited for Naja to continue.

"I was the first one in this group who wore shoes like that," Naja said, "and look what has happened; poor creatures like her start to imitate me. It's so pathetic. Luckily there is no such concern with you, even though you could dress yourself in a more feminine way. So, you're harmless. I could give you some of my old clothes, though, if they would only fit you."

Saia still didn't say a word. However, she couldn't help but wonder how such a creature could have ever come from a person as perfect as Doctor Alauda. It was mind-boggling and if Saia hadn't known better, she would have never believed Naja to be Mari Alauda's daughter.

"Oh! I have another stalker as well!"

"What are you talking about?" Saia asked her, even though she had heard Naja's stories about stalkers so many times that she couldn't bear to hear any more of them.

"I noticed another movement in a window across from our apartment building this morning," Naja explained.

"And?"

"What do you mean?" Naja asked her huffily. "I've already told you about this case many times. This man has been spying on me for at least a year."

"Oh that," Saia said, even though she had no idea who Naja was talking about this time.

"That's right. He hangs around in that building and I am pretty sure he takes pictures of me. It's so amusing. This morning I intentionally left my curtains open when I walked around my room wearing nothing but my underwear."

"Why would you want to do something like that?"

"Because teasing is fun," Naja laughed. "It just amuses me so much how this man suffers because he can't ever touch me. He has to remember his place. Women are worth pursuing and I know the value of my status as a beautiful woman. It's one thing to be a woman but quite another to be a beautiful woman."

Saia didn't know what to say. She replaced the earpieces, opened the news ticker and checked how long it would take until they arrived at Makaira. Another hour. Saia huffed, closed her eyes and blocked the world from her thoughts.

* * *

Saia felt the train slowing down. She looked out of the window, which she had forgotten for a moment due the monotony of the landscape. The emptiness was still there but the landscape looked even more barren than before. The land was still dry and treeless, but much darker than during the first hours of their journey.

"*Attention all passengers*," they heard. "*This train is slowing down due to maintenance work being conducted on this part of the track. We will resume normal speed in a few moments.*"

"Girls," their female supervisor said. "You don't get out of the city often, so I urge you to look outside and remember what you see. The area outside is still so poisonous after the Great War that it is not possible for humans to live here. Unfortunately, there are many such areas all over the world. Remember what you see now so that none of us ever forgets the damage man's destructive power can wreak."

So they were in the wastelands now. Ati, however, had not marked this area on his map and that meant that he had not believed Terra Unionia to be here. It was quite logical because trains passed through here, therefore someone would surely have noticed if there had been any additional settlements here other than the maintenance crews' temporary accommodation.

Saia looked at the view through the window and couldn't help but wonder what kind of place this area had been before the war. Had there been trees? Or had there been a city? Why had this particular area been bombed with poisonous weapons? How many people had died here?

"Why are we being bogged down with history?" Naja snorted under her breath. "Who cares what people did in the olden days?"

Saia decided to ignore Naja's nonsense and she focused on the landscape through the window. When they passed the workmen, the train picked up speed and Saia finally leaned back in her seat and closed her eyes.

It was a while before the train slowed down again. Saia opened her eyes, removed the earpieces from her ears and leaned towards Naja in order to see what was going on outside the window. When the train rounded a bend, an enormous ocean came into view. Saia's jaw dropped in amazement, she had never seen the ocean before. She felt the gentle lurch in her stomach which told her the train was beginning its descent. They were heading towards an underwater tunnel, built between the coast and Makaira.

The windows went dark and Saia felt her ears block. She swallowed a few times before her ears opened again. Now it wouldn't be long before they arrived at their final destination.

The blackness of the tunnel disappeared from the window and Saia noticed that they were once again surrounded by buildings. The train slowed down abruptly.

"*Makaira*," the train's automatic announcement informed them.

"Stay in your seats, girls, until the train has come to a complete stop," their female supervisor announced as some of the girls had already jumped to their feet. "We'll let the Guardsmen check the station platform first before gathering outside."

"Before we leave, we have time to refresh our basic information about Makaira," their male supervisor then informed the group.

Saia looked at the man and hoped he wouldn't make a long speech.

"As we all should know by now, Makaira is one of two ocean cities of the world. This city was founded originally for research purposes. Research carried out here was focused on deep space travel. People were placed in the submerged sectors of the city for a period of a few months and their lives were observed by researchers. Nowadays these submerged sectors are dedicated to testing research devices, which are used to study the composition of seawater. In addition, both magnesium and salt are extracted from the water here. Makaira is 1.2 kilometers long and 0.5 kilometers wide. The current population is 8,000."

"Blah, blah," Naja sighed; she was already bored.

"Makaira's energy consumption is as follows: 60% solar energy, 25% hydro-energy through osmosis, and the remaining 15% wind energy. There may, however, be some fluctuation in these numbers."

After what seemed like an age, the girls heard the doors opening and they saw the Yellow Guardsmen stepping out and start walking along the platform. It took a couple of minutes until their male supervisor received permission from the leading Guardsman to lead them off the train.

"Finally," Naja sighed.

Saia stood up and rushed towards the doors. She wanted to be among the first to get off to put some distance between her and Naja. She wanted to concentrate on seeing and hearing everything about the city, and therefore keeping up with Naja's tricks, which would go against all the Guardsmen's wishes, wasn't part of her plans.

Saia stepped onto the platform at Makaira Station and looked around. She felt a cool breeze on her face. She wanted to rush into the city to see everything it had to offer; it felt to her like she had finally been liberated after a long period of house arrest.

"Miss Motasilla," one of the Guardsmen said. "Remain close to the rest of the group."

"Will we go around the city instead of spending all our time inside one of these buildings?" Saia asked him.

"We will go where we are told to go," the man stated briefly.

Saia pouted. The uncertainty of the situation annoyed her, but she was in Makaira now; a city, which she had never seen before. If Naja would only stay away from her, the day ahead had every chance of being almost perfect.

6.

Jani kept his eyes on Makaira Station through the window beside him. He could see a glimpse of ocean behind the city buildings but unfortunately most of the ocean was out of sight. Now that he really was here, it was a pity he couldn't get off the train to see the city, even though Makaira had, at first, not interested him at all. In fact, the mere thought of leaving Gavialis had felt like a mandatory boring obligation.

Few men got on the train. They had appeared on the station approximately ten minutes after the Yellow Guardsmen had left the platform with the group of girls. One of the Guardsmen had even glared at Jani when he had realized that Jani was staring at the girls, his eyes wide open. The look on the Guardsman's face, the insolence of it, had annoyed Jani; it wasn't as if there had really been any chance for him to inflict any harm on the girls sitting in the train carriage. Not to mention the fact that looking at girls was not yet against the law. The Yellow Guardsmen were simply full of themselves. It was a fact of which Jani had once again been reminded.

Finally, Jani felt a slight jolt. He deduced it meant the yellow carriage had finally been disconnected from the train and therefore it wouldn't be much longer before they were due to depart and head back to Gavialis. Suddenly Jani felt his nerves kicking in. Even though he didn't have to do anything except sit still and wait, he was nervous nonetheless. He checked the time again. For some reason he expected to get caught; that one of the bystanders would realize he was doing something shady. What would be the consequences of him getting caught, he did not know, but Jani assumed it wouldn't be anything good.

"*Doors closing*," the automatic announcement said. "*Next stop: Gavialis, Fourth Corner Station.*"

Jani sighed as quietly as possible. Finally the moment was coming; the moment which had brought him all the way to Makaira. He had no regrets about taking the assignment, at least no very serious ones; he simply wanted to get back to Sixth Circle as quickly as possible. Nonetheless he had some doubts about this covert assignment he had agreed to carry out. It would be just his luck if something went wrong, even though his role in this mysterious task was rather small. All he had to do was sit and wait, pick up the suitcase, and take it to Linai's West Station. Even if the assignment seemed rather simple and straightforward, it had to be more complex than that. Therefore, Jani prepared himself for trouble, arming himself against disappointment with pessimistic expectation.

The train started moving. Jani looked out of the window and saw the Makaira buildings gliding smoothly past. They rapidly picked up speed and, when Jani saw the ocean again, they started their descent into the underwater tunnel through which the train would return to the mainland.

The windows darkened and Jani activated his news ticker. He browsed the latest headlines, which he had already checked numerous times, but there was always the possibility that some new articles would be published in the worldwide news headline feed. All of a sudden, a familiar name caught Jani's eye.

Mari Alauda.

Jani activated the headline in question and a clip appeared on the screen where Doctor Mari Alauda was standing in the middle of a group of men with a wide smile on her face. The caption on the bottom of the screen said "Health Council Management Group." Jani was surprised. Doctor Alauda had been given the opportunity to meet the Health Council Management Group and on top of that; they had given her an award. Jani couldn't imagine any clearer sign of greater success in life. Jani shook his head. He had not even considered that the female doctor he had recently met could be someone famous; that the first woman he ever talked to was a worldwide celebrity.

Jani closed the clip and let the headlines run on his screen again. He couldn't concentrate on reading any of them because he was getting increasingly nervous. He tried to remain calm; the last thing he wanted was to draw attention to himself. He felt his palms becoming sweaty and he kept swinging his leg to release some of the nervousness he was currently suffering from. Luckily, no one was sitting across the middle aisle because not being noticed was extremely important now.

Suddenly the train started slowing down. Jani was on full alert. Why were they slowing down? He activated the general information window from the top corner of the news screen and saw their current speed was only fifty kilometers per hour.

The train continued to reduce its speed.

Jani looked at the nearest man in the car who was sitting a few seats behind him. He seemed to be just as confused about the unexpected turn of events as Jani. Jani turned around and returned to his news screen. Their current speed was only thirty-five kilometers per hour and they were moving more and more slowly with every passing moment.

Twenty-seven kilometers per hour.

Jani shook his head. What was going on? According to the information window on the news screen there could only be one train in the tunnel at a time, so the reason for them to be reducing speed couldn't be about them avoiding another train.

Nineteen kilometers per hour.

Jani was very restless now and he tapped the armrest to his left. He kept staring at the numbers on his screen which were falling continuously. This made him more and more restless. Would they stop completely? Would they come to a complete stop in the tunnel?

Eleven kilometers per hour.

The train was now barely moving and it didn't take long before Jani finally felt the train stop. All he could do was stare at the screen in front of him where the number 0.0 km/h began to blink.

Jani looked around him and he felt extremely uncomfortable. They were hundreds of meters below the surface. Why had they stopped? How long would they have to stay here? And what about the delivery which had brought him here in the first place? Surely the train would soon move again?

Jani switched the general information window back to the news headline ticker because he didn't know what else to do. It took about a minute before a new topic appeared in the headlines.

Train to continent stuck in underwater tunnel 15 kilometers from Makaira

Jani took a deep breath. There was no doubt about it; they had become stuck in this tunnel. Did it mean there was some kind of malfunction on the train? Or was it the tunnel that was causing this? Jani opened the news article which was attached to the news headline. It didn't take long before he discovered that someone on the train had already sent their thoughts to the news service as the following information in the article caught his eye.

... there has been no announcement given to passengers about the cause of the stop, but according to the latest news update, the defect has been identified in the power transmission between the train and the tunnel. The passengers on the train have remained calm, and both rescue and maintenance groups have been sent from Makaira to the train and should reach it within a few minutes.

Jani was beginning to feel more and more uncomfortable. He was late. What if this unfortunate delay would prevent him from getting the suitcase? What would happen then? Would he receive some kind of punishment for his failure, even though the man on the U Train had told him otherwise? Or was the suitcase already on the train? Should he take the risk, go to the sanitary facilities and check the situation out?

Jani took another deep breath to calm his nerves. He had to remain calm, because drawing attention to himself was out of the question. However, the blackness behind the windows caused a heavy sensation in Jani's chest. Jani didn't like either darkness or silence. He barely tolerated the silence in the control room where he worked, but at least the room in question was illuminated and he knew exactly where the exit was. Now, however, he was here, stuck in a tunnel under the sea. There was no way out. On the other side of the windows was a dark tunnel without any oxygen, or at least that was Jani's best guess. Behind the tunnel walls was water. They were deep beneath the surface, so if the train continued to remain stationary, they would be trapped. There was no way out.

Jani closed his eyes. Suddenly the memory of a day he had never really fully forgotten emerged; a day he did not actively think about anymore. It was the day he had met Lu.

He had been less than ten years old when he had visited a food distribution facility in Second Circle, which processed mainly durra and fish as ready meals for the Gavialians. From a child's point of view the place was enormous but extremely interesting. Therefore, the trip to the facility had been a positive change for Jani, who had been glad of the variety. For him the visit had been a much better option than the alternative; spending hours in one of the educational institution's boring rooms listening to his life instructor giving his monologue.

The children had been able to follow carefully how the facility's large machinery operated as one of the employees had explained to them what was taking place in each part of the building. For some reason, Jani had become separated from the rest of his group and he still didn't know what had caused him to wander off. All he knew was that he had wanted to see behind one of the big assembly lines and that he had decided to disappear and come back before anyone had even noticed his absence.

Then he had heard a loud bang and in an instant the entire building had fallen into complete darkness as the walls, machines, and even the roof above him had trembled as if the building was being bombarded. In fact, Jani had first thought the cause of the incident was war, because their life instructor had just recently told them about the Great War. Finally, when silence returned, he realized he was trapped between a wall and one of the machines. It was the machine which had lured him away from his group in the first place.

Jani still remembered how his fear had paralyzed him. He had not been able to see anything in the darkness; he could just hear himself breathing in the silence. He had not dared move, not even in the slightest, because he had been too afraid of causing the walls and roof to fall on him. If the roof had fallen on him, he would have been buried under the rubble and that would have been the end.

It hadn't taken long for Jani to realize that no one would ever find him if he simply remained still and quiet.

"*Can anyone hear me?*" he had finally dared to call. "*Can anyone hear me?*"

But no one seemed to be near and the silence began to fan the flames of his fear. He had started to believe that all the people in the building had already died and that he was the only one left alive. The thought of that had scared him; however, he kept calling, but when he realized no one would answer, he had finally given up and became still and quiet.

At some point he had lost his sense of time. He had merely sat in the darkness holding back his tears comforting himself by hugging his knees tightly against his chest. During that time he knew that he might die without anyone ever finding him and he also understood, for the first time in his life, that there was no one in the world who would miss him if that should happen.

Then, after an eternity, he had finally heard something and when he turned his head towards a sound, he had seen a beam of light in the darkness.

"*Is anyone there?*" a voice asked.

"*Yes,*" Jani had croaked.

Then all of a sudden he had seen a boy's face.

"*Are you alright?*" the boy asked him.

"*Yes,*" Jani had answered, quietly. He was still afraid of the roof falling on him if he dared to move a finger.

"*There was an explosion in the facility,*" the boy had said. "*We are trapped in here.*"

"*We? Are you trapped as well?*"

"*I think most of the people here are,*" the boy replied. "*So, I think it would be best for you to come out from there.*"

"*Okay,*" Jani agreed. "*But what if the roof falls in?*"

"*Come,*" the boy encouraged him instead and then extended a helping hand to Jani. "*You can't stay there because it looks even more dangerous there than it looks in here.*"

Jani had decided to trust the boy and he forced himself to move. Once he had taken the boy's hand, he was pulled from the darkness into the dimness. There had been a broken light somewhere near them, which kept flashing in the darkness, but there had been no sounds of people anywhere in the eerie silence.

"*What happened?*" Jani had asked the boy.

"*I don't know.*"

"*Where are all the others?*"

"*Somewhere near. Some must be badly hurt, perhaps even dead. We two are the lucky ones.*"

"*I suppose so,*" Jani had sighed. "*But how do you know it is safe for us to move around in here?*"

"*We must keep moving,*" the boy had said. "*I think the supporting walls are still standing, so if we are careful, we can find a way out.*"

"*Supporting walls?*"

"*Every building has supporting walls,*" the boy had stated.

"*How do you know?*"

"*I read it. Supporting walls support the upper floors of buildings as well as the roof.*"

"*And the supporting walls of this building have not been damaged in the explosion?*"

"*I don't think so,*" the boy had said, "*because the floors above us are still there, more or less.*"

"*Alright.*"

"*What's your name?*" the boy had asked him next.

"*Jani.*"

"*I am Lu,*" the boy had said. "*I was here with my educational team.*"

"*Me too.*"

Then the two of them had walked around for a while, searching for a way out. In the dimness and the silence of the ruins they had lost their sense of direction; and not just Jani, but also Lu, who had known about supporting walls.

"*I'm scared, too,*" Lu had said at one point, as he saw the horror on Jani's face.

"*So, where do we get out?*" Jani had asked him quietly.

"*Somewhere here,*" Lu had assured him.

Jani had decided to trust him and he had kept following the boy. He chose their path carefully because of all the threatening creaks and cracking sounds which kept echoing all around them.

"*What if the roof really falls in?*" Jani had finally asked Lu.

"*That is why we must find a way out soon,*" Lu had noted. "*The rescue team must be looking for us already, but I think it's wise for us to keep trying to find a way out ourselves, too.*"

"*Are you sure?*" Jani had asked him.

"*I would be more scared to stay put than to search for a way out,*" Lu had said.

"*I guess I would, too,*" Jani had reluctantly agreed.

So Jani had let Lu guide him through the darkness, even though he had not known if the boy really did know where to go and find a way out beneath the collapsing building.

"*How old are you?*" Lu had asked him at one point.

"*Nine,*" Jani had answered.

"*I'm eight.*"

When Jani had heard that, he was a little embarrassed. He was year older than Lu, so he should have been the one to overcome his fears and guide them out of the building, but Lu was much more confident than him. Lu had known how to give the impression of knowing exactly what to do. Therefore, Jani had followed, thankful for Lu's company. He really had not wanted to die that day.

They had been tiptoeing through the rubble for about fifteen minutes when they had finally heard the yells of men outside.

"*We have two survivors here!!*" someone had shouted, as a bright beam of light had blinded Jani for a moment.

The next moments had passed by as if in a dream. Jani and Lu had been lifted up and their fingerprints had been scanned for identification. Grown men had carried them away from the collapsing building to a temporary shelter, where they had been given water and a tablet to swallow.

"*Lu!*" they had finally heard as a tall man in a dark gray uniform had arrived at the shelter.

The man had taken Lu in his arms and kissed the boy's forehead. Jani had watched the two of them quite astonished. He had not understood who the man was or how he knew Lu.

"*Are you alright?*" the man asked the boy.

"*Yes,*" Lu said.

"*Good,*" the man said. "*Now we are going home.*"

"*What about Jani?*" Lu had asked the man.

"*Who?*"

Lu pointed his finger in Jani's direction.

"*I found Jani,*" Lu informed the man.

"*You did?*"

Lu had nodded.

"*Good boy,*" the man stated proudly. "*You are a hero, son. Saving another person's life will gain you five Silver Wing marks. What do you think about that, huh?*"

Lu's face had started to beam and Jani had continued watching the two of them in deep amazement.

"*I am proud of you, son,*" the man said and patted Lu's back. "*You're a good boy.*"

Jani had followed the conversation between Lu and the man without blinking an eye. He had not understood why the man had only noticed Lu when there were other children in the temporary shelter, too.

"*What's your name?*" the man finally asked Jani.

"*Jani,*" he answered somewhat puzzled, since Lu had just said what his name was.

"*Your full name?*" the man specified. "*My last name is Talpa, so Lu's full name is Lu Talpa.*"

"*Jani 821771,*" Jani said.

"*So, you're one of the educational institution boys,*" the man remarked.

"*Why doesn't Jani have a proper last name?*" Lu asked the man.

"*Because Jani doesn't have a provider,*" the man explained. "*I am your provider and my last name is Talpa. That's why your last name is Talpa as well. Jani doesn't have a provider and therefore he has a number. Hasn't your life instructor told you yet about boys who do not have a provider of their own? There are quite a lot of them in the world after all."*

"*No,*" Lu said.

"*Well, then you have now heard it from me,*" the man noted, "*and I am telling you that there are lots of children in the world who have a number instead of a last name, like Jani does. It means that they were born into this world without belonging to any particular man.*"

"*Why are children like that being born?*" Lu asked him.

"*Because otherwise people might completely disappear from this world in the near future,*" the man explained. "*There aren't so many of us left here.*"

"*Because there was the Great War,*" Lu added.

"*That's right. You got it. So if we want mankind to survive into the future, there has to be children in the world who don't have their own providers, and who are being raised in groups. They have to exist, because they are important for all of us.*"

"*Why?*"

"*Because mankind needs more children than there are successful men to raise them.*"

"*Are you a successful man?*" Jani asked the man.

"*Yes I am,*" the man said. "*And Lu here is the proof of that. I am a border guard and Lu will become one, too.*"

"*What does a border guard do?*" Jani asked him.

"*We guard the city's borders,*" the man explained. "*Our job is to ensure that no one crosses the city borders without permission.*"

"*Are there war criminals outside the cities?*" Jani asked the man.

"*Not at all,*" the man laughed. "*There haven't been any war criminals for a long time now.*"

"*Not even when you were a child?*" Lu asked his provider.

"*Not even then, but there are nulls outside the cities. Nulls are unwanted men who have made nothing of themselves, who have not accomplished anything significant. It's our duty to make sure they don't cross the city borders because they have lost their right to live in the city.*"

"*Why?*" Lu asked the man.

"*Because they have not done anything important which would move us all forward. They have accomplished nothing and that's why they have given up. They are simply wasting their lives and it is not our obligation to support anyone like that. We can't let people like that hold us down or prevent us from putting all our time and energy into progress.*"

"*Won't Jani ever get his own provider?*" Lu asked the man.

"*No,*" the man said. "*Jani and boys like him are raised in their institutions where boys don't have providers of their own. They have life instructors instead.*"

"*Life instructors do other things too?*" Lu asked him puzzled.

"*For you, a life instructor only teaches,*" the man said, "*but for boys who are raised in groups, life instructors are also providers. They provide the boys with the basics they need in the same way that I provide for you. Whereas I have only one son, life instructors have an entire group. They teach boys like Jani useful knowledge and skills, just like I teach you. If Jani works hard and he succeeds, he can become a successful man who can apply for an official last name of his own. And perhaps one day Jani can also apply for permission to have his own child. Perhaps one day both of you will be providers.*"

"*Can Jani visit me in our apartment building?*" Lu asked the man next.

"*I don't know,*" Lu's provider answered. "*Typically boys like you don't play with each other.*"

"*Why not?*" Lu asked him puzzled.

"*Because boys like Jani remain in their groups inside the buildings which have been designed for them, and boys like you stay in their apartment building with their providers.*"

"*Can't Jani ever come to visit us at all?*"

"*Would you want him to visit you?*"

"*Yes,*" Lu said.

"*Jani? Do you want to play with Lu?*"

Jani nodded.

"*Very well. If you both want that, I will make it happen somehow,*" the man said. "*I'd do anything for you, son.*"

"*So, you have lots of friends, Jani?*" Lu asked him.

"*I suppose,*" Jani said.

"*Of course Jani has lots of friends. Those who are left alone will become nulls sooner or later. And no one wants to end up like that, right?*"

The boys shook their heads simultaneously.

"*Do you remember the name of the building you live in, Jani?*" the man then asked him.

"*Pentala,*" Jani said.

"*Good boy,*" the man said. "*Come. Let's find your life instructor or one of his representatives. They must have been asked to come here to the scene when the news of this disaster spread.*"

Jani had taken a step towards the man who had been carrying Lu in his arms the entire time. As they stepped outside the temporary shelter, the man had suddenly taken Jani's hand. Jani still remembered how unexpected it had been for him and at that moment he had felt quite uncertain. He had not understood why the man was holding his hand; no grown up had ever done anything like that to him before, but the squeeze of his big hand gave Jani a feeling of safety; something he had not experienced before. For the first time in his life Jani had started to realize how much luckier he would have been in Lu's place. Lu's provider had come to Lu. The man took care of Lu, who obviously meant a lot to him. If Lu had died, the man would most likely have been very sad about it.

And if Jani had died on that day, or if he died now on this train, no one would pay any special attention to it. No one would find it noteworthy in any way; no one except Lu, perhaps. Jani activated his noter and started to type a text-based message.

Lu,

I am stuck on a train in a tunnel under the sea. I have no idea how long we will have to stay here. This incident has brought back memories from many years ago.

Jani

Jani was already about to send the message when he suddenly changed his mind. Instead of sending it to Lu's ID account, he erased it, and closed his noter which he put back in his pocket.

He was in this situation right now for a reason and this reason was something he couldn't tell anyone, not even Lu. So if he died in here, Lu would never know why he had traveled to Makaira in the first place.

Jani stared at a small screen on which the headlines kept changing as the headline ticker kept running from right to left. Suddenly he noticed the name "Makaira" in one of the headlines. Jani quickly froze the news headline ticker and searched for the headline in question by scrolling backwards.

Attack on girl group in Makaira – no casualties

Jani was completely astonished. He opened the news story behind the headline and quickly read its contents. An arrow had been fired towards the girl group in Makaira and one of the girls had been hit in the shoulder. The girl was still alive, but security and safety measures in the ocean city had been tightened.

Jani shook his head. He couldn't understand why anyone would want to attack women. There weren't so many of them left in the world in the first place, so why would anyone want to cause them harm? Women were needed if they wanted to preserve the human race. That much was obvious even for Jani.

Jani took a deep breath. He leaned against the backrest of his seat and cursed his bad luck silently. He had agreed to leave the city for the temptation of Sixth Circle and the one time he had done so, the train had to get stuck in an underwater tunnel.

He shook his head because he had somehow known something like this would happen to him. He had expected that this little trip of his wouldn't be trouble-free; nothing in his life happened without problems of some kind. How could there be so much misfortune in one person's life? His friendship with Lu had been the only thing in his life which had actually worked out well, and even that had begun on a day when a building had collapsed on him.

Jani closed his eyes and memories beyond the years came back to him. For some reason being stuck in a tunnel made him remember another gloomy incident as well, when he had felt most distressed. That summer's day was the day he turned fourteen.

That summer had been a special one because he had just left the educational institution to begin his command education; a two-year program all boys of 14 to 16 had to take part in. The beginning of his command education also meant that a boy faced his descent. It was a significant landmark in a boy's youth, when each one was dropped in the outer circles of the city, no matter what kind of footing they had had in life before that. The purpose of the descent was to bring young men to the outer circles, but the actual circle chosen was determined by the number of Silver Wing marks they had managed to collect so far. After the descent it was each boy's own responsibility to earn their place in the inner circles of the city by succeeding. Jani had been dropped into First Circle, which had not surprised him at all.

That summer, Lu had still been thirteen years old and therefore he was still living with his provider Talpa. At the time, the two of them had lived in Fourth Circle, to where they had moved a couple of years before. Jani would never have had any reason to be in Fourth Circle if he had not known Lu. Their friendship had always been a privilege to him and Jani had often wondered why Lu wanted to spend time with him, when he had nothing to offer the boy in return.

Every time Jani had received access permission to Fourth Circle from Lu, Lu had always been standing outside the station gates waiting for him. And Jani had received such permission almost on a daily basis, so there had been times when he had almost felt like living in Fourth Circle too, even though he had done nothing to deserve it. That summer, Lu had been very curious about Jani's command education and the boy couldn't get enough of Jani's stories about it. This was understandable because Lu had his own descent waiting in the near future. However, unlike Jani, Lu was not going to be dropped into First Circle, he had earned enough Silver Wing marks to be dropped into Second Circle.

"How's it going?" Lu had asked him once as they had walked from the 4.3 Corner Station to Lu's apartment building. *"Is it better or worse than an educational institution?"*

"It's different," Jani had told him. *"I know some of the boys from the institution so the change is not really that big, but the discipline is definitely tighter. My commander isn't as malicious as my crappy instructor was, so you get along with him just fine as long as you do as you are told."*

"So, he doesn't bully anyone around?"

"As long as you behave well and do as you are told, no. He is fair in that way, but if you argue with him, like couple of guys did yesterday, nothing good comes of it."

"So, it's not called command education for nothing," Lu noted.

"You can be sure of that."

"But it really does beat the conditions at the educational institution?"

"Damn right it does," Jani assured his friend. *"Not to mention that I finally have my own apartment."*

"Neat," Lu noted and the two of them high-fived in agreement.

Jani still remembered how telling Lu about his experiences had made him feel good about himself. Lu had always been the one who had known everything, so it was a nice change for him to know something Lu had no experience of; something Lu found interesting. Lu's curiosity and his continuous questions had made Jani feel somewhat wise and he had liked that feeling.

On that summer day, when they had walked from the station to Lu's apartment building, there had been some boys gathered around the main door. Jani had sensed immediately that the boy group would cause them trouble and he had been annoyed by his own insecurities at that moment. He had been older than those kids, yet he had still felt unsure about himself because of them.

"*Talpa is bringing street garbage from First Circle here again,*" one of the boys had laughed.

"*Just ignore them,*" Lu had told Jani.

Jani had managed a watery smile and nodded at Lu's suggestion.

"*Is it fun to live in First Circle, artificial boy?*" the boy, who was obviously some sort of group leader, asked him.

"*I'm sure you'll find out all about it soon enough,*" Lu pointed out.

Jani laughed at Lu's joke, but the boy with the big mouth was not amused at all.

"*What are you laughing about, artificial boy?*" he asked him, clearly riled.

"*What do you think?*" Jani asked the boy instead. "*I'm laughing at you.*"

"*A guy who gets access permission here by giving his ass to his buddy is in no position to laugh at others,*" was the next insult from the boy.

"*Excuse me?*" Lu asked the boy sternly.

At that moment, Jani noticed that Lu had gotten really riled at the insinuation. It was somewhat unexpected because Lu didn't get mad often; the situation was very exceptional.

"*Don't get mad just because I speak the truth,*" the boy said and laughed. "*Why else would you drag that dog here? Everyone knows what the deal is between the two of you and everyone knows that artificial boys in First Circle are easily trained to obey almost every command.*"

Something dark flashed in Lu's eyes.

"*I guess from the bitterness in your voice that you haven't gotten anything more than a hand job from these buddies of yours,*" Jani retorted without knowing why.

"*So, you admit it, artificial boy?*"

"*Dream on,*" Jani had snorted. "*Ask your provider to take you to Lupus in Fifth Circle. I bet he's there even now bending over to share his ass with anyone who asks.*"

"*What?!*" the boy snapped and jumped towards Jani.

However, before Jani had even realized what was going on, Lu had stepped between them and punched the boy in the stomach. The boy had yelped and doubled over in pain as Lu completely winded him.

"*You keep your mouth shut from now on,*" Lu told the boy in anger.

And none of the other boys had even dared move.

Jani had followed Lu inside the building and once they had reached Lu's room he had finally given voice to his puzzlement and shock.

"You hit him!" Jani had exclaimed, not loud enough for Lu's provider to hear him behind the closed door.

"I did."

"Where did you ...?"

"I do martial arts and boxing in my spare time."

"But you're not allowed to hit anyone in a public place! You can get into trouble for this!"

"I know," Lu said, *"But I couldn't help it."*

"He has a crush on you and that's why he spouts all that nonsense."

"I don't care. All I know is that I don't want to see his ugly face ever again. He was asking for it, you know that."

"Maybe he was, but if he tells someone about this ... Worst-case scenario; you will lose some of your Silver Wing marks. Damn if this gets out, they may not even accept you for border-guard training! Old man Talpa is going to go mental with disappointment!"

"That's my problem," Lu reminded him.

"But you wouldn't have hit him if I hadn't been there. If your descent is going to drop you into the First Circle after this ..."

"You don't have to worry about that," Lu said to him. *"If this becomes public, we can always claim that he's involved in gang activity, for instance. He had his buddies with him after all, and they do gather around the main door of this building quite frequently."*

"Who would ever believe me?"

"If we both say so they will believe us. I will say it was self-defense on my part."

"Lu ..."

"That's one option, if that punch becomes public knowledge, but in that case we will both need to say the same thing, you know? We both have to voice our 'suspicions' about them being involved in gang activity, if we end up being interrogated."

"I know, I know," Jani finally sighed.

After this incident, this unfortunate act of public violence, both of them had expected the worst possible consequences but nothing happened. However, during the days of waiting, while Jani was expecting to be called for interrogation, he couldn't remember ever feeling more distressed. Luckily, they had gotten out of the situation without any further trouble, and luckily the boy, who had felt Lu's fist in his guts, had never spoken to them again.

Jani was pulled back from his thoughts as he felt a jolt. He quickly realized the train was moving again. Jani straightened his back and took a deep breath. He was extremely relieved. And almost instantly he noticed a new headline from the news headline ticker:

Train stuck in the Makaira tunnel moving again

Jani checked the time on the screen. He was hoping that the delay wouldn't have the slightest effect on his task. He didn't have any way of anticipating anything like this. The most important thing however, was that they were moving again.

Suddenly an idea popped in Jani's head. Had this unexpected stop in the tunnel been intentional? Had it been one of those safety measures, implemented after the attack on girls in Makaira? Jani searched through all the latest headlines about the Makaira incident as well as news about them being stuck in the tunnel. Only a couple of them contained comments from random readers speculating in this way, as most of the comments refuted such a possibility. The incident on the train occurring so close to the attack on the girl group in Makaira was seen as pure coincidence and nothing else.

Finally, Jani felt the train climbing and a moment later, the train carriage was flooded with daylight. Jani narrowed his eyes. The light was blinding after the time spent in the tunnel but he welcomed it. He decided he wouldn't be leaving Gavialis again for a very long time.

Jani checked the time again. He knew it wouldn't take long before the train slowed down for the maintenance work being carried out on the train track. Jani couldn't help but wonder how many Silver Wing marks the men doing the maintenance work in this location had been given, because those marks were most likely the reason why they had agreed to come here in the first place. Someone had to fix the track in poisonous areas, too.

Jani looked at the view outside the window. The countryside looked pretty desolate. Its emptiness brought the destructive power of the Great War home to him. Because of the Great War, people were packed in the cities now, which had been built in areas where the environment was still suitable for human habitation. So much of the land in the better parts of the two tropics was wasteland. Toxins left behind after the war still remained in the soil, poisoning the environment all over the world. In some areas these toxins had even made the air too dangerous for anyone to breathe. In addition to that, there was all the land between the two tropics; all the barren land which had become desert because of the heat.

All of a sudden the train braked and slowed. Jani's heart skipped a beat but he tried his best to maintain his cool exterior.

"*Attention all passengers*," they heard next. "*This train is slowing down due to the maintenance work being conducted on this part of the track. We will shortly resume normal speed.*"

Jani tapped the armrest with his fingers. He was being tormented by his nervousness and noticed his right leg was swinging constantly. He looked outside and waited. He saw couple of maintenance men outside wearing yellow overalls. Then Jani took a quick look at the other passengers in the carriage. No one appeared to be paying him any attention. Everyone was staring at either the news screens in front of them or the men working outside.

Jani shifted in his seat and waited. It wouldn't be long now before the train resumed speed, of that he was sure. Had one of those men working outside brought the suitcase on board? Or was there an outsider among them who was behind the delivery? How could a man bringing a suitcase onto a train bypass the train's safety mechanism without triggering the alarm? These were questions to which Jani knew he would never have any answers.

Finally their speed increased. Jani knew he had to get to his feet soon and walk to the sanitary facilities, but not just yet. He still had to wait for a moment. He couldn't give the other passengers any reason to suspect him of anything shady, especially now that there had been an attack on those girls in Makaira. At worst, someone on the train could accuse him of organizing the attack in Makaira. Such a thing was well within the realms of possibility if he behaved suspiciously.

Jani checked the time again and again, until nine minutes had passed from the moment they had slowed down. Jani stood up, even though he was one minute early, and walked towards the sanitary facilities. He did not look at any other passenger on the train, he simply continued forward as calmly as he could.

When he finally arrived at the sanitary facilities, he locked the door behind him and started carefully knocking the wall panels. He did it as quietly as he could so that no one outside would hear him. Jani tried to listen to the sounds the knocking made. Behind one of the panels there had to be an empty space for this mysterious suitcase which had brought him here today. Jani got down on his knees and continued knocking and listening. Suddenly, a panel beneath the sink made a different sound from all the others he had been knocking. He immediately started to fiddle with the bolts on the four corners of the panel and noticed them being surprisingly loose.

Jani's heart was beating faster and faster. He placed the bolts he had removed down on the floor next to his knees and then removed the panel, too. Behind it was a small black suitcase. Jani took it without hesitating – it was surprisingly light to hold. He placed the suitcase on the floor to his left and replaced the wall panel exactly as he had found it. Then he replaced the bolts in their holes. He tightened them as tightly as he could with his bare hands before getting back to his feet again and taking the suitcase with him.

Jani studied the suitcase in his hands. He knew its contents weren't any of his business, but he was curious nonetheless. The suitcase was, indeed, very light. When Jani shook it slightly, he didn't feel anything moving inside. Was it empty? Jani shook his head. There had to be something in it, otherwise anyone could have been asked to come here and get it without a covert operation like this. So what could the suitcase contain? What could be so valuable as well as this light, which gave the impression of the suitcase being empty?

Jani put the suitcase on the sink for a moment and looked at his eyes in the reflection in the mirror. He shook his head. The contents of the suitcase did not belong to him. He had agreed to come here to pick it up in order to get into Sixth Circle again. Those had been the terms, therefore speculating about its contents was pointless. Most likely it contained something which had no value for Jani in the first place. Now, all he had to do was to walk back to his seat without anyone on the train realizing he was returning with a suitcase he had not had with him when he left to go to the sanitary facilities. All Jani hoped for was that no one had paid him sufficient attention during the trip. It was the only way to avoid being exposed right now.

Jani opened the door and stepped into the middle aisle. Then he proceeded calmly towards his seat. He held the suitcase behind his right thigh hoping it would draw less attention that way. The first man he passed was studying his news screen and for that Jani was grateful. The men in the back section of the carriage were either doing the same or looking out of the windows at the countryside. None of them seemed to be taking any notice of him, which made Jani feel considerably more at ease.

When he took his seat, he noticed his legs were shaking. He placed the suitcase beneath his seat and took a deep breath as quietly as he was able. He had passed the most critical phase of this journey now, so the worst was over. Now all he had to do was to head to the familiar Linai Station West when he was back in Gavialis.

The rest of the journey seemed to pass by frustratingly slowly. Jani even killed time by studying the results of the latest running races, even though the sport didn't interest him at all. When the train finally passed Albedo, he deactivated his news screen and looked out of the window. It wouldn't take long now before they reached Gavialis and he was now more certain than ever that this trip would be the last of its kind for a long, long time.

"*Gavialis*," the automatic announcement finally informed them. "*Fourth Corner Station. Connecting trains to the Heptagon Line and trains 4A and 4C.*"

Jani straightened up and picked the black suitcase up off the floor. He placed it between the wall and himself and looked outside. Soon, he saw man-made buildings again, whose absence between Gavialis and Makaira had been quite noticeable. The train was gradually slowing down and Jani saw the other passengers already standing and moving towards the doors.

"*Attention all passengers,*" they heard an announcement, this time not generated by the announcement system. "*Due the unfortunate incident in Makaira today we have tightened our security measures. Therefore, all passengers are being inspected at Fourth Corner Station. We thank you for your cooperation.*"

Jani's heart skipped a beat. How on Earth would he explain the suitcase in his hands to the security guards at the station? Jani swallowed and tried desperately to think of some way to avoid the security check, but he knew there was most likely no way around it. Could he hide the suitcase somehow? How would he get it back if he ditched it somewhere in the station? Jani felt his palms sweating. He hated surprises and this security check was the worst kind of surprise he could face right now.

The train finally arrived at the station and they stopped. Jani let the other men get off before him. When he did finally step outside onto the platform at Fourth Corner Station, he saw the other passengers walking through oval-shaped gates, which had been erected near the exit. It was obvious that the gates were scanning them and because Jani didn't know what the security was looking for exactly, he had no other option but to walk through one of those gates without hesitating. All he could hope for was that the suitcase didn't contain anything that the security guards were now looking for. He had no believable explanation why he was carrying the suitcase whose contents was unknown to him. If he said he had found this suspicious-looking suitcase on the train, the guards would confiscate it immediately, and he would be taken in for questioning. At worst, he would get the blame for the Makaira incident and his face would be splashed across the worldwide media in an instant.

Jani pulled himself together. He had to be vigilant now instead of falling victim to his own speculations and fears. If the gate's alarm signal sounded, he had the option of telling the guards that he had found the suitcase on the train, and that he was bringing it to security.

The man walking in front of Jani stepped through the gate and it gave a signal. The man was taken aside and Jani was told to proceed. Jani stepped under the gate and expected the worst with a blank expression on his face. However, by some miracle he got through without a peep and when he realized that, he felt all his strength leave his legs. However, in spite of this, his sudden relief carried him on his way towards another platform from where he could board a train on the Heptagon Line.

Jani heard a train arriving and he quickened his steps. He wanted to part with the suitcase as soon as humanly possible. He boarded the A Train at the last minute and sat down. The train would circle the city clockwise, so before arriving at First Corner Station he would pass all Fifth, Sixth, and Seventh Corner Stations.

Jani pressed the suitcase against his stomach and stared through the window at First Circle. He didn't ever really come to the north side of the circle often, but what he could see from the train was that the north side didn't really differ from the south side at all. So he had lost nothing by avoiding this part of First Circle.

The trip to First Corner Station tested Jani's patience. Getting round to the south side of the city seemed to take forever, even though they were moving at an incredible speed. When they finally did arrive at First Corner Station, Jani rushed off the train and continued without any hesitation towards the platform where he could take the U Train to Linai.

The minutes Jani spent getting from one train to the next felt like a dream and when Jani finally sat down on the U Train, he heaved a huge sigh of relief. Now it would take a further twenty minutes and then he would finally get rid of the suitcase. As he checked the time he noticed it was already almost five in the afternoon. The time was somewhat inconvenient for him, since there had been a change in the shifts in the control room where he worked. All Jani could do was to hope that no one he knew from work noticed him on Linai Station.

The trip to Linai passed by slowly and it was an endless torment for Jani. He was continuously aware of the black suitcase which felt like a heavy burden on his shoulders. He just wanted this to stop. He just wanted to get this over with.

"*Linai, Station West*," Jani finally heard.

Jani stood up, even though the train had not even stopped yet. He stood in front of the doors and watched as the familiar station appeared behind the glass. When the doors finally opened, he got off and walked towards the exit on the east side, just as he had been told. As he walked, he looked around carefully. When he was sure that no one was looking at him, he threw the suitcase under the stairway among other junk that was piled there.

Parting with the suitcase felt extremely liberating. Jani took a deep breath and turned around. He returned to the platform where he could take the next U Train back to the city. Fortunately, the next train was due to arrive at the station in approximately five minutes or so.

When the train finally arrived, Jani got on and sat down. Then he activated his noter. He browsed the basic information of his ID account, but saw no updates. Jani didn't know what to think, but he was feeling doubtful. Had he been tricked? Had he agreed to fetch the suitcase without receiving any compensation? Had he really been that gullible; blinded by the temptations of Sixth Circle? Then a yellow message text began to blink on the small screen of his noter.

ID account updated

Jani clicked the message and suddenly he saw access permission in his ID account. The permission gave him 18 hours in Sixth Circle and, as promised, there was an access key to a room on the 100th floor of Grus Tower in his ID account as well.

Jani took a deep breath. He was more relieved than ever. The suitcase had found its destination and despite all that had happened today, he had succeeded.

7.

Saia heard the door closing. She opened her eyes and looked round in the darkness. Now that her mother had left she stopped pretending to be asleep and activated her information terminal. She had no intention whatsoever of wasting the upcoming night resting, especially now that the girls had been granted a day off from their studies due the incident in Makaira. Therefore she could spend her night doing the things she had been putting off for too many days now.

Saia got up and walked to the window of her room. The thousand lights of the city illuminated the night. One of the brightest was the red tower of Caput Mortuum and the red light instantly reminded Saia of the Makaira incident. Melanitta had been shot with an arrow. It had scratched her arm, but luckily hadn't penetrated it. There had been blood everywhere, though. The Yellow Guardsmen had immediately isolated all of them indoors where Melanitta had received first aid. It had all happened so quickly, now that she was standing in the darkness of her room, the day in Makaira felt almost like a dream.

As expected, Naja had got upset over all the attention that Melanitta had received. When Naja got mad, Saia was usually the one who felt it. This time, Naja had gotten the idea that Saia had a crush on Melanitta and therefore all the girls had looked at her as if she was a madwoman.

"Saia fantasizes about women," Naja had announced loudly. "That's the reason why she is putting on weight and is generally so masculine."

Some other person could have responded by laughing at Naja's words, but Saia had been unable to do so. And Naja had known it, Naja had counted on it. For that reason alone, Saia was such a good victim for Naja to take her frustrations out on because Saia didn't like being the center of attention. When that happened, when all eyes were on her, she lost her ability to speak. Therefore, today, when she remained silent in the eyes of the others, Naja had gotten exactly what she had been aiming for. Saia had been publicly humiliated in the eyes of both the girls and the Yellow Guardsmen. Now everyone in their group believed that she really did fantasize about women, and therefore they would continue to shut her out even more than they had been doing already. Saia simply couldn't understand why it was alright for men to feel affection for the same sex and even display it openly, but women were despised for it.

Saia stared at the city lights and wondered why she didn't feel anything while looking at the view. Instead of the vast luminous sea of lights representing life, she saw the grayness of her own life. Perhaps she had simply been standing at the window of her personal prison, looking at the view, for too long now.

Saia wanted to get out. She desperately wanted to leave this apartment, where even the air within its walls was poisonous for her. She would have done almost anything to have the opportunity to leave, get away to start a new life. She would have done anything to make it happen; anything, but commit herself to a man. She hated the mere thought of sex, which was an issue Naja wanted to talk about endlessly. Now that Saia remembered Naja's face, she suddenly felt her breathing becoming more difficult. She knew she would have to face the girl and the others the day after tomorrow. Why couldn't she just be left alone?

Saia no longer felt happy with the person she was, not at home nor with her studies, and those two were more or less the only places she was allowed to be. So it was no wonder she felt like she had nowhere to run in order to escape. She was trapped in her own anguish and saw no way out, yet she so wanted to escape. Somewhere, there had to be a place where she would feel more at peace with herself. However, she couldn't go anywhere because she was a girl. She would be forever imprisoned in the inner circles of the cities, unless she had the courage to disguise herself as a boy and run away. So far she had not dared do so.

"... *Go and see the world, because if there is a way out of the city for you, you will find it*," Ati had written to her.

Saia walked to her desk and activated her information terminal. She opened her ID account and chose the image option from her profile. Then she projected an image of her brother onto one of the walls of her room.

"Hey, you fool," Saia whispered to the picture and smiled faintly.

She walked across the room to where Ati's picture was projected. He was smiling in the picture. Saia didn't know when the picture had been taken exactly, but it must have been one of the last ones taken shortly before his death.

"You should have stayed a little bit longer, so you could have helped me find the way out of here," Saia told the picture. She felt less lonely that way ...

Suddenly, the words caught in her throat as tears began to spill from her eyes. This was the reason why she didn't look at her brother's picture very often; she still remembered Ati as if she had seen him only yesterday. Knowing that he was no longer in the world still hurt.

"... because I don't know how much strength I have left; how much longer I can stay here," Saia finally continued in a whisper. "Since you've been gone I have had no one to talk to. It sounds pathetic, I know, but you know me. You know I'm not good with people and you know what kind of life I live in this apartment."

Saia began to sob. She shed her tears as quietly as possible, because she didn't want anyone outside her room to hear her. Saia took a step closer to the wall on which her brother's face was dimly projected.

"Why do I believe life would be easier as a boy?" she then asked her brother in a whisper. "I've been thinking about it a lot and that's why I am still angry at you sometimes for going away. You never told me why your life was so difficult and that's why I have no way of knowing when you finally knew you didn't want to go on anymore."

Saia wiped her tears and took another look at the tower of Caput Mortuum, which was glowing brightly like a huge red star in the middle of a thousand city lights.

"When will I know for certain that it's never going to get any better than this?" Saia then wondered. "At what point do I decide I've also had enough? I am sad almost all the time and I hate myself completely. I am ugly and fat and I can't seem to forget this, not even for a brief moment. It feels like there will never be a day when I can just be happy. I have nothing here to live for anymore."

Saia walked slowly back to her bed, lay down and flopped her head against the pillow. She closed her eyes for a moment, but it only made Naja's face appear before her again, and this irritated her deeply. She felt like Naja was always present, even when she was alone in her room, so she tried her best to keep the girl out of her mind.

"She's an idiot," Saia whispered. "Yet you care what she thinks or says about you."

And it was the truth. Even though Saia reminded herself again and again that she shouldn't care what others thought of her, it did matter because she couldn't get away from the girls. She was part of their group, whether she wanted it or not. Therefore what the others did or said, especially when they passed a judgment on her, wasn't totally irrelevant to her. Saia would have loved to have thicker skin and more confidence, but she didn't know what to do to become such a person.

Naja was the worst of them all. Even though no one genuinely liked her, the other girls kept listening to her ideas nonetheless. Saia opened her eyes and stared at the ceiling.

"Why on Earth does she have that kind of power?" she wondered. "Or has she? Who has given her this power?"

The truth was Naja had been stupid when she had told Saia what she had been doing with Lator, extremely stupid on her part.

"Knowledge is power," Saia whispered. "That's what you told me, Ati."

Now Saia knew something about Naja, something Naja had told her without a second thought, and it had not been very wise to do so. Perhaps Naja had told her the truth because it was just weak and quiet Saia, who was also ugly and dumb, but now Saia knew something, knowledge which she could use, but how?

"Time will tell," Saia whispered to herself. "You waited with Doctor Alauda as well before telling her what you knew about her, so don't hurry with Naja now. You will have an opportunity to make this information work to your advantage, you just have to believe it."

Saia felt a smile widening on her face. For the first time she realized she finally had something against Naja. She didn't know quite how use it yet, but she definitely had the ammunition.

"Just block her out of your mind," Saia told to herself. "Don't let that bitch invade the privacy of this room. Just push her aside."

Saia pulled her small portable information terminal onto her stomach and activated the screen. She chose the secure connection and hid her location information. Then she signed in to the closed channel under the screen name of The Fly. She noticed there were three others on the same channel who all were familiar to her. Finally Saia felt like she had come home. It was somewhat comforting to see the familiar screen names on her display. Those names represented people who really knew her in a way.

This was the moment she really felt she could be herself again without feeling bad about it.

The screen name DiseaseBearer took notice of her presence.

<DiseaseBearer: Want to hear something interesting?

The question brought a smile to Saia's face and she quickly wrote her response.

<The Fly: Always.

<DiseaseBearer: There's been 7% fewer girls born this year compared with the number of boys.

Saia was a little surprised. She had not expected DiseaseBearer to be interested in this particular matter, but on the other hand she also found many different kinds of things interesting, so why wouldn't he?

<The Fly: You are right. It is interesting.

<DiseaseBearer: The statistics proving this as fact have not seen daylight yet, but I've been vigilant and made my own calculations from the public information available.

<The Fly: Do you expect it to become public information at some point?

<DiseaseBearer: I don't know. The topic is pretty inflammable considering the current gender distribution of the world.

<DiseaseBearer: But if this information does become public, I am looking forward to seeing which Council gives the official announcement first.

<The Fly: People are going to demand answers.

<DiseaseBearer: And for a reason. The number of girl children should increase drastically or man, as a species, will disappear from this universe for good.

Pause.

<DiseaseBearer: Did that sound dramatic enough? ;-)

<The Fly: It did, but the situation is what it is, and if the number of women continues to drop, there isn't going to be many of us left soon.

<DiseaseBearer: Yellow Guardsmen are getting more days off.

<DiseaseBearer: Or let's ask instead – who would need them anymore?

<The Fly: True.

<The Fly: Are you expecting them to announce all-female years – the XX program?

<DiseaseBearer: If there is any sense left in the heads of the decision makers, they will put every hospital with the fertility program under XX requirements for many years to come.

<The Fly: It's been a while since the last XX years, even though one could assume that artificial wombs should have been used only for girl production for years now.

<DiseaseBearer: There's a conspiracy, believe me. Producing boy children goes against all logic.

<The Fly: Unless the goal is balanced gender distribution in the future. What kind of world it would be, if the majority of people in society were women?

<DiseaseBearer: It would be great!

<The Fly: Ha-ha.

<The Fly: So what else is new?

<DiseaseBearer: I listened to a fascinating audio file today.

<The Fly: Music?

\<DiseaseBearer: Of course.

\<The Fly: I assume you want to share this file?

\<DiseaseBearer: Only with you. Naturally.

\<The Fly: I didn't know you were interested in music ...

\<DiseaseBearer: Why not? You ought to know I am interested in everything!

\<The Fly: Well, of course.

\<DiseaseBearer: I've uploaded the file to The Trough. The usual password will do.

\<The Fly: Copy that.

Saia connected to a service which appeared as an image distribution service for average users on the information network. The image distribution service was quite real, though, for its real users, but there was also something else connected to it. There was a hidden addition to the service, which carried the name The Trough. Saia didn't know how much data The Trough contained exactly, only that is was both created and maintained by DiseaseBearer, and that no one outside of their circle knew of its existence.

Saia typed her password and the image distribution service disappeared from her main window. Suddenly her system informed her of an audio file ready to be downloaded. Saia did not, however, save the file to her own ID Account, but to an account she had created for her "ghost" in order to receive secret material from the network. When the file had been finally saved on her ghost ID account, she opened it and heard faint music.

Saia knew, however, that DiseaseBearer wouldn't send her music for entertainment purposes. Saia muted the sound and started to examine the file more closely. She knew it was encrypted because DiseaseBearer wouldn't have bothered mentioning it otherwise. They had always been honest with each other, as honest as two faceless strangers who had met online could be.

<DiseaseBearer: So how does it sound?

<The Fly: Boring.

<DiseaseBearer: Perhaps you should listen to it through another application?

<The Fly: Would that make it sound better?

<DiseaseBearer: Without a doubt.

<DiseaseBearer: I suggest you filter the extra noise away. What remains is something quite unique.

<The Fly: Like the operetta you sent last year?

<DiseaseBearer: Precisely.

Saia smiled. She finally knew exactly what to do with the file. A year ago she had struggled for a couple of days with an audio file she had received from DiseaseBearer, until she had finally found a hidden conversation by accident. The conversation in that particular file had taken place between two men, one of whom had very likely been the Regional Policy Council Chief.

Saia loaded the audio file and activated the appropriate filter. Then she placed the earpieces in her ears and began listening carefully. The music faded and Saia thought she could hear someone talking. She reset her sound drivers and played the audio file again. The music faded even more but the sub-file within the audio file was still too faint for her to hear exactly what it was about.

Saia tried one more time and when she played the audio file again, she could barely hear the music anymore. Now she could hear a male voice instead.

"*Albedo, this is Beloni. We have entered the atmosphere and we are approaching Albedo from the coordinates zero, seven, six. Estimated time of landing – 12:17.*"

"*Beloni, this is Albedo. Permission to land denied. We are not receiving your transponder signal. Maintain current altitude.*"

"*Albedo, this is Beloni. We have already entered the atmosphere... we must continue our landing sequence.*"

"Beloni, this is Albedo. We are still not receiving your transponder's signal. There seems to be some interference in our communication link. Please respond."

"Albedo, thi... Beloni. We are still approaching from coordinates zero, seven, six."

"Beloni, this is Albedo. A manned vessel is ascending to orbit. Change your course immediately."

"Albedo, this is Beloni. We are requesting permission to continue landing on an alternative route. We have already entered the atmosphere and our landing sequence has been initiated. Our current altitude is 71 kilometers."

"Beloni, this is Albedo — alter to direction three, one, five. Permission to land at Albedo still denied."

"Albedo, this is Belo... We didn't receive your messa... Please repeat your orders."

"Beloni, this is Albedo. Alter to trajectory three, one, five. I repeat; alter to trajectory three, one, five."

Suddenly Saia knew which flight was recorded on the file. She had witnessed its launch into orbit with her own eyes just a few hours ago. She had not seen Beloni, though, which had obviously been descending towards Albedo at the same time. Had their arrival in the yellow carriage caused a change to flight schedules, which had turned out to be a critical problem for the air traffic controllers? How could such a dangerous situation of this magnitude even occur?

"Albedo, this is Beloni. We are continuing our landing sequence. Our current altitude is 64 kilometers. We are still awaiting your directions to proceed with our landing sequence."

"Beloni, this is Albedo. Alter immediately to trajectory three, one, zero or you will collide with ascending vessel. I repeat — alter immediately to trajectory three, one, five."

"Albedo, this is Beloni. We are not receiving your orders or any signal from the vessel approaching our current location. We reque... the... route to Albedo."

Saia bit her nails. How could air traffic control be unable to fix the poor communication link to Beloni? Under what conditions were the vessels sent into space in the first place? When had the last maintenance of Beloni been carried out exactly?

"Beloni, this is Albedo. You are still approaching Albedo on the wrong trajectory. Alter to trajectory three, one, five!"

"Albedo, this is Beloni. We are altering our trajectory to three, one, five."

Pause. The crew of Beloni had finally received the directions from Albedo and were taking action to avoid colliding with the ascending vessel.

"Beloni, this is Albedo. Proceed at current speed and altitude over the polar region."

Silence. Had Beloni received the message from Albedo?

"Beloni, this is Albedo. Please respond."

Silence.

"Albedo, this is Beloni," Saia finally heard. *"We are approaching Albedo on trajectory zero, one, five."*

"Beloni, this is Albedo. Proceed over the polar region. You are not authorized to change your current course. I repeat – you are not authorized to change your current course."

"Albedo, this is Beloni. Repea... last messa..."

"Beloni, this is Albedo. You are not authorized to change your current course. Proceed over the polar region. I repeat – proceed over the polar region."

"Albe... is... loni. There is severe interference in our communication link. Please repeat your orders or we will continue approaching Albedo on trajectory zero, one, five."

"Beloni, this is Albedo. You are approaching Albedo from wrong direction. Alter to trajectory two, seven, zero!"

Saia continued biting her nails. Albedo wanted Beloni to change its course towards the west, but the descending vessel was still approaching the space traffic center from the north.

"Beloni, this is Albedo. Change your course immediately!"

Saia frowned at the severity of the order given to Beloni from Albedo. It almost sounded like landing at Albedo from the north went against world law.

"Albedo, this is Beloni. Repeat your orders..."

"Beloni, this is Albedo. Alter immediately to trajectory two, seven, zero. I repeat – alter immediately to trajectory two, seven, zero. The toxic wastelands of the north will cloud your radar and cause critical error in your landing sequence!"

"What on earth?" Saia wondered. She had never heard anything like it. The mere idea of approaching Albedo from the north being dangerous for space vessels was absolutely unheard of. Not to mention the fact that the toxic wasteland was deemed a risk for space vessels' radars.

"Beloni, this is Albedo. I repeat – alter immediately to trajectory two, seven, zero. The toxic wastelands will cloud your radar!"

"Albe..., this is Beloni. We are approaching... I repeat – we are approaching Alb... direction zero, one,... Estimated time of... – nine minut..."

"Beloni, this is Albedo. Alter immediately to trajectory two, seven, zero! I repeat alter immediately to trajectory two, seven, zero! The wastelands to the north will confuse your radar and endanger your landing!"

Saia heard genuine distress in the voice of the air traffic controller. It was like he was trying to warn Beloni of grave danger. Saia paused the audio file

for a moment and took her world map. She opened it and the background
of the map started glowing in the darkness of her room. There was a tiny
black X on the map, which was drawn on the wasteland area to the north of
Albedo.

"Is it there?" Saia whispered and felt her heart beating faster.

Had she just been given the proof she had spent years waiting for? Had
Albedo's air traffic control and Beloni finally revealed the exact location of
the place she had been searching for all this time?

Saia couldn't wait a minute longer. She clicked the audio file and
continued listening to it carefully.

"Albedo, this is Beloni. Repeat your last message."

"Alter your heading! The toxic wastelands to the north will confuse your radar!"

*"Albedo, this is Belo... Our radar is still functioning normally. We are approaching
from the trajectory zero,... Distance – 40 kilomet..."*

"Alter your trajectory immediately Beloni!"

Static.

"Albedo, this is Belo..."

Static.

Had air traffic control been right? Had the toxins in the wasteland finally
broken the communication link between the vessel Beloni and Albedo, or
was there some other reason for the static Saia was now hearing?

"I don't believe this! ..." she heard Beloni's captain shouting. *"We are flying
over a city! There are people here!"*

Static.

Saia swallowed and held her breath.

"Repeat that, Beloni."

*"There is a huge city here!... millions of people! I don't believe th...! What is this
place?!"*

"Beloni, this is Albedo," Saia heard then, but this time the voice wasn't the
air traffic controller's. *"The Security Council has ordered you to disconnect this
communication link immediately. I repeat – disconnect your communication link
immediately."*

*"Albe... We can see... what is this place?! We must increase our altitude
immediately!"*

"Disconnect this communication link immediately Beloni!"

That was the end of the audio file.

Saia removed the earpieces from her ears and stared at the wall of her
room where her brother's face was still projected. Then she took another

look at the map on her lap. A tear fell from the corner of her right eye and ran down her cheek.

However, the map did not lie. The audio file couldn't be faked either; DiseaseBearer had never tricked her. As she looked at the map she knew for certain there was a huge area of wasteland to the north, about 60 kilometers from Gavialis' border. Unlike on other maps, on Saia's map there was a black cross in an area labeled as wasteland. Both the black cross and the communication between Albedo and Beloni told her that there was much more to be found in that area than mere wasteland. According to her map, the area was huge.

"I've found it," Saia whispered, her voice trembling. "I know where it is."

Saia felt another tear running down her cheek. She wiped it away and returned to her discussion with DiseaseBearer.

<The Fly: That was an absolutely fantastic piece of music.

<DiseaseBearer: I knew you would appreciate it.

<The Fly: When did you find this masterpiece?

<DiseaseBearer: I got it about four hours ago.

<DiseaseBearer: So you are deeply impressed?

<The Fly: Absolutely.

<DiseaseBearer: I expect it will have the same effect on many others as well. The man in this masterpiece has been quiet today, though.

<The Fly: Which one? Swallow or Tower Master?

<DiseaseBearer: Tower Master, but the fate of the Swallow landing among us makes me wonder, too.

<The Fly: I am wondering how something like this could happen in the first place.

<The Fly: Where were Tower Master's eyes and why didn't Swallow hear his directions?

<DiseaseBearer: It is an interesting question ... one could assume Tower Master has seen so many Swallows already that he would have known how to avoid this kind of situation.

<The Fly: Unless the Tower Master in question was inexperienced ...

<DiseaseBearer: That is a possibility, yes.

<DiseaseBearer: But if so, I don't expect that this Tower Master will return to his tower after this.

<The Fly: They have silenced the Tower Master?

<DiseaseBearer: What do you think?

<The Fly: I think this is a masterpiece which will not gain popularity in this world in these times.

<DiseaseBearer: I believe you are right. Because this kind of music isn't for the general public, there is no audience for it either.

<The Fly: Too bad, because I liked it.

<DiseaseBearer: It was quite interesting to listen to. It has provoked many thoughts in my head.

<The Fly: Indeed.

Then Saia got up and walked back to her window. She looked at the lights of Gavialis for a moment, before turning to face the wall again where her brother was staring back at her. Then she smiled.

8.

Jani exited 6.2 Corner Station and found himself in the middle of a swarming crowd. The streets were filled with sounds and voices and were busy with continuous movement. Countless people were walking by enormous buildings and the late evening light made the thousands of signs on building walls glare brightly.

There was a huge news screen across the street on the wall of a massive building, which covered the entire width of the building's outer wall. Jani saw a headline about the upcoming presidential election as well as one about the final games of Capricorn/Cancer, in which only the best sports teams could compete with each other. The finals would start in a few days and Jani wished Lu would have finally some time off by then.

Jani couldn't contain his smile. Sixth Circle was even more impressive at nightfall. Jani was jubilant. He was standing in the place where men with at least 1,000 Silver Wing marks worked and lived. One thousand Silver Wing marks was more than 950 more than Jani had, but despite his lack of accomplishments, he had made it here again. He was in the heart of the bright lights which illuminated the best parts of the city. He was standing in one of the most famous places in the entire world and the feeling Sixth Circle stirred in him was something quite incredible.

Jani didn't want to waste any more time standing next to the station so he left and headed towards Grus Tower, which was only a few blocks away. He decided to go on foot as he wanted to feel like he was part of the Sixth Circle crowd and lifestyle as well. Luckily, Grus Tower was near enough the station so it was constantly within Jani's sight. Therefore, there was no risk of getting lost as the tower loomed taller than all the other tall buildings next to it. It was the tower which was known all over the world, just like Caput Mortuum on the other side of Sixth Circle.

Jani kept walking. Rhythmic music filled the air near the station and there was a crowd of men standing on the next street corner. They were obviously visitors here and seeing them made Jani feel even better about himself. He didn't know how much time those visitors' access permission allowed them, but he didn't have to leave here for another 17 hours and 56 minutes. That was simply beyond great.

On his way to the tower, Jani passed many men on the street as well as a Common Contact Point, restaurants, and different sports facilities. He made sure he remained to the side of the wide street which were for pedestrians because the middle sections of the streets here were full of Zoonas. There were more pedestrians on the narrow bridges over the Zoona tracks than Jani had ever seen before. The dim light of late evening made the lights inside the Zoonas stand out, and the streets full of Zoonas looked like a wide river of lights. It was a sight Jani had never seen before and he was quite impressed.

Jani walked along the narrow bridge and stopped in front of a huge building. There were many different services provided at street level. Jani saw more restaurants, from which a multitude of fragrances filled the air. They were extremely tempting; standard meals in First Circle were pretty similar from one day to the next. Here in Sixth Circle they obviously had more variety when it came to food and therefore all the different aromas teased and tormented Jani's senses. He was hungry, but he decided to wait. In Grus Tower he would most likely get whatever he could ask for, so there wasn't much point in using his weekly points to have dinner.

Suddenly something in one of the restaurants caught Jani's eye. There was a group of Yellow Guardsmen sitting there. Had he, once again, found himself near women? As he observed the Guardsmen for a brief moment, he realized that they were spending their free time together. He decided to continue and as he walked, he concluded that the Yellow Guardsman's easy life would always remain a mystery to him.

Jani was almost intoxicated by the city lights and the swarming crowds on this dark, warm summer night. Everything here was alive, but most of all Jani himself. The longer he kept walking the streets of Sixth Circle, the surer he felt about himself. First Circle and the daily routine had faded quickly from his memory. Here, there was so much to see and feel. Here he felt free.

After walking for a while, he finally came to a stop, realizing that he had arrived at Grus Tower. He began searching for the main entrance, but tried to do it as discreetly as possible, even though he had no idea which direction to go. When he finally found the big main doors, he also saw two guards who were keeping watch over the place. The men were wearing uniforms with a big letter G embroidered on the chest.

Jani walked towards the doors and he noticed the dubious looks on the guards' faces. It was obvious to them that Jani did not belong here in Sixth Circle.

"Good evening," said one as Jani reached them. "Your thumb print, please."

Jani pressed the access permission pad with his thumb, hoping his reward for the Makaira trip wouldn't have mysteriously disappeared from his ID account during the time it had taken him to get here from the 6.2 Corner Station. Then the device in the Guardsman's hands gave a faint peep.

"Welcome Jani … 821771," the man said and looked at Jani somewhat dubiously again.

Nonetheless, he opened the door. The verified access permission didn't need to be called into question.

"Thank you," Jani said and stepped through the door into a vast entrance hall.

He stopped in amazement for a moment and looked around. In the center of the hall was a huge steel bird which had a long neck, long legs as well as a sharp beak. The beak was pointing up towards the ceiling and it was open as if the bird were crying out. The tip of its beak reached all the way to the second floor, which could be reached either by taking the stairs or the elevator.

"Pretty fancy," Jani said.

Then he headed towards the elevator. Once there he pressed a sensor on the wall with his thumb which made the elevator doors open. As he was the only one in the elevator, the guiding system sprang into action.

"*Welcome Jani 821771,*" the automatic message stated. "*Your room is available. Your room is on the 100th floor, B wing. The number of your room: 1214.*"

"Sounds good," Jani said and waited.

The elevator shot up, which made Jani's ears pop due to the change in air pressure. When it finally stopped on the 100th floor and the doors opened, Jani noticed a display on the wall across the hallway, which was activated as soon as he stepped out of the elevator. It was pointing right, towards the B Wing of the tower.

Jani took a deep breath. He was very impressed. He had never even imagined this degree of luxury in First Circle or even in Second Circle. Here, even the hallway floors were covered with soft carpet which cushioned his steps. When he opened the door to B Wing with his thumbprint, he heard yet another automatic announcement, guiding him to his room.

Luckily, Jani's room was located relatively near. Once there, the door opened automatically and Jani stepped in. His mouth fell open. The room was enormous, at least four times bigger than his apartment.

"I guess I should have pursued those Silver Wing marks much harder back in the olden days," Jani said and shook his head.

There was a huge bed in the room and a window on the wall opposite the door which almost covered the entire wall. Jani walked to the window, his eyes wide open. There were no words to describe the brilliance of the view he had. He could even see the tower of Caput Mortuum with its red light in the distance. Jani realized he could see all the way to Fourth Circle, if not even to Third.

"Unbelievable," Jani sighed.

Then he noticed a small table by the window, which had been laid for him. There was a mixture of different snacks on it and Jani took one of the yellow chips between his fingers and took a careful bite.

"Potato and salt," he concluded. "With some sort of spice I guess."

Potato was relatively rare in Jani's daily diet, which consisted mostly of durra, roaches, and fish. He had tasted only a couple of spices during his lifetime, so he had no idea what the spice in these potato chips was, but it tasted good.

Jani sat down on the floor and balanced the little bowl of potato chips on his lap. Then he simply ate and watched the city. Right now, he didn't want to do anything else.

"How can anyone leave here and go back to First Circle?" Jani wondered aloud. "How can I ever go back there again?"

Jani took a deep breath and pondered his good luck. He had been given one of the finest experiences of his life and only because he had agreed to fetch a suitcase from a Makaira train. What on earth had that suitcase contained? What could have been so valuable for anyone to reward him this generously?

Jani took his noter and wondered whether he should write a message to Lu. A big part of him really wanted to tell Lu where he was, what he saw and how he was feeling right now, but how could he explain how he had ended up in Grus Tower tonight?

Jani considered his options for a moment. Perhaps it would be wiser to tell Lu about this face-to-face later on, because he didn't want to leave any traces of his current location on the information network. Of course, no one was likely to find it interesting, but it was better to be safe than sorry. Whatever the black suitcase had contained, it had to be something very valuable. Or the man or the group of men who had organized this entire suitcase-fetching operation had to be extremely powerful. Therefore, it would be better to remain silent. He had even told his supervisor that he was taking some time off because he felt tired. That was all his superiors needed to know about his personal and private affairs.

Suddenly Jani jumped as he heard a loud voice outside. It was a long and deep alarm he recognized, but which he had never heard live and close-up. The voice came all the way from Caput Mortuum and could be heard in the inner circles of the city every night at seven o'clock Earth standard time.

"I can't stay in this room," Jani said then. Even though the view from his luxurious room was most unbelievable, there had to be much more to see in Grus Tower.

Jani stood up and walked to the door. It opened automatically, which Jani found somewhat strange, since he had no ID chip to trigger doors to open automatically when a person with appropriate access permission approached. He shrugged. Perhaps there was some kind of motion detector in his room.

Jani stepped into hallway and waited until the door had closed behind him. When he got to the elevator, the automatic system enquired where he wanted to go. Jani chose a restaurant from the option list and the elevator started its rapid descent. Jani was nervous. He knew he would receive many strange looks during the course of the evening. The men here in Sixth Circle instantly saw through him because he didn't belong here. He decided to try not to worry about such things tonight. He had earned his right to be here.

The doors of the elevator opened and Jani saw he had arrived in a wide hallway, illuminated with purple light. He heard the heavy beat of music nearby. Jani started to walk towards the sound of the music and he found an entrance which led to a restaurant. Above the arch of the entrance he read *Vipio*, which was presumably the name of the establishment. Vipio was a dimly lit place with many round tables, almost all of which were already taken. That caused Jani to conclude that the restaurant had to be pretty popular. On the right-hand side of the entrance was a sign on the wall.

Restaurant Vipio serves durratin. Durratin is an alcoholic beverage, which may cause intoxication. Intoxication is a state of poisoning which disturbs the functions of the central nervous system. Durratin may also cause addiction and consuming it regularly is hazardous to your health. Discontinued consumption of durratin will decrease the risk of falling ill with life-threatening diseases.

Vipio, or the city of Gavialis, is not responsible for the consumption habits of individuals. Vipio personnel reserve the right to refuse durratin to heavily intoxicated consumers.

"Jani?" he suddenly heard behind his back.

Hearing his own name in Grus Tower was totally unexpected and took Jani completely by surprise. He didn't know whether he should turn around at all and face the person who had called his name as he didn't know if it would do him more good than harm. Yet someone had identified him, so pretending to be clueless wasn't a rational way to proceed.

"Jani?" he heard again.

Finally Jani turned around and he saw an older man who was wearing a dark gray uniform.

"Mr. Talpa?" Jani recognized the man at once, astonished.

"*Jaaaaaniiii!*" the man laughed and threw his arms around him.

Jani could smell durratin on Talpa, which only widened his smile.

"What on earth are you doing here?" the man asked him.

"I've been rewarded with a night here in Grus Tower," Jani explained truthfully, since he was unable to make up an appropriate lie.

"Is that so? From work?"

"Yes," Jani replied and swallowed.

"Then you've done something really good!" Talpa concluded. "That's the way to do it!"

Jani smiled and nodded.

"It's so good to see you, son!" the man exclaimed then.

"You seem to be well," Jani stated.

"Don't flatter me, boy," Talpa said and tapped his stomach, which had gotten relatively large since the last time the two had met. "I'm ruining my health with fatty foods and durratin, but I have earned the right to do so, and the doctors can keep their mouths shut!"

Jani laughed. Talpa was very different from Lu, who was much quieter and more reserved than his provider.

"Please, come and sit with me," Talpa said. "Vipio is a most agreeable restaurant. So what would you say to the two of us going inside and having a good old chat?"

Jani nodded and followed the man to the other side of the entrance where dim lighting created a cozy ambience. Talpa led Jani to a free table in the middle area of the establishment.

"Sit down, my good boy," the man stated.

Jani took his seat and looked around, slightly confused. There were restaurants in First Circle as well, but nothing like Vipio, which was spacious and stylish.

"Your first time here in Grus Tower?" the man asked Jani.

"It is," Jani replied.

"Ah!" Talpa noted. "Then we should most definitely celebrate it!"

Talpa snapped his fingers and waved to the waiters working in the restaurant.

"I was not expecting to see any familiar faces here," Jani said.

"You, boy, are the last person on Earth I expected to meet tonight. Do you still live in First Circle?"

"I do, yes."

"Oh ..." Talpa said and shook his head. "You are just the type of man who should have been brought up by a provider instead of one of those uninspired instructors in those petty institutions. A good provider would have gotten the most out of you, and you would have already had clearer goals during your basic education, which would have taken you forward in this world. You could have been something! The instructors in those institutions don't care about boys in the same way providers do."

Jani didn't know what to say so he simply nodded.

"Have you heard anything from Lu?" Talpa asked him next.

"Not in weeks," Jani said. "He has been patrolling for months now without any time off. That's usually the reason why no one hears very much from him."

"He's such a hard-working boy," Talpa stated. "He followed in my footsteps and became a border guard. I am very proud of that boy. He's a good man."

"That's true," Jani said.

"But let's not chat here all night with dry mouths!" Talpa exclaimed, and continued waving at the waiters.

One of the waiters, a young slender man, finally arrived at their table.

"Two Mars Quartzes, please," Talpa said and the waiter nodded. "Have you ever had a Mars Quartz?"

"No," Jani confessed, slightly embarrassed.

"Well, it's durratin made on Earth – nothing more than that – but the drink is served in a glass which is made of Mars quartz."

"It sounds like they are going to whittle away quite a lot of points from your account," Jani said.

"Don't you worry about that, son!" Talpa laughed. "I have 1,977 Silver Wing marks, so the points I earn in a week are more than enough for a couple of Mars Quartzes!"

Jani smiled and nodded. Then the young waiter brought their drinks. The drinking glasses were full of orange liquid, which indicated that the durratin was diluted with an appropriated soft drink. The color orange obviously referred to the iron-based minerals in Mars' soil which gave the planet its reddish color.

"I think Lu is going to reach 350 Silver Wing marks within a couple of years," Talpa said. "When that happens, he might finally move to Third Circle. If he wants to move, I mean."

"You can never be sure about Lu," Jani said. "Even if his standard of living improved in Third Circle, which he would appreciate I'm sure, he has never liked the city or the swarming crowds around him."

"That's true," Talpa said, taking a sip from his glass. "Lu is just like my provider. That man, if anyone, liked silence around him. He was a very patient person overall, calm and extremely honest. He treated everyone around him well and he never raised his voice to me."

"The Talpa name has moved several generations, then."

"Yes, yes," Talpa stated. "but my provider, like me, was an artificial."

"Like the majority of men today," Jani added.

"True, true!" Talpa said and laughed. "I have always encouraged Lu to work hard so he could one day get the opportunity to meet real women and become a provider in that way. Then he could have more than just one child."

Jani listened and nodded. He knew Lu had a realistic chance of reaching that position. He didn't doubt that one bit.

"Lu would be a good provider," the man pondered, "and there are not too many good providers in this world. I have tried not to pressure that boy too much, though, just like my own provider never pressured me to do anything except behave well, but you want only the best for your own son, you know? More than you have managed to do yourself."

"Was your provider a border guard as well?" Jani asked. He had never heard Talpa talking about this man before.

"Of course," Talpa stated. "So, Lu has much in common with my provider in that way as well. That's why I wouldn't be surprised if he told me he would like to stay in Second Circle for the rest of his life, even if he had enough Silver Wing marks to live in Seventh."

"Do you live in this circle now?" Jani asked Talpa.

"Of course," Talpa stated. "Haven't we seen each other during the last couple of years, then? I moved here from Fifth Circle two years ago. Hasn't Lu mentioned anything about it, either?"

"I don't recall him mentioning your move."

"Lu is a good boy," Talpa said again, "but I wouldn't mind seeing him more often. Isn't he patrolling the city border now?"

"I think he said he was about to go to Enovii to guard the power plants," Jani said. "To Enovii or to Rukia."

"Enovii, huh?" Talpa said. "Well, that's right. Gavialis' border guards work in the suburbs as well and men go wherever they are ordered to go."

"That's right," Jani said.

"Who knows; he might even be in Albedo now," the man said and laughed.

"Wasn't there a man in the news a couple of days ago who ran into the Albedo minefields?" Jani asked the man. "I hope Lu wasn't the one who had to clean that mess up."

"It's sad when some men get into that state; that they see no other option than going to the minefield," Talpa said and shook his head. "But I guess men like those were born that way; they can't take other people's success in life."

"Maybe so," Jani said.

"The ones with talent and strength get what they deserve and the weak ones are weeded out," the man added. "And it doesn't hurt to be a hard-headed one, either."

Jani nodded. He didn't know what to say right now, but he was very aware of his own small life right now and the lack of his accomplishments.

"What are you still waiting for, boy?" Talpa laughed then. "Try your Martian! They don't give you an opportunity to enjoy proper drinks served in Martian quartz in the outer circles of the city, believe me!"

Jani smiled and raised his glass. For some reason the passing moment reminded him of Null 497 and he saw the man's face in his mind. Jani had never been that interested in durratin; he did not like the taste of it and the well-known ill-effects of the liquid had diminished his interest in it even more.

Jani swallowed. The taste of the Martian was a little bitter, but the drink was overall better than he had dared expect. He couldn't really taste the bitterness of the durratin because of the orange soft drink in the mix.

"I don't drink durratin very often, do you?" Talpa asked him.

"I don't," Jani confessed. "My weekly points don't cover drinking, not to mention that durratin has never really interested me greatly anyway."

"That's good to hear," Talpa said. "A man can ruin his life with durratin. The key to success is never to drink alone."

Jani put his glass back on the table and nodded.

"They say that's the first sign that you should cut down your drinking," the man continued, "to stop when you want to have a drink alone. You have to remember: take all of life's pleasures in moderation."

"That's right," Jani noted.

"So, when does Lu get some time off?" Talpa then asked him. "The finals are playing soon, so the Bromi Arena is going to be packed!"

"I can't recall the exact day," Jani said. "But I assume he should get off-duty soon because we made plans to go to Bromi Arena. So maybe Lu has done some long shifts recently just to ensure he can get to the finals."

"That could be it," Talpa said. "This year the Gallinula team has been surprisingly good. And Gavialis' victory over Paguna was pure luck, if you ask me. It was a close-run thing that the finals didn't go to Paguna."

"Gavialis was better," Jani agreed.

"You can be sure the team members won't be rewarded with twenty Silver Wing marks like they were couple of years ago."

"Gavialis was unbeatable that year," Jani stated and took a sip from his glass.

"I wouldn't be surprised if victory went beyond the Capricorn Tropic this year. It has been four years, though, since the south celebrated winning the games."

"We will have to wait and see," Jani said and took another sip. "But it would be great to win here in Gavialis for the second year in a row."

"The finals start tomorrow in Gallinula," Talpa said. "What was that city's biggest arena called again?"

"I can't remember," Jani confessed.

"Well, let's see," Talpa said and took his noter from his chest pocket and fiddled with the gadget for a moment until he said:

"Diome Arena. That's right."

Jani smiled and took another sip from his glass. Suddenly he realized the durratin was starting to kick in. He was feeling surprisingly happy and carefree for no apparent reason. Mr. Talpa's company was diverting and the man reminded him of Lu, the only person in the world who really knew Jani.

Without durratin, Jani wouldn't necessarily have been quite so interested in talking about a topic like the finals at length, but the light, easy-going feeling the drink produced in him made everything seem unexpectedly intriguing. Jani's mind was open and he was enjoying the smallest things; the dimness of the restaurant, the music in the background with its heavy beat, as well as the drinking glass made of Martian quartz that he so proudly held in his hand.

"You still work in Linai?" Talpa asked him.

"I do," Jani answered.

"In waste recycling, still?"

"That's right," Jani said and smiled; Lu was the only one who knew where he really worked.

Jani's job in the control room was nothing to brag about but at least he had signed a vow of silence, which made his job at least somewhat exceptional. Nonetheless, the fact remained that the location of Cold Pit's control room was classified information, hence the secrecy.

"Haven't you searched for other jobs?"

"I have," Jani said and this time he was being honest, "but so far nothing interesting has come up. And overall, working in Linai isn't all that bad."

"You get used to anything, I suppose," Talpa said.

"That's true."

"Except to the amount of news about the presidential election once the finals are over and done," Talpa added.

"Campaigning is that close already?" Jani sighed.

"Four and a half years go quickly," Talpa stated. "And soon about six headlines out of ten will have something to do with the elections."

Jani nodded and all of the sudden his head felt very light. So durratin was already numbing his senses and therefore even the presidential elections were suddenly a subject he found interesting enough to discuss.

"Will the candidates be published after the finals?" Jani asked the man.

"As always," Talpa said. "Or rather, let's say their ideas and opinions will be published. Who the actual candidates A, B, and C are remains hidden as usual."

"Except that one of them is Sepiella," Jani noted. "He's held the office now for one entire period, so I'm positive he will want another one, too."

"It is going to be pretty easy to guess who he is among the candidates. At least if all three have different opinions of the world and how things should be."

"And then six months of political wrangling begins," Jani sighed. "Did you cast any negative votes in the last elections?"

"For one candidate," Talpa stated. "The one who thought we artificials should know who our biological siblings are. If that really happened, we would have seen some serious gang activity exploding in all world cities! Where the heck did he get that idea from?"

"It was a pretty unusual theme to come up with in the middle of the campaigning," Jani said and shook his head.

"What's wrong with growing up and finding your place in the world without searching for men who have genetic similarity with you?" Talpa wondered sourly.

"To a healthy person genes are irrelevant," Jani said.

"Damn right. As long as the number of women in the world remains this low, aren't we all more or less related on a genetic level? Why should any artificial know anything about the genetic similarity with some random person? I may have biological siblings here and there, but I don't know them, and I don't want to know them. Why should I? Why should someone know anything about another person's genes?"

"It was a pretty mad idea," Jani agreed. "I'm not interested in knowing who is similar to me on a genetic level, either. It just doesn't matter. Something like that doesn't mean anything to me. Isn't it more important to find people around you with whom you want to spend your time, instead of keeping people around because they happen to share some of their genes with you?"

"Exactly!" Talpa stated. "That sorry excuse for a candidate based his views on research according to which biological siblings growing up with women and their guardians are more prone to compete with each other. That's why he thought that success and getting ahead is easier for men like that than for us artificials."

Jani laughed.

"So, this fool assumed that if artificials also knew about their biological siblings, it would create healthy competition between them," Talpa continued, "and that this kind of competition would speed up progress in different sectors of society. I personally think that an assumption like that is too far-fetched. Today's society encourages men to compete and improve themselves enough and for that reason, candidate A, if I remember his label correctly, got a negative vote from me. I think there were many others who cast the same vote for him."

"Didn't he start to retreat from his views towards the end of the campaign by claiming his words had been twisted and taken out of context, claiming that his original idea had been to give artificials the right to search for their biological siblings if they chose to do so, and that the search results would cover male siblings only?"

"Yes, it was that kind of nonsense," Talpa said. "Either way, there's no way that such a system would have worked. What if some stranger had contacted you just to tell you that he was your brother, even though you never wanted to know about him?"

"It would have been extremely distasteful," Jani stated. "I'm not interested in getting acquainted with any stranger whose existence I'm not currently aware of. I have acquaintances and a good friend, so I do nothing with biological siblings mean nothing to me."

"That is how it should be," Talpa concluded and raised his glass.

Jani raised his glass as well and clinked it against Talpa's before taking a sip. Talpa emptied his glass and waved to the waiters again. They would have another one it seemed, which was not at all an unpleasant thought for Jani. He was very aware of where he was and particularly with whom, even though his head felt very light and his eyelids surprisingly heavy.

Suddenly, the music in the background faded and the majority of the men in the restaurant began to cheer and whistle.

"What on earth?" Talpa wondered and turned around to look towards the back wall of the restaurant.

The wall was covered with a huge screen, on which purple strings had been dancing against a dark background all night. Now, however, the screen had been activated and the following words were visible on it.

Announcement from the Women's Affairs Council

There was a countdown below this message and according to the running numbers there would be a woman on the screen in about one minute.

"I wonder what she is up to now?" Talpa said.

"Could it be something about those attacks against women?" Jani suggested.

"That's right," Talpa said. "The council chief has to address the issue publicly at some point."

"We don't often see her in the public eye."

"That's true, but when this woman participates in the World Council sessions, those broadcasts have millions of viewers, you can take my word for that."

"That's right," Jani said. There had been times when he had also followed a broadcast from a World Council session, just to catch a glimpse of the highest-ranking female in the world among the twelve other council leaders.

Finally, the face of a woman appeared on the big screen and the men in the restaurant started to howl. The woman's brown hair was tightly bound up behind her head and the red of her lips stood out against her light brown skin.

"She is gorgeous!" Talpa said and his eyes glowed.

Jani laughed, yet despite his carefree feeling, he suddenly felt quite touched by the passing moment. Here he was, in one of the Grus Tower restaurants with Mr. Talpa, where they were looking at the face of the Women's Affairs Council. The woman in question had more power than 99% of all the men in the world would ever have. Jani couldn't resist feeling proud, even though he didn't know exactly what of. He also felt deep admiration towards the woman on the screen. Therefore, the passing moment had something quite great in it; something definitely larger than life. If only Lu had been here with them right now.

"Quiet!" someone shouted over the continuous buzz of conversation about the woman.

"Dear world nation," the woman began and looked straight in the viewers' eyes. *"I have been following the news broadcasts and articles around the world over the past week with despair in my heart. I have been dismayed at the fact that there are still those in our society who want to destroy and spread evil instead of building and cherishing what is good in this world. As leader of the Women's Affairs Council, I speak for the entire council when stating that we condemn all the attacks against the world's women."*

Some of the men in the restaurant started to applaud the woman's words.

"We live in a civilized society, whose foundation was created by Gavo Hirunda himself," she continued. *"It is our duty to continue along the path of world peace, otherwise there will be no future for any of us. Therefore, women's safety has to be ensured. Without women, mankind will slowly but surely become extinct. I want to emphasize that the Women's Affairs Council has never judged the Yellow Guard of misconduct or blamed any of the Guardsmen for these attacks, as has been speculated or even impudently claimed in the news. The Yellow Guard is a worldwide organization, respected by every woman in the world, and our respect runs deeper than any words can describe. We are not blaming the Yellow Guard for these recent incidents and we are certain that the guilty one behind these outrageous acts is a disturbed individual who has nothing to do with the Yellow Guard. We are certain that this individual will be traced and arrested by the police. We should never condone murderers among us nor the acts of evil they commit, whether the victims be women or men."*

She paused briefly and the men in the restaurant began to applaud her, even though she could never be aware of such a thing happening on the screen.

"Finally, I would like to express my most sincere regrets for the injured or lost individuals and their families; families whose everyday lives this contemptible murderer has disturbed," the woman added. *"We women will survive this trial, as we cope with all difficulties we may face in life. Women will not be broken in this way."*

Then the communication link was severed and the dark background with the dancing purple strings replaced the face of the council leader on the screen. Many men in the restaurant started to applaud again, until the hum of voices filled the air and the music in the background continued.

"I wonder how long this murderer has run free already," Talpa said.

"What does he want?" Jani wondered. "This murderer, I mean."

"Who knows what these mentally ill individuals think," Talpa said. "But there is plenty of room for this sociopath in Cold Pit as well. The sooner we get to see him thrown in there and banished from this planet, the better."

"I've seen a lot of Yellow Guardsmen here in Sixth Circle," Jani said.

"Have you seen any women, too?"

"I have," Jani answered.

""They are gorgeous, aren't they?" Talpa said. "If there is one thing I will regret on my deathbed, it's that I didn't try hard enough to get on the Apertum list. One of the commanders in the Border Guard Detachment has committed himself to a woman, you know? What he has told us about ... wow! I do envy him."

"He's content with his woman?"

"Content?" Talpa asked Jani, as though he had just heard a bad joke. "That man says he can't live without his woman anymore! He says that every single morning he wakes up with a smile on his face. Can you say the same thing? I can't, even though I have accomplished a lot during my lifetime."

"That's pretty puzzling," Jani noted.

"What do you mean?"

"The stories I have heard about women haven't exactly painted so rosy a picture."

Talpa laughed.

"Let me guess," he said. "Women are child-like and difficult."

"Something like that."

"Well, that's what some men say," Talpa noted. "But I guess there are as many different kinds of women as there are men."

"I can't even imagine living a life like that and maybe it's good that I can't."

"I envy those men, boy," Talpa stated. "I envy them, but I guess that's the purpose of this entire system."

"How so?"

"Obtaining the right needed to meet women is difficult. To get to that point, you have to have accomplished a lot. To get to that position has ensured that both the man and the society he lives in have both already achieved a lot."

Jani nodded.

"However, son; I need to go get some sleep and to sober up. Tomorrow is a new day and for me it means that I am about to pick out hopeful young men who wish to become border guards. I shall drop half of them from the program, because that's my job. The best ones will try again."

"So, you will crush many dreams," Jani laughed. "I *don't* envy them."

Talpa laughed.

"Until next time," Jani said and stood up to shake the hand of Lu's provider. "It was good to see you after such a long time."

"Remember to demand enough from yourself," Talpa added. "And promise me that one day you will get out of First Circle to the Second at least."

"I don't ..."

"Promise that," Talpa demanded and watched Jani from under his eyebrows.

The look on the man's face was not judgmental but encouraging.

"Alright," Jani said. For some reason he felt like he really had a chance of making Talpa's demand come true. "I promise."

"So, I was right about you," Talpa said. "The moment you have someone who expects you to succeed, you start making it happen. You should have definitely been brought up by a provider, boy. Most definitely."

Jani nodded.

Talpa tapped Jani's arm, then left. Jani followed the man walking towards the exit for a moment and thought how lucky Lu was. Then he took a seat and sighed. He realized his thoughts had already got muddled and that he was hungry. The joy he had felt just a moment ago had faded. Then he remembered the upcoming day and decided not to drink another sip of durratin.

Jani decided to leave as well. Remaining made him feel even more tired. He walked slowly and deliberately, as everything around him appeared dreamlike and unreal.

Despite the blurred world before his eyes, Jani still remembered all those times he had seen Null 497 staggering across Linai Station. Luckily he was nothing like Null 497. He wouldn't want to have another glass of durratin tomorrow. He would sober up once he got back to his room on the 100th floor of Grus Tower.

"Hey," he suddenly heard near him.

Jani turned his head and saw a young man watching him, clearly the one who had spoken to him.

"Yes?" Jani asked the man.

"You look like you could eat something."

"Maybe," Jani admitted.

"I just ordered a huge meal," the man said. "I could share it with you, if you want."

"You want to share your meal with me?" Jani asked the man, puzzled.

"Eating alone is boring," the man stated, "and pretty sad in a place like this."

"Alright," Jani said; he really was hungry, and talking to a stranger was no big deal for him right now.

"What's your name?" the man asked him.

"Jani."

"Apus," he introduced himself. "My table is over there."

Then Apus turned around and Jani began to follow him across the restaurant towards the back wall of the place. There was an isolated table to where one of the waiters was already bringing a huge meal on a big plate. Jani sat down and watched the food in amazement.

"What is this?" he asked Apus.

"Potato, seaweed and fish," the man answered.

"Smells delicious."

The meal in his eyes seemed to move slightly, though. Jani's thoughts became even more blurred and he hoped that the man who was sharing his food with him wouldn't notice it.

"Hey, take this," Jani heard next.

"Take what?" Jani asked him and looked at the man confused.

Apus was holding a tiny white strip in his hand.

"You can keep up longer," the man explained. "Your mind becomes clear again."

"N1014?" Jani asked him.

"It's not illegal."

"I know it isn't."

"Have you ever tried it?"

"No," Jani said.

"You must try everything at least once."

"Is that so?"

"Sure. Believe me, you will feel better. Durratin makes you groggy, but N1014 is something else. Once won't make you drop out of the city."

Jani hesitated for a moment, and then took Apus' offering and placed it under his tongue.

"Let's eat," Apus then said.

The man didn't have to ask twice. Jani took one of the plates and filled it with food, which smelled great. Suddenly he felt much lighter. N1014 had started to kick in.

They ate for a moment without exchanging another word. At some point Jani noticed Apus placing an N1014 strip in his mouth as well, until continued with his meal. Neither one of them touched durratin.

But However, N1014 threw Jani's thoughts into chaos. He liked the feeling, though, because it made his tiredness evaporate. Once again he felt carefree. He didn't care where he was right now, or with whom, or what tomorrow might bring. There was only the moment and he seemed to have the power to see and feel whatever he wanted to.

Jani realized Apus was whispering something to him. He didn't really hear what the man had said, because his thoughts kept bouncing back and forth as they blended with each other. He realized, though, that the man had placed his hand between Jani's legs and finally under his trousers as well. Jani was about to push his hand away when he realized he wanted Apus to continue. The pleasure his touch caused took him over, and when he felt the touch of his mouth, the rest of the world ceased to exist.

9.

"Am I going to die?" the woman asked, anguished, as the sweat dripped from her forehead.

"You are not going to die," Mari Alauda assured her. "Everything is going to be just fine, you have to believe me."

"I want to know what it is if I am going to die!" the woman cried out and started to sob again. "Doctor Alauda, please; I need to know!"

"Mrs. Hispida," Mari said calmly and placed her hand on her forehead. "Dying in childbirth is extremely rare. Remember, we are constantly monitoring your physical condition and so far everything has progressed exactly as it should."

"Something will go wrong, I just know!"

"Believe me; the female body has evolved for this purpose only. It is going to hurt, I know that, but so far everything has gone just fine. You just have to calm down."

"I can't take this pain! I will *die* in this!"

"You are not going to die," Mari assured her one more time. "Your child is doing fine and once you have this baby in your arms, you will forget ever even feeling this pain."

Mrs. Hispida started to scream. Mari checked the monitor next to the bed and saw from the image on the screen that the next contraction was about to begin. She waited for the midwife to arrive, even though Mrs. Hispida had wanted her to be present during the entire delivery. After the contraction passed, Mrs. Hispida turned to Mari again and held out her arm. Mari took the woman's hand in hers and looked calmly into the woman's face.

"Me and my man, we didn't want to know what this baby was going to be," the woman then explained sobbing.

"That's nice," Mari said.

"We wanted to be surprised."

"I understand."

"But if I die, I need to know what it is!"

"Mrs. Hisp..."

"Doctor Alauda; please tell me this child is a girl!"

"Mrs. Hispida ..."

"I've said I don't care what it is, but if I die, I want to leave my man behind with a daughter! As the provider of a girl, his chances of advancement improve significantly, even though officially a child's gender isn't a relevant factor! But you know how this world is!"

Mari sighed.

"Are you absolutely sure about this?" she asked Mrs. Hispida.

"I am," the woman sighed. "I want to know whether it's a boy or a girl."

"What if this child is a boy?"

The woman didn't answer.

"Mrs. Hispida?"

"As long as the baby is healthy," she finally said. "I suppose that's the most important thing."

"You will love this baby regardless of whether it is a girl, or a boy," Mari assured her. "And your man will be proud in either case."

"Please just tell me what it is!" the woman asked again as she sobbed.

Mari took a deep breath. Then she placed a thin translucent sensor on Mrs. Hispida's swollen belly and waited for the data to upload to the monitor next to the bed. She honestly couldn't remember the gender of each child from the hundreds of pregnancies she was responsible for. When the device gave a signal, Mari read the data on the monitor.

"The child is a girl."

Mrs. Hispida breathed a huge sigh of relief.

"Congratulations," Mari said. "Now you can relax and let this little girl arrive."

The woman wiped away her tears before her face twisted in pain due to the next contraction. Mari turned around and whispered in a nurse's ear.

"Give her one milliliter of Gesnerin, if she doesn't calm down soon."

The nurse acknowledged the order by nodding and Mari started to walk towards the doors. Once in the hallway she headed towards the elevators, her shoes clacking on the floors as she went. She had a report to write, which was waiting for her in her office a few floors above, and she wanted to start it tonight. It was already almost nine o'clock in the evening, but Mari was in no hurry to get home.

Once in the elevator, Mari stood in the left-hand corner. There was also a young girl in there, a nurse, Mari guessed. She saw quite clearly that the young girl was nervous to be standing next to her. The girl was practically shaking! That kind of reaction was nothing new to Mari; not only was she the leader of the women's department in this hospital, she was also a well-known person across the world, which made her respected and even admired. Young women were often somewhat timid because of the power she had; like them, she was a woman, and therefore she was not as easily manipulated by these young ladies as some men were, and Mari genuinely enjoyed the power that this and her status gave her.

She stepped out of the elevator and continued towards her office. Her Yellow Guardsman, who was sitting in the waiting room, got up when he heard her approaching, but Mari signaled him to take his seat again. They would not be leaving for some hours. The doors to her office opened on the automatic signal from her ID chip. Mari entered the room, walked across it and sat down behind her desk.

She activated her screen and chose a text-based document window from where she was able to find the report draft she had already begun outlining earlier. She had collected data from all the children born during the first half of the current year. So far she had avoided mentioning the total number of the girls cultivated from artificial wombs directly, but she knew she couldn't avoid the issue much longer. It was an ugly truth which she could not disguise, no matter how hard she tried, and she had to put the truth in her report. How to express this truth was a delicate question and one she needed to consider quite carefully. She didn't want the Health Council or any other leading political player to jump on her. On the whole, she didn't like writing reports on issues she had not yet studied in sufficient depth. Therefore, she tried her best to figure out a way to phrase the current state of child cultivation as neutrally as possible. There was no point in fanning the smoldering coals of a situation which was already causing considerable concern.

Suddenly Mari became flushed and hot. She tried to ignore it and remain as calm as possible as she took a few deep breaths, even though she knew there was practically nothing she could do in order to prevent the oncoming anxiety attack. Then her heart began to beat faster. Mari searched for her medicine. If she took some now, she might succeed in averting the worst, like nausea or vertigo.

"Where is it?" Mari huffed aloud in frustration, which she often did when she was unsuccessful in finding a new ampoule for her medicine spray, typically hidden under the tabletop.

Then she opened the second drawer and a medicine ampoule rolled into sight. Mari took it quickly and placed it, hands shaking, in her medicine spray. Then she pressed the spray to her collar bone and closed her eyes. She knew it would take a minute or two before the medicine kicked in, which meant these few minutes before always felt like an eternity.

Mari was genuinely worried about her current condition. She knew she couldn't continue self-medicating endlessly, because her system was adapting to greater and greater amounts of the drugs she used. However, she was very busy at the moment which meant the anxiety attacks were inevitable. She simply couldn't help it. Someday, she would stop taking these drugs and seek the help she needed. She really did need help; she had known that for some time, but how? She was one of the best-known doctors in the world, so if she revealed this weakness publicly she believed it would damage her credibility as a doctor and a professional. Mari didn't like the idea of revealing her weaknesses to anyone. Not to mention that many would perceive her condition to be self-inflected; getting treatment for it would therefore be frowned upon. Many men in particular would see it as unfair, as medical help was much more readily available to women than it was to men with similar needs.

Mari opened her eyes and took a long deep breath. Suddenly she noticed an incoming text-based message in the list of unread ones. It was from Aix. Mari opened the message and read the two lines.

When I see you, you govern all my thoughts. When you're out of sight, you conquer my mind. Where have you been all day?

Mari read the message three times and felt a burning ache in her chest as she did so. Her heart began to beat faster again, but this had nothing to do with the anxiety attack. She felt both joyous and relieved. Aix did have feelings for her. The man really did need her as much as she needed him. Knowing it made her happy in a completely new way. However, she believed she deserved these feelings, especially after she had lived in uncertainty for much too long. Would she finally be able to press herself against Aix's chest and stay in his arms? When would it happen? Mari had the patience to wait, especially now when she knew the depth of Aix's feelings for her.

Mari's hands were shaking as she started a reply. She wanted to confess to having missed being with him, that she was constantly thinking of him even when she couldn't be near him. This was the plain truth and finally she could tell Aix directly. All of a sudden she was pulled back from her thoughts as her workstation signaled an incoming message. Mari switched the window and activated the communication link, even though she would have rather ignored it right now. A man appeared on her screen.

"Doctor Mari Alauda?" the man on the screen asked her seriously.

"Yes."

"I am the Administrative Issues Chief from the Health Council."

"Administrator," Mari responded and straightened her posture. "How may I be of assistance?"

"Some disturbing news has come to my attention, yet I have not yet received a report from you, or indeed from any other medical doctor in the world working on the fertilization program."

"What would that news be, exactly?" Mari asked the administrator calmly, even though she had a very good idea of the reason Administrator Pudu had contacted her.

"It has come to my attention that the birthrate of girls has decreased during the past few years, and that we are talking about very alarming numbers."

"The number of girls has somewhat decreased," Mari responded calmly, as if she were talking about some insignificant everyday event. "I am outlining a report about it as we speak."

"And you have not noticed this trend in the numbers before?"

"If you were to study my previous reports, all the numbers are reported in them correctly. The question is more, why haven't *you* noticed this issue before? Why are you expecting me to draw conclusions from these statistics which are available to all of you, too? Does anyone even read my reports, or am I writing them for nothing?"

"Doctor Alauda; there is no reason to be rude."

"I apologize, Administrator," Mari sighed. "It's been a long day. In fact, there is a woman right now in a delivery room giving birth to a baby girl."

"That's good news."

"I couldn't agree more."

"So, you are composing a report now?" Administrator Pudu asked her.

"I am," Mari said, "and I have indeed noticed that the percentage of girls born is not at the level we would like it to be. I have not reported this particular situation to the council separately because I have not yet had the time to investigate it sufficiently thoroughly. That is the reason why I have not been willing to bring this matter to the council's attention yet."

"What actions are you taking to correct this situation? I understand that we are talking specifically about female fetuses in artificial wombs."

"You are correct," Mari responded. "The decreasing number of girls in the statistics appears to cover only artificial pregnancies, but as you know, the success rate of these pregnancies is not yet close to one hundred percent, so losing fetuses is something we face on an almost daily basis here in the hospital."

"And we are really facing this problem in the XX cases only?"

"According to the statistics, yes," Mari stated. "The fact that the majority of the lost fetuses have been female ones is something I honestly had not realized before. Of course, I have reported each case and archived them in our information systems, but so far I haven't studied this issue in detail or pulled up the statistics for longer time-period cases, due to my busy schedule."

"That is not an acceptable explanation," the Administrative Issues Chief informed her. "It is part of your job and position to monitor these numbers, to know exactly how many children are born. I should not need to remind you that we are in no position to afford losing girls, not even one. Even if the number of girls were to remain at the level it is today, the world population would still decrease significantly – by this I mean millions – over the next twenty years."

"I know it is part of my job and duties. I have just left a young woman a couple of floors down giving birth for the first time. I left her because I have your report to write; a report the Health Council is expecting."

"I don't want in any way to demean the value of the work you do, Doctor," the Administrator then said, much more calmly. "Your expertise and input in leading the fertility program are invaluable. Nonetheless, you must understand that statistics like these make the council's management group take notice."

"Of course I understand that," Mari stated. "And I have been absolutely devastated by what I have learnt, but I don't appreciate the insinuation that

I would have hidden something from the council. I have not knowingly kept this from the Health Council or from any other party involved."

"I understand."

"As the responsible leader of the fertility program I recommend that the Health Council appoints a team to investigate the production of artificial wombs."

"Why would you investigate the devices? Why should we investigate this situation from the technical perspective at all?"

"Because we haven't ruled out the possibility of a technical problem causing the loss of XX fetuses. Therefore it's very important to study the technology of the wombs as well, whereas my team will examine the biological risk factors involved in the artificial pregnancies."

The Administrative Issues Chief took a deep breath.

"It is going to be a long project," he said.

"Can we afford to postpone it any longer? I think not. As I said, there are still too few women in the world for population numbers to remain at the current level. We have a vast collection of ova stored, of course, but at present, artificial wombs are not the solution to the problem of how to increase our numbers. Artificial child cultivation can't even maintain the current size of the world population, so it's inevitable there will be some decrease in population numbers in future. That is the reason why artificial wombs also have to be examined from the technological point of view."

"Very well then," Pudu said. "I will present this issue at the management group's council meeting tomorrow."

"Do you need my statement for this meeting?"

"Yes, I do, and also your report covering the first six months of the current year."

"I will remain here at the hospital to finish it," Mari promised.

"Good," Pudu stated.

Then he disconnected the communication link between them, and Mari's report draft reappeared on the screen.

Mari sighed and leaned back in her chair. She closed her eyes and tried to relax. She was exhausted but this wasn't a good enough reason to postpone writing the report. In addition to her exhaustion, she was also both worried and annoyed. The girl issue had been leaked to the Health Council. How on Earth had Administrator Pudu known this all of a sudden? Had Aix sent him the statistics? Why would he have done so? He was equally astonished, puzzled, and cautious about all of this as Mari herself.

Mari looked out of the window again and stared at the lights of the darkened city. She knew the council management group was going to put pressure on her over the next few months. She was expected to achieve remarkable results; a solution to stop the loss of female fetuses, but she had no idea what was causing the problem. She did not have enough time for thorough research into the issue. Her schedule was full of other tasks such as leading the women's department as well as running the fertility program, to mention just two.

"If you don't have the time do it, delegate it to someone who does," Mari thought. "Someone who knows what they're doing. Someone you trust."

Mari took a deep breath and closed her eyes again. Aix would be the right man for the job. He had been the first to know about the loss of XX fetuses, and he knew how serious the situation was. He was also currently monitoring artificial pregnancies as part of his job, anyway. So Aix had the right kind of knowledge to start investigating this crisis. If Mari put him on the job she could also be sure he would carry out his duties well.

Mari swiveled round on her chair and faced her workstation's screen again. Staring at the half-finished draft of her report wasn't very motivating. She checked the situation in the delivery room and noticed that Mrs. Hispida had finally given birth to a healthy baby girl. The child had weighed 3,553 grams and was 51 centimeters long.

"Overall an average delivery and an average baby," Mari said to herself.

She stood up and walked over to her window as she often did when she wanted to think. She couldn't, however, stop thinking about Administrator Pudu and how the statistics had ended up at the Health Council now, when she had found out the crisis herself just a couple of days ago. How closely was the Health Council monitoring her? Were they under tighter supervision than she had realized?

She turned her back on the city and walked towards the door. She was too nervous now to concentrate on writing her report as her mind was jumping between the Health Council and the artificial womb room. Therefore she decided to go and check the wombs herself, even though she knew the devices were being monitored continuously, with or without her personal involvement.

Mari couldn't even remember the last time she had walked among the rows of artificial wombs. She had time in her schedule to supervise the fertilizations of ova in Laboratory F, in fact she had personally even fertilized an egg herself just a couple of days ago, but she was not a typical sight in the artificial womb room these days. Now, having a few spare minutes, she decided to go there. Her mind was already focused on the artificial wombs, so she might as well inspect some of those devices herself before continuing with her report. Maybe studying the wombs could also pull her closer to the practical level and help her to identify some kind of rational explanation for this XX fetus dilemma.

The door of her office opened automatically as Mari approached it, and the Guardsman waiting outside registered her presence.

"I am not leaving yet," she informed the man. "I just want to visit the artificial womb room quickly, so you may remain here."

"Are you sure you don't want an escort?"

"To the artificial womb room?" Mari asked him amused. "Indeed not, I am quite safe in this part of the hospital."

The man nodded and let Mari go. Mari took a quick look at her Guardsman and she saw the bored expression on his face. The man was most probably not looking forward to the idea of spending yet another night in the hospital, but Mari had a job to do. Therefore feeling sorry for the Guardsman was irrelevant. After all, the man had wanted to become a Yellow Guardsman. He had a job now which gave him status as well as a nice amount of Silver Wing marks, which was significantly more than the majority of the world's male population had.

The corridors of the hospital were silent. Mari turned left and to her surprise noticed that the corridor leading to the artificial womb room was dark. She continued walking and expected the lights to be turned on. In fact, all the lights should have been on.

"What's wrong with the lights?" Mari asked two younger female researchers sitting behind their workstations as she peeked into the nearest room.

"I don't know," the other one said. "They went off about an hour ago."

"Put in a maintenance request then," Mari ordered.

"Yes, ma'am."

Mari continued forward. She arrived at the locked doors and pressed the locking sensor with both her thumb and index finger. The doors identified both her ID chip and fingerprints and opened. Mari entered an empty corridor. The research staff of this department had more or less ended their working day and had left. The nurse on call, whose job it was to monitor the functionality of the artificial wombs, was sitting behind her desk and nodded to Mari as she passed. Mari acknowledged her presence by nodding as well and continued on her way. As she walked forward, she realized she couldn't remember the last time she had seen this department as quiet as it was now.

The light problem in the corridor was the same in the artificial child cultivation department as well. Fortunately, the light system and the artificial wombs received power from separate electrical networks, so at least she didn't have to mention power distribution problems alongside the bleak statistics in child cultivation in her report. Finally she arrived at the doors of the artificial womb room.

She entered the room which was full of row upon row of artificial wombs. From the small shelf next to the door she took a data pad which allowed her to scan how an individual womb was functioning. The information on the pad now indicated that the collective functionality of the wombs was normal and undisturbed. None of the wombs showed any indication of malfunction or failure.

Mari started walking slowly between the wombs. The continuous low hum of the machinery in the background was audible, but Mari was so used to the sound that she barely registered it.

"Boy, girl, girl ..." she began. Something in the silence made her feel uneasy.

Mari didn't like silence – she never had – and it always numbed her mind. It also made people inefficient and that's why she liked spending most of her time at the hospital. She had always something to do here, which also helped her to forget that silence even existed and avoid being useless. Feeling useless had been the worst thing for her while growing up but luckily she had found a man who had saved her from doing nothing, and they had mutually agreed on terms to ensure she would never face being useless again; terms, which she could live with as well.

As Mari passed along the rows of artificial wombs, she inspected the received data from each device carefully. The wombs containing girls seemed to be working perfectly. There was nothing exceptional to be seen from the power usage figures and the water insulated inside the devices matched all the chemical requirements, not to mention that each component of each individual womb was functioning normally and in harmony with every other. In other words, everything was normal.

"So what exactly is the problem?" Mari wondered quietly.

If she observed something exceptional in the wombs now, if a small miracle like that happened somehow, she would have something concrete to report to the council. Yet each womb she scanned seemed to be working correctly, regardless of whether there was an XX or XY fetus maturing in it.

Mari felt the same frustration again. She wanted to find some technical explanation for the loss of female fetuses. It would have been a quick and easy solution to this problem. However, if she were honest, she had known that inspecting the wombs tonight would be a waste of time. If there were some critical errors somewhere in the system, they would have been noticed years ago.

"I'm wasting my time here," Mari sighed.

Reluctantly, she turned round and headed back to the doors. Before leaving, she sent the data from her scans to her workstation, before putting the data pad on its shelf next to the door.

When she stepped into the corridor, Mari suddenly halted. It was as if she had heard a noise coming from the artificial womb room. She turned, and pressed her ear to the door. She held her breath and concentrated on listening to the sounds behind the door. Who had arrived here at this hour? The majority of the research staff had done their day's work and had already left. Had the nurse on call followed her into the room?

She pressed the locking sensor with her index and middle finger and opened the door quietly. She peeked inside. She immediately saw a movement beyond the rows of wombs on the other side of the room. She stepped inside and realized there were two men in the room. Who were they?

Mari closed the door carefully and stood still in order to watch what was going on across the other side of the room. She was furious. The artificial womb room was one of the most protected rooms in the hospital, if not in the entire city. There were not many men out there who were authorized to spend time in this room, and Mari would inform them of it quite soon. She stared and held her breath as the identity of one of the two men became apparent.

Doctor Aix.

Mari's heart leapt and a wide smile appeared on her face, to fade only a moment later as she realized Aix wasn't here alone. He was in the room with a young maintenance man.

Why? Hadn't she just seen from his location status on her screen that Aix was at his desk in his own office? Mari followed his location status whenever she was in her office, so that's why she had assumed she always knew where he was. Now here he was with a maintenance worker. Had one of the wombs started to malfunction? If that were the case, why were the two men standing so close to each other, and why did they keep whispering to one another?

Mari's thoughts became darker, quickly turning black. She knew very well what whispering like that between two men meant. Not to mention the fact that the young maintenance worker kept making a pass at Aix which was impossible for Mari to ignore.

"Excuse me, but this room is not meant for recreational activities like that," Mari pointed out loudly and glared at the two men angrily.

Doctor Aix and the maintenance worker almost jumped and Mari could see how the young man was surprised by her presence even though they were still at opposite ends of the room. Mari finally took a step forward and continued slowly towards them. The clack of her heels echoed round the room, interrupting the almost inaudible hum in the background. The two men stared at her without knowing what to say. Even Aix seemed to be at a loss for words.

"What's the matter?" Mari asked the men sharply, but she directed her question specifically at the young maintenance worker. "Haven't you seen a woman before?"

"N-no ..."the man managed to say.

"Doctor Alauda," Aix finally said.

"Where is her Guardsman?" the young man asked Aix quietly, but Mari heard him anyway.

"Nearby," Aix informed him.

Mari placed her left hand in her pocket and took her emergency alarm in her fingers. All women carried such a device to signal their Guardsmen quickly if there was a sudden need to do so, but Mari was now in a room to which only a handful of hospital staff had access. Fortunately, she had told her Guardsman where she would be, and by luck Aix didn't know she had left her protector outside her office in the waiting room. The young maintenance man was presumably unaware of this fact as well, and was visibly shaken to be in her presence.

"What are you doing here?" Mari demanded to know.

"Mari ..." Aix started in a conciliatory tone.

"This room is closed to outsiders," she reminded him angrily as she continued to glare at the young man. "Get. Out."

The young maintenance man left without protesting, leaving Mari and Aix alone in the room. The speed of his departure boosted Mari's ego; it was always nice to see how her word carried weight.

"What do you think you are doing?" Mari asked, looking deeply into Aix's eyes. "This is the artificial womb room."

"Doctor ..." Aix began.

"Doctor? So we're hiding behind our status and titles?"

"Mari ..."

"You've been using this room for man-love?" Mari asked him angrily. "Of all people, *you* should know better!"

"Is the issue now this room, or the fact that I was here with a man?" Aix asked her instead.

Mari was becoming increasingly angry and agitated. She couldn't remember the last time she had felt anything this strongly; Aix had that effect on her.

"A few moments ago I was reprimanded by the Health Council Administration Issues Chief for the weak success rate in the cultivation of females, so I am not in a very pleasant or understanding mood right now."

"And?"

"And?!" Mari asked him in astonishment. "You ask *and*? You come here to tap some maintenance man and all you can say is 'and'? Aren't there any other places in this hospital, where you can get such needs satisfied?"

"You think I came here specifically for that?" Aix asked her slightly amused.

"You think this is funny?" Mari asked him and took a step closer.

"I think it is ... *surprising* to see you this jealous. Surprising in a good way," Aix said.

"Jealous?"

"You are jealous, aren't you?"

Then he gripped Mari round her neck, pulling him towards her, and kissed her forcefully on the mouth. He forced Mari's mouth open, and in a second his tongue had found hers. Mari wanted to push him away but at the same time she wanted him more than ever before. She had wanted and needed this moment for so long.

"Take off your trousers ..." Aix finally whispered as his mouth briefly left Mari's lips.

She could barely hear him. Aix made her lose all control and she wanted to do everything he demanded. She wanted to be told and to obey. She wanted Aix more than anything she had ever wanted and the strength of her own lust surprised her.

However, there was a crack in this perfect moment of hers. Something deep in Mari's mind resisted this. Something was wrong. She tried to ignore the feeling, but couldn't. Something about this moment she had been longing for was not as it should have been.

"No ..." she whispered.

"Take them off," Aix demanded.

"No," Mari said again, but more forcefully this time.

Then she pushed Aix away from her, even though her every instinct demanded otherwise. When Aix tried to grab her again, she stopped him. She couldn't let him touch her right now; she was not ready to give in and give the man all the control. She still needed to know what was happening.

"What is it?" Aix asked her confused. "You don't want to after all?"

"This is the *artificial womb room*," Mari reminded him seriously. "This is the most protected and valuable room in the hospital; one of the most valuable rooms in the entire world!"

"And?"

"What is wrong with you?" Mari asked him. Her anger started to rise again. "What are you doing exactly?"

"What are *you* doing?" Aix asked her in return and almost equally heatedly.

Then he turned away from her and started to pace nervously back and forth. She didn't know what to think. Aix had been ready to touch her, he had to be frustrated now. It was only understandable. All she could do now was hope that he was able to contain himself and his desires.

"Are you really that high and mighty?" he asked her.

Mari was bewildered.

"Excuse me?" she asked him, absolutely stunned.

"You walk these corridors like you were the most honored and valued woman in the world. Just because you have produced a daughter from between your legs and you live in Seventh Circle, doesn't make you a particularly desirable or admired person."

"What ...?"

"Do you really think you can do anything? That you can use and treat people however you see fit?"

"What are you talking about?" Mari asked him in total confusion.

"What am I talking about?" he said, turning his back on her.

Then he walked to one of the artificial wombs, which was among the group of the latest plantations.

"I'm talking about this," he said as he pointed to one of the wombs, watching Mari with a dark look in his eyes.

"Artificial pregnancies? Artificial pregnancies are part of my job, so why would this room make me high and mighty? What are you trying to say exactly?"

"I am talking about this," Aix said and kept pointing at one of the wombs.

Mari didn't understand what he was getting at.

"You work in this room more than I do!" she finally exclaimed. "You are the doctor I have been working with side by side for three years! What are you talking about?"

"I am not talking about artificial pregnancies in general," Aix informed her, the look in his eyes still dark. "I'm talking about this artificial womb here in particular. Are you really trying to suggest you don't know what this is?"

Mari walked to Aix and kept looking at the man as she tried her best to work out what was happening between them. What did he mean?

"This artificial womb here ... this female fetus, which is maturing in here ... you are going to call her Luna, aren't you?"

Mari's heart skipped a beat. How had Aix found out about this personal and private project of hers? Because she had told no one about it, so how was he aware of it? Had he hacked into her ID account?

"Project Luna," Aix added. "That's the one growing in this womb, isn't it?"

"What do you mean?" Mari asked him with a blank expression on her face.

"I know what you have been up to, *Doctor*," Aix informed her sourly and tapped the translucent cover dome of the womb. "I know who came here in this hospital to visit you just a few days ago."

Mari swallowed and stared at the artificial womb just to avoid Aix's eyes. She was still not ready to admit anything. She couldn't. Luna was supposed to be her personal project, her secret, the embodiment of her love, which should have not been any of Aix's business.

"Did you really think I wanted to know anything about any of my biological descendants?" the man asked her. "And you dragged one of them here to the hospital for this little project of yours!"

"I don't know what you are talking about," Mari exclaimed.

"Don't lie to me," Aix snorted. "Wasn't his first name Jani or something? Yes, I am talking about that pathetic little rat who lives in First Circle and wastes his sorry life without doing anything remarkable; the one who does nothing notable at all. And you dragged him here when you were unable to find a better man with half my genes."

Mari folded her arms across her chest and looked at him sharply from beneath her eyebrows. She had to maintain her cool exterior. She simply had to.

"Fine," she said. "Yes, he is your biological descendant."

"Why?" Aix asked her.

"Why what?"

"Why did you create this embryo?"

"Because I could," Mari answered truthfully.

"And you wonder why I can't stand your arrogance?"

"Since when?" Mari hissed. "Just a moment ago you wanted to have sex with me and now you can't stand me? What do you want, *Doctor*?"

"What I want does not include this monstrosity," Aix said and pointed at the artificial womb next to him.

"But there it is," Mari noted.

"Yes, it is, so you can stop lecturing me about morals and misuse of this room, when you are the one raising a child here whose personal information is forged in the Komeion System."

Mari didn't say a word. She simply had no words to say, because the passing moment felt too unreal for her to fully comprehend it.

"Oh, you have a nerve," Aix stated. "This child is genetically an offspring of you and me. So what did you wish to accomplish with this exactly? Me? Are you out of your mind? I have never wanted a child with you!"

"Don't flatter yourself," Mari told him sourly, even though she could feel her heart splitting into tiny bleeding smitherines.

"What then? Are you after all just an emotional weak woman? This project of yours is something I would expect from a silly young girl with some ridiculous and unrealistic daydreams. I thought you were mature."

"Watch your mouth," Mari told him angrily.

"I could easily report this," Aix reminded. "A couple of scans and the genetic roots of this embryo would be revealed in an instant."

"Report this?" Mari asked him. "Like you reported the loss of female fetuses to the Health Council, before I even had a chance to finalize the first version of my report? A report you should also be composing right now instead of pleasuring some young maintenance boy in this room."

"I have reported nothing to the Health Council."

"You and I were the only ones who knew about those statistics! So don't stand there and claim you didn't report them to the council!"

"You're paranoid! What would I have gained for telling them about this situation?"

"You wanted to cast me in a bad light!"

"The world still doesn't revolve around *you,* Doctor Mari Alauda!"

"And it revolves around you, then?" Mari asked him sneeringly. "Hardly. You are nothing but one man among millions. You're nothing special or even remotely significant."

"Yet I seem to be significant enough for you to falsify data in the fertility program's files because of this Luna you have created. How can I be sure you haven't faked other files as well?"

"Are you out of your mind?!"

"I could ask you the same question."

"What is it that you really want?!" Mari demanded. "My job? Me out of this hospital? Was that the reason you started coming on to me?"

"Me? What about you? You're the one who needs a man here."

"What is it that you want?" she demanded again.

"What is it that *you* want?!" Aix responded. "This Project Luna of yours really makes me wonder what is going on inside your head!"

"So, you are going to diagnose me," Mari snorted. "It wasn't enough for you to hack into my ID account and read my personal files? You have committed a crime!"

"You have created an embryo, which shouldn't even exist!"

"I would be careful, if I were you, Aix," Mari said. "Don't make me angry, or you may end up regretting it afterwards."

"Are you threatening me?"

"You're threatening me!"

"You don't want to go against me, Mari."

"And you shouldn't underestimate me," Mari told him, before finally turned her back on him and walking towards the doors. "Your little plaything gets a transfer from this hospital tonight. He won't maintain any equipment here from this moment on."

"In that case your Project Luna has also come to an end tonight," Aix informed her.

Mari halted and turned around to face the man one more time.

"Is he that important to you?" she asked him, even though she didn't want to hear the answer. "And you tried desperately to claim you weren't in this room because of him."

Aix didn't answer.

"He's gone," Mari informed him. "He can start looking for jobs somewhere else."

When she had said this, she turned around again and continued to the doors.

"In that case this is gone as well," she heard behind her back.

Mari stopped, turned around and realized that Aix was pulling off one of the power cables, which was maintaining the life-support functions of the artificial womb. The dim light which had illuminated the womb in question quickly faded away.

Mari swallowed. Aix had killed her embryo. Mari didn't know what to think, but she knew how she was feeling; bad. She refused to express her anger or shock, she made sure she would show no emotion at all as she maintained her icy cold exterior without wavering. She never let anyone see her weaknesses. She was Doctor Mari Alauda, who felt no fear and did not break down in front of others. She was a woman who had not cried since she was 14 years old. So it took a lot before anyone could truly hurt her.

"I thought you were a doctor," Mari said calmly, "a doctor who preserves and protects life."

"The death of this embryo is your own doing," Aix retorted. "*You* killed her."

"How is it my fault?" Mari asked him. "You are the one who is still holding the power cable in your hand! You are the one who just destroyed life! And you call yourself as a good doctor!"

"If you threaten me, it has consequences," Aix informed her coldly.

"You're mad," Mari said and turned her back on him.

"I defend myself, remember that."

"Don't provoke me into reporting this," Mari said as she approached the door.

"You can't put anything about your Luna in an official report, you fool."

Mari did her best not to react to Aix's words and focused on leaving the room as quickly as possible. She threw the doors open, and breathed in only when she was in the dark corridor. She could still see the young maintenance man in her eyes, with whom Aix had been on the other side of the artificial womb rows. Mari's emotions rose even more strongly and tears began to burn her eyes, but still she did not cry. She had no intention of crying; it was a decision she had made when she was just a 14-year-old girl.

Nevertheless, those last words Aix had said kept ringing in her ears, no matter how hard Mari tried to repress them. She didn't want to relive the conversation between them in the artificial womb room, but his words continued to rankle in her mind. She was able to ignore the slanderous accusations of being ugly because she knew she was a beautiful woman. She could close her ears when someone criticized her position at the hospital because she knew she deserved everything she had worked hard for. However, she couldn't stand it when someone called her a fool. It was the only insult that had pierced her chest like a sharp knife.

Mari decided to hold her head high; she had no time for self-pity. Once she left the dark corridor into the illuminated areas, she continued her determined march towards her office. She knew she had to be extra-careful with her report to the Health Council now, because if Aix was about to defame her, she had to keep her facts straight in order to defend herself.

The entire confrontation in the artificial womb room started to feel unreal for her quite quickly. How had the situation taken this kind of turn? Hadn't she been happy and on top of the world because of Aix's message just fifteen minutes ago? How had the man she loved suddenly become someone else entirely?

"Are you alright, ma'am?" the Guardsman asked her and got to his feet as he saw Mari approaching.

"I am," Mari informed him dryly. "I shall remain in my office to compose a report to the Health Council, so we are not going anywhere just yet."

"Very well," she heard him say.

The door opened and Mari walked towards her desk leaving the Yellow Guardsman on the soft chairs in the waiting room, waiting for their departure. When the door closed behind her, Mari growled and kicked her desk as she finally let her anger out. Who was the real source of her anger now, Aix or herself? She simply couldn't tell.

There was also fear mixed in with her anger. Mari felt exposed, naked. She felt more stupid than ever before. How had she been so easily fooled? How had she not seen the dark side in Aix?

Then she felt the beginnings of another anxiety attack. Mari considered taking more drugs to prevent it; the report on her desk was still waiting to be finalized and she could never know how long these attacks would last, but for some reason she decided otherwise. She sat on the floor instead and let her heart-rate increase. She knew from past experience that the familiar feeling of nausea would soon follow.

Mari stared at the city lights and imagined herself somewhere else. Where such a place existed, she didn't know, but it was a place where there was no Aix, no Health Council, family, or fertility program. It was difficult, even somewhat painful for Mari to confess to herself that she hated her job; it was, after all, her entire life, but at the moment she hated it. She not only hated the responsibility and obligations but also the power she had, which was surely one reason why Aix despised her. He was envious of her.

Suddenly Mari felt the room spinning. She tried to breathe calmly, but was unable to steady her breathing. The nausea grew stronger and sat in the pit of her stomach. With considerable effort, she crawled to her desk, opened a drawer and vomited.

10.

Jani made his way down the stairs at 1.1 Corner Station. Another day in the control room was over and he had no plans other than to return to his apartment to get some rest. The thought of the coming evening wasn't very alluring, though, but he had nothing else to do. He could have taken a quick trip to Fifth Circle, but that thought didn't inspire him much at the moment, either. Today it felt like Fifth Circle was too far away.

The truth was, however, that he had not been particularly excited about anything after returning from Sixth Circle, and the journey back and forth between First Circle and Linai had started to feel even more inane than ever before. It wasn't at all pleasant knowing about things you had to go without. He was certainly aware now that he had been much happier when he had not known anything about the luxuries in Sixth Circle.

Then Jani heard his noter beep. He took it out of his pocket and saw his ID account being updated. Jani couldn't help but wonder if the update had something to do with the mystery of the black suitcase. Had he got caught up in some shady operations after all, in something more long-term than he had first realized? Then he noticed the update was actually new access permission to the Second Circle.

Lu.

Lu had come home.

Jani smiled wider than he had done in ages. He turned around and hastened his steps as he made his way back to the station to take a train back to Heptagon Line. A trip from First Corner Station to Second Corner Station would take only about twenty minutes and when there, a train 2A or 2C would take him to Second Circle in no time.

Jani checked the access permission on his ID account again to see how much time he had been given in Second Circle. As always, Lu had given him more time there than he most likely needed, but this was Lu all right because, on those days when Lu was in the city, Jani felt almost as if he lived in Second Circle as well. Lu had always made sure Jani didn't have to return to the First Circle if he didn't want to. Lu had always been very fair in that way.

However, this time heading to Second Circle and meeting Lu made Jani more pensive than ever before. He pondered how much he could tell Lu about all that had happened while he had been gone. Sixth Circle, women, the black suitcase, Makaira ... what would he share with Lu and what would he keep to himself? His life had been full of surprises lately and all these new experiences were something he would have liked to talk to Lu about. He had always been the one Jani could talk to about anything. He had never judged him or betrayed his trust. Lu, if anyone, knew how to keep a secret. Yet now he was suddenly unsure about whether he should confide in Lu.

Jani got on the train and considered his options during the trip to First Corner Station. The journey didn't seem to take very long, and when he got off the train he felt somewhat pleased to be heading to a different platform from where the U Train to Linai departed.

Jani was able to continue to Second Corner Station almost immediately because the A Train on Heptagon Line arrived only three minutes later. However, because of his anxiety, those few minutes felt like an eternity to Jani.. It would be great to see Lu again after such a long time, but at the same time Jani couldn't still decide what to tell his friend. What would Lu think of his Makaira trip and about the agreement with the shady man which had led to it? Jani knew he shouldn't say a word about it to him, but could he keep it all to himself? Lu was Lu, a man he could trust like no other. Would someone find out if he confided in him? How could they?

When Jani arrived at Second Corner Station he became caught up in the rush-hour crowd. Because of the crowd he was unable to take the 2A to Second Circle and he was beginning to get deeply frustrated. Finally, 2C arrived at the station and this time he did get on and was able to continue his journey to Second Circle.

Jani bit his nails. For some reason the idea of meeting Lu had put his nerves on edge. Jani tried to focus on the news headlines just to forget his upcoming encounter with Lu, but it was pointless. Lu had finally returned to the city and since the last time they had been together a lot had happened. In fact much more than Jani could ever have expected. After a while, when 2C slowed down on its approach to 2.3 Corner Station, Jani's wait came to an end.

Once Jani stepped through the gate of 2.3 Corner Station his restlessness finally subsided and he started to feel better. The wait was over and he was in Second Circle now to meet his friend. He would never have confessed the real reason for his good mood to anyone, but the truth was simply that he was very happy to see Lu. The absence of his only friend had had a major impact on Jani's daily life.

The distance from the station to Lu's apartment was luckily only five hundred meters or so. Despite that, Jani decided to send Lu a message. Instead of talking and letting his noter generate the text-based message from it, he wrote:

I'm in Second Circle. Are you in your apartment?

When the message was sent, it only took a moment before Jani's noter beeped with an incoming message:

I'm in my apartment.

"Good," Jani said quietly and kept walking.

He passed a maintenance worker cleaning the street. They were a rarer sight than in First Corner of the city, so that made spending time in Second Corner even more pleasant. It was also much more peaceful here, even though there were podas on the bigger streets – public transportation vehicles with two or three carriages running almost continuously. Podas reminded Jani of trains but they were much smaller and able to operate in inner circle traffic. They operated at street level and, as Jani walked towards Lu's apartment, he could see at least one poda at any given moment.

Jani arrived at the big building he knew so well and pressed the locking sensor next to the main door with his thumb. A text appeared on the small screen above the sensor:

Jani 821771 – Second Floor

The door clicked open and Jani stepped in. He started to climb the stairs to the second floor and once there, he pressed another sensor next to a door with his thumb. It was, in fact, the only door in the building which would grant him access. The door unlocked and Jani walked through.

The hallway was empty. Jani passed a couple of doors until he finally found apartment 2.044. Then he took a deep breath before knocking on the door. It only took a few seconds before the door in front of him opened, and Jani saw his good friend standing inside.

"Hey," Lu said and they high-fived as friends typically did.

"Long time no see," Jani said and stepped inside. "Why did they keep you on service so long?"

"It was me, actually. I volunteered to take on a couple of shifts from colleagues," Lu explained. "They will return the favor sooner or later."

"So, you have a long break ahead of you now?" Jani asked him and took a scat on a chair by the window.

"Not really," Lu said. "I'm going back the day after tomorrow."

"What?" Jani asked him dumbfounded. "What about the finals? Gavialis versus Gallinula in the full Bromi Arena? You told me you would try to arrange your shifts to get into the game, if Gavialis was in the finals."

"Something else has come up," Lu said.

"What else?" Jani asked him confused. "We have been talking about this for six months now and you have been on duty for two months in a row without any long breaks. Surely they will order you to take some time off soon, if nothing else?"

Lu laughed. "I'm sure they will, but I have one more shift ahead of me."

"Have you become a workaholic?" Jani asked trying to conceal the depth of his disappointment in a joke.

"Sorry, what?"

"You would be the first border guard I know to become hooked on his job," Jani added.

"I have my reasons for getting back," Lu said. "Do you want something? Drink, food?"

"I'm alright," Jani stated.

He observed Lu for a moment and wondered what was going on in his head. In all honesty he was somewhat annoyed with him, because his friend obviously had no intention of staying in the city for a longer period of time. Jani had been so certain that they would go to the finals now that Lu was back, and especially because the finals were taking place the day after tomorrow. The timing had seemed perfect, yet he didn't seem to be interested in the games at all. He didn't even seem eager to talk about the subject, which was somewhat odd. Jani felt hurt, even though he knew it was stupid to feel so. Had something happened to Lu at work?

"So, what's new?" Jani asked him as casually as possible.

Lu took a deep breath, but didn't say a word. Jani observed his friend and it seemed like he was weighing up what to say and where to start. Lu's odd behavior made Jani even more suspicious, because Lu was never unsure about himself. Jani was worried. Something was different this time; there was no doubt about that now. What on earth was going on in Lu's head?

"So, what's new here in the city?" Lu asked him, avoiding Jani's question. "They made this gang arrest near your building?"

"You've read your messages at least," Jani noted.

"I did," Lu said. "Today. I've been on the go almost the entire time."

"In Enovii?" Jani asked him.

"No, not there this time," Lu said.

"Oh."

There was definitely some sort of uneasiness in the air, Jani could sense it.

"In this profession you go where you are told to go."

"Yeah," Jani responded briefly.

Lu sat down and looked at Jani. In fact, it was the first time that Lu had looked him in the eyes since he arrived.

"I went to Makaira," Jani added.

"Makaira?" Lu asked him, both confused and amused.

Jani nodded.

"You actually went outside Gavialis?" Lu asked him and now he was mostly amused. "You, who thinks the world ends beyond Heptagon Line?"

"Yes, me," Jani assured.

"And you've been to Sixth Circle as well," Lu added. "It sounds like you've had a busy week or so."

"There's been a lot going on here," Jani stated.

"So, you've had some time off?"

"Two days," Jani said. "One of which I spent in Makaira and the other recovering from Sixth Circle and all its wonders."

"Even though all you did was the hospital trip?" Lu asked him.

"Oh, that hospital trip was entirely a different thing," Jani said as he realized just now that he had not told Lu about the night in Grus Tower.

"You've been in Sixth Circle twice in one week?" Lu wondered. "You've really had a busy week."

"For once."

"But the Makaira trip is the one I'm most surprised about," Lu said. "Just the thought of you leaving Gavialis voluntarily sounds so unlike you."

"I just decided to get on a train and go," Jani explained.

His courage failed him and Jani realized he couldn't tell his friend the real reason for his visit, even though he had considered telling him everything.

"Did you see any women?" Lu asked him then, "in Sixth Circle?"

Jani nodded.

"You've been lucky," Lu stated.

"I went to the women's side at the hospital," Jani said.

"What?" Lu asked him, astonished. "How did you end up there?"

"My appointment was with a female doctor," Jani explained. "And she seemed to be very competent despite her gender."

"I see. So what was she like?"

"She had long dark hair and quite sharp facial features. And her physical form was very slender, like women usually are. I saw her in the news recently, too. She had been given some kind of award, or something."

"Why would she make an appointment with you?"

"I don't know," Jani said truthfully. "She told me about some research they are doing and that my name had come up for some reason. It was because of my age or something like that."

"How odd," Lu noted.

"Very," Jani agreed. "I won't lie; I was pretty dumbfounded when two Yellow Guards the size of a door came to pick me up from the entrance hall."

"Say what?" Lu asked him amused.

"I arrived at the hospital, went to the registering systems and when I signed in, the damn thing didn't provide me with any directions. All it did was to tell me to wait. So I didn't know what to think at first, until I saw these two Yellow Guards coming to fetch me."

"I don't believe this," Lu laughed.

"Well, believe it."

"What did you think?"

"I didn't know what to think," Jani said, "but you know how it is when you see the Yellow Guards coming at you."

"Yeah. You never expect good news when that happens, do you?"

"You got that right."

"I've never even heard anyone getting access to the women's side."

"Me neither," Jani said, "but it happened. She, the doctor, was called Auda, Alunda, or something like that, and I was sitting on the other side of her desk as she was explaining all this research stuff. I expected her to call her Guardsmen at any second because I think I stared at her almost continuously and pretty intensively, but she seemed quite unafraid. She simply didn't worry at all. She didn't seem to mind my gender at all."

"Maybe it's because women are more used to men than men are to women," Lu suggested. "Because of the Yellow Guardsmen, I mean."

"I suppose so," Jani mused.

"Wow, what a story," Lu stated then. "I bet it's going to be one of those days you will never forget."

"You got that right," Jani said. "I also saw your provider in Sixth Circle, by the way."

"Really?"

"Yeah, in Grus Tower," Jani said. "We had couple of drinks."

"Grus Tower?" Lu asked him suspiciously. "How did you end up there?"

"It was a work-related thing," Jani said vaguely, wishing now he had not said a word to Lu about that particular night in Sixth Circle. On the other hand, it was more than likely Talpa would mention to Lu at some point having seen Jani there, so maybe it was better that Jani brought it up first.

"Work related?" Lu wondered even more suspiciously. "What does Grus Tower have to do with the control room?"

"Yeah, old man Talpa was also surprised to see me there," Jani said then as he ignored Lu's question.

"And how is he?" Lu then asked him.

"Good," Jani stated. "He would love to see you soon."

"I shall have to contact him when I come back here next time. Now I don't have the time to get myself over to Sixth Circle just to meet him."

"Why did you even come to the city now?" Jani asked him. "If all you have is just a few days off?"

"Because I have to talk to you about something," Lu said.

"About what?" Jani asked him, puzzled. "I guess I'm flattered you came back here to talk to me, but …"

"Yes?"

"There's something off here now," Jani said. "You seem … to be … holding back something … somehow."

"You know me pretty well," Lu laughed.

"So, something has happened?"

Silence.

"What is going on?" Jani asked him. "Has something happened to you?"

Lu took a deep breath and Jani didn't know what to make of it.

"Yes," Lu finally told him.

Jani watched Lu carefully but he didn't know whether his face reflected worry, fatigue, or joy. Or perhaps a mixture of all those things.

"Something serious?" Jani asked him.

"I'd rather say … *significant*," Lu said.

"Significant? And what is that supposed to mean?"

"I have to tell you about something and it is going to be strictly confidential. You cannot tell a soul about it."

"Alright … but if it is confidential, why do you want to share it with me?"

"Because you are the only one I can talk to about this."

"Are you in trouble?" Jani finally asked him. "Because if you are, you know I really don't have any means to help you, no matter how much I may want to."

"I'm not in trouble," Lu stated. "Officially."

"Officially?" Jani asked him quietly. "What the heck is that supposed to mean?"

Lu took another deep breath and it made Jani worry even more. What could have had happened to Lu in the middle of his shift? Lu's job was to patrol the city border, or the borders of suburbs, or some specific building complexes which needed guarding. So what could have happened? Had he killed someone? Was this about something like that?

"Have you done something they can legally charge you with?" Jani asked him seriously.

"Possibly," Lu stated.

"What …?" Jani sighed and got to his feet.

He started pacing nervously back and forth not really knowing what to think. Lu had always been an honorable guy. He was the smarter of the two, more successful and better in all aspects of life. So what could have triggered him to do something illegal, if that really was the case? Or something else which could ruin his life?

"I won't be going to Gaskar just yet," Lu said to lighten the tense atmosphere between them, "and hopefully I will never be sent there, not to mention Cold Pit."

"I don't believe this," Jani said. "What on earth have you done?"

"So, that you can fully understand what I am about to tell you, you have to know something about my work in general," Lu said. "And this is strictly confidential, but I need to tell you about it because it will help you to see what is going on and why exactly I wanted to see you today."

"Alright," Jani said and looked at his friend without blinking an eye.

"I haven't been patrolling the city borders, or any suburbs for a couple of years now," Lu finally revealed.

"What do you mean?" Jani asked him confused.

Lu wasn't making any sense now. Lu was a border guard, was he not?

"A couple of years ago I was accepted into a special task force unit within the Border Guard Detachment. The mere existence of the unit is classified information so that's why only a handful of men within the detachment know about it."

Jani's jaw dropped. He had not expected to hear anything like this.

"This unit patrols an area which is located north of Albedo."

"There's some secret research facility there?" Jani asked him.

"No," Lu answered. "This area is not ours."

Jani watched Lu carefully for a moment. He wanted to see if there were any traces of deceit on his face, because none of his words made any sense.

"What do you mean exactly?" he finally asked him.

"I patrol ... a border," Lu said quietly.

"A border?" Jani repeated. "So, there is an unknown city there?"

"An entire country," Lu corrected him.

"What?" Jani asked him and laughed. "What country? What do you mean by *country* exactly?"

"Terra Unionia," Lu said.

"What?"

"Terra Unionia."

"Terra Unionia ...?" Jani asked him quietly.

Then he took a moment to think about what Lu had said. He had heard the name before, or at least he thought so; there was a familiar ring to it.

"Terra Unionia ...? Do you mean that Terra Unionia, which was founded during the days of Gavo Hirunda?" Jani finally asked him.

Lu nodded.

"That place still exists?" Jani asked him astonished.

"Yes."

"And people live there?"

"Yes."

"How many people exactly?"

"Millions."

"Millions?!" Jani yelped. "But … how is that possible?"

"I don't know, but they are there."

Jani took a moment to take in what he had just heard. Lu's words still made very little sense to him, but he knew Lu wasn't lying to him. Lu wouldn't do something like that just to see how he would react to it. Or would he? Was this a joke after all?

"North of Albedo?" Jani asked him.

"Yep. Actually, pretty close Albedo," Lu said. "Surprisingly close, I should add."

"How close?"

"Less than fifty kilometers from Albedo."

"That close?"

Lu nodded.

"But how is something like this possible?" Jani asked him. "How could an area like that exist without the rest of the world realizing it was there? You said there are millions of people there, but how is that possible? Surely someone would have seen them by now, yet no one talks about this place anymore."

"You know what people think of historical issues and topics," Lu said. "We don't talk about the first years after the Great War, if it's not about Gavo Hirunda and his heroic deeds. Nowadays, the known world constitutes our network of world cities. Terra Unionia is not part of this network and that's why no one talks about it. We have a culture of silence when it comes to this particular issue."

"Are you absolutely sure there are millions of people there?" Jani asked him, because Lu's story still sounded quite illogical. "Because this story of yours simply does not sound very believable."

"What part of it?"

"The part saying there is really a huge area like this on our planet that people aren't aware of. How can something like that be possible? Why isn't this place talked about in the media? Not to mention the fact that there are satellites, space stations, and continuous traffic in Earth's orbit, so surely someone would have noticed a 'country' to the north of Gavialis."

"Maybe someone has seen it," Lu suggested. "Maybe some people are aware of it, but they just don't talk about it. I am bound to a code of silence when it comes to this. I am not allowed to tell you about this area at all. People have learnt to conceal all traces of living in Terra Unionia. People there really don't want us to know anything about them."

Jani watched Lu for a moment, feeling profoundly astonished.

"How do you know about this?" he then asked him. "How do you know what these 'Unionians' are thinking?"

"I met one of them," Lu said.

"What?!"

"I told you I have been patrolling this border," Lu added. "I met one of them."

"How?"

Lu got to his feet again and gave an awkward laugh.

"So, men in this covert unit of yours are connected to these people, then?" Jani asked him.

"No, we're not," Lu said. "My job is to keep the Terra Unionians behind the border, and communicating with them isn't exactly what I have been ordered to do."

"It is forbidden?"

"Of course."

"So, seeing these Unionians isn't allowed?"

"No, it's not."

"But you met one of them, anyway?"

Lu shook his head and the smile on his face widened. Seeing Lu doing that made Jani really worry now.

"I neglected my duties when I started a systematic trace on one of their border guards," Lu continued.

"What?" Jani asked him and frowned.

"I traced him for days," Lu continued. "Five days, actually. I thought that he would disappear behind the border at some point and leave me alone but he didn't. He stayed there, because he had also seen me."

Jani was listening to Lu carefully and he couldn't help but shake his head in disbelief. He didn't like the direction this story was taking. It got him worried and afraid at the same time.

"Patrolling a border can get quite boring at times," Lu explained. "And that is the reason why I became so interested in this Unionian when I observed him near the border. Normally there is no one there with me. In fact, I know of no one from our unit who has ever caught a glimpse of any Terra Unionian. That's why the situation was so intriguing."

"So, the other guards in your unit don't know anything about this meeting of yours with this Unionian?" Jani asked him.

"No."

Jani took a deep breath. He still didn't know what to think of all he had been told tonight, but at least he was relieved to hear that Lu's little adventure was not public knowledge in the Border Guard Detachment yet. Was Lu in trouble or not?

"My intention was to keep tailing this Unionian only as long as he remained on the border," Lu continued. "But before I knew it, a day had become two, and then two became five. According to official procedure, I should have informed my superiors of this immediately; it's my job to ensure that none of these Unionians cross the border."

"But?"

"But I told no one."

"Maybe it was the wisest thing to do after all," Jani sighed, "but why?"

"Maybe because I wanted to witness something that the other men in my unit have not or maybe because I didn't see this situation as all that serious. This Unionian border guard was keeping his distance from the border, so I made an estimation of the situation being in my full control, but on the fifth day I finally confronted this Unionian."

"On purpose or not?"

"By accident."

"And?"

"I realized I had gauged the situation wrongly. Facing a Unionian was definitely a serious situation."

"What …?" Jani asked him quietly, even though there were no others in the room.

"We met, face to face, and suddenly I found myself in a situation where we weren't competing in tracing skills anymore but we were fighting for our lives," Lu explained. "I pointed my weapon at the Unionian and the Unionian returned the compliment by pointing a gun at me."

Jani took a deep breath and stared at the floor for a moment. He tried to collect his thoughts but still didn't know what to make of any of this.

"That, however, was not the most shocking thing about the situation," Lu said. "Facing this border guard, I mean."

"What do you mean?"

"The most surprising thing of all was the fact that he was actually a *she*."

Jani looked at Lu and stared at the man for a moment in utter confusion.

"A woman?" he finally asked him.

"A woman," Lu confirmed, and sat down again. "And a very angry one, I might add."

"A woman," Jani said again.

His thinking froze. Learning about Terra Unionia's existence had already been quite a shock for him, but a woman as a border guard was something nearly incomprehensible.

"A woman," Jani managed to say one more time.

"A woman who certainly didn't seem to need any protection from a Yellow Guardsman. She was quite capable of defending herself," Lu added. "And she was fierce."

"Fierce?"

"She accused me of violating the border and told me to back off, pointing her gun at me, even though she was the one who had crossed the border."

Jani kept listening to Lu in shock and finally he shook his head. He was still having a hard time believing that Lu was telling the truth, but at the same time he knew Lu had no reason to lie to him about this.

"How is it possible?" he finally asked him. "That she was chasing you away from an area which isn't even in her territory?"

"Our maps were different," Lu explained.

"What ...?"

"The border is located in different places on our two maps," Lu explained.

"Huh?"

"But before we could figure this out, we had remained in deadlock for hours, pointing our weapons at each other. We were really close to killing each other."

"How did you resolve the situation?"

"I really don't know," Lu sighed. "I've been trained not to accept border violations for any reason; that I should show no mercy to anyone crossing the border. I've been taught that people beyond that border are isolated for a good reason and that they should be kept isolated from the rest of society because they are misfits. Yet as we were standing there together, just me and her, and when either one of us could have killed the other at any moment, something happened."

"What?"

"Before long we both realized we didn't want to kill each other. Both of us had been curious and it was that curiosity that had led us there. It was that curiosity that had driven us both for five days in a row to trace each other. *Five* days. And when we finally stood in front of each other, our anger and fears somewhat faded but the curiosity was still there. Then when we finally started to talk to each other in a somewhat civilized way, I learnt that she had never met anyone from our side of the border just as I had never met anyone from hers."

"But she violated the border," Jani said. "You allowed her to cross the border to our side."

"Did I?" Lu asked him. "According to her, I was in Terra Unionia."

"She was obviously wrong," Jani stated.

"How do you know that?"

"I doubt that you would forget where that border is. You don't make such mistakes."

"But she was quite convinced I had crossed the border and entered Terra Unionia."

"And she was wrong."

"Was she?"

"What do you mean? We are talking about a woman here."

"And?"

"You know how women are. They can persuade men in ways only women can. They can get into your head and play tricks with your mind, finding irrational conclusions and explanations. Such thinking is bound up with their gender."

"I know," Lu said. "I have never forgotten that, but ..."

"But?"

"But something about her was different."

"Lu …" Jani started, worried.

"I know this sounds odd."

"*Odd* doesn't even begin to describe it."

"I haven't told anyone about this," Lu said. "I can't tell anyone this, because it would lead to my immediate dismissal from the Border Guard

Detachment, not to mention that I would lose most of my Silver Wing marks."

"I'm glad you still remember that," Jani said. "Because I was beginning to get worried here for a moment."

"I realize what I have done," Lu assured him. "I am still fully aware of the possible consequences my conduct may have."

"But?" Jani asked him in quite demanding way, because he knew for a fact that a 'but' was coming.

"But I want to go back there."

"Where?"

"To the border."

"Well, aren't you going to go back there, anyway?"

"I mean I want to go back to that specific location where I met this Unionian woman."

"Umm … why exactly?"

"Because I know she will be there."

Jani stared at Lu for a moment and he hoped his friend was joking. Yet he knew their conversation was not exactly the most humorous one, so Lu really meant what he was telling him now. Jani started shaking his head again. There was only one question on the tip of his tongue; had Lu lost his mind?

"You want to see her again?" he asked. "This woman you can't keep in touch with because if the worst comes to the worst, you could face severe sanctions and significant status drop, if anyone ever found out about it?"

"Yes."

"Umm ... come again?!"

Lu smiled and shook his head. However, his apparent amusement didn't cheer Jani up a bit.

"Has this woman mixed your head so thoroughly already that you are incapable of thinking rationally now?"

"Maybe," Lu confessed.

"Then don't make the mistake of returning to that spot anymore," Jani advised, almost demanded, even though Lu wouldn't listen his demands. "Come on! Stay as far away from her as possible!"

Lu nodded, but didn't say a word.

"Maybe there is a really good reason for that border to exist," Jani continued. "I hope you won't lose sight of that now or in the future. And I assume you are still capable of realizing that seeing this woman can't come to anything."

"But I need to see her."

"Why?"

"Okay …" Lu sighed. "I guess I should mention now that all this happened three months ago."

"What? What do you mean?"

"I mean the moment when this woman and I faced each other for the first time happened three months ago."

"And?"

"Three months, Jani."

"And … you have been in contact with her all this time?" Jani asked him then. "Is that the reason you haven't been in Gavialis recently?"

"That's the reason."

"Have you taken an interest in this woman?" Jani then asked him, genuinely worried now.

"She is an interesting person," Lu confessed. "And three months ago, when we decided not to kill each other, we also agreed that we would not talk to anyone about the incident. She would get into trouble on her side of the border like I would on mine."

Jani nodded, but said nothing. He was simply too dumbfounded to know what to say, or even think.

"We argued almost continuously," Lu said and laughed. "The first month passed by exchanging insults and us railing each other. We both have our training and backgrounds after all, so our arguments had a lot to do with how we saw things and I guess how we still do, but after the first month we gradually began to laugh at the ridiculous mockery we kept up. Then one day we simply realized how ridiculous our conversations really were. If we really despised each other so deeply, why on Earth did we keep returning to this location where we had first met?"

"Indeed," Jani said seriously. "Why on Earth?"

"I won't lie; she made my days on the border much more interesting," Lu confessed. "If I am totally honest with you, patrolling the border is pretty mind-numbing work. I walk there in the forest and I keep my eyes on the border, and I don't really see anyone else there, ever."

"Are you telling me you want to keep in touch with this woman just so you can have someone to talk to?" Jani asked Lu slightly sarcastically.

"It's not just about that."

"Of course it's not," Jani sighed.

"The thought of another border guard seeing her and talking to her like I have talked to her irritates me. I wanted to keep her as my own secret."

"So, you feel possessive about this Unionian woman?" Jani asked him.

"Of course I do," Lu said. "Just think about it! I am most likely the first man in the world who has communicated with a Terra Unionian!"

"Sorry, but I can't see that as a great accomplishment," Jani informed him sourly. "I realize this situation is unusual and possibly interesting as well but I am concerned about you."

"Alright. I get your point completely," Lu stated. "Believe me, I do, but unlike you I have had three months to think this over."

"You must still realize and admit that this isn't very wise. I don't care how special this woman is, you have to remember your own place. As a man who has known you since our childhood I am urging you to stop fraternizing with this woman before you end up ruining your life. Soon you will have enough Silver Wing marks to move to Third Circle! Third Circle, Lu! Just think about it and don't lose sight of it! Try to see what you are doing here and whether it is rational to keep in touch with this woman."

"I don't want to," Lu said.

"You don't want to what?"

"Stop fraternizing with her."

Jani took a deep breath and shook his head in disbelief. His concerns were founded then; Lu had lost his mind over this woman.

"You have no idea what I have heard and experienced during the past three months," Lu said. "Everything has changed. And when I say everything, I mean *everything*. Even the way I see the world has changed. I have changed."

"What difference does it make?"

"It makes a lot of difference."

"This can ruin your life!" Jani reminded him. "Don't ruin your life, please! If this neglect of duty gets out there, it won't necessarily send you to Cold Pit, but you will be dropped to First Circle quicker than you can say Gavo Hirunda. You could lose everything you have been working so hard for all these years! Fraternizing with this woman cannot be worth the risk!"

"It is," Lu informed him calmly.

"So, this woman has already succeeded in clouding your judgment," Jani observed and shook his head.

"I wouldn't say that."

Jani continued shaking his head, because there wasn't much more he could do right now. All that Lu had told him made him shake his head. He simply couldn't understand how blind Lu had become; how willing he was to risk every single right he had earned after so many years of hard work.

"Oh come on!" Jani finally snorted. "This is so obvious. This woman has managed to get inside your head and she has already begun to do harm. You should remember women have the ability to drive men to the limits of their endurance, and that is the reason why only the most successful men can handle them. You haven't even received the first Silver Wings on your chest, so you are not competent enough to handle women."

"Don't be ridiculous, Jani," Lu said.

"Ridiculous?!"

"Surely women have other things on their minds than planning how they could make men's lives as miserable as possible."

"Just listen to yourself, Lu! For crying out loud – if old man Talpa knew about this, he would go mental!"

"That's why you are the only one I can talk to about this."

"Just use your head and think about what you are doing!" Jani urged. "Ask for a transfer to some other location and continue living your life as if this had never happened!"

"I can't."

"Yes, you can!"

"She is carrying my child," Lu said.

Jani's jaw dropped. Then an awkward silence fell upon them. Jani looked at Lu without knowing what to say. Was Lu serious? Had he heard him right? What was going on?

"She is carrying my child," Lu repeated.

"So, you slept with her." Jani sighed. "She took advantage of your curiosity and ended up ruining your life in the process."

"Ruined?!" Lu yelled. "She hasn't ruined anything!"

"You have impregnated a human woman without appropriate permission!" Jani reminded him. "You have slept with a woman even though you don't have the right to even meet them!"

"Jani ..." Lu sighed.

"Don't even start to decry what you have done here," Jani told him, "because if this is really true, you are in deep trouble."

"I am telling you the truth."

"Listen to yourself!" Jani shouted. "What's gotten into you?! The Lu I know would never have done something like this! Do you realize that this is more than enough for you to be sent to Cold Pit?!"

"If I'm sent to Cold Pit because of her, then I'll go willingly."

"Come on!" Jani demanded. "Look at the damage this woman has already done to you! The Lu I know would never do anything like that!"

"Her name is Lena," Lu said.

"What?!"

"Her name is Lena," Lu said again. "She is Lena, not just some woman."

"I don't care."

"Lena Vaal," Lu added. "And I love her."

"You what?" Jani asked him unable to believe his own ears.

"I love Lena."

"You *love* Lena," Jani repeated sourly. "Is that so? And what about her do you love, exactly? Do you even know her? Could it be that the thing between her legs has made you see things that aren't there?"

"I love Lena," Lu stated calmly.

Jani growled in frustration and started to pace back and forth across the middle of the room.

"I think about her all the time," Lu confessed. "Now that I am here, she is constantly on my mind, and I want her to be near me again."

"I don't believe this ..." Jani sighed.

"She knows me better than anyone," Lu said. "Even better than you."

"Right," Jani stated sourly.

Lu fell silent. Jani looked at the floor beneath his feet and tried to keep his tongue still. He was very agitated by Lu's stupidity. How could a man like Lu lose his mind so completely? Lu, who had always been rational and levelheaded. Lu, who was always aware of the right thing to do.

So what had happened to him? Had he forgotten everything they had been taught about women? Lu had to be aware of the fact that he didn't really know anything about women, yet he was acting as if he was some kind of expert now, just because this Terra Unionian woman had messed with his head and made him believe all this nonsense she had fed to him. Where was the rational Lu he had always known? The one who never paid any attention to nonsense? The man with him in this apartment now was not the Lu Jani had known since they were kids. Perhaps that was the reason why he felt such deep disappointment. Jani couldn't help it, but he felt deeply disappointed. He had expected more from Lu.

"You should say what you are thinking right now," Lu said next.

Jani turned his face to Lu, looked him in the eyes, and shrugged his shoulders.

"What could I possibly say?" he asked him. "No one can fix what has already happened and if you don't realize, or care about the risk involved in this, then me harping on about it won't help. Frankly I am annoyed. I'm mad because you don't see how blind you are right now."

"I do understand what I have done," Lu said. "I guess I will never find the right way to explain it to you for you to fully understand it."

"A woman is carrying your child, because you slept with her," Jani reminded him seriously. "You don't even have permission to procreate!"

"You're right!" Lu responded. "But she is not one of our women, don't you get it? Her pregnancy won't end up on our records or statistics."

Jani looked at Lu for a moment and he realized he was absolutely right, but it was not much of a comfort, because Lu had still done something he should not.

"But it is not that simple," Lu sighed then.

"Why?"

"Because Lena's pregnancy isn't exactly stored in the information systems in Terra Unionia, either," he added.

"And?"

"It means that we are in trouble," Lu said. "She can't reveal her pregnancy openly in her country, and I can't talk about her or this child to anyone here."

Jani took a deep breath and rolled his eyes.

"Neither one of us was expecting anything like this to happen," Lu said.

"Neither one of you knew how humans procreate?" Jani asked him slightly sarcastically.

"Neither one of us thought about it because we were so focused on each other. I know it sounds odd, but it is what happened. Lena … she's just so incredible!"

"I'm sure she is," Jani said quietly.

"What we are capable of doing together … what a man and a woman can do with each other … there are no words for it!"

Jani didn't understand Lu's excitement and fascination, and it was partly because he didn't even want to. The spark he saw in Lu's eyes was something he had not seen in them before. He couldn't grasp what was going on in Lu's head right now. Neither one of them had ever studied the female psychology or physiology. There had never been a need for it, because official permission to procreate had been so far out of their reach. Now Lu had told Jani that he knew a woman personally; a woman who didn't officially even exist. On top of that, Lu also had feelings for this woman. How could it be? Since when had Lu started to take notice of his feelings?

"Aren't you even little bit curious about what I have heard about Terra Unionia?" Lu then asked him.

"Do you really think I have had any time to wonder about such a thing during this conversation?"

"As I said, there are millions of them," Lu said.

"I heard you."

"And the majority of them are women."

"What?" Jani asked him puzzled.

"You heard me."

"They have millions of women?" Jani asked him again, because Lu's claim sounded too unreal to be true.

"Millions," Lu replied.

"Millions?!" Jani yelped.

"Millions."

Jani stared at Lu and his jaw dropped yet again. Just when he had imagined Lu couldn't surprise him any further, he had told him of the millions of women in the new world. How could it be possible? What would happen if the rest of the world found out about these women?

"Unbelievable," Jani finally said.

"So, do you begin to realize how big this is?" Lu asked him.

"But you have already said, they don't want to be part of our world," Jani pointed out. "They are isolated."

"They are," Lu said. "And because we haven't been in contact with them in generations, even our maps have begun to look different. That is the reason why Lena and I blamed each other for crossing the border, and we both meant it. But we were in this 'gray zone' instead, which is either part of all the world on both sides of the border, or it is a piece of land which belongs to no one."

"So, what is this Lena person going to do?" Jani asked Lu next.

"About what?"

"Is she going to tell these millions of women about you?"

"No," Lu said. "Just one."

"One?"

"Her sister," Lu said. "Her name is Anamona."

"But she's not going to tell her comrades about you in their version of the Border Guard Detachment?"

"No," Lu answered.

"How can you be so sure about that?"

"Because she would get in trouble with her border guard, just like I would in here," Lu reminded him.

"In what kind of trouble?"

"Trouble."

"This is unbelievable," Jani sighed. "This entire conversation is unbelievable and all this feels completely unreal."

"If anything, this country of theirs seems unreal," Lu said and started to smile.

"What do you mean?"

"Well, first of all they have a lot of edible vegetables," Lu said. "The soil in their country is not polluted."

"It's not?"

"No," Lu stated. "So, they grow their own food outside. Lena told me that they eat mainly vegetables for that reason; that they have vast regions of land for this purpose only. Lena has even told me names of these edible plants and such; names I have never even heard of, and once she brought me this round fruit. I believe it was called an apple. Before Lena I had not even heard of an apple!"

"Apple?"

"Yep. It was round and light green, and it tasted sour and sweet at the same time. Lena says that they have red ones as well. In the center of this apple is this hard part, which is usually not eaten. In that part there are these brown apple seeds."

"Apple," Jani said again.

"Here," Lu said and extended his arm under Jani's nose.

Jani looked into his hand and noticed a tiny dark brown object, which was a shape of a water drop.

"This is apple seed," Lu said. "I kept it from the apple I ate."

"That thing came from it?" Jani asked him.

"It sure did," Lu assured.

Jani looked at the seed for a moment and didn't know what to make of it.

"And Lena laughed at me when I told her I would keep this seed," Lu laughed. "She found it amusing, because when she was little, she and her sister had this tree round the back of their house that they got apples from every year. For her, this edible fruit is a normal everyday thing and that's why my fascination over this seed amused her deeply."

Jani didn't know what to say. Lu's stories just kept becoming more and more unreal.

"The name of their biggest city is Pinus," Lu continued. "And what I have heard of it so far makes me want to visit it someday. Lena is in that city right now, I believe."

"What's so special about it?"

"Well, first of all they have integrated a zoo in the city," Lu said.

"What does that mean?"

"They breed and take care of animals, which don't exist in any other part of this world," Lu explained quietly and his eyes sparkled. "They have animals we can only read about! Horses, wolves, colorful fish, and who knows what else! Lena can't even remember all the animals, because she's not from that part of Terra Unionia."

"Why is she there right now, then?"

"Her sister moved there to work," Lu stated. "So, she is having or she will soon have this same conversation with her sister."

"And then what will happen?"

"Then both Lena and I hope that you and her sister will come with us to the border."

"Why?" Jani asked him stunned.

"I want you to meet her," Lu said and smiled.

"What for?"

"Because you are the only one I can talk to about her," Lu explained slightly amused. "For that reason. I want you to meet her, because I love her."

"Lu ..."

"Come with me to the border," Lu asked him.

"I don't believe this ..."

"I want you to meet her. The two of us have created a very unusual situation together, so we must figure out how to proceed with this child coming and all. We need your help."

"What on earth can I do?" Jani asked him. "I'm not a genius who can come up with a solution for a situation like that."

"But you are a man I trust," Lu said. "And that is the reason why I want your help. "

"This is not a good idea," Jani sighed. "If we get caught, we are going to have a little vacation outside of the city and you will lose your Silver Wing marks."

"So will you," Lu said.

"But I don't have as much to lose. You, on the other hand, have a lot to lose."

"I wouldn't ask this if Lena didn't mean so much to me."

"How can you know she's waiting for you there with her sister alone? What if she has alerted her country's border guards and we are taken on their side of the border?"

"She could have done so countless times already, but here I am."

Jani huffed in frustration.

"Jani," Lu said. "Finals come and go, but this is a unique opportunity. Come with me to the border and experience something other men in this world can't."

Jani was curious, there was no doubt about that. But he didn't want Lu to see it. He was annoyed by the fact that the man was able to pull him this way. Meeting women on the border was an extremely interesting proposal which he could not turn down easily or without careful thought. What kind of women will they be? Who was this Lena exactly who had got Lu all mixed up?

Would he see the deceit in this Lena woman? He still believed in the possibility of Lu having been totally blinded by his affection for this woman. Should he take a risk and say yes to Lu's proposal?

"We will leave the day after tomorrow," Lu said, "So, we can spend tomorrow in Fifth Circle and leave the following morning. You wouldn't even have to return to First Circle, if you don't want to. You can stay the night here."

"I've taken lots of time off from work lately," Jani said. "How can I explain yet another day off? They are going to fire me soon."

"You don't have any off days left in your account?" Lu asked him. "We will just make a quick trip to the border and I will bring you back."

Jani sighed.

"Help me, Jani," Lu sighed. "Please."

Those four words hit Jani deep. Lu knew exactly what strings to pull. He couldn't deny his help; as a boy he had helped him escape from a collapsing building, for which he had never asked for anything in return, even though Jani had always felt indebted.

Except now.

Now, Lu was asking for his help. Lu knew Jani could not say no to him now.

"Alright," Jani said, even though he still had his doubts. "I'll come, but I don't want us to get caught."

"We won't," Lu assured him.

"I hope you're right," Jani sighed.

11.

Mari was standing in the middle of a large room located on the top floor of the Main Hospital, and she was waiting. The men behind a long wide desk were all focused on their screens, reading. Evidently, Mari's report had got them all worried, just as Mari had expected.

As Mari continued to observe the men of the Health Council's management group, she couldn't ignore the feeling of loneliness emerging from within. She should have been standing here with Aix by her side today, but the man was nowhere to be seen. Aix had not even contributed a single word to the report and Mari assumed it had everything to do with their fight. Therefore, she had made sure that Aix's name was not mentioned on this report the management group was now studying.

"Doctor Alauda," the head of the council said. "This is not at all what I would call pleasant reading."

"I can understand that."

"We are in crisis."

"I know."

"This is a problem on a worldwide scale, not just a minor internal issue in Gavialis."

"I am aware of that."

"Why hasn't anyone noticed this before now?"

"I can't explain it," Mari answered. "Even if we have had this data all this time."

"And for that reason, someone should have noticed this situation three years ago!" one of the men behind the desk informed her angrily.

"I agree," Mari said calmly. "I can't explain why these statistics haven't appeared on my desk sooner."

"Is this error yours or one of your subordinates?" the head of the council asked her.

"I am the leader of the program, so the responsibility is ultimately mine," Mari stated.

"Indeed it is, Doctor," the man noted.

"We have put continuous effort into producing more female fetuses," Mari added. "Girls have always taken priority, just like this council has ordered, and we obeyed this order even before we realized how bad the current situation is."

"So, why hasn't the deficit in the number of girls been noticed before?" the head of the council pressed.

"I can't explain it," Mari said. "The numbers have been available for some time."

The head of the council studied Mari carefully from beneath his eyebrows. Mari knew the man was trying to break her cool and calm exterior but it would never happen. She didn't crack under pressure. Nonetheless the man's question was justified and it was the one Mari had also been pondering for quite some time now. Why had she also felt like seeing the statistics for the first time when Aix had brought them up?

"You do know the consequences of this."

"I do," Mari said. "An XX year."

"Several XX years," the head of the council informed her. "No boys are allowed to be born from artificial wombs in any world city for the next few years now."

Mari said nothing. She simply nodded at the man with a serious look on her face.

"If this continues, the number of women will halve within forty years and, the way things are looking right now, that number is going to continue falling."

"I know," Mari said.

"That is the reason why I can't stop wondering why, of all the people involved, you failed to observe this trend sooner."

"As I've already said, I cannot explain it conclusively," Mari informed the group. "I am aware I am the head of the fertility program but this title makes me extremely busy as well. I don't lead our unit, I also work as a doctor."

"That is not an excuse."

"It's not, I agree, but I hope it will explain – at least in part – why this issue has been brought to your attention as unexpectedly as it has."

"Very well," the man said. "We will withdraw for further discussion. Please remain in the building until we call you back."

Mari nodded, turned round and left. When the doors closed behind her, she felt more at ease, but not much. It was pretty clear that, in the eyes of the council, she had messed up. She hated taking the blame, but it was part of her role as leader of the fertility program. All she could do now was to come up with a plan to remedy the situation. She really needed to solve the problem of female cultivation soon; the threat of XX years didn't leave her with any other choice. She had to succeed no matter what.

Mari's personal Guardsman noticed her presence and got to his feet. They marched towards the elevator and descended a few floors down. Mari stepped into her office, where her temporary relief after the council meeting faded as she started to worry again.

She sat down on her chair, activated her screen to focus on her work, but the restlessness taunting her made it impossible to concentrate. She had a nagging feeling that something was very wrong now; that there was something happening behind her back.

"Just focus on your work," Mari told herself.

Work had always been the most effective way for her to repress any unpleasant thoughts. However, staring at her screen only reminded her of Aix. She knew he had hacked into her ID account, because there was no other way he could have known about Project Luna. She couldn't prove it but she knew he had done so. And if she blamed him for hacking into her ID account now, she would only expose Luna as well, and she couldn't allow that to happen.

Mari took a deep breath. How carefully had Aix studied her personal files and what had motivated him to do so? How much did the man know about her personal affairs? Had he found something in her records he could use against her now? Was there any choice other than to let him go? Should she fire him?

Mari stared at the doors of her office and took a deep breath. She was not involved in human resources issues so all she knew about Aix was that he had arrived at the hospital three years ago. However, there had to be some documentation in the Komeion System about his appointment.

Mari opened the connection to the Komeion System and searched for Aix's information. He had moved to Gavialis from Tapeti where he had been born. His working history was exemplary and therefore it was no wonder he had managed to get a transfer to Gavialis. However, Mari couldn't see from his personal information whether he had applied for a position in the Gavialis Main Hospital himself or if he had been approached by the hospital's Human Resources department, requesting him to come work in the city.

Mari stood up and walked to her window to look down at the streets below, but all she could see was Aix, holding the power cable of an artificial womb in his hand. He had known about Luna and that was something Mari could not forget.

She could feel the apprehension growing within her. She was irked by the fact that she still wanted to see some good in Aix; she hoped that the man would still want her like she had wanted him, but she knew it wasn't so. She had meant nothing to him. Her feelings towards the man had been worthless. He had shown nothing but contempt towards her and that still hurt, but it also enraged her to have been made to feel such a fool.

She became frustrated at her spinning thoughts. Why couldn't she simply stop thinking about him? She still had her work; she still was one of the leading fertility doctors in the world. She was still the leader of her unit. If Aix disappeared from Gavialis and from her life, she would still have her work, status and accomplishments. She would still be Mari Alauda. Perhaps that was the only solution now. Perhaps she had no other choice than to let him go. Once he wasn't around anymore, she would eventually forget him, too.

Mari turned her back on the window and sat back down at her desk. Then she ran a search for up-to-date organizational information of all the hospitals in the world. Once she found an open position in one of the hospitals in Parus, she applied for the job on Aix's behalf without the slightest hesitation. That was her right as leader of this unit; to apply for jobs on behalf of her employees without first asking their permission. She was doing the right thing now; it was extremely likely that Aix would get the position in question since his record was spotless. As for the motive to apply for the position in question, Mari added "doctor's personal wish to move from Gavialis to Parus."

Once she had saved the relevant information about Aix on the application form, she leaned back in her chair and closed her eyes. A slight smile appeared on her face. If Aix was still spying on her ID account, he would know about his departure soon. Mari couldn't help but feel malicious pleasure just thinking about it. Aix had been a fool to demean her. She forgot no one who ever tried to hold her down or rubbed her up the wrong way. Her next order of business now was to inform the maintenance department about the holes in their workstations' security protocols; if Aix had known how to get into her ID account, there were without doubt serious inadequacies in their safety protocols and information security policies.

Suddenly Mari's workstation sounded a signal. Mari opened her eyes and wondered if Aix had already noticed his upcoming transfer to Parus. She prepared herself to face the man's anger and opened the communication link. However, she saw Saia Motasilla's face on the screen; the girl who had also succeeded in accessing her personal files.

"Doctor Alauda," Saia greeted calmly.

"Saia," Mari said in turn.

"Is everything alright?"

Mari was surprised at Saia's unexpected question and was puzzled.

"Yes," Mari stated. "Why do you ask?"

"I ... forget it."

"What is it, Saia?" Mari asked the girl. This unexpected conversation between them also stirred her curiosity.

"It's nothing," Saia said and forced a smile on her face. "Have a nice day."

"Thank you ..."

Then the communication link between them was severed.

Mari was left to stare at her display without knowing what to think. The odd feeling inside her, which she had had ever since the meeting of the council management group, was getting stronger. Something was definitely wrong now. What had just happened? Or was there something happening right now? Why did she no longer feel in control? Mari hated that feeling. She had been fighting against it her entire life.

Suddenly Mari heard her workstation give another beep, and she looked at her screen and saw the new incoming message on her ID account. She activated the message by touching the screen with her index finger and read:

Parus? We'll see about that.

[Message sent by: Nivalis Aix -10.38.41-SGA]

"So, you're still keeping your eyes on my ID account," Mari said aloud. "And now I have proof of that."

Mari saved Aix's message on an external memory chip together with the application form she had composed on Aix's behalf. Then she ran a search for the contact information of the facility which manufactured artificial wombs. She was still not fully convinced that the reason for the loss of female fetuses was purely biological. It made absolutely no sense whatsoever and therefore it was crucially important that the womb manufacturing process was scrutinized as quickly as possible. They needed to be certain about the condition of these devices; the Health Council was seriously considering designating the next few years as XX years.

Suddenly Mari's display flickered and went off.

"What on earth ...?" Mari yelped and started to tap the data input feed panel, which was integrated into the table top.

Nothing happened. Mari huffed in frustration and kept tapping the input. She didn't know what else to do. Finally her display flashed. She was about to sigh in relief, until the following yellow text appeared against the black background:

Access to Komeion System denied

"Denied?" Mari wondered aloud.

Then her display was illuminated again. Mari followed the system reactivation carefully, expecting the error to be corrected. Then she realized she really did not have access to the Komeion System anymore, only to the general information network and the parts of her own ID account, which were not integrated to Komeion. Suddenly her workstation beeped again as it signaled an incoming message. Mari opened the connection and the Gavialis Main Hospital Chief appeared on her screen alongside Doctor Pika Adustus, a member of the Health Council's management group.

"Doctor Alauda," Adustus began.

"What is going on?" Mari asked him instead. "I'm not connected to Komeion System anymore. I can't access any of my files!"

"Doctor Alauda," Adustus repeated. "You have been temporarily removed from your position as doctor."

"Excuse me?" Mari asked him dumbfounded.

"A very serious accusation has been brought to the Health Council's attention."

"An accusation against me?"

"Yes."

"What is it about?"

"You are accused of the systematic elimination of female fetuses."

"Excuse me?!" Mari yelped and felt panic rising within her and twisting her heart.

"Substantial evidence has been brought to our attention which forces us to remove you from your office until we can investigate these accusations further."

"Let me guess," Mari said in a very low voice. "This accusation originated from Doctor Aix."

"I am not at liberty to discuss the ongoing investigation or any of its details," Adustus informed her. "I'm sure you understand that."

"And I am sure you understand, Doctor, that being suspected of this kind of conduct is more than enough to destroy my career!"

"Please be reassured that we are handling this issue most delicately."

"It is not enough!" Mari exclaimed. "I am being accused of breaking my oath! Even if I was proven innocent, my professional reputation among the leading doctors in the world will have been permanently and irreconcilably damaged!"

"Please calm down, Doctor," the man said calmly. "We are asking you not to leave this building until your escorts arrive to take you out."

"What?" Mari cried out.

She then heard the doors on the far side of her office being locked.

"You are locking me inside my own office?!" Mari yelped.

"I apologize, but the evidence against you is strong," the man said calmly. "We have called the police."

"Police?!" Mari yelped. "Why?! Are you going to officially accuse me of a crime?"

"The evidence suggests that there has been a crime committed. Unfortunately, I am not at liberty to discuss this issue further with you."

"Doctor Adustus!" Mari yelled, but the communication link between them had already been disconnected.

Mari got to her feet and walked to the window. She was scared now. She had never felt fear but now she was genuinely scared. The fear she was facing was real and serious. The police were involved. She would be charged with killing female fetuses. A crime didn't get much worse than that in today's world. Suddenly Mari remembered the five words she had read in a message a moment ago.

Parus? We'll see about that.

"Aix …" Mari whispered in rage. "You did this. You despicable cretin, you did this!"

Mari paced back and forth, deeply distressed. She didn't know what to do. She could have contacted her man, but what good would it do? Alauda would merely start wondering selfishly how this situation would affect his reputation and career. Mari couldn't blame him for that, though, they had always been similar in that way.

Mari slammed her fist against the window glass. She was trapped and she had no means of redressing the situation. Aix had engineered the whole thing. He had retaliated and made his threats real. Mari had not taken him seriously enough and this was the result of her over-confidence. The police were coming and she was about to be taken into custody for questioning. She was being accused of the biggest crime there was; the organized elimination of female fetuses.

Mari finally sat down again and activated her screen. She still had no access to the Komeion System as expected, so she opened the news headline ticker, since she didn't know what else to do. She browsed through the headlines without even noticing what they said; all her thoughts were still circling around the artificial womb room, the Health Council and its management group, Aix, and the police who were already coming for her. Then suddenly Mari saw something in the headline ticker which attracted her undivided attention. It was something most unexpected.

"I can't believe this …" Mari whispered and froze the headline ticker on her screen.

Doctor Mari Alauda charged with organized elimination of female fetuses – How will future generations survive?

It was obvious; Aix had leaked the accusations to the media, for there was no other way the news service could have known about this situation. Mari opened the news article and noticed from its publication data that it had been published online about five minutes ago. Despite its short life span,

871 readers had already commented on it. Seeing that figure hit hard. It made Mari finally realize just how serious her situation was. This was not about her career and status anymore; this was about her life. Before the police had even entered the Main Hospital to collect her, she had already been publicly condemned on the worldwide information network.

Mari didn't want to read the contents of the news article. She browsed the comments sections instead to see what people were thinking about the news. The words Doctor Death, Girl Butcher, and The First Lady of Cold Pit stood out from the endless lines of text.

Cold Pit.

Mari felt a cold wave sweep over her. She knew she would be thrown into Cold Pit because there was no court in the world that would find her not guilty, even if public opinion and the law were officially kept apart. Even if she was found not guilty, she was guilty in the eyes of the world. She had caused the shocking situation of the reduction in the number of girls, unknowingly and unintentionally. Therefore, she was guilty in the eyes of others and her crime was taking its first step along the path towards man's ultimate destruction.

Mari deactivated her screen. She felt more anguished than ever. She wanted to run away but she was imprisoned in her own office. How long would it be before the police arrived? What would happen then? How would she survive this?

There was a knock on the door. Mari snapped out of her reverie and began staring at the doors on the other side of the room. She waited, but nothing happened. Why didn't anything happen? Mari got to her feet and walked to the window. Then she took a deep breath and pressed her forehead against the cool glass. She looked down at the streets of the city where people were walking, free, then she finally heard the door opening behind her.

"What now?" she asked calmly.

"Doctor Alauda?"

Mari turned quickly, and saw Saia Motasilla entering the room. Mari couldn't believe her eyes. What was the girl doing here?

Mari sat down on her chair and tried to keep a calm, neutral expression on her face. She was Doctor Mari Alauda after all; a woman who did not break under any pressure, and she most definitely didn't want to tell Saia about the situation she was currently facing.

"Saia," Mari said and smiled. "I didn't expect to see you today. So what are you doing here?"

"You are in trouble," Saia said.

Mari didn't say a word. She was very surprised at what Saia had just said but was unable to find an explanation for it.

"Why have you come?" Mari asked her.

"Are you guilty?" Saia asked her instead.

"No," Mari said.

"I believe you."

"Why have you come?" Mari asked her again. "How did you know to come?"

"You have got to make a choice," Saia said.

"A choice?"

"You can either stay here to wait for either the police or a public lynching, or you can take a risk and come with me, but if you choose the latter, if you choose to leave this place, you have to leave now."

"Leave where?" Mari asked her and laughed.

Saia's words were making little sense to her.

"We don't have time," Saia reminded her. "So, you need to make your decision *now*. Are you staying or are you going to take a risk and leave with me?"

"How could I leave with you? To where?"

"Away from here," Saia said. "Out of this city. Into hiding."

"Where exactly? There is no place to hide, Saia."

"Are you going to stay or take a risk and leave?"

"If I really take the opportunity to leave, wouldn't that be read as an admission of guilt? I have never killed a female fetus in my life."

"This is no time to start analyzing!" Saia cried out. "The police will be here any minute now!"

"How do you know all this?" Mari asked her confused.

Then she stood up and walked across the room to Saia.

"Who are you?" she then asked her.

"Please don't analyze, don't consider realistic or logical options, or weigh up possible consequences. Just choose. Are you staying or going?"

Mari sighed in frustration. She didn't know what to do.

"I have a way out," Saia added. "If you choose to go, you must trust me enough to follow me."

"Saia ..."

"Please choose," the girl was practically begging. "Time is running out."

"How could I leave anywhere without anyone knowing about it? My Guardsman watches me continuously and so should yours."

"He is sleeping," Saia said.

"Sleeping?"

"He fell asleep over there on his chair."

"What do you mean?" Mari asked her slightly bemused.

"He fell asleep."

"How?" Mari asked the girl most seriously.

"I had some Gesnerin with me."

"What?!" Mari yelped.

Gesnerin was an extremely strong depressant, a drug girls like Saia should have no access to at all.

"He is sleeping now," Saia said. "And he didn't see my face. Look at my clothes, look at me! When he wakes up and the police ask him some serious questions, he will assume that I am a man."

"How did you get in here?" Mari asked her. "Where is your Guardsman?"

"I will tell you everything later, but right now we don't have time!" Saia reminded her in frustration.

"Why are you doing this? Don't you see you can get into deep trouble for this?"

"I know the risks!" Saia yelped. "But you must choose now to either leave with me or stay. Do you really want to stay when all the evidence against you is faked?"

"Alright, alright!" Mari gave in. "Against everything I know to be right, I will choose to get out of here."

"Okay."

Then the girl turned round and opened the door to the waiting room. She was obviously checking whether the route was clear and, after a few seconds, signaled Mari to follow. Mari didn't hesitate anymore; she needed to act now instead of thinking and she almost ran to the door. Once there she noticed the absence of her clerk, as well as an unknown Guardsman sitting sprawled on one of the chairs totally unaware of the rest of the world.

Saia stepped quickly out of Mari's office into the waiting room. Mari followed the girl but decided to make a quick stop by her Guardsman before anything else. Once she reached him, she leaned over his ear. He was still breathing, so when he woke up, his condition would return to normal relatively quickly.

"Thank you for all our years together," Mari whispered. "You have done a good job."

Then Mari turned round and left. She headed quickly towards Saia, who was already quite impatient. Mari was thankful. The girl had unexpectedly become Mari's only way out of the hospital without being escorted out by the police.

"What's going on?" Mari asked Saia. Everything that was happening around her felt too unreal. "How have you engineered all this?"

"I will tell you everything later, right now we have to go," Saia promised. "Now's the time to start running."

"My ID chip won't unlock the doors anymore," Mari pointed out. "I've been locked out of the Komeion System."

"All your rights to the system have been restored," Saia informed her.

"Are you serious?"

"I am," the girl said.

Saia turned left and started rushing towards the artificial womb room. Mari followed her, constantly fearing she would be caught. So far the corridors had been quiet, but that most likely wouldn't be the case for long. How many hospital personnel had already heard about her arrest order?

"How?" Mari asked Saia when she stepped next to the girl. "How did you manage to restore my rights?"

"I have my ways."

"The same ways which made it possible for you to hack into my ID account?"

"More or less," Saia admitted vaguely.

They arrived at the first locked doors. Mari pressed the lock with her index and middle fingers, which opened the doors immediately as if her rights had never been removed from the Komeion System in the first place. They almost ran through the door. Mari slowed down quickly, however, and tugged on Saia's sleeve in order to make the girl slow down as well.

"There are researchers here," Mari whispered. "Someone will see us."

"It's lunchtime," Saia reminded her quietly. "There shouldn't be that many people in these departments at this hour. This isn't the part of the hospital where you take patients in, is it?"

"It's not," Mari said.

Saia stopped.

"Open my backpack, please," she asked Mari.

Mari did as she was told and once she opened the backpack, she noticed that Saia was carrying a yellow outfit with her.

"The Yellow Guardsman's uniform?" Mari asked her puzzled.

"What?!" Saia responded in dismay. "Surely it's not the only thing in there?"

Mari continued digging around the backpack, until she whispered:

"Here are some other clothes as well."

"They should be ordinary men's clothes," Saia explained. "I told Lator to bring me some of his clothes, but I certainly did not ask for his uniform. I have no idea why he put it in there as well. Perhaps he did it without noticing."

"Lator?"

"Naja's personal Guardsman," Saia specified.

"How did you get him to give you his clothes?"

"Your daughter was foolish enough to tell me about certain things which Lator would definitely not want to be leaked in public."

"Has that little bitch let her Guardsman into her bed?" Mari asked Saia enraged.

"No," Saia said. "At least, not yet."

"She will destroy Lator's life, if that happens."

"That's Lator's problem," Saia said.

"Maybe so," Mari sighed.

"Quickly, Doctor Alauda," Saia then whispered. "When we get past all the locked doors, we must look like men. It is the only way for us to get out of the city. We must blend into the crowd and disappear."

"But how?" Mari wondered. "How can we pull this off?"

"We'll manage," Saia assured her. "Your fingerprints will open all the city station gates for next two hours, registering you in the systems as Mar Musca. So we have two hours to get out of Gavialis."

"Where to?"

"To the place where no one knows to look for us."

"But you don't have to ruin your life!" Mari hissed as she was putting the men clothes on.

"Ruin?! When I get out of this city, my life will finally begin."

"What are you talking about?!" Mari asked her as quietly as she could.

"Let's talk about it later," Saia suggested.

"I have to remove my ID chip," Mari said and hid her long dark hair under a cap.

"We need the chip to get out of the hospital doors," Saia said.

"But they can track my movements with it."

"Even if the data from the ID chip is stored in the Komeion System, the police can only use it to trace the door by which you leave the building, not where you go after that."

"So, when we are outside, I will cut it off."

"But then you will bleed," Saia said. "Shouldn't you remove it at a better time?"

"I have to remove it as soon as possible, there simply isn't any other way. If I am about go into hiding, I have to disappear without a trace. My ID chip can leave its fingerprint in the monitoring systems, when I move from one city circle to another, if some random individual station gate happens to scan ID chip signals."

"I didn't think of that in my haste," Saia confessed. "Stupid me."

"Don't worry," Mari said. "Your chip has recently been changed and because of your continuous complaining, its signal has been temporarily turned off. In fact, the time for your chip reprogramming has been booked for next week, if you didn't happen to know that."

"I know."

"The situation with my ID chip is an entirely different story," Mari whispered. "I'll remove the chip and leave it here. Good luck with tracing me then."

"How do you intend to do that?"

"We should pass a few supply rooms before we reach the exit doors. I will numb the muscle of my arm, cut the chip out and close the wound."

"And what about when the numbing effect disappears?"

"Then I will be in pain if I can't find any painkillers."

"Alright, but it's not safe to remain near this hospital building for a long time. The police will be here any minute now and they will realize almost immediately that you're gone."

"It shouldn't take long to remove the chip."

"Good."

"Why are you doing this?" Mari then asked Saia. "Why are you helping me?"

"You're innocent," Saia said.

"How do you know that?"

"I just know."

"What will happen to you, then?" Mari asked her.

"If we manage to escape from the city we will survive and we will be alright," Saia said. "You just have to trust me."

12.

Jani felt the train slowing down. It was a relief because even though Lu had been right when claiming that the train would not at any point accelerate to the speeds of normal passenger trains, travelling in an open wagon was still a very nerve-racking experience for Jani. Now all he could do was to wait and stay put, until he heard a whistle indicating that he should get up and come out.

Everything about the situation he was currently in was mind-boggling. Everything had changed after Lu's return and here he was now, sitting on a thin layer of fine rubble in an open wagon. He had been here by himself since they departed from Albedo towards the north of the area which couldn't be found on any of the official maps in the world.

They had left Gavialis by taking the J Train, which ran between Albedo and Fourth Corner Station, north. Once arrived at Albedo's Main Station, they stayed put, because neither one of them had access through the station gates like the men who worked in Albedo. Even the border guards patrolling Albedo borders remained outside the suburb border. According to Lu, the border guards took care of security at Albedo stations as well as keeping civilians out of the minefield which encircled the area, protecting it from unauthorized outsiders.

Albedo stations were closed environments. Exit was possible either by going through the station gates with the appropriate permission, or by taking the train back to the city. Only border guards and maintenance workers were authorized to step out of the station area boundary, but some people still ended up in the Albedo minefield, as Jani himself had read recently in the news. Men who had let their heads go saw the Albedo mines as being an excellent way to end their days. Men like that could even walk all the way to the minefields from Gavialis. That was a sign of determination, if nothing else.

When the J Train finally made its second stop on the northern side of Albedo, they got off and stayed in the station. They had not tried to obtain access to Albedo with their fingerprints at the station gates; this would have been futile. Instead, Lu had walked to a dark door, previously unnoticed, which was located on the eastern side of the station.

As expected, the door had been locked but Lu had unlocked it with his fingerprints. Once inside, they found themselves in a dark tunnel. Jani was glad to realize that the tunnel was unguarded. Unlocking the door required not only fingerprints, but also a signal received from Lu's ID chip; chips that all border guards carried in their arms. They had been lucky that no one else had entered the tunnel at the same time as they did.

When they had reached the other side of the tunnel, the first thing Jani noticed was a train with two carriages. The first carriage was for passengers but the other one was an open wagon. According to Lu, this open wagon was used to carry rubble to Albedo. That was the official explanation, anyway. In practice, there was no need to take rubble from the northern areas to Albedo.

Lu had taken Jani to the wagon and asked him to climb in and stay at the bottom with some pebbles. Jani had his doubts, but Lu had assured him he would be fine. Then he left Jani alone in order to report back to duty. Before they had left this secret part of the station in northern Albedo, Lu had quickly come by and told him that the trip to the northern area would last about ten minutes. The train wouldn't take them as far as the border, so after their arrival they would still have several kilometers to hike.

The train finally came to a standstill. Jani remained where he was, listening intently to a couple of border guards exchanging words next to the train. Like Lu, these men had come here to relieve other Guardsmen of their duty; Guardsmen who were patrolling a border Jani had not even known about only a short while ago. He had to remain hidden. It took about five minutes before he finally heard the whistle he had been waiting for. He peeked carefully down at the ground and saw Lu standing there alone and waving at him to come down. Jani was more than happy to do so.

"We are alone now?" Jani asked him quietly.

"Yep," Lu responded. "So, let's not waste any time. For now we can walk relatively freely, but as we get nearer the border, you will have to hide again for a moment as I relieve a guy from duty."

"Okay," Jani sighed and jumped down from the wagon.

He took a quick look around him. They had come to an area which was full of rocky, treeless ridges, an uninteresting place. The train which had brought them here, was the only indication of any human presence in the area apart from some footprints in the sand.

They headed north towards one of the ridges. Jani kept looking around him, and the silence of the area was deafening. He was yet again outside the city, even though he had never even really wanted to leave Gavialis. Yet he had to admit that an opportunity to meet two women intrigued him, even if he was still astounded at Lu and his attitude towards his current predicament. Lu was not, however, careless. He had forbidden him from even mentioning Lena in Gavialis, or on the trains they had taken to get out of the city. The topic was simply not open for discussion in public places.

They walked for quite a while without exchanging a single word. When they reached the rocky ridge on their path, they started to climb. Once at the top, Jani saw a vast forest on the other side.

"Oh, wow," Jani said.

"That's where we are heading," Lu said.

"And Terra Unionia is in there?"

"The border is," Lu said and took the first step down.

Jani followed him, and soon they reached the ground on the other side. Suddenly Jani realized he was walking among real trees. The size and the scent of them was something quite new for him; there were no trees in the city. There were some small areas inside Fifth Circle where bushes and a couple of trees grew, but Jani had never seen a forest like this before.

"I didn't expect this," Jani said.

"What?"

"A forest of this size. How much further does this go?"

"I don't know," Lu said. "I go as far as the border and stay there to patrol my area."

"Has this woman of yours told you about what's beyond the border?"

"The forest continues on their side as well," Lu said, "but not indefinitely. They have cities as well."

"As big as Gavialis?"

"No way," Lu said. "They have something like a million people living in their biggest city."

"No more than that?"

"No."

"So, there aren't that many of them."

"The population is around five million," Lu said.

"Of which the majority is women?"

"Yes."

"That's pretty incredible," Jani admitted. "Millions of women. Just think what would happen if the rest of the world knew about them."

"Nothing good would come of it," Lu said.

"I'm sure there would be men who would swarm across the border," Jani speculated.

"They could try," Lu said. "They would face the same fate as those who walked towards Albedo."

"Minefield?"

"Yes," Lu answered. "And an entire border guard authorized to use deadly force. Lena has told me that they are ready to defend their territory from outside infiltration until the very end."

"So, it seems they don't care much for guests," Jani noted.

"They want to be left alone and our policy is to keep them isolated. So I guess the current situation is okay for all parties involved."

"Which reminds me of how serious this situation of yours really is," Jani said.

"I'm sure life would be much easier if I had never met Lena," Lu admitted, "but at this point I don't want things easy. I want Lena and I want my child."

"And that's what I simply don't get," Jani confessed.

"I know," Lu noted, "but that's what I want."

Jani took a deep breath. He didn't want to start another debate on the topic of convincing Lu to see things otherwise because he knew it would lead nowhere. Lu was stubborn and completely blind when it came to the seriousness of his situation. He had decided that keeping in touch with this Unionian woman was a sane thing to do, and therefore Jani's counterarguments fell on deaf ears.

So Jani decided to say nothing as they hiked onward through the forest, where only a few men in the known world had before, and now Jani was one of them. The deeper into the forest they went, the more unreal it felt to Jani. The silence around him, as well as the thought of meeting human women, gave the moment a dream-like quality. Therefore, Jani had trouble understanding that everything around him was indeed quite real. He was really going to meet some women in the middle of a real forest; women who were not protected by Yellow Guardsmen ready to hurl them against trees if they simply dared to look at these women one second too long.

What bothered Jani was how he would talk to these women. So far he had talked to one woman only, a woman who was being called Doctor Death in the media. The discussion he had had with this particular woman had made him feel unsure and awkward. Perhaps for a good reason, though, if there was any truth in the news. However, the women they were about to meet at the border would be different, Jani assumed, because they were Terra Unionians. What were these people like? How would they differ from the rest of the people in the world? Would he even be able to see the difference in them, knowing nothing about women in the first place?

"I wonder what they are going to think of me," Jani said.

"What do you mean?"

"I was just wondering aloud."

"I don't think you will be a big deal for Lena," Lu guessed, "but I don't know what to expect from her sister. Lena wasn't expecting her news to make her sister happy in the slightest."

"I guess that's understandable."

"It is," Lu admitted. "I'm actually quite unsure of meeting this sister of hers myself. Even Lena herself was nervous about telling her sister about ... us."

"Did the thought of telling me make you nervous?" Jani asked him.

"I spent some considerable time thinking about how you would react to the news," Lu laughed. "I could never tell Talpa, though."

"The old man's heart would stop beating," Jani guessed.

"It probably would," Lu laughed. "He would never understand this."

"Not even with time?"

"He has supported and encouraged me so much because he wanted me to succeed so badly. He really wants me to do better in life than he has, and I know his heart is in the right place. This situation would be a total shock for him. It's better that he knows nothing of this; he would only see it as a failure."

"With good reason," Jani pointed out.

"I know. So I can't tell him about this, ever, but it doesn't matter; I can never bring Lena to Gavialis, anyway."

"So, are you really going to keep coming here for the rest of your life just to see her? What if you are transferred somewhere else?"

"I can't think about such things right now," Lu stated. "I need to focus on what is happening now and the time when our child is born. That's the reason you are here now, too."

"And I should know the right words to say to you in a situation like this?" Jani sighed.

"You see things from your own point of view," Lu said. "And Lena's sister sees things from hers. Maybe there's something there, something Lena and I have not yet considered. There's also the fact that the two of you are the only people in this world we can share this thing with. There's no one else."

Jani took a deep breath. He was glad that Lu trusted him enough to confide in him, but he didn't feel he was competent enough to council Lu and tell him how he should proceed. He was, after all, a man worth only 43 Silver Wing marks; a man from First Circle of Gavialis whose job was to monitor traffic in and out of Cold Pit. What on earth could he do to help Lu in a situation like this? It was simply much too big for him, he was out of his depth.

They walked for a while exchanging just a couple of words here and there. Gradually Jani started to lose interest in the never- ending trees around him. The forest was huge; maybe even bigger than Gavialis, which Jani still had a hard time believing. According to all official maps, they should already have arrived at a polluted wasteland, but instead of contaminated soil, the ground under his feet was quite green.

Jani was too exhausted to keep wondering about how green the grass under his feet was. Unlike Lu, he had not got used to walking this kind of distance. His daily exercise involved walking to the stations on paved streets. Here the terrain was hilly and uneven, which made walking unusually tiring for Jani.

Jani already thought about how he would return to Gavialis. How would they succeed? What if he got caught? The riskiest part was the ten-minute trip by train back to Albedo. If he could only get to Albedo's north station without being seen, he would most probably be safe. However, before that many things could go wrong, and before that he was going to meet some women.

He was going to meet some women. He, a man worth only 43 Silver Wing marks.

How had he ended up here? Who exactly was this Lena person? Was she taking advantage of Lu somehow? If so, what were her intentions? Jani had his doubts when it came to women; there was definitely something shady about them. It was said that women's behavior was often dubious to say the least. Even the most competent men were often unable to predict women's reactions. Yet Lu seemed to trust this Lena. Jani had no such liberty. He had to stay alert for Lu's benefit; he had to be the one now to keep an objective point of view.

Finally the moment came when Lu told Jani to stay where he was. Jani sat on the ground and was grateful for the break. However, at the same time he was more nervous than ever before about this secret excursion of theirs. The reason was obvious; Lu was about to meet another border guard, and therefore Jani had to remain still and quiet. No one in the Border Guard Detachment could know about his presence in this area.

Jani got down on the ground and he stayed there, waiting. He was full of anguish, for fear of getting caught. Lu had already gotten used to working in secrecy, but for Jani sneaking around like this was something new.

The silence around him started to feel uncomfortable. Jani didn't understand how Lu could spend day after day in the forest. For Jani, the silence in the control room was often too much to bear, yet he could actually leave the room once his shift was over. Lu, on the other hand, spent days here in the silence.

"Let's go," he heard suddenly, causing him to jump.

"Damn," he muttered.

"What?"

"You startled me."

"You didn't hear me coming?"

"No," Jani said. "I was deep in thought. You've found the other guy already?"

"I have."

"You have?"

"Yeah."

"That was fast. Or I am losing my sense of time in this forest?"

"It didn't take long to find him," Lu explained.

"Right."

"Now we will walk straight ahead for about one kilometer. We will make one stop before we get to the border, so I can hide some motion detectors nearby. There should not be any other guards within a good few kilometers' radius, excluding Terra Unionia of course, but for your sake I am being extra-cautious now. Hence the motion detectors."

"Okay," Jani said. "That doesn't much help abate my fear of getting caught, but I appreciate the effort."

"These motion detectors will tell us immediately if someone approaches the border," Lu explained. "But like I said; no one should be in this area on my watch but I am prepared for any eventuality today."

"So, the border is about one kilometer away?"

"A little bit further than that," Lu said, "but we are pretty close now."

"Right," Jani replied, getting increasingly anxious.

When they had walked for about ten minutes, Lu asked Jani to stand still again. Jani did as he was told and watched Lu as he ran away from him. He was in good physical shape; walking from the train to this location in the middle of the forest had not really slowed Lu down. In fact, Lu had most likely been trying to walk more slowly to help Jani keep up.

Jani wiped the sweat off his forehead and waited. What he was about to see at the border was making him more and more anxious. He hated not knowing what to expect, but he tried to keep himself under control. Only Lu could have dragged him into this madness. Not even the price of a ticket into Sixth Circle could have tempted him here. Jani took a durra roll out of his pocket, which he had saved for a while now.

"Damn you, Lu," Jani muttered, shaking his head.

The silence of the forest only fanned the flames of his restlessness. Each passing moment made him more and more aware of the fact that he did not belong here. His place was in the city where the air was filled with the noise of people and trains, and where men walked on paved streets. Here, the trees and the silence surrounded him and there was nothing else, until they met two women, unknown to the rest of the world.

Lu finally returned and Jani reluctantly got to his feet. The moment had come. They would finally reach this secret border to meet representatives of the female gender. Jani took a deep breath and tried to stay calm. He didn't want to make a nervous or ignorant impression. He was a man Lu trusted, so he had to act as calmly as Lu when they met this woman. Nevertheless, uncertainty regarding the new situation continued to torment Jani and he didn't feel like he was ready to face Terra Unionians just yet.

"Stop," Lu said, halting.

"What?"

"I'll check the border," Lu said.

"Are we there?"

Lu didn't respond.

They waited for a moment and Jani pinned his ears back to listen to the sounds of the forest. He heard nothing.

"They've arrived," Lu said quietly.

"Okay," Jani whispered, "this is it, then."

Then they started to walk ahead. Jani stared at the trees in front of him and waited. Finally he noticed two human beings appearing behind the trees, taking his breath away.

Women.

There really were human women coming out from behind those trees.

"Lena," Lu sighed and Jani saw a wide smile appear on his face.

Jani did not smile. His insecurity was beginning to get the better of him. What was he doing here? One look and those Terra Unionian women would see right through him. What they would see was a man who was less than Lu.

Jani noticed one of the women starting to make her way over to them. She was wearing a dark brown uniform and her hair was light brown. The woman was smiling almost as widely as Lu.

Jani remained behind. When Lu and the woman met, they locked each other in a tight embrace and started whispering to one another. The woman also laughed a little, at least Jani thought so. Jani watched the pair and felt nothing. He was an outside observer; Lu didn't even seem to be Lu anymore. Jani had never seen the man acting like this.

Jani took a quick look at the other woman who had also stayed behind. She seemed almost equally as lost, standing there under the trees. The woman was Lena's biological sister. Jani observed her carefully and wondered what she was thinking now. Finally he saw the woman turn away when Lu and his woman continued embracing. Perhaps she didn't like what she was seeing her sister do now and who could blame her?

"What took you so long?" Jani heard the woman ask Lu, and she pressed her cheek gently against his.

"I placed few motion detectors nearby," Lu said. "I wanted to be extra-cautious tonight."

The woman stared at Lu for a moment until they pressed their foreheads affectionally against each other. Jani was shocked. He had not known Lu was capable of behaving like that with a woman, or with anyone for that matter. But all these displays of affection seemed surprisingly easy for Lu. He didn't seem to be bothered by this woman without a Guardsman, or by her gender. Jani found it strange; he was still waiting for the Yellow Guardsman to come out of his hiding place somewhere nearby.

Jani took a deep breath. Finally he saw the woman let go of Lu. Then she took something from the pocket of her uniform and gave it to Lu.

"Look, Jani," Lu said, "an apple."

Jani took few steps forward to get closer to Lu and Lena. He still couldn't look directly at her. An apple? Was that the edible fruit growing in the wild, that Lu had talked about in Gavialis? Jani nodded and tried to smile. Lu took a bite of the apple then gave it to Jani. Jani explored the fruit with his fingers for a moment, looking at it suspiciously. It felt surprisingly hard. He smelled it carefully, until finally he decided to follow Lu's example and take a bite.

The fruit felt peculiar in his mouth. The taste was somewhat sharp, but also sweet. Despite the relatively hard exterior, the inner part of the fruit was easy to chew. And the more Jani chewed, the more there seemed to be some kind of liquid forming in his mouth. The experience was interesting and the taste good, even if it was a fruit that had been grown outdoors.

"Anamona?" he heard Lu's woman calling.

Then Lu stepped towards the other Terra Unionian woman who had not attempted to approach them. Jani didn't find that odd, because he didn't feel he was in the right place, either. However, he followed Lu who was about to meet Lena's biological sibling, and wondered what thoughts must be running round inside Lu's head right now.

They reached the lone woman and Jani couldn't help but stare. He could barely believe his own eyes; the passing moment felt so unreal. In front of him, just a few steps away, were two human women, and they both looked so petite. They were clearly older then the young girl he had seen in Sixth Circle. The other one also had longer hair than Lena and her skin looked very soft and smooth. Did all women have such smooth and soft-looking skin?

"Here's Lu," Lena said to her sister.

Lena's sister remained quiet and Jani could tell how unsure she was feeling. It wasn't surprising, because the situation was just as strange for him. He didn't know how to make conversation with women, either. The Apertum rights had never been within his reach, so learning about female behavior had not been part of his plans.

"Hi," Lu said.

"Hi," the woman responded quietly.

"And here is Lu's friend, Jani," Lena continued, looking at him.

All of a sudden the attention he was receiving made him lose the ability to speak. It was totally unexpected, since he had seen women before. Finally, Jani succeeded in raising his hand as a sign of greeting and the woman responded in a similar way to his gesture.

Lena and Lu whispered something to each other, before sitting down on the ground. Jani took a step back and sat down on the ground as well, as did Lena's sister. There was silence between them for a while, and Jani started to wish Lu would say something.

"So, how was it in that city of yours?" Lu asked Lena.

"Alright," she told him. "There was quite a lot to see."

"But you wanted to come back here nevertheless?" Lu asked her playfully.

"Of course," Lena said. "I can't image moving there, even though it is a nice place. And this is the best place in the world, you know?"

"Oh, I know," Lu whispered and gently touched Lena's cheek.

Jani was about to yell. When he was near this woman, Lu seemed like someone who had regressed to the level of a child. She kept staring at Lu as if he were some holy relic. Lu's behavior was strange, too; it seemed he was unable to take his hands off this woman even for a moment, and for some reason she didn't resist at all.

"We didn't have any problems getting out of the city, but I guess it is easier for us to come here than it is for you," the woman added.

"The biggest challenge was to get Jani out of the city," Lu joked and took a quick glance at Jani. "Isn't that so?"

Jani threw the apple he had been holding back to Lu. He tried to give a happy-go-lucky impression of himself, even though the moment was extremely forced and contrived for him.

"Is everything alright?" Lu asked Lena, pulling her next to him as he wrapped his arms around her.

"Everything is alright," the woman assured him.

"How long have you prepared to be here for this time?"

"I could stay here for days, but I don't think Anamona is willing to be here that long."

"That's understandable," Lu said.

"She's not usually this quiet," Lena whispered then and took Lu's hand in her own.

"I just don't know what to say," Lena's sister said. "What am I supposed to say now? Or feel?"

"Well, this is an unusual situation," Lu admitted. "I'm sure this must be playing terrible games with your minds, you and Jani."

Jani saw Anamona smiling, but there was no joy reflected in her eyes. It was quite clear for all that the moment was just as awkward for her as it was for himself. Lu and Lena had had time to get used to each other, but Jani and Lena's sister had not been given the same luxury. They didn't know what this was all about; they couldn't comprehend the interaction between Lu and Lena. Jani observed Anamona for a moment and he realized that there had been similar doubts in her mind as had been in his.

"This is stupid," Anamona finally said and Jani was pulled back from his private thoughts. "There's no sense in this whatsoever."

"I agree," Jani said without even thinking.

"This is all I've been hearing for past couple of days now," Lu explained to Lena.

"Me too," Lena said.

"You know the consequences if this become public knowledge," Jani reminded Lu.

He looked at both Lu and Lena. He saw the look in Lena's eyes get darker and he knew his words had been the cause of that, but Jani was not sorry for expressing his opinions. It was about time that these two were pulled from this illusion they had created back into reality to face the facts. Lena's sister agreeing with him was surprisingly encouraging and Jani took that as a good sign.

"But this is the situation nonetheless," Lena reminded them.

"I suppose you have some sort of plan or idea how you are going to proceed with this surprise child?"

"We haven't," Lena replied shortly. "Since that was the reason why we wanted the two of you to come here in the first place, as you very well know. Maybe we needed the support of those who are most important to us."

"Alright," the sister conceded, "but don't expect miracles, Lena. I really don't know how anyone could resolve a situation like this. No recommendations about what to do in a case like this exist."

Jani couldn't help but nod in agreement, surprising even himself. Lu was unable, and more to the point, unwilling to see the seriousness of his situation, therefore Jani found it comforting that there was at least someone in the world who understood his point of view, regardless of the fact that that someone happened to be a woman from Terra Unionia.

"Lu isn't even permitted to have a child," Jani said and looked at Lena's sister.

The woman looked directly into his eyes for the first time and Jani felt a sensation of understanding pass between them.

"Neither does Lena," Anamona said. "In our country Lena is expected to have children, but not like this."

"Anamona ..." Lena sighed.

"To have children, Lena should register on the official fertility program," she continued. "Her pregnancy should be registered because the child's biological father must be chosen carefully. Choosing the right genes is critical since there aren't that many men in our country. However, it seems that the time window to register this pregnancy has already closed."

"Father?" Jani murmured, and looked at Lu.

"It's their word for provider," Lu explained, "or guardian."

Jani nodded at Lu's words but using such a new term felt odd. A provider was a provider and a guardian was a guardian. The roles were very similar but there were also life instructors. Did Terra Unionians have a fourth role for a group of men who were raising children? Jani was confused.

"Provider and guardian?" Anamona asked them instead.

"Umm ... on our side a man who has succeeded in life earns permission to create a child of his own from his gametes," Lu explained. "If he chooses to do so he becomes a provider."

"And the child is always a boy," Jani added.

"What about girls, then? Who takes care of them?" Anamona asked them. "Surely they have this kind of provider as well?"

"Girls have life instructors of their own," Lu said, "who are, of course, women."

"Life instructors?" Anamona asked him.

"Life instructors are adult men and women who are responsible for a group of children in educational institutions," Lu explained. "They guide and teach the children and prepare them for adulthood."

"Ah," Anamona said, obviously still trying to figure out what she had just heard.

"However, if a man has made exceptional achievements in his life, gained a high position in society, for example, an opportunity opens for him to meet women personally," Lu added. "If a woman wants to commit herself to a man and they have children, a man becomes both a provider and a guardian."

"I still don't quite understand the difference between provider and guardian," Anamona confessed and it surprised Jani.

"The difference is whether the child has a mother or not," Lu explained.

Jani nodded.

"How can a child not have a mother?" Anamona asked him confused.

Jani was confused, too. How could all children have mothers? That was a question he would have liked to ask her, but he didn't want to start asking questions now; Lu should take care of the talking, which seemed to be surprisingly easy for him now.

"We have developed artificial womb technology," Lu said. "So, a significant number of children in the world are cultivated in an artificial womb without any participation of a human woman. A woman simply donates her eggs for this process."

Anamona's jaw dropped, and she stared at Lu for a moment, speechless. Then she looked at her sister. It was obvious how profoundly surprised she was. However, Jani was surprised at her being so surprised.

"How is that possible?" Anamona asked them.

Jani kept looking at the woman and was completely thrown by her genuine puzzlement.

"When there weren't that many women left in the world, people had to face up to reality and do something about it," Lu explained. "We had to develop technology able to imitate the womb of a human woman. Therefore, a significant number of children today are artificials, born in hospitals and brought up in educational institutions."

"The first artificial was a boy," Jani added.

"Pavo 000001?" Lu recalled and looked at Jani.

"That's what I'm thinking, too."

"Do children mature as normal human beings in these fake wombs?" Anamona asked them.

"Jani and I were both cultivated in an artificial womb," Lu said.

"Excuse me?" Anamona asked him.

"Believe it," Lena said to her sister. "It's true."

"I don't know what to say," Anamona said slightly amused, but there was also a hint of nervousness in her voice. "That sounds so unreal."

"It's understandable," Lu said, "but it's quite common for us. In fact, there are departments in every Main Hospital in each world city for these artificial wombs. It would be odd from our perspective if this weren't the case in some of our cities. "

"It would turn out to be a worldwide scandal," Jani said.

There were still traces of astonishment and disbelief visible in Anamona's face.

"That sounds like ... some fictitious story," she finally said.

"For us it's quite real," Lu replied.

"What do they look like, these artificial wombs?" she asked.

"They are about one meter long, oval shaped, closed devices," Lu described, "I think."

"You are right," Jani assured him, even though he had only ever seen them in pictures.

"So, you both had a provider, because you were born from these artificial wombs?" Anamona asked them.

"Lu has, I don't," Jani said.

"So ...?"

"Lu's provider, Mr. Talpa, is a man of many achievements. Therefore, he was awarded permission to procreate," Jani explained.

He felt quite silly explaining something so obvious, but he also felt unsure of himself telling the women that Lu had a provider when he didn't. It had never been an issue that artificials liked to talk about.

"He is not committed to a woman, though," Lu added. "He has not achieved enough to be allowed to meet women."

The woman stared at both Lu and Jani, expectantly.

"In other words, Lu has a father and his name," Lena said. "Lu's full name is Lu Talpa. The last name indicates whether a child has a provider or not. A provider is also a guardian, if a child has a mother in his life as well. However, Lu was cultivated in an artificial womb and therefore he doesn't have a mother."

"Ah," Anamona managed to say.

"I don't have a provider," Jani said. "So, I was brought up in an educational institution."

"So, you have had this instructor?" Anamona asked him.

"Yes," Jani said, "a life instructor."

"And instead of a last name you have ...?"

"An identity number."

"So, your full name is ...?"

"Jani 821771," he answered.

"That is really your name?" Anamona asked him genuinely confused.

"Yes."

"That is so odd," she said and looked at her sister, shaking her head slightly. "Why are motherless children being created in this world?"

"Because otherwise humans will become extinct," Lu said.

"Ah," Anamona answered.

"We really do need artificial wombs for this," Lu added.

"Pretty amazing, isn't it?" Lena said and smiled at her sister. "their system is so different from ours."

"Sounds like it," Anamona said quietly.

"On our side the main difference is that only mothers raise the children," Lena explained in turn. "And big families are valued."

Now Jani was the one who was surprised. Women were, of course, good at raising children, but hardly alone. They always raised their children with the men they were committed to.

"We have a similar situation," Lu said and Jani waited for him to continue. "Women are encouraged to make a commitment to a man and have as many children as possible."

Jani nodded in agreement.

"It's understandable," Lena said. "In our society women are not explicitly encouraged to have children, because it is taken for granted that everyone is heading in that direction. Motherhood is an integral part of adulthood for every woman."

"Is that so?" Lu asked her with a goofy smile on his face, and he pulled Lena tighter towards him.

Lena laughed and nuzzled Lu. Jani was completely baffled by the childlike behavior of the two. Even Lena's behavior seemed silly, despite the fact that he didn't know the woman personally. He still didn't know what to make of Lu, who was behaving as if he had been transformed into someone else under Jani's very eyes. It was easier for him to stare at the ground beneath his feet than to look at his friend.

"Shouldn't we be getting back to the original topic so that we can actually leave here at some point?" Jani asked the others, wanting Lu to remember why he had dragged him here in the first place.

"Alright," Lena said.

"I've been talking to Lu about this," Jani started. "He seems to be very committed to Lena and this child, which doesn't come as a surprise to me as I've known Lu for quite some time now. Despite Lu's feelings, it seems that the wisest course of action is to let this child be born on your side of the border."

"No," Anamona replied almost immediately and shook her head. "Like I said before, Lena's pregnancy is not registered. That is a problem."

"A problem?" Jani asked her skeptically; he suspected the woman was exaggerating. "Can't this registration be faked somehow?"

"No," Anamona said briefly.

"The fact remains that Lena is more bound to this child than Lu because of her gender alone," Jani pointed out. "For that reason, the birth should happen on your side. So you should resolve all the practicalities by yourselves because Lu and I are bound to our side of the border."

"Right," the sister noted sourly. "Sounds like you just want to push this entire thing onto our side of the border so that you can return home and forget this ever even happened. You have no idea, what kind of trouble Lena will be in for this."

Jani was getting frustrated.

"Are there any other options here?" he asked her. "Giving birth on our side …"

"I will never let Lena cross the border," Anamona informed him severely.

"Anamona …"Lena said, trying to calm her sister down.

"So, this child has to be born in Terra Unionia," Jani concluded and felt slightly better. "We are in agreement then."

Anamona took a deep breath.

"Alright," Lu said. "What problems will Lena face on your side exactly?"

"Her life will be ruined," Anamona told him briefly.

"So would Lu's, if this were exposed on our side," Jani pointed out. Jani didn't want the women to forget the seriousness of the situation for Lu, either. "What kind of problems would Lena face exactly? Lu would lose everything he has. He would most likely lose all his Silver Wing marks and he would be dropped from the city!"

"Why would it be so bad to live outside the city?" Anamona asked him.

"Why would it be so bad?" Jani replied, stunned. "There is *nothing* outside the city."

"What do you mean, nothing?" Anamona asked him.

All of a sudden both Lena and Lu hissed at them simultaneously, the signal to be silent. Jani forgot the debate they had just started and started listening to the sounds of the forest.

"What ...?" Anamona asked the others quietly.

Lena lifted her right index finger, indicating that they should be quiet. Jani watched both Lena and Lu and he realized the order to keep it down was not a good sign at all. What on earth was going on?

"We are no longer alone," Lu informed them quietly.

"What?!" he heard Anamona whispering to her sister.

Lena responded to her sister by lifting her index finger to her lips, the universal signal each of them understood. Jani and Anamona exchanged looks. She was scared; Jani could see that clearly from the look on her face. Jani felt charged as well. What would happen if they were found here? He would most likely be thrown out of the city and end up sitting on trains with Null 497 all day. Lu might keep his citizen status but he would most likely be cast out to First Circle at the speed of light. Of course, there was always the chance that they would be taken to Gaskar; fraternizing with Terra Unionians was something totally unheard of.

Jani took a deep breath. He should have known this. He had known that coming to the border had not been a good idea. Nothing ever happened to him without him facing problems in the process, he had seen that so many times before already.

"On the ground, now!" Lu suddenly hissed, "and don't move."

Jani practically threw himself on the ground and once there, he saw Anamona flat on the ground as well. Then both Lu and his woman started moving towards the pond nearby. They proceeded almost silently; impressive, had it not been for the sinister circumstances.

Lu and Lena started communicating with each other by exchanging hand signals. Jani couldn't make out exactly what messages were being sent to and fro between them but he was still hoping the two border guards would be able to deal with the situation as quickly as possible, and that no outsider would notice them here at the border. He was a civilian after all, who should not have known anything about Terra Unionia. Both his and Lu's lives would be ruined if word of this meeting got out, and seeing two human women in close proximity was definitely not worth that.

Lena and Lu rolled on the ground in opposite directions. Then they stopped and remained still in order to listen to the sounds echoing from the forest. Suddenly, Jani heard footsteps. He looked at Lu and noticed his woman lifting two fingers. Lu nodded. So there were two people approaching them, Jani concluded from the signals Lu and Lena were using. Since when had border guards patrolled in pairs? Didn't Lu always talk about being on duty alone? Jani continued to follow Lena and Lu carefully, and suddenly he noticed the two exchanging surprised looks. Lu said something to Lena and shook his head. Lena nodded.

Jani took a deep breath and waited. Finally he noticed Lena raising her thumb, then her index finger and finally her middle one. She had counted to three, but what for?

Suddenly Lena jumped to her feet and pointed her weapon towards the pond.

"STOP," she commanded loudly.

Jani was surprised. Why had Lena jumped up? Were there more Terra Unionians in these woods? Were Terra Unionian civilians allowed to walk here near the border? Or had more border guards from Terra Unionia appeared here? If that were the case, why would she point her weapon at them? Jani was overrun with questions.

"Who are you?" Lena demanded to know.

So the two new arrivals weren't border guards; she would have recognized her colleagues.

"Interesting," Jani heard next and the voice belonged to a man.

A man? Jani was really surprised now. What was going on?

"I asked you a question," Lena informed the man.

Silence.

"Answer me!" Lena ordered angrily.

"Who are the other three you are here with?" she was asked instead.

Jani took a deep breath. They had been exposed. Why had he said yes to Lu's request? What would happen now? It depended, of course, on who these people were. Would he and Lu have an opportunity to escape and hide now? Would Lu leave his woman behind? Even more questions.

"You're not asking questions, just answering them," Lena informed the stranger.

Suddenly Lu got to his feet. Jani was shocked, what was he doing? Why was he exposing himself voluntarily to these outsiders, whether they had seen all four of them or not?

"We almost missed you two," Lu said. "You have obviously learnt to avoid the border guards."

Silence. Jani did, however, continue listening to see what would happen next.

"Drop your suitcase and step back," he heard Lu demanding.

"Well, isn't this a surprise," a man said. "Both a Hirundian and a Terra Unionian border guard side by side. I didn't know the two countries had established diplomatic relations with each other."

"QUIET," Lu shouted. "I want to hear names now."

Jani took a quick look at Lena's sister, who had lifted her head from the underbrush to get a better view of them.

"He told you to state your names," Lena informed the strangers angrily. "So, let's hear them!"

No answer.

"Which side of the border do you belong to?" Lu demanded to know.

No answer.

"Which one?" Lena also demanded.

Now Jani really was surprised. Didn't Lu and Lena know who they were dealing with? What was going on?

"Who are you and what are you doing here with a woman?" Lena asked next.

Woman? Jani just kept getting more and more stunned. If there was a woman at the border, she had to be from Terra Unionia, because all the other women in the world were safe in the luxurious inner circles of the world cities.

Suddenly Jani noticed Anamona starting to drag herself closer to Lu and Lena. Jani watched her going and shook his head. He tried to signal to the woman to remain still, but she didn't seem interested in his warnings. Typical. Didn't they say that women often behaved in an illogical manner? Jani became annoyed by Anamona's irrationality. Didn't she realize she could make the current situation worse if she were discovered?

When Anamona had crawled a couple of meters, she stopped and lifted her head carefully. All Jani could do was to hope she wouldn't make any fatal moves.

"NAMES!" Lena demanded and the aggressiveness in her voice surprised Jani.

It was quite clear that no one messed with the woman. Finally Jani started to understand the situation Lu had faced when meeting Lena for the first time. Lu had not been joking when describing how serious it was.

Even though Lena had no Yellow Guardsmen near her, she seemed more than capable of taking care of herself.

Suddenly Lena's sister got to her feet. Jani was about to yelp, but it would have been pointless. Nothing was holding Anamona back anymore, because she had already stepped behind her sister. Jani pressed his head to the ground and sighed. He was the only one left who was still hiding. Why? Hadn't the man already said he knew there were four of them here?

Finally Jani stood up as well and he looked in Lu's direction. In addition to Lu, Lena, and Anamona, there were two other people here now; an older man and a woman. Jani looked at the new woman without knowing what to think. Another one, he noted. For all the years without a sight of a single woman, they had begun to pop up everywhere he looked. How was that possible? Who were these two who had arrived here?

Why did that black suitcase that the man was carrying seem so familiar to him?

13.

Both the man and the woman, who were considerably older than anyone in their little group of four, sat down calmly on the ground. They did so reluctantly, however, as Lena kept her weapon trained on them. Lu followed the situation attentively. He trusted Lena and knew she was more than capable of keeping these two civilians under control; the civilians who had appeared so unexpectedly at the border. However, controlling was one thing, getting rid of them was another. Lu was aware of the precariousness of the situation and this made him angry. He didn't like this sudden turn of events at all.

"Is this really necessary?" Lu heard Anamona asking Lena.

"It is," Lena told her briefly.

" Don't you know her?" Anamona asked her sister.

"No," Lena said. "Should I?"

"That's Tilia Linum," Anamona whispered.

"Who?" Lena asked her; a question to which Lu wanted an answer as well.

"She used to live next door to us in Avena when we were young. I met her in Pinus about a week ago."

Lena took another look at the woman who was sitting on the ground. The woman looked back and gave her a faint smile. Then she glanced at Anamona before looking back at Lena. Lu knew she was about to say something.

"So, you are from Terra Unionia," Lena said. "Have you forgotten that being on the border zone requires permission from the Border Guard. Show me your permission immediately."

But Tilia Linum and the man who was accompanying her didn't make a move, which spoke volumes as far as Lu was concerned.

"So, you haven't applied for permission nor has it been granted," Lena noted, "which does not surprise me, as border zone passes are granted only in exceptional cases and usually for research groups."

"We are a research group," the man informed her and Lu was surprised at his bare-faced insolence.

"You are not," Lena retorted, "because if you were, we would have a group of border guards here, assigned to escort you to the border for your own safety."

Lu knew that Lena was referring to the minefield, which circled Terra Unionia.

"Does *she* have her border zone permission?" the man sitting on the ground asked her and nodded towards Anamona.

Lu noticed the man's attitude a second time. He wasn't sure what he had been expecting from Terra Unionian men but it certainly was not the smugness he was now observing in the man sitting on the ground.

"You are Lena?" the woman, Tilia, asked her.

Lena didn't answer.

"This is Lena?" the woman asked Anamona now.

Lu glanced at Anamona and he noticed her hesitating. Finally she nodded.

"But what on earth are you doing here?" Tilia asked her.

"That's none of your business," Lena informed her. "Now, I want to see your border zone permission or we will leave immediately and I will escort you to the nearest border station. Civilians, who have intruded into the border zone without appropriate permission, are to be punished."

"I will show you my permission right after Anamona Vaal shows hers," the man informed her.

Lu took a deep breath and studied the man's face. He was defiant, even though he was in no position to be. Lu hoped the man would not provoke Lena too much.

"Border zone permission, please," Lena demanded, but still relatively calmly.

"Why are there two Hirundians here?" the man asked instead. "I'm seeing two Hirundians and two Terra Unionians. Imagine that."

The word Hirundian was still something Lu had not got used to, even though he had been aware of such a term's existence for months now.

"I demand to know how you two have managed to avoid the mines," Lena announced.

Tilia and the man exchanged quick looks, but neither of them spoke. Their silence triggered Lena to take three steps forward bringing her level with the pair.

"Here," Lena stated and extended her left arm in front of the man's eyes while her right still held her weapon.

"Excuse me?" Tilia asked her.

Lu followed the situation carefully. He still didn't feel the need to step in and support Lena; she had the situation under control.

"You two have a mine detector," Lena explained. "Don't even bother to deny it. I know you have one, or you would already have been sprayed all over these woods in small pieces. Hand it to me."

But the couple remained still and silent.

"I'm not asking again," Lena informed them. "Give the device here or …"

"Or what?" the man asked her.

Lu glared at the man. He was really starting to annoy Lu.

"Tilia," Anamona whispered and looked at the woman on the ground quite beseechingly.

Lu also looked at this woman called Tilia and he waited for the situation to be resolved. For now, Lena had managed with the two Unionians, but Lu was still prepared to step in at the first sign of trouble. He paid special attention to the man; his defiance promised no good.

Then he noticed Tilia take a deep breath and poked her male companion in the ribs. The man looked at Tilia for a moment and grunted under his breath before taking a small device from his pocket. He handed it to Lena, who took a step back and started studying the device while Lu continued watching the two strangers.

"What on earth is this thing?" Lena wondered as she fiddled with the odd-looking device in her hands. "Interesting."

Then she looked over her shoulder at Lu and threw the little device to him. Lu caught it and also studied it closely. The device reminded him of Lena's locator. There was a green dot blinking on its small screen, which was a hidden Unionian mine near the pond.

"I can't allow unauthorized civilians to wander around here," Lena began. "I'm sure you can understand that."

"But she is a civilian as well," Tilia pointed out and nodded towards Anamona.

"And what about these young Hirundian men, then?" the man asked her. "Who are they?"

"Their identities are none of your concern," Lena snapped.

"I disagree," the man said.

"I don't care what you think," Lena replied.

"As a Terra Unionian citizen I have the right to know why a border guard, who should be protecting our country, is allowing Hirundians to stray on our territory."

"Oh, be quiet," Lena retorted sourly, "no one here is interested in satisfying your curiosity."

"Is that so?"

"Lemmus," Tilia said and looked at the man pleadingly.

She obviously wanted Lemmus to stop. So Tilia was wiser than her male companion.

"I think it would be wise to stick to the relevant issues," Anamona said.

"I agree," Tilia responded and watched Anamona calmly.

"Anamona Vaal," Lemmus said and began to observe Lena's sister.

Lu got curious. The man knew Lena's sister? How could that be? Lu took a quick look at Anamona who appeared not to have even heard her name spoken. If she knew this man, why was she acting as if she didn't? He had, after all, told Lena that he knew Anamona and he had even announced her name to the others.

"You know him as well?" Lena asked her sister and by doing so gave words to Lu's private pondering.

"Unfortunately," Anamona sighed.

"Unfortunately?" the man yelped. "And I thought we were friends!"

Lu's confusion was deepening. Who was this man and how did he know Anamona? Was he a threat?

"What is our nice little lady from Avena doing here in the middle of this forest with two Hirundian men?" Lemmus asked her sarcastically. "I thought you didn't like men at all."

Lu looked at Anamona and saw the look on her face darken. The man was intentionally provoking her, so her facial expression was quite understandable.

"Quit being nosy," Lena told the man quite sharply after noticing the look on her sister's face.

"If you really are her sister," the man said and looked up at Lena, "I am really surprised."

"Your being surprised means nothing to me," Lena informed him rudely.

"Anamona," Tilia said. "You demand answers from us but surely we have the right to get some from you as well? Like us, you are also a civilian, so you being here is definitely an exception to official procedure. Your being here now is just as forbidden as ours."

"And what made you draw that conclusion?" Lena snapped.

"Like us, she is here without official permission," Tilia noted. "If she had it, she would have shown it to us by now."

"You assume too much," Lena snorted.

"I believe that's the case," Tilia said.

"And her being your sister doesn't really qualify as official border zone permission," Lemmus added. "So, it's my guess that every single one of us here is unauthorized, including those two Hirundian men."

Lena said nothing. She simply kept staring at Lemmus and Tilia from under her knotted eyebrows. Lu knew too that each one of them was aware that no one here tonight had come to the border on official or permitted business.

"What's in the suitcase?" Lena asked the man next, changing the subject.

"Cones," the man said.

"Right," Lena scoffed, "and I am a one hundred-year-old grandmother from Hirunda."

Lemmus looked at Lena blankly and shrugged his shoulders.

"Is the suitcase coming or going from the country?" Lena asked him.

The man still said nothing.

"Why are *you* here?" Tilia asked her. "Anamona?"

"Don't ask Anamona anything," Lena snapped. "She won't talk to you."

"Lena," Anamona said, trying to calm her sister down.

"Don't let her take advantage of you just because you happen to know each other."

"I used to know you, too," Tilia reminded Lena.

"Maybe so," Lena noted, "but I hardly remember you and right now I have no reason to trust you. You are a Terra Unionian woman who has been caught wandering round the border with a man."

"But you are here as well," Tilia pointed out. "And with Hirundian men."

"It's none of your business."

"But it is," Tilia replied, "because I am here as well. All six of us are here. So either we stay here for the rest of our lives demanding answers from each other, or we make a conscious decision to talk to each other openly."

"How can I know you will tell the truth?"

"We simply need to trust each other," Tilia stated.

"Right," Lena scoffed and rolled her eyes. "I don't believe anything that comes out of that man's mouth."

"Mine?" Lemmus asked her innocently, but with a sly smirk on his face.

Lena remained silent, but Lu could sense she was tense.

"Do you trust me?" Tilia asked Lena. "If I promise to tell you the truth, will you trust me?"

"I don't know," Lena told honestly. "I don't know you, either."

"But Anamona does," Tilia pointed out.

"Do you trust her, Anamona?" Lena asked her sister, without turning her face away from the pair.

"I don't know," Anamona sighed. "I don't know anything anymore."

Then Anamona sat down on the ground and took a deep breath. Her frustration was apparent even for Lu, even though he barely knew her.

"She doesn't trust you," Lena informed Tilia.

"And therefore all six of us are going to stay here to wait and see what will happen next?" Tilia asked her. "For how long? Days? Weeks? Months? I'm sure the Border Guard will eventually send out a search party for you when you fail to return."

Lu's memory of his first encounter with Lena came vividly to mind.

"She's right," Lu said and took a step towards Lena. "We have to resolve this. They shouldn't be here, but they are."

Lena took a quick look at Lu. She looked into his eyes and hoped that his proximity would give her the strength to remain patient.

"I agree," Tilia said. "And we must remember, despite our suspicions and doubts, the practical level of things here. If I returned home and told people about what I have seen here, how could I do that without revealing myself? So yes, I confess; I don't have border zone permission, neither of us has, therefore I have no reason whatsoever to tell anyone about what I have seen here; I would gain nothing from informing the authorities about you."

"That's true," Lu said.

Then he looked at Lena and nodded in assurance that the situation was still under control.

Lena sighed and finally lowered her weapon.

"Thank you," Tilia said.

Lena looked at the woman and nodded.

Lu observed Tilia who had remained calm the entire time. Her calmness was quite astonishing for him.

"So, would you like to tell us why you are here?" Tilia asked Lena.

"We wouldn't," Lena informed her.

"Yet you demand an explanation why we are here," Tilia pointed out.

"I am a border guard," Lena reminded them. "It's my business to know such things."

"Is it?" Lemmus asked her, "because, even if you are a border guard, you have broken your oath many times now. First, your sister is here without official permission and second, you are fraternizing with enemies of the state."

"It doesn't obligate me to tell *you* why we are here," Lena replied.

"So, do *we* have to tell you the reason for *our* presence here just because *you* happen to carry a gun?" the man demanded. Lu didn't like his tone of voice at all.

"If you want answers, we have to start trusting each other," Tilia pointed out. "This would mean all of us telling each other what we are doing here."

"Fine," Lena said. "We won't tell each other why we are here."

Tilia looked at Lena, astonished.

"But I will confiscate that black suitcase of yours," Lena told them.

"I won't allow it," the man informed her.

"I'm not asking your permission."

"You aren't authorized to confiscate this suitcase."

"Oh, I am," Lena answered.

Lemmus was holding the suitcase even more tightly, but Lena lifted her gun and took aim.

"Lena!" Anamona exclaimed afraid.

"Give it to me," Lena demanded.

"Not going to happen," the man mocked.

"Ah, the suitcase is important enough for you to guard it with your life?"

"So it would seem," Lemmus stated.

Lu's patience had also run out. He took his weapon and like Lena, aimed it at the man.

"You too?" the man asked him and looked at Lu.

"A Terra Unionian border guard asked for your suitcase," Lu stated.

"Stop it!" Anamona exclaimed. "We are here to find a solution to our situation, not make it worse."

"Anamona!" Lena hissed at her sister's sudden outburst.

Tilia looked at Anamona, then Lena.

"Tilia and Lu are right," Anamona said to her sister. "We must trust each other if we are ever going to go back home. That's what you did with Lu back then."

"Lu? And that would be you, then?" Tilia asked him and looked straight into Lu's straight eyes.

Lu didn't answer or even look at the woman. He was too focused on Lemmus who had a very suspicious air about him. If the man threatened Lena in any way, he was ready to shoot.

"Lower your weapons," Tilia implored, "please."

"Lena ..." Anamona said and took a step towards to her sister. "That black suitcase can't be worth a human life."

"He's ready to die for it," Lena said. "So, it must be valuable."

"But are you ready to kill for it?" Anamona asked her. "You don't even know what's in it!"

"We should resolve this situation without violence," Tilia said. "Lena, please, put down your gun."

Lena stared at the woman for a moment, then she suddenly complied. She lowered her right arm and let it hang next to her thigh, Tilia was visibly relieved. Lu also lowered his weapon. He trusted Lena's assessment of the situation.

"They still don't need to know everything about us," Lena reminded her sister.

"I agree," Anamona replied.

"So, are we obliged to say everything?" Lemmus asked her. "You already have my device, so we can't cross the minefield without you. Are you asking for this suitcase as well?"

"Possibly," Lena stated.

"Then we demand to know why the four of you are here," the man informed Lena.

"Lena asked me to come here," Anamona suddenly said. "And that's the reason why I am here. That's why Lu is here with his friend."

Lu took a deep breath. Anamona had opened a real dialogue now, but luckily without revealing too much.

"How is this possible?" Tilia asked them amazed. "Two Hirundians and two Terra Unionions?"

"I've learnt today that there are many things in this world which are possible, no matter how impossible they first seemed," Anamona sighed and Lu wondered what exactly she meant.

She didn't like Lu. Perhaps it was because she was so protective of Lena, something Lu could both understand and accept. However, he remained hopeful that Anamona's negativity towards him wouldn't make Lena doubt the strength of their emotions.

"Your appearance here is most unfortunate," Lena said. "Only we four were meant to be here tonight, but now we have four Terra Unionions and two Hirundians instead and frankly, I wasn't expecting this evening to turn into a major conference of the two nationalities."

"But this is wonderful," Tilia said and her face was beaming.

"Wonderful?" Lena asked the woman, confused, and Lu was also quite surprised by her choice of words.

"Well, isn't it?"

"In what sense?" Lena asked her.

"You have cracked the border," Tilia said.

Lu looked at the woman in confusion.

"You're talking and listening to each other," Tilia added. "Don't you see how amazing that is?"

"Amazing?" Anamona asked her and shook her head.

"Well, how can it be anything but amazing?" Tilia asked her.

"I don't even know what this is," Anamona replied, frustration audible in her voice.

"This is a catastrophe," Lena sighed. "That's what this is."

"And that's why I am worried," Anamona said.

"You are worried because you always worry about everything," Lena said.

"And you're not worried about this at all?" Anamona asked her sister. "Tilia and that man found this place. How can we know for sure we won't get caught when we get back?"

"How could we get caught?" Lena asked Anamona instead. "I won't tell anyone about this. If someone lets the authorities know about this, it will be one of those two, most likely him."

"Me?" Lemmus asked her. "What could possibly motivate me to tell anyone about this?"

"How should I know?" Lena asked him, "but there is something really odd and shady about you."

Lu nodded at Lena's words. He totally agreed with her.

"Huh?" the man said, but Lu could not gauge how genuine his confusion really was.

"Who could he tell?" Tilia asked Lena. "Lemmus would most likely get into much more serious trouble than Anamona or I would if this were revealed in Terra Unionia."

"Why?" Lu asked her. Lena had never really told him much about Terra Unionian men.

"Because I am a man," Lemmus said.

"And you are bound to different laws?" Lu asked him.

"The law is the same for all," Lemmus stated, "but in some cases men don't receive the same degree of understanding as women often do."

Lu looked at Jani for the first time since the arrival of the Unionians. Jani returned his look and there was confusion in his eyes, confusion he had been feeling for some time.

Then Lena sat down on the ground next to her sister. The tension, which had floated upon all of them, started to dissipate. Lu decided to follow Lena's example and he too sat down next to her. He could still sense the tension in her, so he put his hand on her back and hoped his touch would somewhat calm her nerves.

"Oh, I see," Lu heard Lemmus then noting. "The two of you are lovers."

"What?" Tilia asked him dumbfounded.

Lu glared at the man from beneath his eyebrows. He simply didn't understand how to keep his nose out of other people's business. Lena huffed and shook her head.

"Now I can say, in complete honesty, that I am *very* surprised," Lemmus informed them. "More surprised than I have ever been during the last twenty-seven years, but this explains nicely why there are both Terra Unionians and Hirundians here right now."

"Why twenty-seven?" Lena asked him instead.

"Oh, nothing," Lemmus laughed.

"Why twenty-seven exactly?" Lena asked him again. "If you want me to trust you even just a little, you have to be able to answer a simple question like that."

"He doesn't have to say," Anamona said. "Let him tell us what's in the suitcase instead."

Lu glanced at Anamona and wondered why she had suddenly taken Lemmus' side.

"But I want to know," Lena stated.

"I will tell you later," Anamona said and glanced in turn at Lemmus.

Lu couldn't help wondering what exactly Anamona knew about Lemmus. It was quite obvious it was something she didn't want to bring up publicly. Lu was beginning to become suspicious of Anamona. He loved Lena, but her sister's furtiveness was making him wonder. He could only hope Lena had been right about Anamona and her trustworthiness.

"I don't see why we can't tell the truth," Tilia said and surprised them all.

Lu looked at the woman and waited for her to continue.

"So?" Lena asked her.

"Lemmus is Hirundian," Anamona informed them. "He has been living in Terra Unionia for over twenty seven years now."

Lu couldn't believe his own ears.

"Defector?!" he yelped.

He remembered the moment he had met Lena for the first time. Even then Lena had hinted at the possibility of defectors, which had been extremely offensive to his ears. Lena had retracted her words, which had been enough for him at the time but now he realized Lena had been right after all. Lemmus had crossed the border into Terra Unionia and Lu didn't know what to think about it. He looked at Jani again and noticed the shock on his face.

"So, now that the truth is out, Mr. Lemmus may very well tell us what he has got in his suitcase," Anamona continued.

"You know you are much more cunning than you appear," Lemmus said and looked at Anamona.

Anamona shrugged her shoulders. Lu stared at the defector and noticed a faint smirk. The man obviously had some unfinished business with Anamona. He had no idea what it was about, neither did he want to speculate on it further. He was still coming to terms with the fact that the man was a defector.

"We weren't supposed to end up here at all," Tilia explained. "We got lost."

"You got lost?" Lena asked her. "Now why does that sound like a lie?"

"Because you have decided not to trust us," Lemmus suggested.

"Maybe," Lena confessed.

Lu would have said the same thing himself.

"Is the suitcase going into Terra Unionia or coming out?" Lu asked them.

"It's going to Terra Unionia," Tilia said.

"But it originated from Hirunda?" Lena asked her.

"Yes," Tilia answered.

"Smuggling," Lena noted and sighed.

"I didn't know there were goods crossing the border," Lu stated.

"It's news to me, too," Lena said.

"And I didn't know border guards patrolling here spend their duty-time kissing each other," Lemmus informed them.

Lu was running of patience. He was close to shouting a few well-chosen words at the defector, when he suddenly felt Lena place her hand on his arm. Her touch was a signal to calm down and it also had the power. Instead of shouting, he took a deep breath and contained himself. However, he could not forget the defector. If the man had crossed the border he had to be a criminal. Other than a trial, sentencing, and being thrown into prison, what else would have motivated him to hide in Terra Unionia? Lu decided to stay close to Lena, just to be sure.

"What's in the suitcase?" Lena asked the man again.

"Actually we don't know," Tilia said instead.

"You don't know?" Lena asked her. "Right."

"We haven't opened it yet," Tilia added.

"Then we can open it together," Lu said.

Tilia and Lemmus exchanged looks. Then they leaned over to each other and whispered something. Lu kept his eyes closely on them.

"Very well," Tilia said.

"You'll open it?" Lena asked her surprised.

"Only if you tell us why all four of you are here exactly," Lemmus said. "And especially why Anamona and that other Hirundian man are here."

Lu waited for someone to say something.

"Alright," Lena then agreed, against the expectations of all the others.

Lu looked at Lena to see if she was serious.

"You really agree to these terms?" Lemmus asked her quite surprised and Lu wanted to hear the answer as well.

"I do," Lena assured him.

"Why does it feel like I shouldn't trust you?" Lemmus asked her and there was a suspicious look in his eyes.

"Maybe you should avoid asking questions like that now when we have obviously made some progress," Tilia pointed out quietly.

Lemmus looked at the woman and nodded.

"So?" Lena asked them.

"I come to the border a couple of times a year when I receive a message about a delivery like this," Lemmus explained and showed the black suitcase in his hand.

"Delivery?" Lena asked him.

"It's about small things," Lemmus said, "mostly artifacts which are not popular in either Terra Unionia or Hirunda."

"What artifacts?" Anamona asked him.

"Artifacts from the time before the Great War," Lemmus said.

"What?" Jani, who had remained silent for some time now, wondered.

Lu glanced at Jani and noticed a look in his eyes he couldn't identify. Jani was surprised, that much was clear, but why he had reacted so strongly to the issue was beyond Lu's immediate comprehension.

"Anamona," Tilia said. "When you visited me on your first day in Pinus, we had a cup of tea."

"Yes?"

"Those tea cups we drank from ..."

"Are from the time before the Great War?" Anamona asked her surprised. "You got them from Hirunda's side of the border?"

Tilia nodded.

"Unbelievable," Anamona said. "There was not a single crack in them."

Tilia smiled. Then she looked at Lemmus, apparently waiting for him to continue.

"There are men in Hirunda who share our passion for studying the times before the Great War," the man explained.

"Why would anyone want to know anything about that time?" Lu asked her, "I can't imagine how anyone could be interested in that era at all. Isn't it enough that we know the war happened and that mankind learnt its lesson from it?"

"It seems to be enough for most of the human population today," Lemmus admitted.

"But not for you," Lena noted.

"This era of world peace is, of course, the most important thing there is," Tilia noted, "but I can't help but wonder why this world is the way it is today."

"I'm interested in history," Lemmus stated. "Tilia too. I find history absolutely fascinating. They don't teach that subject in Hirunda and as you may well know, it's not discussed in depth on our side of the border, either."

"I think it's important for all of us to know where we have come from so that we can really know who we are right now," Tilia added. "We don't think history should be concealed just because it's been a bloody one. We have to learn from it or we as a race won't evolve."

"But we have evolved," Lu noted. "We've evolved tremendously."

"That I don't deny," Lemmus said, "but if we know nothing about our past, how can we be sure the progress we are making now is heading in a sensible direction? We simply can't!"

"Our past is derided and even despised for nothing," Tilia said. "The years of the Great War obviously constitute one of the darkest eras of this world, but that doesn't mean that there wasn't anything good in the past as well."

"Like what?" Lena asked her.

"That's what we want to find out," Tilia stated, "and during the years Lemmus and I have been working on this, we have found out a lot, including details about the time when Terra Unionia and Hirunda were still one."

"I still don't quite understand why," Lena said.

"Me neither," Anamona confessed.

"You're not at all curious about why the world is the way it is today?" Tilia asked her. "You're not interested in the reasons why Terra Unionia and Hirunda are two separate nations?"

"Are they separate?" Jani asked her.

"That is a very good question," Tilia said. "And the answer to it depends on which side of this border we are."

"Which reminds me," Lemmus said, "which side of the border are we on now exactly?"

"On Terra Unionia's, obviously," Tilia said and smiled as she looked at Lemmus.

"If that's the case, why are there two Hirundians on this side?" Lemmus asked her. "And our Miss Border Guard Vaal is not amazed by it at all."

"We're not on either side," Lena informed them. "Or we are in a place which belongs to both sides."

"Say that again?" Lemmus asked her confused.

Lena and Lu exchanged looks and Lena's facial expression softened in amusement. Lu knew she was thinking about the day they had met for the first time.

"How is it possible?" Tilia asked them.

"Lu and I met here by accident," Lena said, "and when we finally started to trust each other enough to exchange our maps, we noticed they were different."

"In what way?" Tilia asked her, even though she must have guessed the answer already.

"The border," Lena continued. "On my map, on Terra Unionia's official map, the border is located a couple of hundred meters further south than on Lu's map."

"Interesting," Lemmus noted briefly.

"So, you decided to trust each other and exchange maps instead of shooting each other," Tilia concluded.

"It took hours," Lena said. "Days even."

"I'm very impressed nonetheless," Tilia confessed. "You both are trained in a certain way and I can already imagine the education about Hirundians that Lena was fed during her training."

"The enemy," Lu said.

"So, you know," Tilia noted.

"Lena has told me."

"I am proud of you," Tilia said, "that you really made the choice to talk instead of killing."

"Curiosity had something to do with it as well," Lena said and laughed.

"Curiosity?" Tilia asked her, grinning.

"I had never seen a human woman at such close proximity as I did on that day," Lu explained.

"I can believe that," Lemmus stated.

"And I hadn't seen a human man," Lena added.

"When did all of this happen?" Tilia asked them.

"About three months ago," Lena said.

"Amazing," Tilia said, "absolutely amazing."

"Indeed," Lemmus noted, "to be honest, I never believed that I would one day witness something like this in my own lifetime."

"Me neither," Tilia confessed. "Hirundians and Terra Unionians interacting with each other … this is fantastic!"

"This is a crime," Lena stated.

"But you keep breaking the law because you are in love with him," Lemmus pointed out.

Lena didn't answer and Lu tried to keep a cool exterior as well. Their love was no business of outsiders, particularly that defector.

"It's quite obvious so you don't have to deny or admit it," Lemmus added.

"Fantastic," Tilia said again.

Anamona, however, huffed in frustration.

"Ah," Lemmus noted. "The sister here isn't the most understanding sort."

Lu glanced at Anamona and saw from the look on her face that the defector had been right. Anamona was just like Jani; doubtful of him and Lena. Lu knew it was only natural, nonetheless it was still frustrating.

"She'll get used to the idea," Lemmus added.

"And what do you know about that?" Anamona snapped.

"Oh, I know a lot," Lemmus informed her. "I've lived in both Hirunda and Terra Unionia after all. Which reminds me; do Hirundian women still live in the inner parts of the cities?"

"Of course," Lu replied briefly, not interested in a profound discussion with the man.

"Well, of course," Lemmus said. "Are you both from Gavialis? It is the nearest city from here after all."

Jani nodded and Lu as well.

"What kind of place is this Gavialis?" Anamona asked them.

"Gavialis is the capital city of Hirunda," Lemmus said. "It means that the World Council is assembled in Gavialis."

"It's the biggest city in the world," Jani continued. "You can't tell from one side of the city where the other side is because it looks like it goes on forever, and the buildings, especially in the inner circles, are enormous both in width and height. There are people all around you and wherever you are, you can hear the sound of traffic and people. That's why the silence of this place is so odd for me."

Anamona nodded.

"You feel so proud walking the streets of Gavialis where you can see what mankind has accomplished," Jani added, "the huge buildings known all over the world make you feel so proud. This is the case especially in the inner circles."

"Circles?" Anamona asked him.

"Gavialis is built in the shape of a heptagon," Lemmus explained. "So, when observed from the air, it looks like a perfect heptagon. The city is divided into seven circles. The inner circles are considered more precious than the outer ones so all those huge buildings we already mentioned as well as all the latest technology can be found in the inner circles. When I was still in Hirunda, the population of Gavialis was around twenty million."

"Twenty million?" Anamona asked him and her jaw dropped.

"It's so much more than the entire population of Terra Unionia," Lena said.

"Unbelievable," Anamona said and stared at the ground, her eyes wide open.

"How many people live there now?" Tilia asked them watching both Lu and Jani.

"It's about the same," Jani said.

"And there are equally big cities elsewhere in Hirunda as well?" Anamona asked them.

Lu could see that Anamona found exactly the same things astonishing as Lena had done a couple of months ago, when they had begun to tell each other more about their countries.

"The world population is clustered into big cities all over the world," Lu explained in a relaxed manner. "The cities in the south are located on the better side of the Capricorn tropic and the cities in the north on the better side of the Cancer tropic. We also have two ocean cities, but they are considerably smaller."

"Ocean cities?" Anamona asked him.

"One on the Great Sea, the other on the Blue Sea," Lu said. "They were originally built for research purposes, but nowadays they each have a few thousand people living on them."

Anamona listened carefully and Lu could tell she was struggling to take it all in.

"Well, I knew that Hirunda was bigger than Terra Unionia," she said, "but I never fully realized how many people there really are out there."

"How could have we known?" Lena asked her. "We haven't been told about Hirunda in our learners' circles at all. No one talks about Hirunda unless the topic is protecting our environment or guarding against invasion."

"Lena is right," Tilia said. "Hirunda is not talked about on our side of the border. The little we talk about it is usually very negative."

"That's one way of keeping the curious ones away from the border zone," Lemmus commented.

"Did you visit Gavialis often when you lived in Hirunda?" Tilia asked Lemmus.

"Maybe a couple of times a year," Lemmus said.

"Where are you from then?" Lu asked him.

"I've lived in many places but I was born in Erasmia," Lemmus said.

Lu nodded. He knew very well where Erasmia was, even though he had never visited the city himself.

"How far away is Gavialis from here?" Anamona asked him.

"It's surprisingly near," Lemmus said, "maybe sixty, seventy kilometers away?"

Anamona nodded and began thinking about what she had just been told.

"What are you thinking about?" Lena asked her as she noticed the distant look on her sister's face.

"About never being able to see any pictures of Gavialis," Anamona said. "We have no pictures of the world beyond this border."

"That's surprising," Lena said. "Just yesterday you didn't want to know anything about Hirunda."

"There are many things I didn't know yesterday," Anamona pointed out.

"I can bring Lena few pictures, if you want," Lu offered.

It was quite apparent that Anamona genuinely surprised by Lu's offer, which Lu took as an encouraging sign. If bringing pictures of Gavialis would help this woman to like him a little more, he would bring all the pictures he could get his hands on. He would do anything to make Anamona see him in more positive light.

"Is it true that most land masses on this planet are contaminated?" Anamona asked them.

"A significant part, yes," Lu said.

"Some of the land is useless because of the Great War," Lemmus added, "some because of the extreme weather. The land masses on both sides of the equator are mostly inhabitable because of floods or desertification which stretch to the tropics and beyond. So the world population is clustered together in the cities, connected to each other via a network of trains and aviation."

"But if I continued south from here on foot, I wouldn't die because of environmental toxins?" Anamona asked them.

Lu and Jani exchanged looks. Lu was amused at Anamona's peculiar question.

"You wouldn't," he finally said.

"I don't see what was so amusing about my question," Anamona snapped.

Her sharp tone of voice surprised everyone but most surprised was Lu who sensed he had messed up.

"Your question caught me off guard," Lu said calmly, "that's all."

"I suppose Hirundians believe strange things about us too?" Tilia asked them. Lu was relieved by her attempt to steer their conversation towards another topic.

"As a matter of fact, yes." Lena laughed. "On our first days here Lu asked me if Terra Unionian women really cut off their breasts to be genderless."

"Really?" Tilia asked her and laughed.

Lu was suddenly embarrassed.

"Some border guards have said they've seen women like that beyond the border," he explained. "We take talk like that for urban legends but of course some men keep speculating."

"It was so amusing," Lena laughed. "I mean when he tried so discreetly to observe my chest. Finally *I* had to ask *him* what it was all about."

"She thought I was going to ask her to remove her clothes," Lu added. He too laughed at the memory of the situation.

"I never expected to have an assumption like that," Lena said.

"Well, our border guards have been told all kinds of stories about Terra Unionia," Lu explained, "So, it's easy for us to believe almost any story involving women. Over these past few weeks I have learnt that most of the talk is either completely fictional or at best an exaggeration."

"Not to mention the fact that the men patrolling this border are told that we are a crazy bunch of fanatics with mental issues," Lena added.

"It's an effective way to keep men on our side of the border. You do the same by calling us a military enemy."

"That's true," Lena said.

"And that is exactly the reason why I told you earlier that I was proud of you," Tilia said. "The fact that you started talking to each other instead of firing your weapons is a far greater accomplishment than either one of you can possibly imagine."

Suddenly Lu was on the alert. He took a small data receiver out of his pocket, a device carried by all Guardsmen equipped with motion detectors.

"What is it?" Lena asked him.

Lu looked worriedly at the small screen.

"Someone's approaching the border," he said and got to his feet.

"What?!" Lena exclaimed.

"Yep ... there's definitely some movement in the border zone," Lu informed them.

"On Hirunda's side?"

Lu nodded.

"Someone has activated the motion detector," he added.

"Distance?" Lena asked him as she got to her feet, too.

"Approximately seven hundred meters," Lu said and showed Lena the device in his hand. "The target is moving southwest."

"That's close," Lena huffed and shook her head.

"Defector?" Jani asked him quietly.

"Possibly," Lu stated.

"What now?" Anamona asked him.

"The three of you will withdraw into Terra Unionia territory," Lena told Anamona, Tilia, and Lemmus and beckoned the group to stand up.

"And I'll stay here alone?" Jani asked him, confused.

"Wait here, all of you," Lu said. "We may very well get out of this situation without anyone noticing. The distance between us and the target is still far enough. I will go and check the situation out and hopefully guide this person to another route. You must remain silent and as still as you possibly can."

"Alright," Lena said.

Lu nodded and left. He headed briskly southwards and did not stop running until he was about a hundred meters away from the others. He looked back and was relieved when he couldn't see Lena and the others anymore. Then he checked the direction from his data receiver and noticed his target moving in direction two six four. In other words, the intruder was to the west.

Lu kept running. He wanted to reach the target before it went beyond his reach on the other side of the border. If the target really was a defector, he would not necessarily be aware of the minefield on Terra Unionia's side. Once those mines started exploding, all the Unionian border guards would be on alert, which would trap Jani and the others right where they were. It was also very likely that another Terra Unionian border guard would find this defector before he arrived at the minefield. That would also put them on alert, which was neither desirable for Lena nor the others. The only way they could get the situation under control was for him to catch the defector before he crossed the border.

Lu stopped and checked the data he was receiving from the motion detectors. His target was moving, about two hundred meters away from Lu's current position. He set off again and ran towards his target as quietly as he could. After a one-hundred-meter run he stopped again and checked the location of his target one more time. The distance between them was less than hundred meters now. Lu put his data device back in his pocket and grabbed his weapon. The time to act had come.

Lu chose his steps carefully as he approached the target. He stopped a couple of times in order to hear what was going on around him. Finally he heard steps nearby. Lu waited for a moment, until he saw the first glimpse of movement behind some trees. Instead of one man there were two of them walking towards the border.

"Oh no," Lu whispered.

Suddenly the situation had become more complicated. Detaining two men instead of one required much more effort. All he could do now was hope that the men respected authority when confronted with it. Then without analyzing the situation any further, he jumped from his hiding place and placed himself between the men and the border.

"STOP," he announced.

The men halted. Lu watched the two for a moment, holding his weapon tightly. Both of them were wearing dark clothes and they had hidden their faces beneath large hoods.

"You are not authorized to be in this area. Place your hands on your heads and turn around. You are under arrest."

Silence.

Neither one of them made a single move.

"This is your final warning," Lu informed them. "Put your hands on your heads and turn around."

"Why?" the shorter one of the two asked him.

Lu frowned. The man's voice had sounded quite odd. He was a younger man, but why would a young man, who had his whole life ahead of him, want to get out of the city?

"I don't need to explain my reasons," Lu informed them. "All you need to know is that you have been given an order by a border guard. Put your hands on your heads, turn around, and proceed south."

"We followed you here," the boy then said to him.

Lu was stunned.

"Excuse me?" he asked him.

"You came here with some other man," the boy added.

"You're mistaken."

"No, I'm not," the boy insisted.

Lu took a deep breath and thought quickly about what to do next. He didn't like the idea of him and Jani being followed. Damn! He should have been more careful. However, the only thing on his mind had been Lena and the first meeting of the four on the border. This was the result of his inattentiveness. Lu had never felt dumber than he felt right now.

"What are your names?" Lu asked them.

But the two remained silent again.

"YOUR NAMES," Lu shouted, but neither of the men said a word.

"Fine," Lu said. "Put your hands behind your backs so I can bind them. You are now heading back towards Albedo."

"Then we will tell the others you are here with a civilian," the boy said.

"I am not here with a civilian," Lu informed the boy.

"Yes, you are."

"You are mistaken."

"We both saw you. You are wearing a border guard's uniform, he is not. The other one is civilian."

"You saw something that was only in your imagination."

"He is a civilian and he is somewhere nearby. If you take us back to Albedo we will speak publicly about what we have seen here. We will talk about a border guard who brings civilians here which, according to you, is a restricted area."

"Maybe this imaginary civilian has permission to be here," Lu said.

"I didn't imagine him. He is here with you and before you came over the ridge to get into these woods, you made sure the other border guards didn't see him. That's why I'm sure he's not authorized to be in this area either, if we are not allowed to be here. So if you take us back to Albedo, we will tell everyone else about you."

"You are trying to blackmail me?!" Lu yelped.

The boy shrugged his shoulders.

Lu considered his options. Had the boy been serious about his threats? If so, he had to reconsider his position. If Jani had been with him right now, they could have taken the two men back south. On the other hand, these two knew Jani was a civilian. Therefore, they would get caught themselves if they escorted these two men back together. If they were to tell someone in the Border Guard Detachment about a guard bringing civilians here, he would most likely have to say goodbye to Lena, too.

If he lowered his weapon now to bind the hands of one, the other would most likely run away. So what was there to do?

"Alright," Lu said. "Turn right."

"Where are we going?" the boy asked him.

"I will take you to my friend," Lu informed them.

Which was the truth. It wasn't a good decision, but it was less bad than the alternatives.

The two men, who were still hiding their faces beneath large hoods, took the first steps in the direction Lu was pointing. Then they proceeded slowly without exchanging another word.

Lu was deeply annoyed. The sudden appearance of these two men had not been part of his plan, but the same applied to the Terra Unionian woman and her defector friend. So perhaps the only viable option was to take these two men to the others and decide together what to do next with Lena by his side. Lu wasn't very keen on shooting the two here and hiding the bodies in these woods. However, if they caused problems he might have to do so. The thought was not a pleasant one but he would do whatever it took to protect Lena and his own position in the Border Guard Detachment's special unit.

"What are you going to do to us?" the boy asked him.

"Be quiet," Lu said angrily. "We are not here to talk, we are here to walk."

And luckily the boy seemed to hear him. Lu was grateful for the silence; he didn't want to answer any more of their questions. He also expected one of them to try to escape at any moment but neither one of them seemed too eager to leave the other behind. It made Lu wonder a little but he could understand it. It made his task much easier.

When they finally came close to the spot from which Lu had started running, he gave the two men the order to turn left.

The men did as they were told without protesting. Then he saw the familiar-looking pond behind the trees. As they came closer, he didn't see anyone near it. He assumed Lena had heard them approaching and told everyone to get on the ground and remain still.

"It's me," Lu informed the others.

"Lu," he heard Lena's sigh of relief and suddenly he saw her standing up.

Also Anamona raised herself into a sitting position, as did Jani, Tilia, and the defector. Once Lena realized Lu was not alone, she instinctively grabbed her weapon.

"Who are they?" Lena asked him.

"They refuse to tell me their names," Lu said, "but they said they followed me and Jani as we were heading north. They knew we were here."

"Is that so?" Lena noted.

"Damn it!" Lu growled. "Why didn't I notice them sooner?!"

"I didn't realize they were following us, either," Jani said, trying to calm Lu down.

"Either we lost these two from our tail or they changed direction intentionally when they reached the border zone," Lu added, "otherwise they would have been aware of my motion detectors."

Jani nodded. Then Lu pushed the other man onto his knees.

"Get down," he stated.

"Another two defectors in one night?" Jani wondered aloud. "What is wrong with men these days?"

Anamona, Lena, Tilia, and Lemmus followed the situation quietly. Suddenly Lu noticed that the other man he had brought with him was staring at Jani most intensively.

"You know him?" Lu asked Jani as he knew for certain the defector had taken an interest in him.

"Who?" Jani asked him confused.

"This one here," Lu said, and yanked the hood off the man's head.

To everyone's surprise, instead of a man, a dark-haired woman was revealed under the hood.

"Doctor Alauda," Jani said, his eyes wide open.

"Who?" Lu asked him.

"Mari Alauda," Jani said again. "I went to see her in Gavialis Main Hospital a few days ago."

"Mari Alauda?" Lu wondered where he had heard the name before. "Mari Alauda from the news?!"

"The news?" Lena asked them.

"She is a wanted criminal!" Lu exclaimed.

"Criminal?" Lena asked him, surprised. "What has she done?"

"She's accused of sabotaging the artificial wombs," Jani said, and shook his head.

"What kind of sabotage are we talking about exactly?" Lena asked them.

"Thousands of female fetuses maturing in artificial wombs have been killed," Lu sighed, "and she's the main suspect."

"Oh goodness," Tilia sighed and covered her mouth with her hand.

"They call her Doctor Death," Jani said, "her pictures have been distributed right across our information network all over the world. She managed to escape and disappear from the police."

"Well, we don't have to wonder anymore where she went," Lena noted.

"The media circus around her is one of the biggest in years," Lu added. "She's most likely the first woman in the world who will be judged in a public trial."

"Great," Lena sighed and rolled her eyes.

"I'm innocent," Mari Alauda informed them.

"If you're innocent, why didn't you stay in Gavialis to await your trial?" Lu asked the woman sourly. "Why are you here running around in these woods? Where did you think you were going?"

"My intention was to stay in Gavialis," Mari stated, "because I didn't know about any other options."

"What other options?" Lu asked her.

"Terra Unionia," Mari said.

"And what's that?" Lu asked her.

"Oh don't even start with me," Mari said and glared at Lu.

"I really don't know what you are talking about," Lu insisted.

"Yes you do."

"You are mistaken," Lu replied. "Has this boy told you about Terra Unionia?"

Then Lu took a step closer to the boy who was on his knees.

"Who is he?" Lu asked Mari Alauda, "your favorite Guardsman? I didn't know that the Yellow Guard had recruited men this short."

Mari didn't answer. She simply looked fearlessly at Lu, her eyes filled with defiance.

"So, you are here because of him," Lu continued. "Who are you, boy, and how did you know to come here? I'm convinced you followed me all the way from Gavialis."

The boy on his knees remained silent and kept staring at the ground.

"Answer me or I'll drag you back!" Lu told angrily.

"And you would risk him telling the entire border guard detachment about this little conference in these woods?" Mari asked him.

"You are in no position to make threats right now," Lu retorted. "Who do you think the border guard detachment would rather believe; me or a wanted murderer?"

"I am not a murderer," Mari informed him, the anger flashing in her eyes.

"If you were innocent you would still be in Gavialis awaiting trial," Lu reminded her.

"And what justice would be served when the evidence against me is fabricated?" the woman asked him sharply.

"Of course it is," Lu said sarcastically, "that's what the guilty always say!"

"Let her be," Tilia asked him and stood up. "Leave her be, Lu. Please. Accusing her is not going to resolve this situation now."

"You don't realize the magnitude of the crime she is being accused of," Lu told the woman seriously. "Eliminating female fetuses is an unheard-of crime, more cruel than anything mankind has seen since the Great War. That's the reason why I can't ignore these accusations now."

"I understand," Tilia said and took a step closer, "but try to remember the rest of us as well."

"What do you mean?"

"We shouldn't be here either," Tilia added.

"Is that so?" Mari Alauda asked them.

Lu glared at Mari and pushed her to her knees. Mari yelped.

"She's in pain," Tilia said direction, indicating her with genuine concern in her eyes. "Look at her sleeve. Is that blood?"

Lu noticed a dark spot on her sleeve. There was no doubt in his mind why it had appeared on the garment.

"That blood just proves beyond any doubt that this is Mari Alauda," he said.

"Why?" Lena asked him.

"According to the news, Doctor Alauda's ID chip was found near the Gavialis Main Hospital. In other words, she had cut it out of her arm."

"How severe is your pain?" Tilia asked the woman.

"Not so bad yet," Mari informed her. "The arm is still partly numb, though, but the bleeding has almost stopped. So I'm going to be fine."

"I have to take her back to Gavialis," Lu said.

"I'm not going back there," Mari stated.

"You are a criminal," Lu said and pointed his gun at the woman.

"Lu," Tilia appealed.

"I am duty-bound to do this," Lu told.

"Right now she is not threat to anyone," Tilia pointed out. "And I'm quite sure we must remember a few things about jurisdiction."

Lu took a look at Tilia and he knew exactly what she was talking about. And she was right. No one knew which jurisdiction applied at this spot on the border. Lu, however, was still having difficulty accepting that there really was more than one set of legislation in the world, but he knew Terra Unionians would see the situation quite differently.

"Lu," Lena said quietly.

That was Lena's way of confirming that Tilia was right. Lu looked at Lena for a moment, seeking her assurance that she was serious, then he nodded. He took a step back and placed his hand on Lena's back. Lena really did know how to calm the storm within him.

"Let's try to remain calm," Tilia said. "None of us trusts anyone here and every one of us has something to hide. We can agree at least on that."

"Yes," Lena said.

"Good," Tilia responded. "So, let's try to get along without any extra fights which will lead us nowhere. None of us is here with permission. Every one of us has violated the border in some way, regardless of our background."

"True," Lena sighed.

"Border?" Mari asked her.

"Border," Tilia said without defining the concept more accurately.

Then Tilia kneeled down to the Hirundian boy.

"What border?" Mari Alauda asked them.

No one answered. Not even Tilia, who had already begun studying the Hirunda boy, still hiding beneath his hood.

"Wait a minute," she said.

"What?" Lu asked her.

"He's not a boy."

"What?!" Lu yelped stunned.

"We have a girl here."

"A girl?!" Lena exclaimed.

Lu had a hard time believing his own ears. Was Tilia absolutely sure what she was seeing? Maybe she wasn't used to young boys and therefore she was confused.

"I don't believe this," Jani said to himself and shook his head. "Two women outside the city without their Guardsmen?! What is this world coming to?"

"Hey," Tilia said and removed the girl's hood from her face. "Who are you?"

No response.

"Leave her alone," Mari suddenly told her.

"You be quiet," Lu told Mari angrily.

"I won't hurt her," Tilia assured the woman.

Mari said nothing more, but observed Tilia carefully.

"Are you here because you want to find Terra Unionia like Mari here?" Tilia asked the girl.

The girl nodded.

"How did you get out of that city of yours?" Tilia asked her.

"Are you from Terra Unionia?" the girl asked Tilia instead.

Tilia looked over her shoulder and watched both Lemmus and Lu. Lu was keeping his cool exterior; he had no intention of revealing the women's current location.

"You are a woman so you have to be from Terra Unionia," the girl said.

"Why?" Tilia asked her. "Why do you assume that?"

"Because you are a woman and you are here without Guardsmen. So Terra Unionia is here as well."

"But you are here, too," Tilia pointed out. "And you came here with another woman."

"You are from Terra Unionia," the girl still insisted. "I know that. That woman is wearing a different uniform from that of the guard who came to us, so she is from Terra Unionia as well. I am sure of that. And you said something about a border. So we are on Terra Unionia's border now."

"There could be many explanations for my different uniform," Lena pointed out, trying to turn the thoughts of the Hirundian girl away from the border.

"Like what?" Mari Alauda asked her.

Lena glared at Mari, but said nothing.

"If you tell me your name, I'll tell you where I come from," Tilia told the girl.

The girl hesitated for a moment.

"My name is Tilia," she said. "And you have come here with Mari Alauda. So your name is?"

"Saia," the girl finally said. "My name is Saia."

"Saia what?" Lena asked her.

"It's none of your business," Mari told her.

"You're not in charge here," Lena informed Mari Alauda.

"Then who is? That *little man* dressed as a border guard?" Mari asked her, insulting Lu.

Something dark flashed in Lena's eyes and suddenly she pulled out her gun and pressed it against the woman's forehead.

"Lena!" Anamona exclaimed and moved towards her sister. "Don't."

"Lower your guns now!" Tilia demanded loudly. No one present was left doubting whether she was serious or not. "No one is going to shoot anyone here! Bloodshed will only make things worse!"

Lena and Lu exchanged glances. Lu wasn't willing to shoot anyone, nor was Lena. The wisest thing was to do what Tilia had commanded.

Finally both Lu and Lena lowered their weapons and Lu calmed down. Perhaps they should give Tilia a chance to resolve the situation her way.

"Mari and Saia," Tilia said and looked at Lena and Lu over her shoulder. "Their names are Mari and Saia. We know that now and it didn't take a gun to find that out. So I hope that none of us has to see those things again tonight."

14.

"Why would you, a young woman, want to get away from the city?" the border guard called Lu demanded as he kneeled in front of Saia.

Saia was at a loss for words. Even if she hadn't been she wouldn't even have wanted to say a word. She knew she was in deep trouble and that was enough to silence her.

"Hey," the red-haired woman said gently to the border guard, "try to be less demanding. She is obviously not used to being around men."

Saia glanced quickly at the woman. She seemed friendly, unlike that man Lu who had found the two of them in the forest.

"Girls are constantly surrounded by Yellow Guardsmen," Lu said. "And they are men. So she's used to men."

"But you are not one of those Yellow Guardsmen," the woman who had introduced herself as Tilia reminded him, and she was right. This Lu person had no idea how girls and Yellow Guardsmen interacted, because he was a border guard. It wasn't the same to being around Guardsmen. Those men were different.

"How did the two of you get out of the city?" Lu asked them.

Saia still remained silent and so did Doctor Alauda. Both of them were fully aware that, no matter what they said, each word had to be chosen carefully. Lu and his friend had identified Doctor Alauda as Doctor Death, and this worried Saia. However, luckily for them, this Tilia woman seemed to be keeping the men under control; no mean feat in Saia's opinion.

"This woman told us that she had heard about Terra Unionia only a couple days ago," the female border guard said, referring to Doctor Alauda.

"Her name is Mari," Tilia said.

"Fine," Lena said. "Mari heard about Terra Unionia only recently and I believe she heard it from you, Saia. So exactly how did you know to come to this spot here?"

Saia continued to look in silence at the ground beneath her feet. She didn't want to talk. Everyone was staring at her and this was making her feel uneasy and distressed. Why couldn't she just be left alone?

"It's a good question," Lu's friend said, "because Terra Unionia is not on our maps."

"So, where did you get the idea to come here, girl?" Lu asked her. "What made you think Terra Unionia would be here?"

"Is that really an important issue here?" Doctor Alauda asked him instead. "Isn't it more relevant that we are here?"

The border guard glared at her but said nothing. Saia was still frightened about what they were going to do to Doctor Alauda.

"We are interested in how widely Terra Unionia is discussed around the world," Tilia explained.

"It's not a popular topic of discussions by any means," Doctor Alauda said.

Lu sighed and rolled his eyes. He didn't trust Doctor Alauda at all.

"No one wastes their time thinking about a place that is mentioned only briefly in some old texts," Doctor Alauda added. "though I do remember hearing about Terra Unionia during my studies as a young girl. It wasn't anything revolutionary. Believe me, Terra Unionia isn't important for the majority of people at all."

"That's a relief," the young woman next to Lena noted.

"However she found it interesting enough," Lu reminded the others, pointing at Saia, "because you are here."

Saia finally found the courage to speak.

"So, it is true," she said. "Isn't it? You admit that Terra Unionia is real and that we are in Terra Unionia now."

"We are not in Terra Unionia," Lena said.

"Then who are you people?" Saia asked her and looked at Lena, "especially you. I have never seen a brown uniform like yours. Not to mention that you are a *woman*. We are in Terra Unionia, I just know it."

"Not necessarily," Doctor Alauda said.

"How so?"

"He is a border guard. We've seen men like him in the city as well," Mari said and nodded towards Lu.

Saia fell silent. Doctor Alauda was right. Yet despite Lu she was still quite sure that this was Terra Unionia and that Lena was a Terra Unionian. Tilia, being a woman, had to be as well, otherwise how could she be here in this place which, according to the map, was supposed to be contaminated wasteland.

"Oh all these secrets," laughed an older man, sitting a little further away. "A girl who won't say how she came to be here with a woman who's accused of multiple murder, together with a mysterious foursome who are still saying nothing about why they are here in the middle of the woods in the first place."

"Not to mention the contents of your suitcase," Lena reminded him.

Saia glanced back at the man and noticed he was holding a small black suitcase. Then she glanced at the Terra Unionian border guard and saw doubt in her eyes. She and the older man were clearly not friends, was Saia's assumption. She regarded herself as pretty good at assessing inter-personal relations.

"This is not going to work now," the woman next to Lena sighed. "This entire situation is farce in its purest form."

"You can say that again," Lena said. "I'm sorry I dragged you here."

The woman looked at Lena and nodded.

"I suggest every one of us sits down on the ground," Tilia said. "If we don't calm down now, we will never figure out a way to get out of this forest."

"Sounds good," said the older man.

"I agree," the younger woman added, clearly exhausted.

"This is a nightmare," Lena commented.

"Let's sit down," the older man said and smiled, "and let's join together like our ancestors used to do, round the campfire back in the olden days."

"Sarcasm won't help now," Tilia pointed out.

"He knows no other way of talking to people," the younger woman quipped.

"Sit down, Anamona," Tilia commanded her.

Saia saw the younger woman – Anamona – take her place next to Tilia. The name sounded pretty strange, but it was pretty strange that she was here in the first place. Saia had never seen women without their Yellow Guardsmen, but Anamona was protected by no one.

Lena found a place to Anamona's right. The border guard Lu sat down on Lena's right and Jani sat next to him. Doctor Alauda placed herself between Jani and Saia, for which Saia was grateful. However, the older man sat on her other side. Saia tried her best to ignore him and therefore kept her eyes firmly focused on the ground.

"We can't let this turn into a free-for-all," Tilia said, "So, let's try to keep to one speaker at a time."

"I second that," Lena said.

"You can be the chairperson for us now," the older man suggested. "For some reason everyone here is willing to listen you."

Saia glanced furtively at Tilia. The man was right. Tilia really seemed to be the only one here the others had no issues with.

"Alright," the woman said.

"So, what now?" Lena asked her.

"Now we are doing something prohibited," Tilia informed the others, scanning the circle of people present. "We will all tell each other why we are here and each one of us is going to tell the truth."

Lena took a deep breath and looked at Lu. Doctor Alauda glanced at Saia and the older man stared at Tilia with a dumb-founded look on his face.

"So, my name is Tilia Linum," Tilia started. "This man here is Lemmus, my friend. The names Saia and Mari we heard a moment ago. Next to Mari we have Jani."

Saia looked at Lu's friend who nodded.

"And next to Jani is Lu who is a Hirundian border guard," Tilia added.

Saia frowned. Hirundian? What did Tilia mean by that word ?

"Then we have the two sisters here, Lena and Anamona," Tilia added, the link between Lena and the other young woman finally being revealed to Saia as well.

Then Saia her gaze to the ground in front of her. She didn't want anyone paying her any special attention, but she was listening intently to every word being said, trying to burn each one of them into her mind.

"So, Lemmus and I got lost in these woods and we ended up here by accident," Tilia explained.

"And that's the truth," Lemmus added calmly.

"Alright," Lena noted.

"Once here, Lemmus and I met these four; Anamona, Lena, Lu, and Jani," Tilia explained. "We were sitting here together when Lu realized there was movement in the forest nearby. In other words, he had spotted you two."

"I see," Doctor Alauda said.

"Before you came here, neither of the two groups had got as far as telling the other why we had come here tonight. I think the moment for that discussion has arrived. We all have to speak truthfully. Nothing that is said here will ever be repeated outside this circle when we leave."

Saia glanced quickly at Doctor Alauda who was listening intently to what Tilia had to say. Saia admired her calmness. She was being accused of horrible murders and on top of that she had a deep, self-inflicted wound on her arm. Then there was the fact that they had been caught on their way to Terra Unionia, but Doctor Alauda still hadn't lost her composure. She was as calm as she ever was. Saia wanted to be like her but she knew it was only an impossible dream which could never come true.

"How can we be sure that no one here will say anything about this evening to anyone?" Lena asked her.

"We can only give our word," Tilia said, "and as far as I am concerned, I can't talk to anyone about this without it causing me serious problems."

"Same goes for me and Jani," Lu said, "and I assume these two new arrivals can't really announce publicly where they have been and what they have seen."

"Good," Tilia noted.

"I can talk to no one," Lena added, "and I don't think Anamona can say a word about this to anyone, either."

"True," Anamona confirmed.

"So, we just have to trust that everything that is said here tonight, stays here," Tilia noted.

"I guess that's the only option we've got," Lena said.

"Okay. So I'll go first," Tilia said. "I will start by telling you why I am here tonight and once I've said all there is to say, the next person can take over. Do we agree that this is the wisest course of action to take?"

Saia looked at the others and she noticed how Tilia looked at all seven in the group. Each one of them made a gesture of acceptance.

"Great," Tilia said. "I am here because my friend Lemmus asked me to come here. Our plan was to find that black suitcase Lemmus is holding now at a predetermined location. This is not the location; after we found the suitcase we got lost."

"What's in it?" Lu asked her calmly.

"That can wait for a moment," Tilia deflected. "Anamona; why are you here?"

"I am here because my sister asked me to come and meet Lu and Jani."

"Alright," Tilia said. "Jani?"

"Well, I'm here because Lu asked me to come. Honestly, I'd rather be at home in Gavialis right now."

"And Mari and Saia are here because they are searching for Terra Unionia," Tilia added.

Saia nodded, until she found the courage to raise her hand.

"Saia," Tilia invited her to speak.

"Is Terra Unionia here?" Saia asked hopefully.

Tilia glanced quickly at Anamona and Lena. Lena nodded.

"Terra Unionia is behind me," Tilia finally confessed.

Saia's heart skipped a beat.

"I told you so," she said to Doctor Alauda feeling most relieved. "I knew it."

The doctor smiled faintly and nodded.

"Mari," Tilia said. "Is it true you are accused of murder?"

"It is," Doctor Alauda responded baldly. "Unfortunately it is true."

"Have you committed the crimes they accuse you of?" Tilia asked her.

"No," Doctor Alauda stated without any hesitation.

Saia knew she was telling the truth. She would have shouted it to the world if she had had enough courage. She simply didn't know what Alauda would think if she started to arguing her innocence to the others. She didn't want to make the situation worse so she decided the best thing for her to do at the moment was to remain silent.

"Lena," Tilia said. "Why did you ask your sister to come here?"

"If I tell you why, you must tell us what is in that suitcase," Lena said.

"Hadn't we more or less agreed that already?" Tilia asked her.

"Good, but the agreement also binds Mari and Saia. You two have to tell us how you heard about Terra Unionia."

Saia looked at Lena before turning to look at Doctor Alauda. They exchanged glances, and finally Saia nodded in agreement.

"Good," Tilia said. "So, first Lena will tell us why she is here with her sister and then I will tell you about the black suitcase in Lemmus' hands."

"You will?" Lemmus asked her one more time and looked at Tilia.

"We have no other choice," Tilia pointed out. "Not if we want to return home and continue living our lives as before. Lena is the only one of us who can navigate through the minefield. She confiscated your little device, remember?"

"How could I forget," Lemmus said sourly, glaring in Lena's direction.

"Those are my terms," Lena informed the two.

"Please," Tilia said.

"Alright," Lena agreed, "but if that black suitcase isn't opened once I'm done, I will shoot it open, which will most likely destroy its contents."

"Understood," Tilia said.

Lena cleared her throat again and looked at each member of the circle before continuing.

"I asked my sister to come here because I wanted her to meet Lu," Lena began. Saia was curious to know what would follow. "Lu and I met a couple of months ago, in itself a breach of both our oaths. I assume you understand that I am forbidden to make contact with an enemy representative on my own. In addition, I am under strict orders to kill the enemy if he crosses the border. However, Lu is still very much alive as is his friend Jani, not to mention Saia and Mari. So it must be pretty apparent now that I have bent some rules and regulations. If this became public knowledge in Terra Unionia, I would be in serious trouble."

"That's understandable," Tilia noted. "Anamona already told us that she is here because of some problematic situation. If that is the case, then what is this problem exactly?"

"It's about me and Lu," Lena said awkwardly, "the situation is … well, … that … "

Saia, along with everyone else, noticed that Lena was searching for the right words. She seemed hesitant but at the same time determined. Saia didn't know what to expect. Lena continued.

"The situation is … I'm pregnant," Lena managed to say.

Silence fell on the group. Tilia's and Lemmus' jaws dropped. Saia looked around and realized Doctor Alauda was looking at her, stunned. She had never expected Lena to tell them anything like this.

"Excuse me?" Lemmus finally asked her.

"I'm pregnant," Lena said again. "And the child is Lu's."

Tilia and Lemmus turned their heads slowly and looked at each other. Suddenly Saia noticed a smile creeping over Anamona's face.

"I'm glad you find this a laughing matter," the venom in Lena's voice was clearly audible.

"Your situation? Hardly."

"What then?"

"I never imagined I would ever see Lemmus that confused," Anamona said and covered her mouth with her hand.

Saia turned to look at the man and noticed him looking at Anamona. Finally he said, amused:

"You really don't like me, do you?"

"Not so much, no," Anamona confessed in front of the others and Saia was taken aback by her honesty.

"Too bad," Lemmus said. "We have so much in common after all."

Anamona laughed and shook her head. Saia didn't know what to make of the banter between the two.

"You are expecting a child by a Hirundian man?" Tilia asked Lena, seeking confirmation that this was no joke.

Hirundian? Once again that odd expression caught Saia's attention.

"Yes," Lena said. "I guess you're all beginning to understand how unusual my situation is."

"Unusual?" Tilia asked shaking her head. "What on earth are you going to do?"

"I don't know," Lena said. "All I know is that the child is coming."

"How far gone are you?" Doctor Alauda, the childbirth expert, asked Lena.

Lu turned to face her and there was coldness in his eyes. Saia was worried. What was going on in his head? Was he about to attack?

"It's none of your business," the man barked at her.

"Well, I'm sorry I asked!" Doctor Alauda exclaimed.

Saia was scared. The air between them had suddenly become much more threatening. Her heart had started to beat faster and she felt all her strength draining out of her legs. She looked at Tilia and hoped that the woman would do something.

"Lu," Lena calmed the man down instead and Saia was grateful for his patience.

"She doesn't need to know anything about our child," Lu said quietly.

"She is a doctor," Lena pointed out.

"And?"

"Do you see any other doctors here?"

"She's been accused of *murder*!" Lu whispered.

"I know," Lena said, "but she is here now and she's the only doctor on this entire planet who knows I am pregnant."

"And?"

"What do you mean, and?" Lena asked him confused.

"I don't trust her."

"I trust no one here but myself, you, and Anamona, but this situation forces us to take the others here into consideration, particularly Mari because of her profession."

"I don't know what good my professional skills can do right now," Doctor Alauda said. "I may be a doctor, but here I have nothing but the clothes I am wearing. So I can't examine you."

"Not yet," Lena said and lifted her index finger while the others waited for her to continue, "but if you were to defect to Terra Unionia ..."

"Hey ..."Anamona reined in her sister.

Saia took notice. Were they heading to Terra Unionia after all? For the first time that evening there was true hope in her heart.

"If I have understood correctly, she isn't a particularly popular person on Hirunda's side of the border," Lena told her sister.

"Lena!" Anamona exclaimed.

"Alright, alright," Lena said and raised her hands. "It was just an idea, you know."

Anamona was against defectors, then. All Saia could hope for was that Lena and Tilia would more receptive to the idea of them coming to Terra Unionia.

"I don't think Lena's idea is entirely impossible," Tilia said and Saia felt even more relieved. "She could really be an asset in this situation of yours."

"What?!" Anamona yelped.

"Just because she is a doctor?" Lu asked sourly. Saia didn't like his tone of voice at all. "Surely you have other doctors on your side of the border?"

"Of course we do, but not the kind of doctors who would have good reason to keep this pregnancy to themselves," Tilia explained. "If Mari defected – and I'm not saying yet that she should – but if she did, she would be in no place to announce publicly how she ended up in Terra Unionia. Surely they would interrogate her, wouldn't they?"

"Yes," Lena said.

"So, in such a situation the wisest option would be for her to speak truthfully, but saying as little as possible. Mari is here tonight, so she already knows about your child. She is a doctor who knows what she is doing medically, regardless of her background."

"Thank you," Doctor Alauda said.

Saia was pleased as well. She was growing to like Tilia more and more with every passing minute.

"The truth is that Lena can't talk publicly about her pregnancy," Tilia said. "I can't emphasize that enough, that's the way things are on our side. In that light alone Mari would be the most rational choice to monitor Lena's pregnancy and even help her deliver the child when the time comes."

"It's true," Lena said and looked at Lu. "And she has not been convicted on your side of the border."

"How can she be convicted of anything if she can't be tried?" Lu asked her.

Saia was beginning to get cross with the man. He had already made his mind up about Doctor Alauda being guilty, even though he knew nothing about the issue. His attitude simply proved the point that people believed blindly what they read in the news headlines.

"I would like to state one more time, though it's most likely pointless, that I have not committed any capital crimes of any sort," the doctor pointed out. "Just because the news network spreads pictures of me and they publish stories of these allegations, that doesn't make me guilty."

Saia nodded at Doctor Alauda's words.

"However, this wouldn't have become public in the first place if there had not been a strong case against you," Lu reminded.

Saia was really most annoyed now but she knew Doctor Alauda was capable of defending herself.

"My so-called guilt was leaked to the news network before I was even called to the Health Council to answer these allegations. My reputation was ruined even before the police had arrived at the hospital to read me my rights!" the woman explained. "Don't you find that just a little bit odd?"

"It shouldn't happen like that," Saia added quietly. "At least not in public cases."

"Surely you realize your words alone are not enough to convince me," Lu said.

"Oh, I do," Doctor Alauda assured him. "But you should understand that I was very frightened when I realized what was going on, and that I am still scared. When the entire world condemns you as a murderer, you wouldn't want to stay in the same city either, waiting for a trial where the case against you was built entirely on fabricated evidence. You would lose faith in the legal system, too, and you would run away. You would run as if your life depended on it."

Lu didn't answer, but Saia knew he still had doubts when it came to Doctor Alauda and her story. Like most people in the world, he, too, had already condemned her.

"Are you ready to defect to Terra Unionia?" Lemmus asked Doctor Alauda.

"I don't believe I could be more ready than this," she said. "I have nothing in Gavialis anymore. It's all gone. As unbelievable as it sounds, I have lost everything. Even though I can talk about this with a smile on my face, I'm serious. I'm just too astonished and angry to do anything else."

"You have a man in Gavialis," Jani said, "a man you are committed to, otherwise you wouldn't have been allowed to work at the hospital. Do you have children with him?"

Saia pricked up her ears. How could Jani know anything about Doctor Alauda's personal life?

"That's a private matter," she informed the young man.

"Surely there is someone you are leaving behind, someone who will miss you?" Lena asked her.

"Who is going to miss Doctor Death?" Doctor Alauda asked her, sarcastically. "A monster of a doctor who committed the ultimate crime when she began systematically destroying female fetuses? Hardly."

"Not even this man of yours?" Lena asked her confused.

"Let's just say that my man has always preferred male company over mine," Doctor Alauda laughed. "And that the particular arrangement always suited us both equally well. He will be able to move on without me."

Saia noticed that Anamona's mouth had fallen open. She was clearly having some difficulty understanding Doctor Alauda's choices. The doctor's life was not the most ordinary example of average female life outside Terra Unionia, but Doctor Alauda was an exceptional woman; she was strong and intelligent. She had never been mediocre.

"I defected to Terra Unionia decades ago," Lemmus said.

Saia was surprised and turned to face Lemmus. So defecting to Terra Unionia wasn't entirely impossible. There really was a chance for her and Doctor Alauda to defect. Then she looked at Doctor Alauda and saw confusion in her eyes.

"Thinking about leaving it all behind and defecting may give you the impression it's easy, but the first few years in a new country are surprisingly hard," the man continued. "I speak, of course, from a man's point of view. Gender is a significant factor here."

"I don't think I have any other option," Doctor Alauda said.

Lemmus nodded.

"Back to Lena and Lu's situation," Tilia said. "How we deal with Mari's situation is obviously an important issue to talk about but I think it has become quite clear what we have to do in her case."

"I agree," Lena said.

"Are you serious?" Anamona asked her sister.

"Mari has no other option," Lena pointed out, "and there's no denying that her professional skills may prove to be invaluable."

Anamona sighed.

"And from what I've heard so far, it seems that she can't return to Gavialis," Lena added. "Should she stay here then, in this no-man's land between the minefield and Hirunda?"

Hirunda.

Why were the Terra Unionians talking about them as Hirundians and the world as Hirunda? Saia found this very odd. For her, Hirunda stood for Gavo Hirunda, the great hero of the past. He had been the man who had brought peace to the world after the Great War.

"So, I will defect to Terra Unionia?" Doctor Alauda asked them.

"So, it would seem," Lena replied.

Saia breathed a huge sigh of relief. Life in Gavialis was finally over.

"Don't worry, love," Lena whispered to Lu, "we need her."

"I don't like this," Lu said quietly.

"Me neither, but I have to take her onto our side."

Saia glanced at the border guards but when Lu saw her looking at him, she turned her head away and continued staring at the ground by her feet.

"Have you thought about the time after this pregnancy?" Tilia asked the pair. "On which side of the border will this child be raised?"

"I don't know," Lena said.

"Have you considered terminating this pregnancy?" Tilia asked them.

"You too?!" Lena snapped. Her reaction to Tilia's question got everyone's undivided attention, Saia's included.

"That was the first option I came up with," Anamona explained to Tilia.

"Terminating a pregnancy is never an easy option," Tilia said, "but it happens, even though it's not publicly acknowledged on our side of the border. In this situation ..."

"I would like to consider other options," Lena informed the woman sharply.

"Alright," Tilia noted. "I only brought it up because in your situation it would be the easiest way out of this."

"Easiest?" Lena asked her.

"You are bound to Terra Unionia and our laws, Lu is bound by Hirunda's. A child whose parents are from different sides of the border will not fit into either society. There are no procedures or recommendations in existence which can instruct or guide us in a situation like this. From a jurisdiction point of view, this child is a problem. Would it be right to give this child up? Of course not, but we have to accept the world the way it is, and we have to accept the rules and regulations which apply beyond our little area of neutrality here at the border."

The look in Lena's eyes darkened. Saia noticed Lena turning her eyes towards Doctor Alauda.

"I don't know what you expect from me," Doctor Alauda said as she noticed Lena's stare. "Without the appropriate medicine or instruments my ability to help you is limited."

"Do you know how to terminate a pregnancy?" Tilia asked her.

"Yes," the woman told briefly. "How far gone are you?"

"I don't know," Lena said quietly, "I've been pregnant for a couple of months or so but that is just a rough guess."

"The reason for me asking is the rules I won't break," Doctor Alauda explained. "Even if we were in Gavialis Main Hospital now, I would not terminate a pregnancy that has progressed normally beyond a certain point. I am bound by both legislation and my own oath. Terminating a pregnancy beyond a certain time limit is considered a crime in Gavialis and, contrary to public opinion, I am *not* a murderer."

"In Terra Unionia the operation in question has gained more or less illegal status," Lemmus explained to the others.

"More or less?" Doctor Alauda asked him curiously.

"Officially it is not acceptable for a woman to even ask for a pregnancy termination in any circumstances, if the pregnancy has progressed normally," Tilia said. "But the operation itself is not totally forbidden under our law."

"However, you said terminations are still conducted?" Mari asked her.

"Yes," Tilia said. "And if a woman wants a termination, it is carried out discreetly; anyone knowing about it could create serious problems for the woman concerned."

"That's true," Anamona sighed.

Saia listened carefully to what was being discussed and absorbed every word. She couldn't hear enough about Terra Unionia, the people who lived there, and their habits. She wanted so badly to cross the border but was afraid to show her enthusiasm openly.

"Anyway, no one is going to touch our child," Lu said angrily. "This is my only chance to have my own child."

"Yours?!" Anamona suddenly exclaimed. Saia was surprised at her outburst. "Yours?! Is that all you can think about?! You selfish …!"

"What?" Lu asked her stunned.

"You should be thinking about Lena!" Anamona snapped. "This pregnancy could ruin her life!"

"Anamona!" Lena exclaimed.

"Let's all calm down!" Tilia chimed in. "Let's all just calm down."

"He's only thinking about himself!" Anamona said pointing at Lu.

Saia looked at the woman, admiring her courage to talk to a man in such a way.

"Excuse me?!" Lu asked her huffily.

"Anamona, Lu – be quiet!" Lena shouted at the two. Saia looked at the woman in surprise. "The situation is that *I* am carrying this child. *I* am about to become a mother, therefore, *I* am telling you that *I* am not going to give this child up. I know what kind of world we live in. I know how tricky this situation is, but I can't terminate this pregnancy."

The group fell silent and Lena took a deep breath. Saia swallowed and hoped they could avoid further similar conflicts.

"Alright then," Tilia finally said. "Lena is keeping this child so terminating the pregnancy is not an option. This means that you have to consider other options."

"That's why we are here," Lena commented with a dark look in her eyes. "That's why Anamona is here and why Jani is here. We both know what kind of trouble we are in. We're not stupid, but we want to keep this child; it is our baby."

"Why can't she give birth normally in Terra Unionia?" Doctor Alauda asked them. "Why exactly do you need to hide this pregnancy from others?"

That was definitely a question worth asking, Saia thought.

"It has not been registered," Anamona said briefly.

"So, pregnancies are closely monitored on your side as well," Doctor Alauda noted.

"Very closely," Anamona stated. "We must register all pregnancies during the first three weeks. Typically, the registration is carried out by the doctor who carried out the fertilization operation."

"Ah," Doctor Alauda noted with interest, "So, in Terra Unionia women are only fertilized in a doctor's office? You don't have any so-called natural fertilizations?"

"If you are referring to the way Lena got pregnant, then no," Anamona said, "under no circumstances, no, no, and no."

Saia glanced across at Doctor Alauda again and noticed how she was observing Anamona in confusion.

"Men are not involved in raising children in Terra Unionia," Lemmus explained. "The percentage of men in the whole population is negligible and when it comes to procreation, girls are preferred in general. There are many reasons for this, perhaps we shouldn't get in to them right now, but the point is that women are fertilized under the doctors' watchful eyes."

"How marginal is the number of men, then?" Doctor Alauda asked the man.

It was a question that had made Saia curious as well.

"Very marginal," Lemmus stated.

"So, you, for instance ...?"

"I most likely have many biological offspring in Terra Unionia, but I know none of them personally," Lemmus said.

"Aah ..." Doctor Alauda managed to say.

" That's also the case in Hirunda, is it not?" Lemmus asked.

"That's true," Doctor Alauda noted, "but as you know there are also men who are well aware of their own biological children's identities."

"That's right," Lemmus noted. "In Terra Unionia the men have been 'freed' from this obligation which the rest of the world perceives as a privilege."

"Interesting," Doctor Alauda mused.

"As Hirundian women are obliged to donate their ova, so are Terra Unionian men obliged to make similar donation of their seed," Lemmus added.

"Naturally," Mari said. "If the population is female-biased, it's only logical."

"Terra Unionia is a matriarchal society," Tilia recounted, "So, there is really only a handful of men in our heavily female-dominated population."

"That's unbelievable," Doctor Alauda said, thereby giving word to Saia's puzzlement as well. "So, you have a situation which is the direct opposite of the whole of the rest of the world. Where we are desperately trying to raise the number of women, you are limiting the number of men."

"That is exactly the situation," Tilia concurred. "Girls are preferred."

"As in other parts of the world, too," Doctor Alauda added making Saia nod. "If only more girls were being born."

"Why aren't more girls being born?" Anamona asked her.

"That was a mystery I thought I was trying to solve until I realized I was being accused of murder," Doctor Alauda said.

"The main problem in Lena's situation is the DNA scan," Tilia said bringing the focus back to the original topic. "The DNA of every Terra Unionian man is saved in our national information system, and we don't have any DNA data matching Lu's."

"That's right," Doctor Alauda said.

"What exactly would happen to Lena if this pregnancy were exposed?" Lu asked the Unionians.

"The child would most likely be taken away from her," Anamona said.

Saia was surprised. How could it be? She looked at Tilia who nodded at Anamona's words.

"Why?" Lu asked her.

"As we've already said, this pregnancy is unregistered and therefore illegal," Lemmus continued, "there is no law in Terra Unionia forbidding pregnancy termination, but there is the concept of an illegal pregnancy as defined in our law. So if a child's biological father's DNA cannot be found in our information system, it will alert the authorities immediately. Something like this simply cannot happen in Terra Unionia. Lena's fraternizing with an enemy would be exposed immediately as soon as this child's DNA had been scanned and she would most likely be punished for an illegal pregnancy. The child would be taken away from her and she would be confined under house arrest."

"The child would survive?" Lena asked the others.

"The child would survive," Tilia said.

"But Lena would have to live in public disgrace," Anamona added, "So, if this became public knowledge it would completely ruin her life. She would become an outcast, isolated from all others. This is the accepted course of action in such a situation."

Doctor Alauda nodded. Saia knew exactly what it felt like to be an outcast living in disgrace.

"What if Lena defected to our side of the border?" Jani asked the Unionians.

"Over my dead body!" Anamona snapped.

Lena looked at her sister.

"It was just a suggestion Anamona ..." she soothed.

"But it is out of the question," Anamona informed the group. "It will never happen. Lena is my only sister."

"What kind of life would Lena have in Hirunda?" Tilia asked the others.

"Tilia?!" Anamona exclaimed.

Saia understood Anamona's reluctance completely. Lena would be making a huge mistake if she defected to their side.

"I'm curious, that's all," Tilia explained. "It can't hurt to discuss the possibility."

Saia noticed how Anamona huffed and then looked at her sister.

"You're not defecting," she told her angrily.

Lena wrapped her arms around Anamona to console her. This act of compassion surprised Saia who had never witnessed such closeness between two women. She couldn't imagine hugging her own sisters; she barely even knew them.

"I'm not exactly sure what would happen to Lena, I don't know if such a thing has ever even happened on our side," Lu said. "I suppose Lena would be taken to be with the other women in the inner circles of one of the cities."

"Would she be able to keep her child?" Tilia asked him and Doctor Alauda.

"Probably," Doctor Alauda replied.

"So, then it is an option," Tilia concluded.

Anamona glared at the older woman.

"I'm sorry, Anamona, but Lena has to consider this option as well."

"What would happen to Lu is an entirely different issue," Lemmus pointed out then.

"Indeed," Jani noted seriously.

"What do you mean?" Anamona asked the man.

"Lu has slept with a woman and managed to inseminate her. Procreation without official permission is not something that is taken lightly," Lemmus explained. "The company of women is a privilege for only a small handful of men."

"*Successful* men," Doctor Alauda added.

"That's right," Lemmus said, "So, if this were revealed, Lena and the child would most likely never see Lu."

"And Lu would lose all his Silver Wing marks," Doctor Alauda added. "He would lose everything; his position, his work, and all the rights he has earned so far."

"Not to mention the fact that he would get a one-way ticket there," Jani said pointing to the sky.

"Where?" Tilia asked the man.

"To Cold Pit," Jani said.

"What is Cold Pit?" Anamona asked him.

Saia was surprised at Anamona's ignorance.

"It's a prison on the moon," Lemmus said. "A prison from where there is no return. The worst criminals are sent there."

"Who are these worst criminals then?" Anamona asked him.

"Mostly men who have taken the life of another person," Lu said.

"Aren't there different degrees of those acts?" Anamona pointed out.

"Not in our society," Lu stated. "If a human life is lost in circumstances other than an accident, that's enough for a man to make his first and last trip to Cold Pit."

"That's the way it goes," Lemmus said. "Cold Pit's coldness is legendary."

"It's a big enough threat for many men who are prone to test the limits of the law. Unfortunately, there will always be a few sociopaths in society who can't help their impulses," Lu added. "Like we have seen in the headlines recently."

"Really?" Lemmus asked him curiously.

"And I am not referring to you," Lu added, looking at Mari, "even though there are those who say you are responsible for those crimes as well."

"I know," Mari said sourly, "I can read."

"What crimes have been committed then?" Anamona asked him curiously.

"There has been some major crimes committed in world cities recently," Lu said. Saia nodded.

"By the same perpetrator?" Anamona asked him.

"Most likely," Lu said.

"How many victims are we talking about? Tilia asked him.

"Three, four?" Lu guessed and looked at Jani.

"The victim in Makaira survived," Jani reminded them.

Saia could still see the blood that Melanitta had shed. She knew she wouldn't forget that sight for the rest of her life.

"So, people are taken to the moon?" Anamona asked the men, to be sure she wasn't being tricked.

"There have been people on the moon for decades," Lemmus said.

"I know people go there but I have never really thought they would stay there for longer periods of time. There must be permanent settlement there."

"There is," Lemmus said. "Alongside Cold Pit, there are power plants on both polar areas and energy is brought from there to Earth as well."

"Cold Pit is a closed facility for criminals," Jani added. "Whoever goes there stays there and they will die there."

"And they would send Lu there just because he is the father of my child?" Lena asked the others.

"It's possible," Lemmus said.

"It's a choice between Cold Pit and Gaskar," Jani said.

"Gaskar?" Anamona asked them.

"The island of Gaskar, whose southern tip is located directly on the Capricorn tropic. The island itself is uninhabitable due to the extreme weather but they managed to build a prison there," Lu explained.

"When I was a child, Gaskar was the only prison in the world," Lemmus revealed. "I can still remember when Cold Pit was being built. It was a long project but unfortunately a necessary one. Men can be freed from Gaskar once they've served their time."

"That's true," Jani said.

" There are criminals who simply have to be kept separate from the rest of the population," Lemmus added.

"So, defecting to Hirunda is not an option," Lena stated. "No, no, and no. Lu and I want to be together."

"Yes, but what you want and what is possible in this world may well be two different things," Anamona reminded her.

"I refuse to believe there is no way to resolve this situation so that both Lu and I can keep our child," Lena stated. "Look at us! Look where we are now! We have three Terra Unionians here, one defector from Hirunda, two

Hirundian men, and two Hirundian women, of whom one is about to defect to Terra Unionia. If someone had told me six months ago I would be sitting here tonight, I would never have believed it. Yet here we are, each one of us, regardless of the law and the regulations set by the people outside this place. So even though this child is a problem from a legal standpoint, there has to be a way for it to fit into this world. There has to be some way."

Saia looked as Lena and empathized with her. Her situation was not an easy one.

"If a way exists it won't be found quickly and easily," Lemmus said. "I'm sure you both understand that this is something you have to think through carefully and plan for, and the planning part is going to take significantly more time than we have in this corner of this forest tonight."

"You can say that again," said Lena flatly.

However, Saia didn't see Lena's situation as particular problematic. She wondered for a moment whether to speak or not, but summoned up enough courage and began to speak.

"What if Lena's information was altered in your information system?"

Everyone present fell silent and Saia started to feel extremely awkward because of the sudden attention. She regretted immediately having opened her mouth.

"And who would be able to do something like that?" Anamona asked her.

"I might be able to do that," Saia said.

"Really?" Anamona asked her. "And we should just give you access to fiddle our national information system?"

Saia heard annoyance in her tone of voice.

"I'd need a connection to your information network," she added. "I'm sure your systems differ from ours, but they're still made by people. I'm sure I'd learn pretty quickly how to use them."

"No," Anamona said. "Absolutely not."

"But if I am coming to Terra Unionia with Mari anyway ..." Saia began. She knew that if she could help a Terra Unionian now, it would work in her favor sometime in the future.

"Mari is going to defect to Terra Unionia, not you," Lena said.

Saia's spirit was crushed.

"What ...?" she asked, deeply confused. Going back to Gavialis without Doctor Alauda was inconceivable. "But why?!"

"Because I say so," Lena informed her bluntly.

"But …"

"Let's talk about that later on," Doctor Alauda interrupted.

Saia protested in frustration then fell silent. For her the matter was far from closed. If Doctor Alauda defected she would most definitely accompany her. She had no intention of returning to Gavialis ever again, especially not without Doctor Alauda. She would plead with Tilia; that woman seemed to be the most understanding of them all.

"So, you have known each other for a longer period of time?" Lena asked Doctor Alauda.

"I've known Saia for years now," Doctor Alauda said.

"She's my doctor," Saia said quietly.

"Saia," Tilia chimed in, "thank you for your suggestion. We may come back to it, if necessary. It is, however, good to know that this kind of option exists."

Saia looked at Tilia and nodded. There was some room for negotiation with Tilia, she sensed.

"What if Lena simply disappeared?" Doctor Alauda suggested. "When her pregnancy starts to show, couldn't she simply disappear?"

"Hide where?" Lena asked her.

"I can't answer that for you."

"That option should be considered as well," Lemmus noted.

"We have to consider it, don't we?" Lena stated.

"But it still wouldn't resolve the issue of giving birth, how and where Lena would deliver her baby," Anamona reminded. "She can't just push the child out under some tree and wait for her bleeding to stop. What will happen after the child is born? There has to be some official records or other documentation, this child has to show up somewhere. What about when the child is growing up? What nationality will it have? Who will educate it, and where?"

"One step at a time," Lena said calmly.

"The gender of this child is also a relevant factor," Lemmus reminded.

"How so?" Doctor Alauda asked them.

"Girls and boys are raised differently in both Hirunda and Terra Unionia," Lemmus specified. "When the gender of this child is known, you two have to decide where the best place for the child to grow up is. I suggest you think it over carefully, because the answer will not be self-evident."

"Doesn't a small baby need its mother?" Jani said. "Doesn't this bind the child to Terra Unionia?"

"Possibly," Tilia answered, "but if we don't figure out a way to avoid a DNA scan ..."

"It means trouble," Lemmus noted.

"And if Lena gets caught carrying this child, you can be sure that Lu won't see her ever again here on the border," Tilia said.

"What if Lena's personal information were altered on *our* systems?" Doctor Alauda asked Saia, "would you be able to do something like that?"

Saia looked at the doctor for a moment, then nodded.

"Who are you?" Jani asked her from the other side of Doctor Alauda.

Saia took a quick glance at the man but quickly averted her eyes and stared at the ground. She didn't know how to communicate with men; not counting Ati, she never had.

"What are we talking about here exactly?" Anamona asked the others.

"Saia could create an ID account for Lena on our information system," Lu explained.

"So, in principle defecting to Hirunda isn't an impossible idea after all. Lena could live her life in Gavialis," Tilia said.

"What?!" Anamona snapped angrily. "Absolutely not! Haven't we already dismissed this option?"

"Anamona ..." Lena sighed.

"You are actually considering an option like this?!" Anamona asked her sister, shocked.

"I have to," Lena replied. "I have to think about Lu and my child."

"I understand the child, but ..."

"Please don't end that sentence," Lena interrupted her sister, "please."

"Well forgive me, but you asked me to come here so I will say what is on my mind," Anamona replied defiantly.

"Anamona," Lena raised her voice, "don't."

Saia watched the two women carefully and waited. She knew that the tension between them would soon erupt.

"How can you know that Lu will still want this child in a year from now?" Anamona asked her sister.

"Excuse me?" Lu asked her, the irritation in his voice was audible.

"You have known each other three months," Anamona said. "Three months! That is more or less 12 weeks. So forgive me if I'm having a hard time believing in some great love story at this point!"

Saia had to admit to herself that there was some sense to Anamona's words.

"I am committed to Lena and this child," Lu informed her.

"That is what you're saying now," Anamona retorted.

"And I mean it."

"You are a *man,*" Anamona pointed out.

Saia was taken aback by her remark.

"And?"

"Men don't care about children or take any responsibility for them," Anamona informed him. "The male psyche is different. Forging an emotional bond with children does not come as naturally to you as it does to women. Men are unable to love their children like women love them."

"What?!" Lu exclaimed.

Saia was also in shock when she heard what Anamona said but remained silent.

"Anamona, be quiet!" Lena told her sister. "You don't know what you are talking about!"

"And you do?!" Anamona asked her, "all this talk about moving to Gavialis, altering personal information et cetera – it's all pointless! You have no guarantee that Lu will still be interested in you and your child in the future."

"You don't know me," Lu pointed out seriously.

"You are a man!"

"So what?!"

"It is a biological fact that male behavior is controlled by their sexual instincts! You wanted to copulate with a woman so congratulations; you have achieved your goal, but don't start claiming that you have any interest in Lena or this child! You are a *man!* You can say all you want about caring about Lena and being committed to this child but it is a lie! You are saying all these things just to ensure that you will be able to continue copulating with her!"

Even though Saia didn't know anyone here, she could understand Anamona's point of view. Even Lator had been ready and willing to risk everything because of Naja, which was still mind-boggling to Saia.

"Have you lost your mind?!" Jani exclaimed. "You have some nerve blaming this on Lu! If anyone is to blame it's Lena; she used Lu!"

"How could Lena ever take advantage of Lu?!" Anamona snapped. "What on earth could she gain by carrying Lu's child?!"

"The female psyche is narcissistic! Lena manipulated Lu because she is a *woman*!" Jani claimed and Saia's jaw dropped. "She was a Terra Unionian border guard bored with her daily patrolling routine and she wanted to try something women on your side obviously don't experience very often! She wanted something different compared with other women, women constantly compare themselves with other women! Lu was too gullible to say no, so he provided this perfect opportunity for her to do so! Your sister lured Lu with her female tricks without caring at all whether she would ruin his life in the process! And now she is blackmailing Lu with this child; she doesn't want to terminate this pregnancy because her situation is exceptional and it gives her the one-up on all other women!"

Saia noticed that Lena's mouth had dropped open, staring as she was at Jani, eyes wide.

"You have developed this odd affection for that woman without even thinking what her true motives could be!" Jani shouted at his friend. "All she wanted was for you to bring some variety into her life here on the border! She doesn't need you for anything else!"

"What?!" Lena exclaimed.

"Oh, Lena's life is so in order now that she's carrying the child of a Hirundian man!" Anamona yelled sarcastically. "Your allegations have no grounding in reality!"

"Most likely Lena planned this so-called surprise pregnancy, in the process ruining Lu's life as well!" Jani claimed loudly.

"How is Lu's life ruined now?! He is not biologically attached to this child like Lena is!" Anamona yelled. "He can disappear behind this border whenever he wants and leave Lena alone with this situation! I am sure that is exactly what is going to happen! As soon as Lena doesn't want to copulate with him anymore, his interest in Lena and this child stops immediately!"

"Will you two shut up!" Lu shouted. "Neither one of you knows what you are talking about!"

"Lena has used you!" Jani told his friend, beside himself with rage.

"In what way exactly?!" Lena demanded to know.

"Lena is the one who will have to raise this child!" Anamona snapped. "This child is Lena's! Lu has no rights when it comes to this child!"

"Excuse me?!" Lu asked her. "I do have rights to my own child!"

"Not in Terra Unionia!" Anamona informed him.

"This child is not Terra Unionian!"

"Well, the child is not Hirundian, either!" Anamona informed him, "and never will be! This child is Terra Unionian because Lena is Terra Unionian! The child is *Lena's*!"

"And I'm nothing?!" Lu asked her angrily. "I have full rights to my own child! That is what is written in World Law and Terra Unionia is part of the world, whether *you* like it or not!"

"We have our own laws and regulations! Why are you refuting Lena's full rights to this child? Men don't care about their biological children!"

"Why shouldn't a man want to raise his own child?" Lu demanded. "I had a provider and he raised me! He never even entertained the idea of abandoning me!"

"Your motives are controlled by your sexual desires!" Anamona hissed. "You are a slave to your instincts! Sexuality and violence are the main driving forces behind your behavior! For now Lena has satisfied your needs but what about that day when she says no to you? What will happen then? You will force her to bend to your will by using physical force! It has happened to women before and it will happen again, but you can be sure that the very moment you raise your hand to hit her, she will hit you back and she will hit you back hard!"

"WHAT?!" Lu yelled. "Have you lost your mind?!"

"You are a man!"

"So what?!"

"You have your limitations!"

"And you don't?!"

"I bet you want to hit me now, don't you?" Anamona asked him. "Come on, then, show your true colors!"

Saia was beginning to get frightened. Anamona wasn't serious, was she?

"Look how she is provoking you!" Jani interjected. "That's exactly what women do! That's exactly how they get in your head!"

"Stop it, now!" Tilia erupted. Saia hoped that her instruction would reach the four.

"Lu is not violent towards me!" Lena yelled to her sister.

"Not yet! Don't you remember anything you have been taught about men?! Is this how quickly you forget everything? You already let him between your legs! One day he will hurt you physically, too!"

"Are you insane?!" Lu's face was purple with rage.

"You had the opportunity to copulate like some animal and that was all you wanted! The mere thought of you two wanting to raise this child together is beyond ridiculous! You are not able to do that because you are a man!"

"The only thing that is beyond ridiculous is you!" Lu informed her. "You don't know what you are talking about! All those ideas, your attitude towards men, it just proves you really are totally selfish! "

"LU!" Lena shouted in shock.

"Your head is all mixed up because of that woman's manipulation!" Jani said to Lu. "You defend her, you can no longer think straight because of the damage she has done! You should have been more careful back then when you realized she was a woman!"

"Silence!!!" Tilia suddenly shouted.

The feuding foursome finally fell silent.

For a moment there was perfect silence in the forest. Saia glanced at Tilia whose face was full of anger. Then she looked in turn at Anamona, Lena, Lu, and Jani who were still eyeing each other up suspiciously. Saia waited and held her breath.

"What a show ..." Lemmus finally said quietly.

"I understand that this situation is emotionally highly charged but what do you expect to accomplish by all this?" Tilia asked the four, voicing her disapproval. "Just listen to yourselves."

Silence.

"Lu, Jani – try to understand that on our side of the border men really don't participate in raising children and unfortunately we have this commonly accepted belief in our society that men are unable to form an emotional bond with their biological children," Tilia explained. "This may be the result of men not being aware of their children but this is not the time to go into that."

"But ..." Anamona started.

"You'll be quiet now, Anamona," Tilia told her. "You have already voiced your opinions. You have been taught to be cautious near men, like every other Terra Unionian woman, but now the time has come to question your own views, whether you want to or not."

"My alleged violent urges are still a real concern in Terra Unionia," Lemmus added. "I am still being carefully monitored, even though my behavior has been exemplary for over 26 years. The expectations and attitudes run deep."

Saia looked at the man to see if he was really serious.

"I've known Lemmus for almost twenty years now," Tilia continued. "And he has never had the slightest urge to physically attack me. This has nothing to do with these regular meetings with a psychologist, does it?"

"I would never hurt you," Lemmus confirmed, "never."

"So, maybe your sister has recognized something she still needs to work on," Tilia pointed out to Anamona. "Is Lena's stubbornness wise? Not really, when we consider the circumstances, but Lu isn't the biggest threat to your sister, the law and the people's common beliefs are."

"I still don't trust Lu. I just can't believe that a man could ever want a child. You don't have to take my word for it, would you be interested in fathering a child?" Anamona asked Lemmus then.

"Me?" Lemmus asked her confused. "Why?"

"I want to know where you stand."

"Well to be honest I don't know."

"When Lemmus and I met for the first time, he it made perfectly clear that he couldn't care less whether I was his biological child or not," Anamona told the others.

"And it was the truth," Lemmus confessed, "but I am me. If I still lived in Hirunda and had somehow achieved all these great things to be viewed as successful enough to have earned official permission to procreate, I wouldn't necessarily use the privilege. I am not that kind of person. These are just my own views, not the views of all men and especially not Lu's."

"Thank you," Lu said.

"You have to understand, for your sister's sake, that men are not unable to love, and that the love that men feel does not always manifest itself exclusively through sexual behavior," Lemmus added. "Men do have similar feelings to women and a man can fall in love with a woman. If this were not the case, how could there be love between two men?"

Saia realized Lemmus was right. He had raised a good point.

"I find it extremely important to emphasize now that affection between a woman and a man is taboo in Terra Unionia," Tilia said. "In fact, the affection between Lena and Lu would be considered a mental disturbance. Only mentally unbalanced or unstable women fall in love with men. That's why Anamona has difficulty understanding and accepting her sister's affection for Lu."

"You don't have to defend me," Anamona said.

"Yes I do," Tilia stated.

"Why?" Anamona asked her.

"Well, if we don't talk openly about these issues now, we will never understand each other. It is important that we are all fully aware of the cultural differences which influence our thoughts. Our cultural backgrounds dictate how we perceive Lena and Lu's relationship. It is important that Lu understands where your resentment comes from and that you would cast out any man near Lena, not just Lu. Lu simply happens to be the person here who has fallen in love with your sister."

"Vice versa," Doctor Alauda finally said. "I was not surprised to hear what Jani had to say about the female psyche; on our side of the border, men see women in a certain way, good or bad."

Saia nodded. Doctor Alauda knew what she was talking about.

"So, we have to talk these thing through," Tilia continued. "Let's try without any further quarrelling. We have our different views because we come from different backgrounds with our values, norms, and ways. We are different and that's why we have to talk about these things together, in order to learn to tolerate our differences. We are by no means exceptional people here; it is also difficult for us to tolerate dissimilarity, but for this reason, keeping our thoughts to ourselves will help no one."

"All I can say is that I am committed to Lena," Lu stated. "If my word is not enough then so be it, but it is the truth."

"And I believe you," Tilia said. "However, you must understand that Anamona needs more time to accept this. Jani too, he is like a brother to you. Anamona has her doubts for a reason. She loves her sister and she is scared for her. Her fears are justified, not because you are a bad person, she's afraid of what will happen to Lena in Terra Unionia."

"I understand that," Lu noted.

"Good."

"And when it comes to your claims, Jani, you are mistaken," Lu said. "Just because you can't understand the affection between Lena and me doesn't mean it doesn't exist. You or Anamona not being able to grasp it doesn't render it non-existent. It is very real for both of us."

"Do you honestly think that Lu and I would have started something like this on the spur of the moment?" Lena asked the others and by doing so grabbed Saia's undivided attention. "Is that how stupid you really think we are? I had absolutely no intention of feeling these emotions for Lu. I didn't want to fall in love with him. When I met him for the first time I was so afraid I felt physically sick. There's a very long way from that point to feeling love for this man! These feelings of mine didn't evolve in a moment!

They are not even through choice. I didn't choose to fall in love with Lu – I didn't even know I was capable of loving a man – but it happened. On the day that I found out I was pregnant, I was scared. Yes, I considered terminating this pregnancy – the mere thought of an illegal pregnancy scared me half to death – but knowing this child exists made me happy, too. This pregnancy feels like a natural extension of the love I feel for Lu."

Suddenly Lena covered her mouth with her hand. Saia noticed she was trying to hold back her tears. Lu looked at Lena and pulled her to him as he wrapped his arms around her. Saia didn't know what to think of the sight. She had never imagined that a man committed to a woman could care for her so tenderly.

"It is obvious you're having a hard time understanding this," Lu said. "It will take time because you haven't been here the last few months. I can't imagine my life without Lena. My sexuality plays a major role in us having this child but I am capable of other feelings, too."

"I am also capable of sexual desire," volunteered Lena, turning to face Anamona. "Desire, in my case directed at Lu. I want it too, not just the other way round. It is also part of my psyche and my personality, whether it is classified as insanity in Terra Unionia or not. I don't feel abnormal or exceptional in any way. Lu has never forced me to do anything."

Saia felt she shouldn't have been privy to this intimacy. Lena's confession and all this public analysis of people's desires, was totally unheard of. All she could do was hide her embarrassment and awkwardness by continuing to stare at the ground.

"When it comes to female sexuality," Tilia said, "its existence is of course acknowledged in our society, but it is perceived as similar to thirst or hunger, something completely natural for us. It is a biological need which must be fulfilled and girls of a certain age are taught how to fulfill this need for themselves."

"I think female sexuality is over-rated on our side," Doctor Alauda said. "The fact that there are so many more men than there are women has led to the way of thinking that females have all the power when it comes to sexuality in general. That's why I am not at all surprised to hear these claims that women are great at manipulating men. Perhaps we do behave differently from men in relationships than men do, but over-emphasizing the female sexuality is entirely understandable in our cultural context. A man is the one who is given permission to approach a woman, who in turn allows a man to touch her guarded body, if she wants to. A woman's ability to carry a child gives her great power, even though many women don't realize that."

Saia cast a guilty glace in Doctor Alauda's direction. Was that last sentence for her benefit?

"And only the most successful men are allowed to step humbly among women to compete for their attention," Lemmus added. "So, women are treated as if they were the most valuable treasures on the planet. That's the reason why only a few chosen men earn the right to enter this treasury of women. And therefore women are often seen as spoilt, proud, and sometimes even self-centered."

"So, if Lena came to Gavialis, Lu wouldn't be able to see her," Doctor Alauda added to change the direction of their conversation. "Lu is not a man of great advancement; he's not successful enough to have the right to see Lena often. They would live in different parts of the city and Lena would spend her time with other people, not Lu, even if Lu's role in this pregnancy escaped the authorities' attention. They would meet only occasionally and only in certain parts of the city, and even then Lena wouldn't be alone. She would be constantly guarded by the Yellow Guardsmen."

"Better than never seeing Lena and the child," Lu pointed out.

"Of course," Doctor Alauda said.

The whole group fell silent for a moment. Saia observed the others closely and waited.

"I guess I have to face facts; there isn't really a solution to our problem which would satisfy all parties involved," Lu said.

"Are you losing hope?" Lena asked him.

"I think this is more about my suspicions becoming real," Lu said to her, "suspicions I didn't want to believe, but I guess it was too good to be true after all."

"Maybe we can still figure something out somehow," Lena tried to console him.

"I hope so," Lu said, "but I'm not counting on it. I think I am going to lose you and the child."

"Don't say that," Lena begged.

"It's true."

"I won't accept it."

"Maybe we can still figure something out," Tilia said, trying to encourage the young pair. "The child isn't going to be born tomorrow or even the day after that."

Lena looked at Tilia and nodded. Then she turned to face her sister, pulled her close and wrapped her arms around her.

"Let's not fight anymore," Lena said. "Things will work themselves out somehow."

"I hope so," Anamona said, an empty look in her eyes. "I'm sorry I got so worked up, but I don't want you to defect to Hirunda. I just don't want that to happen."

"I know," Lena whispered.

"You're all I've got," Anamona reminded her quietly. "You have to stay in Terra Unionia."

Saia could feel Anamona's fear. As someone who had lost her own sibling she knew exactly what Anamona was feeling.

"Like we've already said, this pregnancy won't show for a while yet," Lena reminded her. "So, for now this situation is still under control."

"We are not in control of this situation because we already know what will happen to you in the forthcoming months as the baby grows inside you," Anamona pointed out. "Since when have you been the rational sister?"

Lena laughed.

"We have to exchange roles every now and then," she joked.

Anamona smiled then placed her head on her sister's shoulder.

"As sad it is, this child is a problem," Anamona said. "This child simply has no place in either society. There is no social niche for this baby. Someone is going to have to make a considerable sacrifice."

"I know," Lena said quietly. "I know."

15.

Jani took a deep breath and tried to calm his nerves. He had not expected things to come to a head in such a heated argument. However, he had to stand by Lu now, seeing as the man himself seemed to have forgotten the risks involved in fraternizing with Lena. As Tilia brought their argument to a close, he was able to breathe more freely again.

Then he remembered the cursed black suitcase, in the hands of the defector. It was quite familiar, it had to be the same one which had taken him all the way to Makaira.

"Should we move on?" Lena suggested. "I think we have already discussed my current condition enough."

"I agree," Lu said.

"So, who's next?" Anamona asked the others.

"The man with the black suitcase," Lena said nodding at Lemmus.

"I second that," Lu stated.

Jani's ears pricked up. This was the moment he had been waiting for. He noticed Tilia nodding as well which he interpreted as a gesture of compliance. Jani observed the woman for a moment and wondered at her unusual manner. She had presence which made people pay attention when she was talking. It was a quality he had missed in his life instructor as a child.

"Alright," Tilia finally said. "To recap, we really don't know who this suitcase is from. That is the truth. We also can't tell you who delivered it to the border, either. All we know is when a delivery is scheduled to take place. We go to the border and collect. Well, usually Lemmus takes care of that. My presence here tonight is actually quite exceptional."

"Lucky you," Mari Alauda said.

"You can say that again," Tilia noted.

"So, you communicate with Hirundians in some way," Lena asked Tilia.

"Yes, but communication is one way only," Tilia said. "we have no means of sending messages out of Terra Unionia so all messages come from Hirunda in our direction."

"On what channel?" Lena asked her. "Have the Hirundians penetrated our network?"

"No," Tilia assured her. "The messages are not sent via the information network."

"That's a relief," Anamona noted.

"So, you come to the border and get these deliveries from a particular place?" Lena asked them.

"Yes," Lemmus said. "These so-called deliveries typically float down the river from Hirunda's side."

"Well, of course they do," Lena stated. "I should have realized that. The river provides a way for the person on Hirunda's side to avoid getting too deep into the border zone."

"True," Lu noted.

Jani listened to the conversation carefully and with great interest. There was some sort of organized activity behind the suitcase delivery, just as he had suspected.

"The river is without question a security weak spot from Terra Unionia's perspective," Lena sighed. "In the Border Guard we call it the 'bleeding wound' in our line of defense."

"The river must be monitored on your side, though, surely?" Lu asked.

"Of course," Lena confirmed, "it's monitored with sensors right through the entire border zone, but I suspect suitcases like that cross the border under the surface of the water, so they are not easily detectable. Because the first water purification plants are situated beyond the border zone, where larger pieces of debris are removed from the water during the screening process, suitcases like that may float down the river through the border zone without anyone noticing. Our sensors monitor mainly movement on the ground, not underwater."

"You are correct," Lemmus said.

"How exactly do you avoid our sensors?" Lena asked him.

"We try to stay as far away from the river as possible," Lemmus said.

"But you must have retrieved that suitcase somehow," Lena pointed out, "So, what's your secret?"

"Well ..." Lemmus started.

"How do you locate these deliveries?" Lena interrupted. "With the same device you locate and avoid the mines on the border zone?"

"Yes," Lemmus confessed.

"Interesting," Lena noted. "I bet you used this same device to locate the suitcase as well. It must send a weak signal of some kind."

"You're right," Lemmus stated.

"Does this signal also disturb the monitoring sensors?" Lena asked him.

"Very much so."

"So, you blind our sensors," Lena stated. "The suitcase itself creates a disturbance which enables you to locate it and pull it out of the river."

Lemmus and Tilia exchanged glances, then looked at Lena again. Jani knew for certain that Lena had deduced the situation correctly.

"Organized activity," Lu stated. "Someone from our border guard has to be involved in this because, if these suitcases are delivered to the river by civilians, some of them would already have been caught."

Lu was right, Jani knew that.

"You don't let civilians near the border zone?" Lena asked Lu.

"We don't really have to forbid it," Lu said. "People remain in the cities. They are not interested in exploring what might be found outside the train track network, especially when a significant part of the land is still uninhabitable after the Great War. People also believe that visiting these areas could even be a health risk due to the environmental toxins."

"That's why no one dares to come here," Saia suddenly said, and her voice attracted everyone's attention, including Jani's. "According to official maps, this area is nothing more than contaminated wasteland, a health hazard."

"Really?" Tilia noted interested.

"That's the surest way to keep the nosy ones out," Lemmus explained.

"Not very effective, it seems," Tilia laughed, nodding in Saia and Mari's direction.

"Which just confirms that someone from the Border Guard Detachment is involved in this delivery chain of yours," Lu added. "It's pretty obvious now."

"I don't know any names," Lemmus confessed, "and I have never asked any of them. These men work discreetly and undetected."

"So, is this illegal, then?" Anamona asked them.

"As much as maintaining contact with someone living in Terra Unionia is considered illegal in Hirunda," Lemmus explained. "Whether it is illegal exactly, that I can't say. When it comes to the exact word of law from the Terra Unionian perspective, I'm sure my actions are blatantly illegal, but my conscience is clear because we aren't exactly exchanging weapons here or anything like that."

"That's good to hear," Anamona said.

"So, what is in that suitcase, then? You told us earlier that these deliveries are about some old artifacts, but what artifacts are so important that you two have come here despite the risk of getting caught?" Lena asked Lemmus and Tilia.

Jani took a deep breath. He wanted to know, too, what had been so important for him to be rewarded with a night in Grus Tower in Gavialis' Sixth Circle. Finally, Lemmus turned the suitcase over in his hands and unlocked the clasp. Jani waited on tenterhooks for its contents to be revealed.

"Whatever is in this suitcase will be a surprise for me and Tilia as well," the man added. "It is always a surprise."

"Understood," Lu said.

Lemmus opened the suitcase and stared at its contents in silence. Jani tried to keep the expression on his face as neutral as possible. He didn't want anyone to realize he had seen the suitcase before. He had promised to keep it to himself after all.

"What is it?" Lena finally asked him.

Lemmus kept his eyes on the contents of the suitcase, then laughed.

"Well, tell us," Lena urged.

"A bottle," the man said.

"Bottle?" Lena asked him.

Jani was taken aback. A bottle? What the man serious?

"It feels quite hard," the man offered as he touched the bottle inside the suitcase. "My guess is that this must be made of an oil-based plastic."

"Oil-based plastic?" Lu asked him.

"Before the Great War plastic was made from oil," Lemmus explained. "Oil is a liquid in the soil which has a high carbon and hydrogen content, which originates from ancient organic material."

"We know," Anamona sighed.

This information was, however, new to Jani.

"In this case this oil-based plastic bottle is a significant find because plastic does not decompose in soil," Lemmus said.

"At least not very easily," Tilia added as she was becoming increasingly curious about the bottle with every passing second.

"These plastic bottles can remain in the ground for 450 years," Lemmus guessed. "It is a long time."

"So, the bottle in question must be old," Lu noted.

"It could be very old," Tilia pointed out.

"This bottle is the reason why you came here all the way from Pinus?" Lena asked them. "Sorry, but I'm having a hard time believing that anyone would take the trouble to get to the border just because of a bottle."

Jani agreed, but on the other hand he had gone all the way to Makaira without even knowing what was in the suitcase.

"Like I have already said, we never really know what is being delivered to us," Lemmus reminded them.

"Well, I guess this time it wasn't worth the trouble," Lena guessed.

"This is not just any bottle," Tilia said as she inspected the suitcase in Lemmus' lap.

"What do you mean?" Lena asked them.

"There's something inside it," the woman answered.

"What?" Lena asked her curiously.

"Hmm ..." Lemmus said and took the bottle out of the suitcase so that all the others were able to see the object being discussed.

Then he placed the black suitcase on the ground next to Tilia and started to turn the bottle in his hands to inspect it more carefully. Jani watched Lemmus intently.

"Is there a paper roll in there?" Anamona asked them.

"It would seem so," Lemmus stated.

"So, that piece of paper is the reason you took the trouble to get here?" Lena asked him confused.

"This paper must be important," Lemmus said, giving the bottle to Tilia.

Tilia took the bottle without hesitation and studied the paper roll inside with great interest.

"Must be?" Lena asked him. "You're not sure?"

"Like I said, we don't usually know what is being delivered," Lemmus explained. "But we are more than just collectors of ancient trash even though this bottle may give you that impression. I have always believed, however, that piles of trash from the time before the Great War would most likely contain many interesting finds which would reveal a great deal about the past."

"That's true," Tilia said as she studied the bottle in her hands. "There's written text on this paper," she observed.

"So, my eyes didn't deceive me, even though the light is poor," Lemmus stated.

"They didn't," Tilia assured him. "There is definitely some writing on this paper."

"Can you distinguish words on it?" Anamona asked her.

"Hmm … it's hard to say since the paper is rolled but there are definitely individual letters here."

"Are you going to open the bottle?" Jani asked the two.

Tilia and Lemmus exchanged looks.

"Let's do it," Tilia said.

"Are you sure?" Lemmus asked her. "Here in the middle of this forest?"

"You think we should wait until we get back to Pinus?"

"We have no way of knowing how fragile that paper is," Lemmus said. "If it crumbles, we will never know what was written on it."

"This paper has most likely been covered inside this bottle for a long time and therefore it has been protected from sunlight and moisture as well," Tilia said. "So, it could take some careful handling, but I wouldn't touch it with bare hands."

"I have my gloves with me," Lemmus said. "What shall we do?"

Tilia observed Lemmus for a while, then said, "Let's open it."

"Are you sure?"

Tilia nodded.

"Open the bottle," Lena said impatiently.

"Oh, so Miss Border Guard is also interested in what is written on this paper?" Lemmus observed and smirked.

"I am interested in finding out why the two of you have come to the border in the first place," Lena explained.

Lemmus took his gloves out of his pocket and put them on. Then Tilia gave him the bottle.

"This is most likely a screw cap," Lemmus said.

"It would seem so," Tilia noted.

Lemmus clenched the cap with his right hand and twisted. The cap seemed to be sealed tightly, but the man was able to loosen it. When the cap was off, he placed it carefully in the suitcase and looked Tilia in the eye. She nodded, which signaled Lemmus to pull the tiny paper roll out from the bottle into his hand.

"Be careful," Tilia told.

"I will, I will," the man assured her.

Lemmus placed the bottle back in the suitcase, then unrolled the piece of paper. Jani saw Tilia leaning over him in order to see the sheet more closely.

"You can hardly read this anymore," Lemmus said.

"Let me see," Tilia asked him and leaned in even closer.

"I can't make head or tail of this," Lemmus sighed in frustration.

"Because you can't read it," Tilia informed him, "it's written in one of the ancient languages."

"Ancient languages?" Lu asked her.

Jani was surprised as well. What languages was Tilia talking about?

"There are many people in Terra Unionia who study dead languages as a hobby," Lena explained, "even though we only speak two official languages."

"Two?" Jani asked her. "I thought all the people in the world shared just one language."

"Terra Unionia is a bilingual country," Tilia explained as she studied the piece of paper.

"Odd," Jani said. "Doesn't it make daily life complicated?"

"Not really," Anamona stated.

"Can you all speak both of these languages?" Jani asked the Unionians.

"Yes," Lena said. "All Terra Unionians are bilingual."

Jani didn't know what to think. He couldn't image that there were two entirely different languages spoken in the world. It simply felt too complicated to work on a practical level. Yet knowing this made him also wonder whether there was someone in Terra Unionia who would be able to read that book he had seen in the museum in Sixth Circle.

"The fact that there is only one spoken language worldwide has its roots in a conscious decision," Lemmus said. "After the Great War there was the need to unify the world and therefore one language was chosen as the official language of the entire human race. This language was taught to the next generation. In fact, it was made law and thereafter all the other different languages disappeared and died out after just one generation."

"Do you understand the language written on that piece of paper?" Anamona asked Tilia.

"I do," Tilia replied.

"Well, what does it say?" Lemmus asked her.

Jani watched Tilia take the black suitcase from between her and Lemmus and place it right beside the man. Then she stared at the piece of paper while Lemmus held it up in front of her.

"I think this is what it says: *I am alone. All the people I have ever talked to are gone. I am the only one left, on the edge of these ruins, as I watch the world coming to an end. We have already destroyed all there is to be destroyed, but we continue to destroy what has already been destroyed. This is all we can do. If someone finds this message once I'm gone, they should tell those who are still hiding this destruction that we did not deserve this world. Mankind is one huge disappointment.*"

"Wow ..." Lena sighed. "Grim."

Jani agreed.

"From the days of the Great War, I presume," Anamona said.

"That seems to be the case," Lemmus noted, "this *is* a great find."

"You can say that again," Tilia said.

"It is?" Lena asked them.

"Well, of course it is!" Lemmus exclaimed. "A message from the past, beyond the grave!"

"But we all already know about the war without even reading that message," Lu pointed out. "So, I can't really see its value."

Jani nodded at his friend's words. He was also having difficulty understanding Tilia and Lemmus' fuss over one piece of old paper.

"The value of the paper is very evident to me," Tilia said. "This message is unique. There is not a similar one anywhere in the world, and it is most likely one of the few things we have on this planet from the days of the Great War."

"Not counting the environmental toxins," Lemmus added.

"Do you receive things like this without sending anything back?" Anamona asked the two.

"We do deliver some things in return," Tilia said.

"Really? So what did you give in exchange for this message?" Lena asked her.

"Seeds," Tilia told her.

"Seeds?" Anamona asked her amused. "Are you serious?"

"What seeds?" Jani asked her in turn.

"Herb seeds," Tilia specified. "Basil, mint, rosemary ... these are valuable rarities in Hirunda."

"Herbs?" Anamona asked her again.

"We take herbs for granted," Tilia explained, "but that's not the case in Hirunda. Or can any of our Hirundian representatives present say they have tasted basil, for instance?"

"I've never even heard of such a thing," Lu confessed.

Jani also shook his head. He had no idea what they were even talking about.

"Ladies?" Tilia asked the two women from Gavialis.

"I can't say," Mari Alauda said. "I know nothing about herbs."

Saia didn't say a word but communicated by shaking her head.

"How do you deliver them across the border?" Lu asked the pair.

"It's obvious we can't deliver anything from the same place where we retrieve our deliveries because the river only flows in one direction," Lemmus said.

"So, you deliver your goods up north," Lena said and nodded slowly, "in Pinia Sector where the river continues to Hirunda."

Tilia nodded.

Then, activating the small light she was holding in her hand, Lena pointed it at Lemmus.

"There's something on the other side of that paper of yours," she informed them.

"What are you talking about?" Tilia asked her.

"Take a look at the other side," Lena suggested and pointed the light towards the piece of paper Lemmus was holding.

Lemmus and Tilia did as they were told. Suddenly Jani saw how Tilia's jaw fell. What had she seen on the paper?

"I don't believe this ..." she managed to say at last.

"What?" Anamona asked her.

Suddenly Tilia practically yelled in joy. Then the woman jumped on Lemmus' neck and even the man's smile was wider than ever.

"What is it?" Lena asked them, puzzled.

"This insignificant-looking piece of paper has just proven something which we have only speculated about before," Tilia explained as she smiled and wiped her eyes.

"Amazing!" Lemmus exclaimed. "For this they should have been given the entire herb garden! Amazing discovery! Just amazing!"

"I'm so ecstatic!" Tilia yelled out and clapped her hands. "I can hardly believe this!"

"How can we be anything but ecstatic over this," Lemmus said. "Finally Tilia! After all these years!"

"I know!" Tilia exclaimed, still grinning from ear to ear, and hugged Lemmus one more time.

Jani observed her joy in wonder. What on earth had she seen on the paper?

"Could you perhaps share this exuberance of yours?" Lena inquired. "What is this about?"

"A reaction like that is making even me curious," Mari stated.

"Alright, alright," Tilia said and tried to contain herself. "Where should I begin?"

"Don't ask me," Lemmus said. "My brain isn't functioning anymore. I can stare at this text and wonder about how it is possible but nothing else. This is true. This really is true."

"This is true," Tilia assured him quite excited.

"What on earth is there on that paper?" Lena wondered aloud.

"Have you ever heard of a work called Yesterday's Final Book?" Tilia asked them.

"Yesterday's Final Book?" Lena repeated, puzzled.

Jani shrugged his shoulders to signal his ignorance, no one else seemed to know anything about the book the woman was talking about.

"I've never heard of it," Mari informed her.

"Hesternus – Yesterday's Final Book," Saia suddenly said.

Silence.

All seven turned and looked at Saia. Silence fell.

"So, you have heard about it?" Tilia finally asked the girl.

"I have," Saia said.

"You are full of surprises, did you know that?" Mari noted. "Unbelievable."

Jani agreed with Mari. There was clearly much more to this quiet girl than her blank exterior.

"I thought it was nothing more than a legend," Saia continued, her eyes still on the ground, "So, I never searched for any details about it because I didn't believe I would find anything even remotely truthful about it."

"So, this text really exists?" Mari asked Tilia.

"Yes," the woman said.

"How do you know that?" Anamona asked her.

" Because Lemmus and I have a part of it in safe-keeping," Tilia said.

"What?" Saia asked her, finally raising her eyes from the ground and to Tilia.

"Lemmus and I have the first part of it," Tilia said. "We have it hidden because it is absolutely one of the most important finds we have ever had."

Saia stared wide-eyed at Tilia like she had just witnessed a miracle.

"We are talking about handwriting on paper," Lemmus specified. "Not some symbols stored in an information databank, but a handwritten text."

"What does that mean exactly?" Jani asked them.

"It means that the writing in this particular text has been written on paper by a person using a tool which can be used on different surface materials, like paper for instance. Just like in the case of the message on this paper roll. These writing tools were called 'pens'. In the case of Yesterday's Final Book the person who wrote with a pen called himself Hesternus."

"How do you know this?" Jani asked him.

"Yesterday's Final Book begins with a review where Hesternus explains his decision to write his book on paper. According to him it was the only way he could ensure that his writing would remain outside the information system and networks."

"So, he draws the letters on paper?" Jani kept asking.

"Yes," Lemmus answered, "but with a pen one could actually make more precise marks than with brushes and therefore a pen was most likely the preferred tool when writing small letters by hand."

"So, it was the precursor to our drawing stylus?" Mari asked him.

"Very much so," Lemmus said. "A pen simply leaves its mark on the surface you are writing on instead of transmitting the marks of your hand movements to your workstation screen."

Jani tried to recall whether he had seen one of these pens during his museum visit. It was unlikely, because he felt he would have remembered such a thing.

"Do you still use these pens?" Lu then asked Lena.

"We do," Lena said. "I believe some art circles still use them."

"That is correct," Tilia said. "Pens are not used so much for writing nowadays, but artists do draw with them."

"What did this Hesternus write about then in his book?" Mari asked.

"About the years after the Great War," Saia replied before Tilia had even opened her mouth.

Jani took a look at the girl and wondered what else she knew and was concealing.

"Have you read his works?" Tilia asked the girl.

"No," Saia replied, "but according to what I have read about the book, it must have been written during the first years of peace."

"You are right," Lemmus said.

"So, all those rumors were right then," Saia observed, "imagine that."

"I would have never believed you would know about this," Mari said. "I'm impressed."

Jani nodded. The girl really seemed to know a lot.

"What does that paper roll of yours have to do with this ancient book?" Lena asked the two.

"Hesternus writes about the history of mankind, of which there are no other records, thanks to the organized destruction initiatives after the war," Lemmus began, then he looked at Tilia.

She continued: "Among other things, Hesternus writes about the suspension of all religious activities. This means of course that, after the war, all religious groups were banned and therefore almost all the stored information on religious rituals was destroyed as well."

"Religions were unions of people who shared similar spiritual views and who practiced collective rituals, which had something to do with supernatural powers," Lemmus said. "Activities of this kind were banned by law after the Great War because they were only seen as inciting hatred in the world. Gavo Hirunda's goal was to unite all people, religion was considered one of the biggest obstacles to the success of this process."

Jani nodded. He remembered seeing the picture in the Hirunda Historical Museum illustrating this peculiar-looking building which was being dismantled; a building which had been used in religious rites and which was called a church.

"Gavo's decision was widely supported among the survivors of the war," Tilia continued, "and that's not just my speculation; this is what Hesternus writes in Yesterday's Final Book. His writing style is a little sarcastic; in the early days, practicing a religion was about maintaining peace and living a good life."

"Only humans can twist the concept of peace into a reason to start annihilating their own kind," Lemmus elaborated, "or at least this was the case when the idea of peace was delivered in the form of a religion. According to Hesternus, religions were an exceptionally effective way to get the masses supporting one ideology and we all know what might have been the result of that."

"So, Hesternus writes quite a lot about how we started to bury our own history during the first few years after the Great War," Tilia continued. "The only knowledge that was allowed to be preserved from the past was physics, chemistry, mathematics, biology, and medicine. From the many languages, one was chosen as the official language of all people as well as a language called *Latin,* one of the ancient dominant languages in the world. Its vocabulary and syntax were preserved. Some information about technological innovations and development was also preserved, but all the war technology expertise employed in the Great War against mankind and this planet were erased and forgotten."

"In his book, does this Hesternus say anything about the technology used in the Great War?" Anamona asked.

"No," Tilia said. "He simply states that Gavo Hirunda's decision to erase all knowledge of it was the right one. He felt it was unwise to leave any traces of it for future generations. It would have been too grotesque for all those who had died, whose lives had been claimed by the war. I have to agree with Hesternus on this."

"So, this Hesternus censored himself, too," Anamona noted.

"To a certain degree, yes," Tilia said, "but he perceived the topics he writes about as too important and valuable to be lost forever, even if the rest of mankind wanted to close its eyes to the past. The knowledge of the world before the Great War on political, sociological, and cultural levels were all issues that Hesternus felt were important enough to be preserved."

"Among other things, Hesternus mentions the concept of a United Nations in his book," Lemmus said.

"What does it mean?" Lena asked him.

"He doesn't define or describe the concept very strictly but Lemmus and I believe that it was some sort of coalition of different nations that had come together to promote worldwide peace. The exact number of nations in existence at that time is still a mystery to us, but one can presume that there were several."

"That was one of the reasons the Great War was declared," Anamona added.

"It was certainly a factor, I'm sure," Tilia admitted.

Jani nodded. He had been born into a unified world nation, so despite Terra Unionia, the thought of there being other nations felt most strange. Such an artificial division of people couldn't have any positive consequences, that much he felt was obvious.

"When Hesternus mentions the United Nations, he also quotes a document of some sort he calls the Charter of the United Nations," Lemmus continued. "The quote is not long, but it says a lot nonetheless."

"What does it say?" Anamona asked them.

Tilia cleared her throat and began.

"The Charter begins with the following words:

We the peoples of the United Nations have determined

— *to save future generations from the scourge of war, which twice in our lifetime has brought untold sorrow to mankind,*

— *to reaffirm our faith in fundamental human rights, in the dignity and value of each individual person, in the equal rights of men and women and of nations large and small, and ...*

Silence.

"And?" Lena asked her.

"That was all Hesternus quoted from the Charter," Tilia said.

"What does that quote tell you, then?" Lena asked her.

"'The scourge of war, which twice in our lifetime has brought untold sorrow to mankind ...'" Mari repeated what she had just heard. "Untold sorrow."

"Exactly," Tilia said. "So, mankind didn't fight wars continuously before the Great War as is often assumed nowadays."

"But there were wars," Anamona pointed out.

"Two," Tilia stated. "Two within a short period of time."

"What the conflicts leading up to those wars were about we can only guess at," Lemmus continued. "But we can assume that the United Nations was created as a result of those wars. Maintaining peace was very important if a coalition such as the United Nations existed in the first place."

"The quote in question also proves beyond any doubt that in the past, mankind really considered things like human rights and the equal rights of nations regardless of their size," Tilia added.

"Even though Hesternus didn't quote more than forty or so words of the Charter in his book, these forty-odd words tell us a great deal about the ancient world," Lemmus assured them.

"About this period in history we have no other source of information other than of Hesternus' book, excepting, of course, the few ancient artifacts we have gathered from that time," Tilia reiterated.

"But how can you be sure this Hesternus was telling the truth?" Lu asked them. "What if he was some crazy old man who had lost his mind in the war and just made up these deluded stories?"

"That's always a possibility," Lemmus admitted.

"That wouldn't explain why the book was hidden," Tilia pointed out. "If his work was simply the result of an overactive imagination, why was the book divided into three parts and hidden?"

"Is that what really happened?" Anamona asked her.

"We have reasons to believe so," Tilia said.

"Does he reveal the reason why the Great War broke out in the first place?" Anamona asked her.

"We don't know that," Tilia said. "I assume Hesternus didn't want to preserve that information to ensure that no one in the future would ever have reason to turn against a certain group of people based on something he had written. However, he does mention scourges that tested the world and which also paved the way for the Great War. For example, the rapid loss of fresh water and the unequal division of goods and welfare, as well as rapid climate change. The latter caused massive changes in the environment, mostly in the form of desertification, so that huge areas of land were rendered uninhabitable within a generation."

"So, how is that piece of paper of yours connected to all this?" Lena finally asked.

"Well, Lemmus and I have been interested in the role of the Charter, specifically the part about fundamental human rights," Tilia began. "Also, Hesternus himself mentions the concept of fundamental human rights but he doesn't go into any further detail. The two of us have speculated about that particular concept for a long time now; what those rights might have been and whether they were part of the Charter or if they had been explained in some other document. If that is the case, we want to know whether there is anything left of that document."

"So, is there something in your bit of paper about these rights?" Anamona asked her.

"Yes," Tilia announced, beaming. "As unbelievable as it may sound, that little piece of paper finally proves beyond any doubt that these fundamental human rights were indeed declared and documented."

Jani straightened his posture. He was more curious than he would have expected.

Lemmus turned the piece of paper over carefully and Lena shone her torch on it. Everyone saw the paragraphs that had quite clearly been written on it at some point in the past.

"That one is Article Twelve and that one is Article Thirteen," Tilia said pointing at the paper but without touching it, "and in these two articles the intrusion into a person's privacy as well as a person's freedom of movement are mentioned."

"So, now we know that there were at least thirteen articles in which these rights were defined, about which we could only speculate before tonight," Lemmus explained, "and that one article could have been divided into many parts like this Article Thirteen has been here."

"So, you understand what it is saying?" Lena asked Lemmus.

"This is written in a different language from the writing on the other side that Tilia interpreted earlier," Lemmus said, "a language we here all understand."

"Well, what do these articles say exactly?" Mari asked them.

Lemmus turned the piece of paper over and read:

"Article Twelve: *No one shall be subjected to arbitrary intrusion of his privacy, family, home, or correspondence, nor to attacks upon his honor or reputation. Every individual has the right to the protection of the law against such intrusion or attack.*"

"Sounds reasonable," Anamona noted.

Jani was nodding. The article sounded very logical. It was something he took for granted.

"I am sure that similar, corresponding laws can be found in both Hirunda and Terra Unionia today," Lemmus pointed out, "So, privacy laws were not just something invented after the Great War, or by Gavo Hirunda. Mankind thought about these issues long before that."

"Read Article Thirteen please," Tilia asked Lemmus.

"Article Thirteen, Paragraph One," Lemmus continued. "*Every individual has the right to freedom of movement and residence within the borders of each state.*"

"Naturally," Lena noted. "That's taken for granted in Terra Unionia."

"Paragraph Two," Lemmus continued,

"*Every individual has the right to freedom of movement between countries, including his own, and to return to his country.*"

"Ha!" Lena huffed. "That will be the day."

"Hirunda sees itself as the only 'country' in the world so this is unnecessary under Hirunda's law," Lemmus pointed out.

"Terra Unionia could disagree on that," Lena reminded. "The border is closed. Period."

"So, based on this article, we can draw the conclusion that world development after the Great War has not been entirely positive?" Tilia asked the others.

"No, we can't," Anamona stated.

"Why not?" Tilia asked her.

"Because, unlike in the past, there is peace on Earth," Anamona replied, "and because no one in Terra Unionia wants to leave our country, we don't need a law granting us that right."

"Interesting," Tilia noted.

"What do you mean?" Anamona asked her slightly charged.

"Your answer is very good," Tilia assured her, "but it is very Terra Unionian. What if the border were open? Would you, Lena, like to visit Hirunda knowing for sure that you could still come back to Terra Unionia?"

"Of course," Lena told.

"You would?" Anamona asked her, "even after everything you have heard here tonight?"

"I would love to see where Lu comes from," Lena said, "it is a significant part of Lu's life. I don't have any opportunity to see it, therefore part of Lu will always remain hidden from me, even though he has told me so much about his world out there. I would also love to take Lu to Avena and Pinus."

"I'd love to go with you, you can be sure of that," Lu stated. "All that you have told me about Terra Unionia sounds like some fictional fairytale place for me."

"Now I am surprised," Jani informed Lu.

"Why does that surprise you?" Lu asked him. "Are you honestly not interested in seeing what Terra Unionia is like, especially now that you know it really does exist?"

"I've always been happy in Gavialis," Jani said.

"Well, that's true," Lu noted.

"So, this Article Thirteen does not really apply to today's world," Tilia said. "Whether we interpret it as a sign of progress or regression is a different discussion entirely."

"Even if the border were open, surely people wouldn't be allowed to come and go as they pleased," Jani commented. "Surely such movement would be monitored just like they monitor movements between the city circles at the moment."

"Possibly," Tilia stated.

"But if that were the case, if people really did cross borders freely, would Article Thirteen still apply?" Anamona asked.

"It's a good question," Tilia said. "Having the right to move from country to country doesn't really specify how this movement should be dealt with on a practical level. These are interesting questions which provoke us into thinking about alternative systems."

"It's extremely unlikely that Terra Unionia would ever open the border," Lena sighed. "Unless Hirunda forces them to."

"Why would we do that?" Lu asked her.

Jani nodded. The mere thought of Terra Unionia appearing in the news headlines struck him as absurd.

"It may well be that those in power on our side don't want this border open, even if it were not an issue on your side. Terra Unionia is officially a hazardous zone which we want to keep isolated from the rest of the world," Lu added.

"That's unbelievable," Anamona said quietly shaking her head.

"So, this really is the only place we can meet each other," Lena said and looked at Lu. "It also means that Article Thirteen is just some pointless verbiage from the past instead of something Lu and I could use as a basis for our plea to spend more time together."

"It's odd that you really want to go to Hirunda," Anamona said to Lena. "I can't get over it."

"I don't find it odd at all," Lena said. "I'm curious, especially now that I know Hirundians are not just crazy militarists. That's why the idea of visiting Gavialis, for instance, is so intriguing."

"Wouldn't you want to see Gavialis, then?" Tilia asked Anamona. "The city which was built in the shape of a perfect heptagon with almost 20 million people in it? For a Terra Unionian that sounds like a fictional fairytale, just like Terra Unionia sounded to Lu."

"I admit that the thought of this particular city is intriguing," Anamona confessed, "and especially after everything I have heard here tonight, the place has begun to interest me more, but I guess I see things from a more practical point of view. Therefore I can't lose sight of what is really possible and what is not. Because I'll never get the chance to go to Gavialis and see it with my own eyes, and because Terra Unionia and Hirunda don't have diplomatic relations, I refuse to waste my time entertaining the idea, not the mention the fact that going to Gavialis is quite a horrifying thought in some ways."

Jani was surprised at Anamona's choice of words.

"In what ways?" he asked her.

"Well, at the risk of hurting someone's feelings, I confess that the thought of millions of Hirundian men milling around me makes me want to stay in Terra Unionia," Anamona confessed. "I'm sorry, but that's how I feel."

"You wouldn't have to walk alone among the men," Jani pointed out. "Women on our side don't wander around without their Yellow Guardsmen."

"But these Yellow Guardsmen are also men, are they not?" Anamona asked him.

"It's not the same," Saia said. "Yellow Guardsmen become acquainted with us, so being around them and with them in public places is entirely different from being around other men."

"That's true," Mari noted. "Guardsmen are there but you don't really see them as men, even though they are. It's difficult to explain."

"I will roll this piece of paper up again carefully and put it back to the bottle," Lemmus said, cleverly changing the subject. "I'm sure you won't mind if Tilia and I want to keep the paper as untouched as possible."

"Keep it," Lena agreed.

Lemmus rolled the piece of paper up and dropped it carefully back into the bottle, Tilia watching his hands.

"How did you two get involved with this ring searching for these ancient artifacts all over the world?" Anamona asked them.

"Good question," Lena noted.

"Were you involved in this activity while you still lived on our side?" Lu asked Lemmus.

"I was," the man confessed without blinking an eye.

"And that is the reason why you defected to Terra Unionia?" Lu asked him.

"That chapter in my life is an entirely different story," Lemmus said, evading the question.

"Why have the two of you dedicated your lives to this?" Mari asked them.

"Why does anyone do what they do?" Lemmus answered her. "Why did you want to be a doctor? Or why did Anamona want to move to Pinus? A person does nothing if they don't feel it is rewarding – consciously or unconsciously – and this work is extremely rewarding for Tilia and me."

"Even though you can't use this information you have uncovered for anything?" Lu asked them, "because no one cares about history anymore?"

"We are interested in it," Tilia said. "I am an endlessly curious person, I always have been. I don't understand people who care nothing beyond their own life's little circles. One of the topics I am interested in happens to be our past and especially the time period before the Great War, but the first few years after the war also interest me greatly."

"Why?" Lena asked her.

"I want to understand why Terra Unionia and Hirunda are two separate nations and why there are no diplomatic relations between them. I refuse to believe the argument that we are simply too different to live together peacefully and therefore this friendship between Lena and Lu is all the more amazing if you ask me."

"Thank you," Lena said.

Lu nodded as well.

"Have you found the answer to that question? I mean the one about us being separated?" Mari asked them.

"Possibly," Tilia stated.

"From Yesterday's Final Book?" Anamona asked her.

"Where else?" Tilia said.

"Well, why are there two nations in the world today?" Mari inquired, holding her arm tightly where she had removed her ID chip.

"Have you ever heard of the Two Sector Riots?" Tilia asked.

Lu and Jani looked at each other and shrugged their shoulders simultaneously. Anamona shook her head, as did Lena.

"I haven't," Mari said. "Saia?"

Saia also shook her head.

"It's no wonder," Lemmus noted. "The riots in question don't really fit nicely into the official Hirundian picture of how the current era of world peace started on this planet."

"There were commotions in Terra Unionia?" Lena asked him.

"Both Terra Unionia and Australandia," Lemmus told.

"According to Hesternus, that is," Lu added.

"Precisely according to Hesternus," Tilia agreed. "So, according to him, peace after the Great War was not achieved in a single moment, which I'm sure sounds logical to all of us. After the war, mankind went through a certain transition phase, during which the instable and isolated societies tried to find a new footing. There weren't very many people left after the war, only a few hundred million, so the groups of survivors were located relatively far away from each other geographically. The wisest course of action was to found one unified nation, which would deal with all human issues all around the world. This is how the first World Government was founded and its purpose was to stabilize order among the survivors of the war who had to continue living on a planet which had more or less been completely destroyed."

"Australandia wasn't, however, very keen to join the others in this new and still loose union, similarly the female communities of this particular area which could in a way be seen as the early Terra Unionians," Lemmus explained.

"These all-women communities were probably one of the biggest civilian groups which survived the war. Most male survivors were ones who had fought in the war," Tilia added.

Suddenly Jani realized he was listening carefully. He discovered to his own surprise that he found it all most interesting.

"In the case of Australandia, the area's isolation may partly explain why the locals weren't too eager to trust and seek support from people in other parts of the world," Lemmus explained. "Especially after the Great War, when the distrust between the different peoples was running very deep."

"But most world citizens supported the founding of 'one world, one nation'," Tilia added, "and eventually most Australandians came to the same conclusion and they started supporting it as well."

"Wasn't Gavo Hirunda one of the most influential people in this?" Jani asked.

"Yes," Lemmus replied. "World peace is still very much attributed to Gavo Hirunda. He paved the way for it."

"And we Terra Unionians still call your nation after this man," Tilia said.

"Well, that's what I have been wondering about," Mari said. "I just didn't want to say it out loud. You see, no one on our side of the border sees themselves as living in a country called Hirunda. We live in cities which are part of the world nation on this planet."

Jani nodded. He had noticed the same thing about the Terra Unionians; the way they referred to the rest of the world beyond their borders.

"Really?" Anamona asked her. "I have never thought of Hirunda as anything else but Hirunda."

"I found it odd that *you* talk about Hirunda," Mari said to Lemmus.

"I have lived in Terra Unionia for almost 30 years, so I have absorbed this expression into my own vocabulary," Lemmus explained.

"If I remember correctly, Hirunda was originally called Hirundanlands," Tilia said.

"Hirundanlands?" Mari asked her.

"Yes."

Suddenly a realization struck Jani.

"I recently visited a museum in Sixth Circle of Gavialis," he said.

"You?" Lu asked him amused, "you in a museum?"

"Yes, me," Jani assured his friend, trying to hide his smile.

"Are you serious?" Lu asked him, deeply amused. "Where is this museum?"

"Near the city's Main Hospital," Mari told them.

"The museum is called Hirunda Historical Museum," Jani continued, "but the museum itself is not dedicated exclusively to Gavo Hirunda and his accomplishments, there are also many things there about the building of world cities and developing technology and so on. The name of the museum could also refer to a nation called Hirunda, not just to this great man who once lived here."

"That's interesting," Tilia said.

"You're saying no one on your side of the border ever says they live in Hirunda?" Anamona asked them.

"No way," Mari assured her. "I am a Gavialian, because I live in Gavialis."

"In the city which was named after Gavo Hirunda," Lu elaborated. "Gavo, Gavialis."

"Gavo's city?" Lena suggested.

"Very much so," Lu confirmed.

"Well, it seems he certainly was well-respected and highly valued," Lena remarked.

"Surely Gavo Hirunda is known in Terra Unionia as well?" Mari asked the Unionians.

"I was told about Gavo Hirunda in my learners' circle, but I don't know if it is still part of our children's curriculum today," Tilia said.

"They taught us things about Gavo Hirunda, too," Anamona said. "Briefly though and in conjunction with the place Hirunda; what sort of place it is, where it got its name from, and so on."

"Right," Tilia noted.

"What were you taught about Gavo, then?" Mari asked the women. "What are the official facts about him in your country?"

"That he was a great charismatic leader after the Great War who helped build hope in the people traumatized by war," Anamona said. "Gavo Hirunda had an amazing ability to encourage people and get them to work together for a better tomorrow. That is the reason why he is one of the most central figures in the history of permanent world peace."

"Yet according to Terra Unionian history, Gavo Hirunda was also an extremely strict and draconian leader who showed no understanding towards those who disagreed with his views or objected to his draft proposals," Tilia added.

Mari listened and nodded.

"It may well be true," she said.

"It most likely is," Lemmus added, "because after the Great War there was, without a doubt, an urgent need for a leader who was both inspiring and rigid."

"Yet despite Gavo's charisma, there was unrest in two places in the world which needed to be resolved in order to achieve world peace," Tilia said. "The other place was Australandia."

"But Australandia did not isolate itself," Lu said.

"Australandia needed the support of the other sectors to rebuild its society, so the minor political turbulence subsided relatively quickly. Terra Unionia, however, was an entirely different case," Lemmus explained.

"And like we have already said, there was a relatively big group of civilians in the Terra Unionia area after the Great War. This collective consisted mainly of women and children," Tilia added. "Just like our society still is today."

"When they started building the world nation, the temporary government consisted mainly of men who had a military background," Lemmus continued. "This was not seen as advantageous for all parties, especially not in the area of Terra Unionia. The military may have played an important part in maintaining order as it rooted out criminal activity after the war, but once the situation had been stabilized, the temporary government's priorities did not meet the people's needs at all."

Jani kept listening carefully. It still felt like he was listening to a fictitious story though he knew Tilia and Lemmus were deeply serious.

"Not to mention the fact that within female communities there was deep distrust of men with military backgrounds," Tilia continued. "Lemmus and I have estimated that during the years of the Great War, billions of people died in either direct bombardments or as a result of natural or biological weapons. Many civilians also had to defend themselves against soldiers who had lost their minds in the war. Much of the Great War was not fought by the armies alone, the civilian population was also butchered in unimaginable numbers."

"So, there were billions of people in the world back then?" Lena asked them.

"The population of Hirunda is around 150 million these days," Lu said. "How could have there been so many people in the world in the past?"

"Those were different times," Tilia said. "Who knows why there were so many people in the world and how many there might have been had it not been for the Great War. These are things we will simply never know. That knowledge has been lost for good."

"In any case, the temporary government was not trusted and this distrust was greatest in the area of Terra Unionia, where most women survivors lived in their individual communities," Lemmus continued.

"At that time, those in power had one goal over all others – to make the world a better place than it had ever been during its entire history," Tilia continued. "They finally wanted to take mankind to other planets. Instead of fighting wars, there was a mutual desire to focus all technical development on scientific breakthroughs. Space travel was one of the main applications for technical innovation. Female communities criticized this waste of valuable resources. According to them, mankind was heading for imminent collapse if technology remained the number one priority. All other aspects of modern life – education, health care and cleansing the Earth's biosphere – were secondary. Women wanted to invest more in those 'secondary' areas."

"We don't know exactly what triggered the turmoil in the Terra Unionia area; Hesternus does not go into much detail," Lemmus said, "but he does mention the deep distrust between the female communities and the rest of the world."

"He also mentions briefly the violence against these women as well," Tilia added, "to which the women's response was equally cruel."

"For example?" Anamona asked them.

"Hesternus mentions men being shot in the genitals and left hanging from their feet scattered around the outskirts of female settlements," Lemmus explained. "Among the women themselves was a wall of silence. No individual act of violence could ever be proven, regardless of whether it was believed to have been committed by a man or a woman. Gavo Hirunda was losing his control over these communities in which the women felt they had the right to maintain their own code of justice."

Jani didn't know what to think. He had never linked women and physical violence together before.

"Hesternus also mentions that Gavo Hirunda had no other choice but to take the risk and disband these women's communities," Tilia added.

"One can assume that this particular decision was the one that triggered the rioting, which in turn led to all the violence," Lemmus said. "In Terra Unionia this turbulence was seen as a demonstration against the temporary government. Hirunda, as it was then known, saw this as a rebellion against peace. According to the female communities, 15 people were killed during these riots but according to Hirunda only four."

"So, it is quite obvious that the vast women-based communities and the temporary government didn't see eye-to-eye," Tilia explained. "Unlike in Australandia, which, at the time was relatively isolated in the south, the geographical location of Terra Unionia and its resources made it possible for the women's communities to isolate themselves from the rest of the world. So these communities decided to break away from the temporary government's control. According to them, history had already proven that patriarchic social systems did not work. Mankind's past had already proven beyond any doubt that patriarchic societies had always been the cause of some form of war or another. Therefore, power and order had to remain in women's hands if the world was ever to leave the era of endless fighting and the brutality behind it."

"The women's communities blamed the temporary government – who were relying on their military strength – for trying to maintain order through violence, and this was seen as nothing other than an extension of the ravages of the Great War," Lemmus added.

"These communities did not want to be part of such a world," Tilia specified.

"The Hirunda of that time perceived these communities as fanatic sects," Lemmus continued. "So, Hirunda did not recognize the founding of a new state; the unwavering belief in a one world nation was the only guarantee of permanent world peace. If there were only one nation in the world, future wars could be avoided. That was seen as the only way to maintain peace. However, when the women's communities closed their borders and communication between the two parties ceased, Terra Unionia slowly began to be regarded as a closed area of Hirunda, as a reservation."

Jani saw Lu nodding. He assumed Lu had heard similar stories about Terra Unionians before he had been sent to the border to patrol for the first time.

"Distrust towards the rest of the world is a characteristic of our society still very much in evidence today," Tilia said. "We are still waiting for the invasion."

"Our children are raised to wait for it," Lena stated quietly.

"And what I've heard from Lu, in Hirunda they still regard us as a sector of society which has to be isolated from all others," Tilia said.

"That's true," Lu noted.

"And public sentiment is shifting from one generation to the next. That's why it feels to me like Terra Unionia's role of the underdog in Hirunda's shadow is consciously nurtured in Terra Unionia," Tilia said.

Lena watched Tilia for a moment, and then said:

"You know, you might be right."

"Well, let's think about the flyover for a moment," Lemmus said. "It was a shock for everyone, which is understandable of course, but have you really noticed how people are talking about it? Terra Unionia defines itself as Hirunda's victim and as such, a significant part of the nation's identity is its persistence and willingness to survive in the shadow of its evil neighbor Hirunda."

"A flyover?" Jani asked her. "What exactly are you talking about?"

"A Hirundian vessel flew over Terra Unionia," Tilia said.

"What?" Jani stated and watched Lu.

"So, you knew nothing about it?" Tilia asked him.

"Well, no," Jani said.

"Lena told me," Lu stated. "Otherwise I wouldn't have known about it. I didn't pay any attention to it when I saw it."

"Which direction did the vessel appear from?" Jani asked the Unionians.

"From the north," Lemmus said. "It flew from north to south."

"To Albedo, then," Lu said.

"Well, of course," Jani replied. "It was coming in to land from space."

"Albedo?" Anamona asked them.

"One of the suburbs of Gavialis," Lu explained. "It's a space travel center."

"So, it was a civilian vessel?" Anamona asked.

"Yes," Lemmus replied. "A vessel like that is not meant to be used in war, even though it has weapons installed."

"We don't have vessels which are purely warships," Lu added.

"You don't?" Anamona asked him slightly suspiciously.

"No, unless you count a couple of old wrecks you will find in Albedo," Lu said. "And even they are seen as nothing more than quaint relics these days.

"I find it extremely interesting that there was no open discussion of this flyover on your side. Its unexpected appearance in our airspace caused nationwide uproar," Tilia said.

"I've heard nothing about this," Jani said. "There has been no mention of it in the news headlines."

"However, there is an audio file," Saia said.

And once again the whole group turned and looked at the quiet girl.

"There is?" Tilia asked the girl.

Jani looked at this quiet girl who kept asking questions. She was an enigma, timid and quiet but at the same time she had world-shattering information the others knew nothing about.

"Saia?" Mari asked her.

"How else would I have known where to look for Terra Unionia?" Saia pointed out quietly.

"So, you have an audio file where this flyover is discussed?" Lena asked the girl.

"It's been distributed across the information network," Saia said.

"What are you talking about?" Jani asked her suspiciously. Saia's claim sounded rather far-fetched.

"Of course not publicly but it's available if you know where to look," Saia stated.

"What is it like?" Anamona asked her.

"It contains the exchange between the landing vessel and Albedo," Saia explained. "The vessel should not have come in to land from the north but another vessel, which was already ascending into orbit, forced it to change its trajectory."

"So, it was an accident," Tilia stated to Lemmus. "As you suspected."

"It *was* an accident," Saia assured them. "Albedo tried desperately to guide it along another route, claiming that the toxins would interfere with the landing vessel's radar as well as its communication with them, but the vessel took the forbidden course anyway – they seemed to be experiencing interference with their communication link - and at some point the man flying the craft saw a huge city with millions of people beneath them."

"Pinus," Lena said.

"Pinus," Anamona repeated.

"The man in the vessel was shocked by what he had seen and once he told traffic control about it, the communication link between Albedo and the vessel was severed almost immediately," Saia explained.

"So, Terra Unionia is known outside my unit in the Border Guard Detachment as well," Lu said.

Jani didn't know how to take what he had just heard. He found it amazing that even after such an incident as this, Terra Unionia had still not appeared on the news for the rest of the world to talk about.

"I think Terra Unionia might be a secret of those in power," Lemmus speculated. "Or how else could you explain that not one satellite or the station in Earth's orbit has detected Terra Unionia from out there?"

All Jani could do was nod at Lemmus' words. He had asked that very same question of Lu when he had heard about Terra Unionia for the first time.

"We know how to blend in with our surroundings in Terra Unionia," Lena explained. "During the darker hours the cities are not illuminated. Only if someone walks along a street does the light go on. If we consider the main railway line, for instance, the trains run underground most of the time."

"True," Tilia said. "The greenhouses in Taurusia are as green as the environment around them."

"And if there are any signs of human settlement visible all the way into space, those keeping the secret in Hirunda could easily claim them to be the old ruins of a toxic environment where no one should go wandering around," Lemmus added.

"Who knows how many people on our side know about your existence," Lu said. "But Terra Unionia is not discussed publicly and even if the name were familiar to some, they would most likely assume there were no people left, since no one hears anything from you anymore."

"So, the flyover was not a sign of an approaching threat?" Anamona asked them.

"It was not," Lena assured her sister. "Hirunda is not planning on invading Terra Unionia tomorrow."

"Does Hirunda have any plans at all regarding Terra Unionia?" Tilia asked them.

"That I don't know," Lu said. "All I know is that it is my job to guard the border and ensure there is peace on Earth."

16.

Jani stared at the black sky above him and noticed one bright spot moving among the stars. It was either a space station in Earth's orbit or a vessel either approaching or departing from Albedo. As he stood there looking at the black sky above, Jani couldn't stop wondering about the men who had stared at the same stars in the past. They had died a long time ago but because of them, the world was as it was today. His thoughts astonished him; when had he ever pondered things of this nature?

"What are you thinking?" Lu asked him.

Jani was pulled from his wandering thoughts and he turned to face his friend. Alone at last, the two men were able to talk openly and freely with each other about the evening they had just experienced.

"I don't know," he answered honestly. "My thoughts are all over the place."

"Yesterday's Last Book," Lu said. "I had never even heard of it."

"I don't think there are many people who have," Jani reassured his friend, "but that girl over there is one of them."

"She seems to know quite a lot," Lu noted.

"And she still wants to go to Terra Unionia," Jani said. "Even after everything I have heard I still have difficulty understanding why anyone would want to escape from Gavialis as badly as she does. Especially her; she has all she could ever want in the city. Her life is an easy one."

"Aren't you at all curious about the world beyond that border?"

"I am, I'm not denying that," Jani confessed. "But if the price of my visit was never to be able to return to Gavialis, I would choose Gavialis."

"I don't know what I would choose," Lu said.

"So, you are still undecided?" Jani asked Lu.

"I am," Lu said. "Gavialis is not the center of my world."

"But Lena is," Jani pointed out quietly.

"Lena and the child, both of them."

"And you are really willing to choose them over Gavialis?"

"Yes."

"That's crazy."

"Maybe."

"I'm sure there would be plenty of nulls who'd be glad to have the option, but you have accomplished things. Your life in the city isn't a bad one."

"It's not," Lu agreed, "but it's incomplete without Lena and the child. So if I knew I would be treated differently in Terra Unionia, I would cross the border tomorrow. If I can't live together with Lena in Terra Unionia, there wouldn't be much sense in defecting."

"So, the only place you can be together is right here," Jani said and took a look at the darkened forest. "Is this where you are going to raise this child? Is that possible?"

"I don't know," Lu sighed. "It seems I don't know anything anymore. And more I think about it, the more complicated if feels, but if I think about the childhood this baby would have in Terra Unionia, I become more convinced that's the place for this child to be."

"Why?" Jani asked him puzzled.

"They seem to have all sorts of things there, which we have to do without."

"Like?"

"First of all fruit, the clean environment, and live animals in their capital city. Those are wonders this child would never experience on our side of the border."

"You make it sound like we don't have anything remarkable on our side of the border."

"Sure we do," Lu admitted. "But Terra Unionia still sounds like the better option for this child. On our side he, or she, would end up in an educational institution without an opportunity to ever even see Lena. Can you honestly recommend life in an educational institution?"

For a moment Jani didn't know what to say.

"I didn't know better," he finally conceded, "but at least I was taken care of. Every child is taken care of, you know that."

"But is it enough? As a man who is about to be a *father,* that option just doesn't seem enough. I want my child to have more."

"Maybe Terra Unionia seems like a better choice for this child because you don't know exactly what the child's life there would be like."

"That's a possibility," Lu admitted, "but the most important thing is that both Lena and the child have a healthy and stable life."

"So, you would be ready to let Lena withdraw behind the border and keep the child without ever seeing them again, if that really were the only option available?"

"If that's what she wanted or what we needed."

"Are you sure?"

"If for some reason she failed to show up here one day, I would have no power to dictate what I want. She would have made her decision."

"Do you think she will disappear someday without coming back?"

"It's always possible," Lu confessed. "I know that, I'd be a fool to think otherwise, but at the moment she wants to come here to be with me, that much I know. However, if the day comes when she no longer wants to, I'd be powerless to change that, and I honestly don't know what I would do then."

"Maybe you would forget her eventually?"

"I wouldn't," Lu assured him.

"Are you sure?"

"About a month ago I thought she had had enough," Lu then said.

"What made you think that?"

"She didn't come for a couple of days," Lu explained. "And I have never gone through such a turmoil as I did during those few days."

Jani didn't like what he was hearing but he let Lu talk without interrupting him.

"Because of the uncertainty, I was close to losing my mind. I'm serious, Jani, I was even considering crossing the border, even though I knew the chances of surviving through the minefield ahead were minimal. Yet I seriously considered it, not knowing where she was or whether anything had happened. That's how bad it was; I was ready to risk my life for her. I guess it's madness to be attached to another person so intensely, but I can't help it, she is in my thoughts all the time. And if I don't know where she is or when she is coming back to me, I just lose it."

"That sounds ..."

"Crazy, I know, but that's just the way it is."

"And you still believe you have this situation under control?" Jani asked him quietly. "That having this relationship with her is worthwhile?"

"It is worthwhile," Lu assured him.

"It doesn't sound like it."

"It is, because only now has life started making sense."

"Yeah, so much sense that you're ready to defy a deadly minefield ahead of you just to get near that woman," Jani pointed out. "Listen to yourself!"

"It sounds crazy," Lu admitted, "but if you have never experienced something like this, I don't think you can comprehend why I can't live without Lena."

"I hope I will never be in that position," Jani informed him. "I never want to."

"Maybe you're lucky then; not knowing what you are missing."

Jani sighed. Lu was lost to him. Concerning Lena, he had been truly blinded and as a result, he was also beyond the reach of Jani's help.

"A part of me still expects her to just not show up one day," Lu confessed.

"If her pregnancy is discovered in Terra Unionia, she won't come back, she won't be able to. At least that is how I have understood it."

"I know."

"So, maybe it would be wise to take that option into consideration and to start preparing for it."

"A part of me doesn't want to think of the future, only to focus on what I have in my life right now," Lu explained, "but I can't ignore this feeling of apprehension that the thought of the future stirs up in me. That's why I am grateful for every moment she's here with me; I know only too well that things can change in an instant. I still don't understand what Lena sees in me. I honestly don't know why she wants to be with me, but she does. She doesn't care about which city circle I live in, she's not interested in the number of Silver Wing marks I have earned, or me advancing my social status. She loves me because of me and that is simply amazing. I don't know what I have done to deserve her in my life."

Jani remained silent; he genuinely didn't know what to say. The thought of a woman, or any person for that matter, who didn't pay any heed to the number of Silver Wing marks was revolutionary. Before now, he had not even considered that there were millions of people in the world who didn't care about collecting Silver Wing marks, or who didn't judge and rank people by how many they had earned. What could it mean exactly? What sort of person would he be in a society without the Silver Wing mark system?

"I am also worried about her sister hating me," Lu finally said.

"Oh ..." Jani replied.

"She hates me," Lu laughed and the man sounded tired. "I guess I shouldn't be all that surprised. I guess I shouldn't have expected anything else in the first place."

"She hasn't painted a very rosy picture of herself," Jani pointed out, "even though I have to admit that I partly agree with her on certain issues."

"Right."

"She doesn't understand Lena's feeling for you as I don't understand yours for her," Jani said. "I just don't understand you, Lu. It's as if you're not the same person anymore. I have no idea whatsoever what keeps you in this place. I understand she is a woman and having sex with her is ... *interesting*, but I don't understand this strange urge of yours to keep her close to you at all times. I just don't get it."

"I love her," Lu said. "That's what all this boils down to. Three months ago I didn't even know what that word meant, but now I do. And I have also began to realize that she may well disappear from my life, and for the first time I feel like I could lose something I can't live without. It's a realization I have not had to struggle with before but which I have to get used to. It's a thought which torments me continuously."

"Does she know about this?"

"She's aware of my feelings," Lu said, "and she knows I don't want to lose her."

"Does she know you were ready to defy the minefield?"

"No," Lu said. "And I don't think she needs to know about it, at least not now."

Jani took a deep breath and nodded.

"So far I have her," Lu added.

"Then why aren't you happy?"

"I am."

"Are you?"

"Yes."

"Even though you're worried about these things?"

"Having her here and near me compensates for all that."

"Does she have similar thoughts about losing you?"

"I don't know."

"What do you think?"

"I know she misses me when we are apart," Lu said, "she tells me that every time we return here, but I also see it in her eyes; in the way that she looks at me when we meet here after spending some time apart, and I feel it when we kiss."

"So, if this commitment of yours really lasts, would her coming to our side of the border help your situation at all?"

"I doubt it," Lu sighed. "We both know I would lose her regardless."

"But if the girl from Gavialis knows how to create a fake ID account, why couldn't she create one for your child as well?"

"I suppose she could," Lu said, "but why would she?"

"You can always ask," Jani pointed out.

"It wouldn't be much of a solution, though. Getting Lena to Gavialis would only introduce a list of other practical issues to resolve. How would I see her and the child? Should I give up my life completely to be with them? Would I have to cut Talpa out of my life permanently, so he would never find out about this? And so on."

"You're sure the old man wouldn't understand?"

"Never," Lu replied. "He would never understand this. If he saw me here now he would probably lose it completely."

Suddenly they saw Lena and Anamona getting to their feet. Jani watched them for a while, expecting the two to come over to them, but the women walked over to Mari and Saia instead, which surprised the two men. Jani watched them sit down again and start talking to the two Gavialians. The four women were too far away for Jani and Lu to hear what they were discussing.

"Wonder what they are talking about," Lu mused.

"Probably just women's stuff," Jani guessed. "After all, there are four women from two different sides of the border. I bet they must be curious about each other."

"Wonder what the men in Terra Unionia are like," Lu pondered. "I mean those few who exist, and I'm not counting that man over there as one of them. His roots are in Erasmia."

"Defector," Jani noted sourly. "Before today I didn't even know that word applied to anyone except nulls who managed to get inside the city border."

"Maybe his life was in danger back in those days," Lu speculated. "That's the reason why that female doctor is crossing the border."

"That's why it would be interesting to know what he has done in his past," Jani said. "What could have been a big enough reason for him to cross the border? Did he simply want some variety in his life or had he just had enough of collecting Silver Wing marks? What job did he do back then?"

"The reason for him to leave must have been a crime," Lu said. "Mark my words; that man is a wanted criminal."

"Do you think he's with that Tilia woman like you are with Lena?"

"Can't say," Lu said. "They seem to be friends but if there's something else, it's hard to say."

"Can a woman and a man be friends?" Jani wondered.

"I have no idea," Lu replied. "Maybe. Maybe you will end up falling for that Anamona over there."

"Unlikely," Jani informed Lu sourly.

Lu laughed and punched Jani's arm in a most amicable way. Jani looked at him with a sour expression on his face. He didn't find Lu's joke amusing at all.

"Do you really want to be a provider?" Jani asked him, "or if Lena is still in the picture, guardian even?"

"I do," Lu said. "That's the reason why the thought of not seeing my child at all feels … well, awful really."

"But there are many men in the world who may have biological offspring, yet they don't seem to care about them."

"That's different."

"How?"

"Because of Lena," Lu said. "This child is not just some random biological offspring, he's ours. This child belongs to both of us. That's why he is important. I can't say it in any other way."

"You've made quite a mess here," Jani said. amused. "You're a man who didn't care about anything, other than being a border guard."

"She's the only one I need," Lu said. "Lena and our child. She's the first person who has made me wish that the world would be different."

"Different how?"

"Well, I'd like it if Article Thirteen still existed, for starters," Lu stated. "I would like to go to Terra Unionia to be with Lena and go back home again, if I chose to. The world is not like that anymore and knowing that it used to be makes me feel as though something fundamental has been taken away."

"But it's not like that," Jani said. "Nothing has been taken away from you; that Article ceased to exist before we were born."

"I know," Lu conceded, "but I still feel we should have something similar. The border is closed and Terra Unionia hidden, that's why I can't be with Lena in any other place than this small spot in the middle of these woods. This is the only place where I have the opportunity to live life to the fullest."

"What if Terra Unionia became public knowledge?" Jani pondered.

"I don't see that happening," Lu said, "but if it did happen, they would most likely just tighten the border control even further as there would suddenly be a huge bunch of maniacs to contain in the area known as Terra Unionia. That's how the powers that be would most likely see the situation. So I would lose Lena and the child in that case as well."

Jani sighed.

"Why be sad about something you can't change?" he asked Lu.

"Aren't you ever sad, then?" Lu asked him.

"What do you mean?"

"I bet you were excited to get access permission to Sixth Circle not once, but twice. Weren't you just a tiny bit upset when you had to return to First Circle after finding out exactly what lies beyond Fifth Circle?"

"It wasn't nice," Jani admitted.

"So, you did spend some time thinking about how you would love to stay there even though you logically knew it could never happen?"

"Alright," Jani confessed. "You've caught me."

"Equally, it annoys me that I can never have Lena," Lu continued. "I just keep borrowing her for a while each time she comes here and every time I have to leave this place I feel it."

"Feel it?"

"Like someone had reached their hand inside my stomach and was squeezing my guts. That's how it feels."

Jani took a deep breath and stared at the dark forest. He didn't know what to say. As expected, he had not figured out a solution to Lu's problem. He had known as much since the very first moment Lu had asked him to come here but luckily he wasn't the only one who had no answers. Yet despite his lack of usefulness tonight, he could still appreciate the experience. He had never even dreamt of facing a situation like this, yet here he was with seven others, four or five of whom were people he would never see again. He was, however, sure he would remember each one of them for the rest of his life.

Suddenly Jani noticed Lena and Anamona getting to their feet again. The two left Doctor Alauda and Saia alone and exchanged a few words with each other as they walked slowly towards Terra Unionia. Then Lena nodded towards Lu and him and Jani knew she would come to Lu soon.

When Lena found her place next to Lu, he nuzzled her neck. Lena laughed and took Lu's hand in hers. Jani felt extremely awkward in their presence. He was clearly someone whose company was not needed right now.

"I want to apologize," Lena said.

Lena's words pulled him back out of his private thoughts. Had she spoken to him?

"Yes I'm speaking to you," Lena said with a smile, as if she could read his thoughts.

"Why?" Jani asked her, puzzled.

"Why am I speaking to you?"

"Why apologize," Jani specified.

"You wonder why?" Lena asked him, amused. "I might have said things to you earlier tonight, which I didn't necessarily mean. Okay, that's not quite right … I *did* say things I didn't necessarily mean. I know I can't take any of it back, but I hope we can get along nonetheless."

Jani was stupefied, completely lost for words.

"I think the most important thing for us right now is to try to get along," Lena said.

Lu pecked her cheek and pulled her closer to him.

"Alright," Jani finally managed to say.

"And I'd also like to apologize for my sister, she is still pretty shaken up because all of this," Lena added. "I know it doesn't justify her behavior, but maybe it explains it a little."

"Well, she hasn't been the only one who's been upset," Jani said.

"I understand that too," Lena said.

"As long as you treat Lu well, we are pulling on the same rope," Jani volunteered.

"Good," Lena noted. "Then we are going to be pulling on the same rope in future as well."

Jani nodded.

"Well, now that's over with … let's rest before the sun rises again," Lu said and pulled Lena with him onto the ground.

Lena didn't resist and found her place next to Lu. Lu seemed completely content. Jani remained still and looked away. He had never imagined Lu with a woman and as a result he didn't know how to behave exactly as the pair displayed their affection for one another. He knew, however, Lu wanted to spend some time alone with Lena. He got up and went for a walk near the pond close by. Perhaps it would do him some good to be alone for a moment to help clear his mind. A great deal had been said this evening and he wanted to try and make some sense of it alone.

He got up and left. Lu didn't even notice which annoyed him a little bit. It was obvious Lu couldn't see anything but Lena anymore and Jani couldn't help feeling like an outsider who had no purpose or place anymore. He didn't like it, but he was powerless to change the situation.

Jani walked slowly and he struggled to maintain his calm exterior. He didn't want anyone around him see how he felt inside; his private thoughts were his own. When he reached the pond, he stopped and stared unseeingly at the calm water in front of him. He could still sense a dreamlike veil over the night. Here, on the border of Terra Unionia, sharing this place with women, some of whom were Terra Unionians. He couldn't ever have dreamt about a night like this. His world had changed but it was too early to tell how remarkably, or indeed whether it was a turn for the better or for the worse.

All of a sudden Jani felt another person's presence near him. He turned round and saw Tilia standing a few meters away. Jani swallowed. Why had she come? Did she want to talk? If so, how should he act with her? Only once before had he had a private conversation with a woman.

"This is not easy for you," Tilia said and took a step closer.

"Excuse me?" Jani asked her, despite already having a pretty good idea of what the Terra Unionian woman was talking about.

"You and Lu are close," she continued. "So, his need to be near Lena is very confusing for you."

"Possibly."

Tilia stepped closer to Jani and remained there as she stared into the dark water before them.

"You have to allow yourself to feel uncomfortable about it," she continued. "If a change doesn't feel uncomfortable, it's not an important change."

"Maybe I don't want things to change," Jani said.

"None of us do, usually," Tilia confirmed, "at least not unexpected change, but we are in constant change, all the time. All our experiences, all the people we meet along the way, all that changes us."

"What if the change makes you worse than you are now?"

"That may happen," the woman admitted, "but I don't think that's the case this time."

Jani glanced carefully at the woman. Tilia saw this and said, "I just sense it."

Jani nodded.

"How long have you known Lu?" she then asked him.

"I met him when I was a child," Jani said.

"So, he is like a brother to you."

"Almost."

"But you are not brothers?"

"Not genetically," Jani said.

"Not all families are based on genetic similarity," she said. "Sometimes we find a family in the most unexpected places."

"Do you have a family?" Jani asked her in turn. He didn't want their discussion to focus on his life alone. In his opinion, there was not that much to say about it in the first place.

"No," Tilia said.

"What about that defector?"

"His name is Lemmus," Tilia pointed out.

"Is he like a brother to you?"

"He is a good friend."

"Is it true that there are real animals in your biggest city?" Jani then asked her. "Animals which don't exist anywhere else in the world?"

"Has Lu told you that?" the woman asked him and looked at Jani pleasantly surprised.

Jani nodded.

"Yes, it is true," Tilia said.

"That's pretty … amazing, I guess."

"The Pinus Zoo is quite a marvelous accomplishment."

"And no one in the world knows about it," Jani said, "your people excluded, of course."

"What do you think is the best thing about Gavialis?" Tilia asked him in turn.

"I don't know," Jani answered quietly. "Its vastness, the size. Maybe the energy you feel all around you there, especially in its inner circles."

Tilia looked at Jani and smiled.

"It would be great to see all that with my own eyes someday," she said. "However …"

"Yeah," Jani said. "Article Thirteen expired a long time ago."

"Indeed."

Then they stood for a while in silence looking at the pond in front of them. Suddenly Jani was surprised to realize that having Tilia standing next to him wasn't uncomfortable at all. There was something about her that made the awkwardness simply disappear. Tilia was different. Did her age have something to do with it; the fact that she was significantly older than he was? Maybe. Maybe age also made women's status more authoritative, just like with men. Yet Tilia didn't have a single Silver Wing mark. In the world's eyes she had made no significant advancement whatsoever. Despite all that, there was still something about her which made Jani treat her with respect.

"You are the second woman I have talked to alone," Jani then confessed not really knowing why.

Something about Tilia made him open up even though she was a woman. Maybe it was her tranquility, maybe the fact that she did not confirm any of the prejudices he had towards women. Tilia was so different from his expectations. She had something really manly about her, even though she was also very feminine.

"Only the second?" she then asked him. "Who was the first, if you don't mind me asking?"

Jani nodded behind them.

"Who?" Tilia asked him confused. "Mari Alauda?"

Jani nodded.

"Are you serious?"

Jani nodded again.

"Talk about a coincidence," Tilia whispered, surprised. "That she ended up here on this very spot as well."

Jani didn't know what so say so he shrugged.

"It happened just few days ago," he added. "When I realized it really was her who had come here, I couldn't believe my eyes."

"I'm sure."

"So, the point is, more or less, that I'm not very good at talking to women," Jani added.

"You are doing fine," Tilia assured him. "At the end of the day, talking to women is pretty much the same as to men."

"Well of course, but I am not accustomed to women," Jani explained slightly embarrassed. "Don't you find it strange talking to men?"

"No," Tilia replied flatly.

Jani kept getting even more surprised at Tilia's sense of calm. Then he stared at the water again. When he took another quick look at the woman, he saw her staring at the pond, too. She was clearly lost in her own thoughts.

Jani couldn't stop thinking about her. There was something about her presence which made him feel much more self-confident, more important. How did she do that? He was mystified.

"I was one of those men who delivered that suitcase for you," Jani finally said without even knowing why.

Perhaps he just wanted to get it off his chest. Perhaps Tilia was the only person in the world he could talk to about it.

"Excuse me?"

"An unknown man approached me on the U Train and asked me to spend my day off taking a trip to Makaira. I said yes because he promised me something I really wanted as a reward. My assignment was to pick up a black suitcase and take it to Linai station. I wasn't allowed to open the suitcase or talk about it to anyone. Not even Lu knows about this."

"You're serious, aren't you?" Tilia said as she studied his face carefully.

Jani looked in the woman's eyes and nodded.

"So, Mari Alauda was not the only odd coincidence for you tonight," Tilia concluded. "No wonder you were so silent at times."

Jani took a deep breath and nodded slightly.

"Don't tell Lu," he said. "Please."

"This will remain between the two of us," she assured him.

"You don't plan to tell Lemmus?"

"Do you want him to know about this?"

"I don't know."

"Well, until you do, this shall remain between us."

"Alright," Jani said and he truly believed Tilia was being honest.

And suddenly he felt lighter than he had in days. He felt relieved and grateful.

"I guess Mari Alauda will really cross the border," Jani continued.

"Seems so."

"Do you think it is a good idea?"

"You don't?"

"I don't know."

"I don't think she's guilty," Tilia said.

"Why not?"

"It's just a feeling I have."

"For your sake I hope you're right."

"You think she should return to Gavialis?"

"It would be the right thing to do," Jani said.

"Would it?"

"Why wouldn't it be?"

"Let's make a deal," Tilia said. "If the birthrate statistics are public, follow them for a while. If the number of girls born is still decreasing at the same alarming rate after Mari is gone, you will know whether she has been telling the truth or not."

Jani looked at Tilia for a moment, then nodded. Maybe he really would. If the loss of female fetuses suddenly came to an end, Lu could urge Lena to bring Mari back to the border to be returned to their side, if it was possible. For now Doctor Death would get a moment to catch her breath after the charges and media circus she had left behind in Gavialis.

* * *

Jani opened his eyes as he heard Lu walking near him. He looked up at his friend who nodded. It was a sign that they would go soon.

"Finally," Jani sighed quietly and got up on his feet.

"We will all leave together as one group," Jani heard Lena informing the Unionians.

Jani collected his thoughts. Had he been the last one to wake up? Why hadn't anyone stirred him?

"That means me, Anamona, our newcomer, and you two," Lena added.

"Alright," Tilia said.

Jani turned to face the Unionians. They really were leaving, and so was Doctor Alauda. Jani got to his feet. He didn't know why, but he couldn't take his eyes off the Unionian group. This was it. This was the last time he would see any of them. From this moment on he would have no idea what happened to any of them, except Lena. Lu surely would keep him informed of the latest news where Lena was concerned.

"I will guide you through the minefield and point you in the direction you should walk to get to the main train route," Lena informed the group.

Main route? Jani wondered what Lena had meant by that.

"What is the closest station?" Anamona asked her sister.

"Populus. It's less than ten kilometers from here."

"Ten?" Anamona sighed.

Jani knew where she was coming from. He had a long hike ahead as well, before he reaching the train to Albedo.

"I can't remember it. Is it in the Taurusia Sector?" Tilia asked Lena.

"Yes," Lena said. "Populus is one of the stations on the main route, but it should be empty during the midsummer festivities. I would be very surprised if there were any other people there beside you."

"Good," Anamona noted.

"So, prepare to leave," Lena said before getting to her feet and leaving.

"Finally," Jani heard Lemmus sigh.

Then he saw Mari Alauda take her place among the Terra Unionians when the group split. Jani looked at the woman and wondered what was waiting for her across the border.

"Terra Unionia is waiting," he heard Lemmus say to Mari.

Jani didn't envy Mari. He could not have even imagined crossing the border and leaving Gavialis behind for good. Doctor Death did not have very many options. Finally Lena informed her group.

"It's time to go."

Then Jani noticed her turning one last time to Lu and waving goodbye. Lu responded by mouthing silently the words *love you.*

Then Lu turned to face Jani and Saia and waved them to follow him. Jani did as he was told and took a deep breath. The thought of returning to Gavialis felt good, but it also worried him. They could still get caught sneaking around in a restricted area.

Suddenly Jani saw something quite unexpected. Saia turned on her heels and ran away. Jani turned around as well to see what the girl was doing exactly and he noticed everyone else was on alert by the sudden turn of events as well. Everyone knew almost immediately what Saia was doing; she was running towards Terra Unionia.

"HEY!" Lena yelled and started to run after the girl.

Lu did the same.

It was Lemmus who jumped towards Saia and managed grasp her arm, preventing her from reaching Terra Unionia territory.

"LET GO!" Saia yelled and struggled to free herself from Lemmus' grasp.

"What on earth do you think you are doing?!" Lena asked the girl.

"I won't go back to Gavialis!"

"Don't be insane!" Lena snapped. "I won't take you to Terra Unionia! What's so difficult to understand in that?!"

"Then I will go there myself!" Saia announced stubbornly.

"Oh no you won't!" Lena told to the girl.

"I'm got going back to Gavialis!"

Jani watched the scene unfold from a distance, barely able to believe his eyes.

"Young lady," Lemmus, who was still holding Saia's arm tightly, began, "one just doesn't go to Terra Unionia. Don't you understand there is a life-threatening minefield ahead of you?"

"I'll take the risk!"

"Not today," Lemmus told her. "You have no reason whatsoever to cross the border."

"You know nothing about my reasons!" Saia snapped.

"I know a thing or two about defecting," Lemmus snapped back, "and the day you cross the border, you had better be officially dead to every person who knows you. Right now, you are merely missing."

"I don't want to go back there!"

"Your disappearance could expose us all!" Lu reminded the girl.

"How?!" Saia asked him in anger.

"Saia," Mari Alauda sighed.

But Saia refused to listen to anyone.

"Hey," Lemmus tried a different tack. He placed his hands on her shoulders, leaned over and looked deep into the girl's eyes.

"We need you in Gavialis," Lemmus said.

"Why?" the girl asked him crossly.

"You have skills that others here don't."

"Like?"

Then Lemmus whispered something into the girl's ear.

"What that's supposed to mean?" Saia asked the man.

"Find out," Lemmus told her. "You are a girl with unique abilities to find out almost anything from the information network, so find out."

Jani watched closely as the two exchanged glances. After a few tense moments, Saia gave in.

"This way," Lu told the girl as he took hold of Saia's arm and pulled her towards the south; the direction in which Gavialis was waiting for them several kilometers away.

Saia yanked her arm loose and looked angrily at Lu.

"Young lady," Lemmus said, "this is not over for you. You still have a chance to get to Terra Unionia, but not today. Your day will come. Be patient."

Saia didn't say a word, instead just snorted in anger. Then she leaned against a tree and folded her arms across her chest, angry. There were seven people blocking her path to freedom.

"Silly girl," Jani heard Lena sigh, but I guess no more undisciplined than I was at her age."

Lu pulled Lena into a final embrace and covered his face with her light-colored hair. Jani didn't want to watch their last sentimental moment; a public display of intimacy was still something he had to get used to. He didn't know yet whether he would ever get used to this new Lu but perhaps this would be the last time he had to witness this behavior.

"Put the rock on a stone when you're here," Jani heard Lu saying.

"Alright," Lena noted and took Lu's face in her hands.

"See you soon," Lu whispered, "and be careful."

"You too," Lena said and finally detached herself from Lu's arms, "and try to keep that girl with you."

Lu laughed and said, "She's going to get back to the city if I have to drag her screaming."

"Good," Lena laughed.

Then she let go of Lu and stepped back towards the group she was about to lead back to Terra Unionia.

"Let's go," Jani heard Lena announce to the others.

" Doctor Alauda!" Saia called.

Doctor Mari Alauda turned around and took a last look at the girl.

"See you," the woman said with a faint smile.

Jani noticed a dark look in Saia's eyes.

"Let's go," Lu commanded and pulled Saia with him. "Come on."

Saia was reluctant to move.

"Go," Mari mouthed silently to the girl, the distance between the two of them already several meters.

Then the woman waved Saia goodbye one last time, turned her back on them and continued with the others towards Terra Unionia.

"Let's move, people," they heard Lena giving orders to the others, breaking the silence of the forest around them.

Finally Lu turned his back on the woman he loved and took the first steps to lead the disinclined Gavialian girl further from the border. The girl kept looking over her shoulder, inspiring Jani to do the same. The group following Lena to Terra Unionia disappeared behind the endless line of trees and their shadows.

"I'll escort you Albedo's North Station," Lu informed them. "From there you will have to figure out a way back to Gavialis."

"You're not coming back, too?" Jani asked him.

He had assumed Lu would return to Gavialis as well.

"I can't," Lu stated. "I'm still on duty, patrolling the border."

Jani could hardly believe his ears.

"I have to return to the city alone with her?" he asked Lu.

"It'll be fine. No one will see she's a girl," Lu assured him. "She'll hide her face beneath her hood and when she travels with you, everyone will automatically assume she's a boy. That's how she did it when she left from Gavialis, so the trick must work the other way around, too."

"So, you are really going to send me back there alone?!"

"I don't have any other options," Lu stated calmly. "You know where to go and what to do."

"And you obviously want to get back to the border to be with Lena," Jani pointed out sourly.

That was the last straw. Lu had not mentioned even once that he wouldn't be returning with Jani. It would have been much less of a problem, if he could travel from Albedo to Gavialis alone but suddenly he had to travel not only without Lu but also with a girl in tow. If he had known this he would never have agreed to come to the border in the first place.

"You can let go now," Saia finally informed Lu, who was still holding her arm tightly.

"I most definitely can't," Lu retorted.

Jani looked at the two and saw Saia trying unsuccessfully to pull her arm lose from his grip.

"So, you are really leaving me to take care of her?" Jani sighed and shook her head.

"I don't need your protection," Saia informed and glared at him.

"Good," Jani replied rudely.

They walked for a while without saying another word, but the air between them was tense. Jani wondered what had made the quiet girl suddenly speak out so loud. Perhaps it was anger that had given her the courage to express herself more freely.

"How long are you going to hold my arm?" Saia finally asked Lu. Jani was once again surprised.

The girl was definitely unusually talkative even though she was alone with two men in the middle of a forest.

"I will walk alongside you, until I'm sure we are far enough away from the border," Lu said. "You can still make a run trying to cross the border."

"I'm not stupid," Saia said.

"Running mindlessly towards a minefield doesn't really give the smartest impression," Lu pointed out. "You have obviously developed an obsession with Terra Unionia."

"And what if I have?"

"Pull yourself together and think rationally," Lu commanded her.

"What's that supposed to mean?" Saia asked him sourly.

"It means forget Terra Unionia, go home, and continue living your life."

"Right," Saia sighed.

"Why were you with that doctor in the first place?" Lu asked her.

"I helped her," Saia said.

"You helped a wanted criminal escape from the city?" Lu said, "why would you do something like that?"

"It's called conscience," Saia snapped.

"Well, you had better keep your mouth shut about seeing her now that charges against her have been made," Lu reminded.

"I know," Saia answered.

"So, you can't tell anyone about the two of us, either," Jani then said. "I really don't want to be connected to her at all."

"Didn't you go to see her at the Main Hospital recently?" Lu asked him.

"I did," Jani sighed.

"If I were you, I would expect the police to come and ask some questions about her in the near future," Lu added.

"Especially if the police have realized you aren't currently in the city either," Saia said somewhat amused.

Jani stopped and stared at Saia, confused. The girl had said something he had not even considered himself, but now he couldn't help but wonder whether her words had any truth in them. Jani simply couldn't know what was currently waiting for him back in Gavialis.

"No-one will connect you with her disappearance," Lu assured him, seeing the look on Jani's face.

"I hope this trip doesn't put me in the situation where I have to lie to the police," Jani whispered.

"Unlikely," Lu calmed him down. "You are a man from First Circle, she's a woman from Sixth."

"Seventh," Saia corrected.

"Either way," Lu continued, "the fact is that you two have lived completely different and separate lives far away from each other. No one will connect the two of you. Not to mention the fact that she must have met a lot of other people during the week."

"But I am a man," Jani pointed out. "How many men did she meet on regular basis? We have no way of knowing that. As a man I can get out of the city without anyone paying any special attention. She's a woman so her movements are followed more carefully. At some point the search for her is going to extend beyond the inner circles and even the whole city and when that happens, the men she had been in contact with are suddenly going to become more relevant to the police investigation. A woman simply can't disappear from the inner circles of the city without a trace."

"Despite that, I hardly believe you will be among the main suspects, so quit worrying about it," Lu told him. "It is very likely they are still looking for her in the inner circles of the city, so it's going to take some time before the police start to include the outer circles in their search. Sixth and Seventh Circles where she has access will be searched first and these circles are huge. That's why this search is going to take time even if the police plough all their resources into this search. The thought of a woman getting out of the city is surely too far-fetched an option for them to even consider."

"The city may be big, but so is the police force," Jani pointed out. "And she is Doctor Death, so searching for her will be active for quite a long time."

"You will not be a suspect in this case," Lu sighed. "You are a man from First Circle. Where could you have taken her, to First Circle? The police aren't going to find her there. To Linai? She's not there, either. To Albedo? You don't have access permission there in the first place! And if someone is going to get suspicious about you, they can check the security records of the stations. You have not been to any public place with her, so that's that."

"That's true," Jani concurred.

"So, you are worrying about nothing."

"Let's hope so," Jani sighed and took another step forward.

"I must say, though, that I won't miss the media fuss which is waiting for you in the city," Lu said. "Luckily for me, I am on the border out of reach of all those news stories."

"I don't think Doctor Death will disappear from the news for some time," Jani guessed. "She was the most written-about topic worldwide yesterday and I don't think it will come to an end any time soon."

"You can be sure of that," Lu said. "People don't forget a thing like this very quickly."

"Doctor Death ..." Jani sighed.

"Her name is Mari Alauda," Saia informed them.

Jani took a quick look at the girl and he noticed anger in her eyes.

"You just won't quit defending her," Lu pointed out.

"Why should I?" Saia snapped. "She's innocent."

"Whatever," Lu said shaking his head in amusement.

"If you are so sure of her guilt, why did you let her cross the border with this woman of yours?" Saia asked him.

"I am not sure of her guilt," Lu stated.

"Yet the tone of your voice says otherwise," Saia said.

"In my opinion, running away in her situation is irresponsible. Not to mention the fact that I would expect each world citizen to trust our legal system enough to be sure that innocent individuals will not be found guilty. If she is innocent as you claim, she should have nothing to worry about."

"You are naive," Saia snorted. "Innocent men are being condemned for crimes they didn't commit. I bet there are plenty of them in Cold Pit as well, paying for the crimes of others."

"Is that so, Miss Conspiracy Theorist?" Lu asked her and rolled his eyes.

"Don't mock me."

"So, there is not even the tiniest doubt in your mind that these allegations towards Alauda are unjustified?"

"No," Saia informed him sternly.

"You don't see that confidence in another person very often," Lu said. "I didn't know women on our side of the border were capable of that kind of loyalty to another woman."

"What do you mean, on our side of the border?" Saia asked him sourly. "You know practically nothing about women."

Lu laughed at Saia's argument.

"You being committed to this Lena Unionian doesn't suddenly make you an expert on all women," Saia informed him. "I happened to see on my own screen, in the privacy of my own room and in real time, how certain sensitive records on Doctor Alauda's ID account were altered in order to cast her in a bad light. Then these same records were conveniently forwarded to people who have more power than you could ever imagine."

"What are you talking about?" Jani laughed.

"I saw it all at exactly the moment it happened. So you two can just stop trying to convince me right now – and everybody else for that matter – that she could actually be guilty of the atrocities she's being accused of. She is innocent and there is a conspiracy behind it."

"Are you serious now?" Lu laughed.

"I am," Saia informed him and finally yanked her arm away from Lu's grip, "but I failed."

"In what?" Lu asked her.

"Not getting it on my memory chip," Saia said. "I always have memory chips within my reach when I'm online, but for some reason when I saw this happening I couldn't get it on an external memory chip. I failed and let Doctor Alauda down in the process. I could have saved her reputation, instead I failed."

Jani observed Saia for a moment and he saw desperation reflected in her eyes. She really was serious. And she was obviously blaming herself for what had happened, even though no one expected her to take responsibility for it.

"If I had found a memory chip, even just one, I would have had proof of someone tampering with the metadata of certain records to make sure there were traces of Doctor Alauda in them. Someone hacked into her ID account."

"In addition to you?" Jani asked her.

"Yes," Saia confessed.

"Why did you hack into her ID account?" Lu asked the girl.

But Saia didn't answer.

"Do you do that sort of thing often or was Doctor Dea… Alauda the only one for some reason?"

Silence.

"Where did you learn the skills? What do you use them for?" Lu asked her.

"I learnt them all by myself," Saia replied, "and I have never done anything like this to anyone before. I have no such evil in me."

"Has she talked to you about this? Does she suspect someone in particular?" Lu asked her.

"She believes she knows who's behind this," Saia said, "but like me she doesn't have any proof."

"Who is it?" Lu asked her.

"One of the doctors at the Main Hospital," Saia answered.

"Who?"

"You don't need to know that."

Lu observed the girl for a moment, then said, "You're right. That information has no relevance or importance to us, at least not now."

"So, how did you get out of the city with her?" Jani asked her in turn. "Did you walk all the way from Gavialis?"

"Of course not."

"How then?"

"We came via Albedo," Saia said.

"The stations are closed and there are guards patrolling the edge of the minefield," Lu reminded.

"We walked through the station gates in Albedo."

"How?"

"The same way we got out from each and every station in Gavialis."

"So, your hacking skills extend far beyond ID accounts. You can access the extremely well-protected servers which run these personal information systems as well," Lu noted.

Saia didn't say a word.

"There's no point denying it anymore," Lu continued.

"How did no one notice you leaving the city?" Jani wondered.

"They were disguised," Lu reminded him. "Men's clothes."

"No one in Gavialis expects to see two women without their Yellow Guardsmen," Saia said. "We walked among hundreds of men, yet no one saw anything. We were basically hidden in full view."

"I suppose that's really it, especially in the outer circles of the city," Jani said.

"But surely you left some data on the information system when you walked through the station gates?" Lu wondered.

"Of course," Saia stated, "if there are no matches to our fingerprints in the monitoring systems at stations, that alone would have triggered a common alarm and locked every single gate in the station. It's something that would happen to your girlfriend, too, if she decided to come here and try to open a station gate with her fingerprint."

"I know," Lu said.

"So, in other words, you can get back to the city with a fake ID identification now as well?" Jani asked her.

"Not exactly," Saia said.

"Why not?" Lu asked her.

"Because I added a so-called 'ghost' to the system," Saia explained. "This ghost ID simply appeared on the system and disappeared from it after couple of hours."

"Bottom line?" Jani asked her.

"My ghost has not been in the system for over 24 hours now," Saia explained. "All I can hope is that no one paid any attention to it while it was there and that they don't connect its fingerprint data to my real ID information. While this ghost identification exists, I don't. It overwrites my real ID information while it's on the system."

"So, you can't get back to the city with the same fake ID information, because it doesn't exist anymore?" Lu asked her.

Saia nodded.

"So, how *are* you going to get back to the city?" Jani asked her.

"I didn't plan on coming back," Saia said, "So, there was no need to think that far."

"You better come up with some way, *Brains*, and fast," Lu retorted. "Luckily for you, Jani is with you."

"So, I have to get her through the gates," Jani sighed.

"That's the only option," Lu said. "We can only hope there aren't too many people on station duty at this hour in the morning, who would see you two pushing through the gates with one ID identification data."

"If Albedo is not going to be a problem, Fourth Corner Station will," Jani sighed. "There are always people on every single Gavialis station. They are never empty and even if they were, they are continuously monitored by security services. Not to mention the fact that I am heading to First Corner Station where the gates do actually open with my fingerprints. She is on her way to Sixth or Seventh Corner Station."

"Sixth Corner Station," Saia said.

Lu took a deep breath.

"There must be a Contact Point at Albedo station," Saia said.

"There is," Lu said, watching the girl carefully.

"What are you going to do?" Jani asked her.

"Another ghost," Saia said. "I can't see any other option."

"You can make one at a Contact Point's communication terminal?" Jani asked her slightly worried.

"I will have to," Saia said. "I haven't done anything like that before because Contact Points are always monitored but we need to keep our faces, as well as the display of the terminal we are working at, hidden while I'm working. Not to mention that I have to encrypt my location information to avoid the alarm being automatically triggered."

"Because you are a woman who is not in the city?" Jani asked her.

"Exactly."

"Alright," Lu said. "This is starting to sound like a plan."

"I still don't like it," Saia said. "I've never walked the city streets alone."

"And?" Lu asked her.

"It scares me!" Saia yelled in her defense. "It shouldn't come as a surprise to you, should it?!"

"I suppose not," Lu admitted, "but doesn't playing around with information systems scare you, then?"

"It does," Saia confessed, "but it's like playing with fire. Walking the city streets without a Guardsman is like someone had forced you to stand in the fire instead. I haven't done it before."

"But today you have to," Lu said.

"Shit," Saia whispered.

Jani looked at her carefully and suddenly felt sorry for her. The poor girl was genuinely scared, even if it was of her own doing. If she had been ready to help Doctor Death in her escape, she should surely be able to find the courage to walk home from a station in Sixth Circle.

They continued their journey. They walked in silence as each of them pondered the situation.

"What's going to happen now?" Saia finally asked them.

"What do you mean?" Lu asked.

"We won't ever return to that place on the border again?"

"Why on Earth would you want to go back there?" Lu asked her puzzled.

"To meet the others," Saia said. "Maybe Doctor Alauda could also return there some day."

"Maybe," Lu mused, "it's hard to say."

However Jani didn't share the girl's wish to return. Getting back to the city was the only thing on his mind right now. He could even visualize the control room in Linai. It was the place he most wanted to return to as soon as possible.

"Am I ever going to see you both again?" Saia asked them.

"I don't know," Lu said. "I haven't thought about it."

"I think you should carry on with your life as if you had never met us," Jani said. "We have nothing in common so there's no point in keeping in touch."

"I think that's the wisest thing to do," Lu agreed, "we met on the border by accident, we spent some time there. Let's leave it there. It's for the best, for all of us."

"I think so, too," Jani replied.

"Not to mention the fact that you live in Sixth Circle too, so your day to day life has nothing in common with ours in that sense as well. So it's very unlikely that we will meet again."

"What about keeping in touch online?" Saia asked.

"Why would you want to do that?" Lu asked her laughing. "don't you have better friends than us two?"

"I don't," Saia replied.

Jani was surprised and he looked at Saia. Was she serious? He watched her carefully for a moment out of the corner of his eye until he was sure that she had really meant what she had said.

"Why would you want to keep in touch with two guys from First and Second Circles?" Lu asked her.

"What difference does it make?" Saia asked him in return.

"I think it makes a big difference," Lu replied. "You have your own life and routine going on, I have mine and Jani has his."

"So, that means you want to get rid of me," Saia deduced, "what if I don't want to go home anymore, what if I want to live as a man from now on?"

"Why would you ever want to do something like that?" Lu asked her bemused.

"Because I want to."

"Are you insane?" Lu laughed. "Why would anyone want to escape from Sixth Circle? Have you ever even been to the outer city circles? Do you even know what those places are like?"

"There are no women in those parts of the city, that's for sure," Jani reminded her.

"So what?" Saia asked him defiantly.

"So what?! You have just told us that you are afraid in public without your Guardsmen."

"If I were alone," Saia added.

Jani didn't like the direction this conversation was heading in.

"I would stay in Sixth Circle without ever contemplating any other option if I were you," he informed the girl.

"What's so special about Sixth Circle?"

"Well, first of all you have everything you could ever need there," Lu started. "You have the company of other women and, because you are a woman, life is easy for you. You just exist in this world and yet you still live in luxury. Most men in this world have to work extremely hard for a very long period of time in order to achieve a similar standard of living you have been given for free."

"Maybe so," Saia said quietly, but her tone of voice revealed clearly how little she valued her life in Sixth Circle.

And it annoyed Jani. He didn't like the way Saia regarded her privileges so casually.

"You are ungrateful if you can't see that," he said.

"Ungrateful?!" Saia exclaimed.

"Be happy for all those things you have," Jani told her. "Be happy for the fact that you were born as a woman."

"You know nothing about my life!" the girl announced angrily.

"Excuse me, little missy, but a woman's life is pretty easy compared to a man's. If you are bored by your daily routine, or lack of one, and imagine that impersonating a man would bring a significant change to your life, you are gravely mistaken. Be happy for what you have been given."

"What do you know about what I have been given?"

"Oh, I know," Jani stated. "You are nothing but a spoiled little girl who has too much time on her hands."

"You know nothing about me!" Saia hissed and started pacing forward leaving the two behind her.

"You being able to hack into the information system just proves my point. You are nothing more than a bored girl with too much time on her hands," Jani added.

"Believe what you want," Saia retorted. "Perhaps I am bored and spoiled. Perhaps I am privileged, but that's not what I have asked for from anyone, and that's why I owe nothing to you or anyone else, just because of my gender!"

"Who says you do?" Lu asked her puzzled. "All I am worrying about from this talk of yours is that you won't go back home. I can't even begin to understand why you would even consider an option like that."

"Maybe I just don't get why you are willing to risk everything you have for one Terra Unionian woman," Saia replied. "You must already have some Silver Wing marks from your job, and on top of that, you are quite tall so you are not discriminated against because of your height, but what are you doing? You are sleeping with a woman who should not even exist. You are having a child whose information is not registered on the Health Council's system nor that of the Inner City Issues Council. If I were you I would worry about me first, then others."

Jani burst out laughing.

"You two have something in common, I see," Lu noticed and looked at Jani.

"Sounds like it."

"And she doesn't seem like the shy little girl we saw at the border last night," Lu added.

"Most definitely not."

"Quit talking about me as if I weren't here," Saia insisted.

Lu and Jani exchanged amused looks.

"What did that defector whisper to you?" Lu asked Saia.

"It's none of your business," Saia snapped.

"Why are you protecting him?" Lu wondered.

"I'm not protecting him."

"So, why won't you tell what he whispered to you?" Lu pressed.

"Why are you so curious?" Saia asked him instead. "You're so annoying."

"The feeling is mutual," Lu informed her.

Jani laughed.

"What's so funny?" Lu asked him.

"This whole thing," Jani said. "This entire situation and how absurd it really is. Here I am, walking in the middle of a forest in an area which, according to official maps, is contaminated wasteland. I am walking with my friend, who is about to become a provider without official permission and on top of that we are walking with a girl who is without her Yellow Guardsman and who wants to either go to Terra Unionia or start impersonating a man in Gavialis. At what point exactly did my life become this insane?"

Lu's smile widened slowly before he began to laugh as well.

"This is quite unusual," he then admitted.

"Being around you without my Guardsman is undeniably strange for me," Saia said instead, "but I'm not as pretty as your girlfriend so I guess I'm safe without extra protection."

"And what is that supposed to mean, are you insulted because we treat you like a human being?" Lu asked her amused.

"No," Saia said.

"Are you sure?" Lu asked her.

"Your girlfriend is beautiful," Saia continued, "it's easy for the pretty ones."

"What are you talking about?" Jani asked her confused.

"Yeah, shouldn't you be happy that you can be around us without being afraid?" Lu added.

"Okay, whatever," Saia said.

"Well, just so you know, I have not ranked or classified your looks into any category," Lu informed her, "and that is the truth."

"Same here," Jani added.

"Right," Saia sighed sarcastically.

"Okay, what is this exactly?" Jani wondered. "Am I the only one who's lost here?"

"You are not," Lu said.

Jani saw Saia turn to face them, observing them for a moment.

"Fine," she finally said. "Maybe my expectations of you were false. I have simply been taught that men see a woman's beauty first and foremost, and not much more beyond that."

"I see …" Jani managed to say.

"All I see in you at the moment is a problem which needs solving," Lu stated.

"A problem?" Saia asked him.

"You are a girl," Lu said. "We are two men. You are really not supposed to be here with us at all, yet here you are, and now we have to get you back to the city and get rid of you without anyone even realizing we have even had any dealings with each other. That's at the forefront of my mind, when I think of you, nothing personal."

Saia nodded. Jani interpreted from the look on her face that Lu's words had not hurt her feelings. For a moment they walked on in silence. Jani sensed some tension between them once again, hardly unexpected, but he was getting tired of all this. He was even starting to wish he could be home in First Circle as soon as possible.

"He whispered me a name," Saia suddenly said.

"What?" Lu asked her.

"The defector," Saia said. "Lemmus."

"What name?" Jani asked her.

"I think it's the name of the person who can help me, if I can find him on our information network."

"Why would he tell you his name?" Jani wondered.

"I don't know," Saia said. "Maybe he wants me to find the means by which he was able to escape to Terra Unionia back then; how he officially became dead in the world's eyes."

"I wonder how he found out about Terra Unionia back then?" Lu pondered. "I learnt about it from work and Jani heard about it from me."

"How many people know about Terra Unionia overall?" Saia wondered instead.

"Where did you hear about it?" Lu asked her.

"From my brother," Saia answered.

"Does he know you are here now?"

"He's dead," Saia said briefly.

"Oh."

"It happened years ago," Saia added, "but he knew about Terra Unionia, even though he didn't know the exact location where it would be. He had marked five pretty good guesses on his map."

"And that's basically how you ended up here with Alauda," Lu asked.

"That's right."

"Even we happened to meet in those woods it doesn't make us friends now," Lu then reminded the girl as kindly as he could. "I know that you know my secret, but remember that I know yours as well. I know you helped Alauda out of the city and that is a crime in itself."

"Are you threatening me?" Saia asked him.

"No," Lu said, "I'm simply stating that we all share information which we all should keep to ourselves. Despite that, our journey together will end after today. Jani and I have been friends for years but we can't have anything to do with you from now on. I'm sure you understand that."

"I see."

"Don't take it personally," Lu added.

"Fine," Saia said briefly. "Then I won't look for your contact information when I make progress in my research."

"What research are you talking about?" Jani wondered.

"The search for the other part," Saia said.

"What other part?" Jani asked her again.

"Now that we know that a part of Yesterday's Final Book is in Terra Unionia, the other two pieces must be somewhere else. And I intend to find at least another one of them."

"Are you serious?" Lu asked her.

"I've never been more so," Saia replied.

"What are you expecting to accomplish with that?" Lu wondered.

"Not to mention the fact that there might be others searching for that text, too," Jani added, "others who may have more power than you can imagine."

"I want one of those lost pieces," Saia announced.

"How do you know they have not been found yet?" Jani asked her. "Maybe someone already has them in his possession."

"Maybe Lemmus hinted something," Saia said.

"Did he?" Jani asked her.

Saia didn't respond.

"You are a woman," Lu reminded her. "Your means of searching for the pieces of this so-called book are limited. Don't even start assuming they will be in Gavialis. It's a big world out there."

"I'm not expecting that."

"Then why would you even begin such a search?" Jani asked her. "If I were you, I would drop it."

"On the day I hold the second piece of this book in my hand, Tilia and Lemmus will convince Lena to take me across the border. On that day I will go all the way to Terra Unionia."

17.

Saia woke up. She felt her legs aching after the long hike, but there was also a nasty pain all across her back. Her mother had beat her the very moment she had set foot inside the apartment. According to her, putting on men's clothes and pretending to be a boy was a sure sign of mental instability, but Saia had also disappeared for a couple of days. Therefore, she now believed that Saia had been wandering round Sixth Circle as a man; an act which was extremely shameful and embarrassing for her. Therefore the boy had been beaten out of her; something Saia's painful back reminded her of only too well.

Saia sat on her bed for a while. She was both upset and sad, and hated both feelings. She had held back her tears since yesterday and she was still too proud to sob, even though she was alone in her room. If she did cry, her mother would have won this little battle and that was the last thing she wanted, not after everything she had seen, heard, and experienced. Her mother was a small player in the world which had opened up before Saia's very eyes.

Eventually Saia stood up and walked over to her desk. There she activated her terminal to see the news headline ticker and noticed that Doctor Mari Alauda was still the most widely written-about topic all over the world.

Saia browsed the headlines for a moment and concluded that in seeking Doctor Alauda, wide scale searches had been launched. As a matter of fact, she was also being sought in other cities of Capricorn Tropic, which, at this relatively early stage, was very surprising. Like Lu and Jani, Saia had not expected the police to start searching for Doctor Alauda outside of Gavialis for weeks, but because the allegations against Doctor Alauda were so severe and previously unheard of, it seemed the police simply weren't taking any chances.

"Keep searching," Saia said sourly.

She kept browsing the headlines and noticed that the leader of the Women's Affairs Council had also given a public statement about the Mari Alauda case. Saia was curious now. She selected the headline and glanced through the text.

According to the news article, the leader of the council was shocked by the news, but was urging Doctor Alauda to surrender and trust the legal system. There were thousands of comments in the article which Saia chose to ignore. She was too tired to read slander now. Instead, she closed the news window and let the headlines run across her screen once again.

Doctor Alauda still missing

Search for Doctor Death expanding

Doctor Alauda sighting in Erasmia proven hoax

Women tell all – Mari Alauda was cold and heartless young woman

Torment of Mari Alauda's man – "I'm not Mari!"

Mari Alauda – First Lady of Cold Pit?

Doctor Alauda's ID chip still puzzles criminal investigators

Saia clicked the last headline open and started to read with interest the article attached.

Doctor Mari Alauda, sought by the authorities for some days now, keeps hundreds of policemen and criminal investigators busy in all cities of Capricorn Tropic. One of the greatest mysteries surrounding the doctor's disappearance is her ID chip, which was found in the Gavialis Main Hospital area near the gate leading out from the hospital. The ID chip found was most likely removed by Doctor Alauda herself, presumably having cut her arm with a surgical knife. According to the police, the blood-stained chip was found in the immediate proximity of an empty anesthetic ampule.

The removal of the ID chip has proven to be a puzzle for investigators working on the case. How did the doctor leave the hospital without it and the protection of her Yellow Guardsman? If Mari Alauda has left the city's Sixth Circle, how did she get through the station gates without her ID chip or fingerprints? How did she manage to disappear without a trace?

According to the latest statement by police, the investigators are continuing their work under the assumption that Mari Alauda had received outside help in order to escape. However, despite the assumed outside support, her movement around the city without an ID chip continues to confuse the investigators. Where is Mari Alauda and how has she, the most wanted woman in the world, managed to trick the numerous information systems, without leaving any trace of her movements?

All sightings of Mari Alauda should be sent to the police immediately so that the doctor can be brought before a court of law to face the allegations against her.

Saia closed the news article and sat still for a moment, staring at the surface of her desk. She didn't know what to think. She felt guilty about the fact she hadn't succeeded in recording the only proof of Doctor Alauda's innocence on a memory chip.

"*Don't worry about it now,*" Doctor Alauda had said as they had approached the tree line, following the two young men far ahead of. "*You have done more than I could have ever have asked of you.*"

"*But it's not right what has happened to you,*" Saia said.

"*It's not, but it has.*"

"*Do you know who has done this to you?*"

"*Yes. He's one of the doctors at the hospital; Doctor Aix.*"

"*Why did he want to ruin your life?*"

"*Because in a way, I was about to ruin his. I didn't expect him to go this far, that was just plain stupidity on my part.*"

"*Well, he's going to remain in the past now. We are going to start a new life in Terra Unionia. I assume these people are not connected to our information network, so they don't know anything about our background.*"

"*Let's hope so. Are you still sure the place is here?*"

"I am. And if we keep following those two men over there, they will lead us to the border via the safest way possible without any other border guards realizing we are here. I hope that's the case. I think we were extremely lucky when we saw those two."

"We have been lucky throughout this entire journey. I would have never believed I could get out of Gavialis without anyone noticing my departure."

Saia closed the new ticker and changed the window to the main menu of her ID account. She chose the search service and typed the name she had heard as a whisper in her ear. In an instant, a list of news headlines from the distant past appeared on the screen. The truth was that, according to official data, a man who had been known under such a name had died 26 years ago. This only proved that Saia had found the legitimate trace of this mysterious defector, currently a citizen of Terra Unionia. And according to official data, this man had died in Australandia. Just before his death he had been charged with crimes of …

Saia almost jumped as she heard a knock at the door. She quickly turned her screen off and turned to face the door.

"Are you dressed?" she heard.

"No," Saia informed her angrily.

"Ten minutes," her mother said. "Then you will be taken back to your studies."

Saia didn't bother to respond. She turned around to her workstation, reactivated it, and chose a common document template. Then she began to write a short message she would send to DiseaseBearer and others to read. Those people, if anyone, loved conspiracy theories and alternative points of view.

Mari Alauda – Doctor Death or a victim of a treacherous conspiracy?

Mari Alauda – the woman who, according to the latest news, is a heartless monster. She is a woman who has endangered the future of mankind by systematically destroying female fetuses. Mari Alauda is a monster, a cold-blooded murderer who hates mankind enough to take its future away one little piece at the time.

Since the Great War, no crime this ghastly has been committed. The entire world is following the news headlines and waiting for the moment when Alauda is taken into custody. Everyone wants her to be dragged into court to face up to her crimes. No one is allowed to destroy innocent fetuses, we all know this, especially not the most valuable of all fetuses – girls.

Has anyone, however, asked the question why? Why would a woman like Alauda – respected worldwide among medical doctors, and dedicated to her work – want to do anything like this? What was her motive? Why is no one asking these questions, instead of remaining horrified at how cruel this woman – now known as Doctor Death – was? How many of us really knew Mari Alauda? How many of us came into this world through her hands?

Who has the most to gain personally in the event of Alauda's disappearance? This is the real question that the police should be asking throughout their investigation.

Saia read her writing through and decided to work on it again later on. For the moment she had to leave and pretend that nothing in her world had changed. She deactivated her information terminal and walked to her closet. As usual she chose something loose to wear yet something demure enough to hide the bruises her mom had given her.

Saia stood still for a moment staring at her reflection in the mirror. She had never liked the way she looked, but this morning she disliked herself a little less than usual. Today, her life had some sense to it. This morning she had goals.

"I'm as strong as Doctor Alauda," Saia said to her reflection. "She never broke down. She was strong and she has to be strong now, too, as she starts her new life. I'm also starting a new life and that's why I too have to be strong."

Once she had said all this, she turned around and walked across the room towards the door. In the hallway she walked resolutely towards the main exit. She passed her mother's room and knew she was in there, yet Saia didn't turn her head to look at the woman; she had nothing left to say to her.

"You don't look feminine," she heard.

Saia didn't respond, instead she chose to ignore the woman and continued towards the door. If her mother wanted a feminine daughter, she should go to the hospital and tell the doctors to make her a new one. Suddenly Saia started smiling, because she finally realized she was on a completely different level from her mother. Even down to the smallest thought, they were completely different. She was wiser and more sensible and for that she was proud. She never wanted to be like her mother. She wanted to be like Doctor Alauda – confident, strong, and educated.

The Yellow Guardsman sitting in the hallway got to his feet to escort Saia to the elevator and beyond. Saia didn't greet him, because the Guardsman was new. After her sudden disappearance her mother had let her previous Guardsman go, even if the man had known nothing about her escape. Or perhaps that had been the exact reason to fire him. Once the elevator doors were shut, Saia took a quick glance at the new Guardsman.

"What?" Saia asked him, when she noticed the Guardsman observing her.

"Are you alright?"

"Why wouldn't I be?"

"I heard you arguing with your mother last night."

"Arguing?" Saia asked him, amused. "She beat the heck out of me. It wasn't the first time, though, and most likely not the last, either."

An awkward silence fell upon them and it filled the entire elevator.

"It's not right," the Guardsman said.

Saia was confused. She took another look at the Guardsman and saw a look on his face she didn't quite recognize.

"What isn't right?" she asked him.

"The way she treats you."

"It doesn't happen that often," Saia explained. "So, quit thinking about it. I guess she never really believed I would actually run away dressed like a man, even if she has shown me the door a few times. She just lost her temper."

"Quit making excuses for her," the Guardsman told her. "Something like that should never happen."

Saia took a quick glance at the Guardsman and suddenly had a strange feeling. It was a sensation she couldn't quite place, but she liked the feeling.

"The uniform suits you," Saia said.

"Thanks."

"Why aren't you pleased?"

"Why would I be?"

"You are a Yellow Guardsman."

"I am not a Yellow Guardsman," Jani pointed out. "And eventually someone is going to notice."

"No they won't," Saia assured him. "I trust you can remember your story?"

"I am Atis 461890 from Paguna. I was transferred to Gavialis the day before yesterday."

"That's right."

"And this new ID information is permanent now? This is not another one of your ghosts?"

"Yes, it's permanent. You are Atis now."

"And you don't think anyone will notice that my name has changed?"

"How could anyone know that?" Saia asked him.

"You assume much."

"I do," Saia said and suddenly she felt a smile creeping across her face.

For a moment it had felt like she had been standing side by side with her brother again. It was a feeling she had not felt in a long time.

"Jani 821771 has disappeared," Saia continued. "He's gone. There are no traces of him anywhere so your true identity is safe."

Jani took a deep breath.

"But someone did search for your ID information yesterday," Saia then added, even though she had contemplated whether to mention it to Jani at all.

"What ...? Who?"

"I don't know, but the search came via Komeion System."

"Komeion?"

"It's the huge internal system for all the world hospitals," Saia explained. "Whoever did the search didn't realize that it would leave a trace."

"Who could be interested in my personal information?" Jani wondered.

"Whoever it was he must have been quite surprised to find that Jani 821771 simply does not exist. He's nowhere on this planet."

Jani took a deep breath.

"So, now what?" he asked her next.

"Your first day as a Yellow Guardsman begins right here," Saia said, stepping through the open elevator doors to face a new day. "Welcome to the madness of Sixth Circle."